MOUNTAIN MAN
2ND PREQUEL

Also by Keith C. Blackmore

Mountain Man
Mountain Man
Safari
Hellifax
Well Fed
Make Me King
Mindless
Skull Road
Mountain Man Prequel
Mountain Man 2nd Prequel: Them Early Days
The Hospital: A Mountain Man Story
Mountain Man Omnibus: Books 1–3

131 Days
131 Days
House of Pain
Spikes and Edges
About the Blood
To Thunderous Applause
131 Days Omnibus: Books 1–3

Breeds
Breeds
Breeds 2
Breeds 3
Breeds: The Complete Trilogy

Isosceles Moon
Isosceles Moon
Isosceles Moon 2

The Bear That Fell from the Stars
Bones and Needles
Cauldron Gristle
Flight of the Cookie Dough Mansion
The Majestic 311
The Missing Boatman
Private Property
The Troll Hunter
White Sands, Red Steel

MOUNTAIN MAN

2ND PREQUEL

THEM EARLY DAYS

KEITH C. BLACKMORE

Podium

Cover design by Podium Publishing

ISBN: 978-1-0394-4991-6

Published in 2023 by Podium Publishing, ULC
www.podiumaudio.com

Podium

MOUNTAIN MAN
2ND PREQUEL

1

He woke to the smell of strawberry shampoo in Tammy's hair. He had one arm draped over her, her fingers loosely tangled with his. The rest of her was mashed against his body for warmth. She snored, little rips that came in a comforting rhythm, so he just lay there, relaxing in her scent, sounds, and softness. The warm bed they shared was something he didn't want to leave.

He listened to her sleep, breathing in time with her, their heads sharing a pillow.

Morning light outlined the window on the other side of the bed, but the dark curtains kept everything shadowed. Wind blew softly, sounding cold even for late October. Halloween was a few days away, and Gus sleepily wondered what the plan would be. He was going to be moving in a couple of weeks, finally leaving his basement haven after so long. Chris the landlord understood the move. The bottom floor was old and drafty, and as much as Gus hated to leave, he had to because of rising heating costs. Come winter, the new place would be much warmer and energy efficient. It was also much bigger, with beautiful laminate flooring, in-floor heating, and a rustic feeling that relaxed him the moment he unlocked the front door. It was definitely more enticing, perhaps even enough to persuade Tammy to move in with him. That was the plan, at least. He'd seen how her face lit up when he showed off the new place. She very much approved.

And for Gus, making her happy was becoming an increasingly big deal in his life.

She stirred under his arm, enough to make him think she was waking up. She didn't, however. Fine with him. He focused on the window and his mind quieted, perhaps on the verge of returning to sleep.

The light around the curtains fluttered, catching his eye.

The light flickered again, and continued, as if a branch were waving outside. The wind blew a little harder as well, just a few decibels more, enough to stir up visions of surprise snowstorms. The curtains remained closed, but the activity behind them became jumpier. Gus lifted his head a little higher.

Something was out there. On the lawn.

The apartment was the downstairs half of a duplex, and his bedroom window looked out onto a healthy patch of grass. One night last year, in late spring, Gus had heard something plop down just outside his window, scaring the living shit out of him. Whispers followed, low but audible, prompting him to investigate. A couple of drunk students had decided his lawn was the perfect place to drop and rest for a bit, not three feet from his bedroom window. Gus confronted them, and they surprised him by getting to their feet, apologizing for the disturbance, and moving on.

Gus hoped he wasn't having a repeat incident. Not with Tammy in bed and wearing only a t-shirt. That shit wouldn't fly.

He propped himself up on an elbow and stared, the cold air nipping at his bare torso.

"What is it?" Tammy asked, sounding mostly asleep.

"Something outside the window."

"Students?"

"Hope not. Maybe a dog."

The flickering around the edges continued.

Goddamn, Gus thought. It was bothering him now. He slipped towards the edge of the bed.

"Don't go," Tammy whispered.

"Got to," he answered.

"Don't. It's cold."

He got out as carefully as he could, without losing any warmth in the bed— warmth he fully intended on returning to once he checked outside.

Tammy whined as he adjusted his side of the blankets and sheets.

The window waited, the outline dimmed by shadows, as if a parade were marching by. The wind rushed in Gus's ears, his skin prickling with the drop in temperature. He stared at that covered portal and thought he heard movement outside, like someone crawling around on their elbows. The ceiling creaked overhead, but that was fine. That was only Chris, shuffling across the floor with his slippers on, so as not to disturb his tenant below. Maybe he was about to take care of matters. Be decent of him if he was.

Gus moved to the lower corner of the bed, eyes locked on the window.

"Don't open the curtains," Tammy whispered, her words surprisingly clear in the stillness.

But Gus intended to do just that. Peek around the edges first and, if he could, scare the unholy milk squirts out of whoever was crawling around out there. Because, indeed, it sounded like someone was pulling themselves along by their elbows, right up to the glass. He could hear it, even as the wind picked up just a few decibels more. It was either a person or a sick dog, or a really fat gopher.

"It's cold," Tammy pleaded.

"Back in a minute." Gus hitched up his lumberjack pajama bottoms. Barefoot, he rounded the base of the bed, kicking away his t-shirt that had fallen to the carpet.

Overhead, an unknown weight thumped in his landlord's apartment. There was a muffled scramble, growing more intense, sounding almost like a wrestling match. Gus stopped and stared at the ceiling.

The curtains darkened, as if whoever was outside had moved closer. The wind changed weirdly, becoming strained and wheezy. He sized up the dusty curtains, listening, listening, expecting contact with the glass. Outside, that morbid, single gasp of wind stretched into an impossibly long, undiminishing note.

Gus reached for the curtains.

"Don't open them," Tammy whispered.

Gus looked back at her. The room had darkened. He could barely see the tangled mass of the bed, and Tammy was little more than a twinkle of eyes peeking out from an unkempt mop of hair. Her fingers clenched at the pillow, their crooked lengths grey and stark.

"Please don't open them…" she repeated, and Gus wasn't sure if she was asking or if it was just his imagination.

More rustling outside, closer now. There couldn't be much space between the glass and whoever was out there. Had to be students. Passed out drunk and only now just waking up. No doubt on their way back from the bar just down the street. One of the reasons the rent here was so cheap.

But whoever was out there continued to issue that disturbing, unending hiss. That sound should have compelled him to check on Chris the landlord, but instead, Gus pinched one corner of a curtain, the cloth rough and unpleasant to the touch.

"Don't open," Tammy again, her voice at his ear.

All had gone quiet overhead. The temperature dropped further, and Gus's pulse quickened. Something made contact against the windowpane, a soft, rhythmic tapping that might've been a fingertip. The wheezing wind changed again, splitting into otherworld mewlings, as if issued from cancerous throats. The fingertip beating mutated into a scrabbling of nails across the glass.

Dread flooded Gus.

"Please don't…" Tammy pleaded, her voice muffled, as if speaking through a pillow.

The seams around the window creaked as the mysterious presence outside pressed against the glass, increasing the pressure. All the while, the clawing grew stronger, rushing towards a breaking point.

Taking a deep breath, Gus faced the curtains again—

—and yanked them apart.

2

He woke with a gasp.

Gus lay on the sofa, staring at the bare wooden beams overhead, his pulse thumping and uncomfortable. Otherwise, nothing—not a sound. Nary a creak of timber or floorboard. Nothing moved within the house, no sound save his own breathing. Empty. Abandoned.

As he lay there, recovering from the dream, the ominous quiet did little to comfort him. The silence, the very absence of life, had to be the loneliest, most desolate thing ever.

A strengthening daylight marked a grey October morning. Gus rubbed his cheek, his palm sliding down thickening stubble. His stomach felt fine, though he hadn't tried sitting up yet. That would be the next trick. He rolled onto his side with all the grace and majesty of a beached walrus and plopped onto a hardwood floor. He tried catching himself at the last second, but gravity was greedy and pulled him down. Glass bounced somewhere—the empty bottle of Captain Morgan was rolling away, stopped eventually by the leg of a coffee table.

Gus stared at the bottle. He waited for a warning shout from the owners as they finally returned home. A shout of anger, perhaps. Maybe even outrage.

Nothing, however. Just more of that terrible, unending silence.

He sighed, and even that sounded miserable.

The morning caught him at a low point. To be brutally honest, he felt downright shitty. This little bit of movement woke his stomach, and it seemed to ask him, quite pointedly, if there had been a couple of doused cigarettes in those last few rum shots. There hadn't, of course. At least he was pretty much sure there weren't, but his guts weren't buying the story and continued twisting.

He blamed the rum. But then, after yesterday and last night, he was glad the rum was there. Damn glad. He felt lucky, too.

The drink served as a tether—to reality and, dare he say it, sanity.

And Gus very much needed that.

The coffee table was at eye level, littered with the single wrapper of a Cherry Blossom candy bar. It was the only thing he'd eaten all night. He looked past the wrapper to the wide windowpanes facing the city. The deck was out there, along with furniture, and nothing else except the tarnished face of Annapolis and its increasingly diseased color. The city looked greyer than usual. Hazy. As if the place had taken a couple dozen artillery shells.

Maybe it's better now, he thought. Maybe the cops finally got things under control during the night. Maybe…maybe the army rolled in and laid down martial law. Such thoughts did little to settle his stomach, or withdraw the nails that gouged his temples with every heartbeat.

Cringing, he used the sofa to get to his knees, then his feet, and took the spin that came with the rise in altitude. He couldn't remember the last time he'd been hungover and knew he should just stay put for a while, to let his stomach settle. He needed to check on things, however. He swayed and clutched at his sizeable midsection, just before reaching for his nuts and adjusting matters down there. While he was at it, he scratched where needed, his attention drawn to the view outside his window. Gus expected the owners to burst through the doors and start shouting, threatening to call the cops. All things considered, he *hoped* the owners would return. He'd be damn glad to see another face. Another *living* face.

He stepped around the coffee table, unintentionally kicking the rum bottle. He flinched at the contact and glared at it. "Don't give me a hard time. Not this morning. I'll toss you if you do."

Meaning every word, he left the bottle and plodded towards the sliding glass door. He stopped and stared, his bulging gut not an inch away from the glass. Smoke rose from Annapolis. A lot of smoke. Far to the right, but drifting across the city.

Gus slid opened the door. A blast of cold air shocked him, even felt a little good, but did little to quell the queasy aftershocks of a night of hard drinking.

Still wearing yesterday's painter clothes, Gus stepped outside and shuffled towards the deck, and that dangerous drop of maybe forty or fifty feet. He stopped at the last chair facing the railing and the city beyond. There, he shuffled to the right and stepped up to the edge of the platform. He undid the front of his painter overalls, pulled out his lad, and let drift.

He peed long and hard, cheeks puffing at the release. The flow was a hard one, so hard that he got dizzy.

"Ah no," he muttered, squeezing his eyes shut. "Don't do it. Last thing I need is to piss myself. To *puke* and then piss myself. Then pass out. Christ, what a picture."

The image forced him to open his eyes and smile sadly.

That time, he was channeling his inner Toby.

And thankfully, *mercifully*, the dizziness faded. The other shitty feeling remained, however, but he'd deal with it.

Finishing his business, he tucked himself away and exhaled. He'd spent last night out here, watching Annapolis, listening to the city self-destruct, hearing the far-off screams and the barely audible shouts for help. The noise had been disturbing, to say the least. There had been gunshots as well, and flashes of light, like firecrackers going off under a carpet. At one point there'd been an explosion, a muffled *pop* of energy that held his attention for long seconds. Nothing else came of it.

Except for the smoke coming from that one quarter, the city now seemed far more subdued.

Hand on his belly, Gus watched, and listened.

A few hazy streamers rose into the air from other sections, adding to the pillowy opaqueness drifting over Annapolis. It definitely wasn't industrial smoke, but some fire that had started during the night and was finally dying off. There were no birds. No crows or seagulls, as if the wildlife sensed shit was going down and had the good sense to stay clear, until things had played itself out.

Not a bad idea in the least.

Still no noise. Not a single car horn or a scream. Maybe it was intermission for the plague. Or maybe folks were done barricading themselves inside their homes or wherever. Maybe they were holed up in their basements, like he and Toby had been after escaping Mollymart East, peeking out from behind curtains as their neighbours strolled by in their slippers, their flesh gray, their mouths slack. The stillness was unnerving. Untrustworthy. Like the rancid eye of a mighty shit storm enveloping the city.

Judging by what Gus had already seen, the dead would wait out any hiding survivors. Not because the dead were smart, but because they were dead, and possessed the eternal patience of the deceased and none of the needs, or fears, of the living.

He leaned back and realized with a start that he'd sat down on a lawn chair, one of two cushy perches on the deck. Didn't even remember planting himself, so absorbed he'd been in the state of Annapolis. Even the grumblings of his own stomach had been shut out by his city gazing. He felt his belly, grimaced at the growing mutiny there, and continued his surveillance.

Nothing. Just smoke and clouds and the irregular angles of thousands of rooftops. There weren't any skyscrapers, and the tallest apartment building couldn't have been any higher than seven stories. From South Mountain, the city looked flat, in a bomb blast sort of way.

Toby would have had a few choice words on the matter, if he was around.

That was enough to rip the bandage off the deep and still-fresh wounds that were memories of Toby, Gord, and, of course, Tammy. Gus had mourned the loss of all three the night before. The rum had helped him through, but at times, it also made matters worse. His friends were gone. The love of his life was gone. Goddamnit, Benny and the regional manager with the weird nasally voice were probably gone.

Everyone was gone. All gone.

A great and terrible ache overcame him then. Gus hung his head between his shoulders and let it happen, let it flow. And when his shoulders came close to stopping their trembling, the sadness would surge up again, his crying doglike, a blubbering, snotty mess.

"God *damn*," he whispered, dragging a sleeve across his face and grimacing at the results. "Oh god damn."

He wiped his hands on his coveralls, snorted, and blew out watery ribbons. "Damn it," he ejected. "I'm gettin' all fuckin' runny here."

When he finally got himself under control, the city remained.

"Yeah," he said, needing someone to say something, even if it was only him. "Yeah."

Gus bent over, placed elbows to knees, and let the silence drone on in his ears. When he figured he had a handle on his grieving, *their* faces would crowd his memories, and that would set him off once more. He hated doing it, knowing full well that Gord would chew him out for doing so. Toby, well, Lord only knew what would come out of Tobe's mouth, but it would probably be surprising. Tammy…

"Oh god," Gus whispered.

Then he firmed up, blowing out his sinuses and getting to his feet. "Fuck this," he swore softly. "Fuck this…"

He sized up Annapolis.

"I need a drink," he said.

3

Back in that modern kitchen, which was really the size of his old living room, Gus threw open the cabinet doors where he'd found the supply of alcohol.

The rum was all gone, and frankly, he couldn't remember drinking it.

There were others, however. Not rum, but Jack Daniel's whiskey. A bottle of cherry brandy stood next to that, as well as a quart of gin. A pint of vodka and a pint of cinnamon whiskey were also tucked in there, along with four loose cans of apple cider. That was all on the top shelf. Below that was a case of generic cola and ginger ale. The cheap stuff. About eight cans were missing from the cola, as Gus had used those to mix with the rum. Somewhere during the night, he'd switched over to straight sips, too smashed to bother with mix.

Reeling, no, *rotting* from the after-effects of the rum and his grieving, Gus pulled out the whiskey and placed the bottle on a nearby kitchen island. The counter and the bottle shook when he slapped down the case of ginger ale.

It felt like that kind of day. Was gonna *be* that kind of day.

Gus eyed the pop and, pursing his lips, cracked open a can and downed most of it. It was warm but sparkling fine.

All the while, he wondered.

They can't be all gone, he thought. *Had to be someone left. Definitely some cops. All those cops that tried shooting their way through the zombie mob? Some of them had to get away. Had to. Odds were someone did, right?*

He belched, reloaded on air, and stared off into space.

There had to be someone alive. The other folks from Mollymart for one. Some of them had to have gotten home. Probably hiding right now, just like he and Toby had done. Staying low and keeping quiet.

Gus looked in the direction of the living room. So what if there *were* people alive? What could he do? Could he save them? After the overwhelming display of zombie might he'd experienced firsthand?

A chill went through him.

"Fuck that," he whispered.

An old-fashioned phone hung on the wall. A prized piece of antiquity, and the only means of communication in the whole damn house. If it weren't for old movies, he wouldn't have a clue as to how to use it.

Gus went to the receiver and picked it up. No dial tone, same as yesterday. He was cut off. Alone. And stuck on the side of a mountain. Given the high-quality construction of the place, however, he'd lucked out. Whoever owned the place would be back, though. They had to come back.

If they were alive.

He finished his drink and went to the sink. Needing more in him than just sugar, he grabbed a coffee mug from a cupboard, filled it with water, and downed that as well. Gasping after that intake, he topped off the mug again and drank that.

His belly sloshed dangerously, warning of a possible revolt.

Fine. Gus cupped his stomach and his mug. He walked into the living room, thought better of it, and returned to grab another can of pop just in case.

That was when his guts rolled and heaved. His poor suffering belly had had enough, and whatever it held now decided to take the express elevator up. Through force of will, he managed to swallow against the surge, to send it back down as he raced for the nearest bathroom.

He crashed off the doorframe, dropped to his knees and, for all of a second, beheld the pristine white toilet bowl.

Before opening his mouth and fouling it all.

He yarked twice in succession. Groaned, cringed at what had come out of him, then barfed again, pouring a gruesome stream of vegetable beef soup into that porcelain receptacle. He turned his face away from the depths, gasping for air, and clung to the can like the life raft it was.

His eyes widened. His colon was about to eject its load as well.

"Christ." Gus struggled to his feet while turning, undoing his overalls and clenching hard. Dropping his clothes and drawers, he crashed down on the toilet, hard enough to leave a bruise. *The booze.* Not used to drinking, he knew. Plus he'd been walking around all morning ignoring the signs. And now his body was on the mutiny, a second away from a very violent discharge.

He squared himself on the toilet seat and fired one. Then two. Then three. Great billowing salvos that rocked him and sent stars across his vision. Honest to Christ *stars.*

And even as he voided in one direction, his stomach sought to unload in the other.

Gus swallowed, sending back down whatever bubbled up his throat. Except his stomach would have nothing of the sort. It returned-to-sender once, but not twice.

Then the absolute worse happened—it exploded from him, firing from all ports in a hurricane surge of force.

It was over in seconds, but the damage would linger much longer.

A dazed, deflated Gus sat back, shocked by what he'd spewed into the nearby sink. There he rested, composing himself, drawing in cleansing gasps of air and tasting the foulness polluting his mouth. That got him leaning into the sink again, spitting what he could into the basin. He settled back down on the crapper and checked on the toilet paper—nearly a full roll. *Gonna need that*, he thought. *All that and more*, he knew, feeling unclean all over.

Never again, he swore to himself. Never again.

There he sat, head hanging between a set of hairy knees, staring at a plush beige mat that had escaped the blasts. Gus stayed that way, listening to the drips, hoping he was getting better, and relieved when his innards appeared to relax.

"Thank you, lord," he whispered, holding onto his head. He glanced around and shuddered, knowing he had some cleaning to do.

And clean himself up he did, slowly, stopping every now and again when his stomach rumbled.

The painter duds didn't escape the shitstorm, so he waddled into the laundry room, stripped down to his blue Fruit of the Looms, doffed them as well, and chucked everything into the washer. Feeling dirty, he made the journey back to the shower in the same bathroom he'd just devastated, and slumped against the wall while rinsing off.

The warm water worked magic.

He didn't have a repeat episode, and he ended the shower fifteen minutes later. An unstained towel hung nearby, and a quick sniff told him it was fresh. He dried off, wrapped the towel around his waist and made his way to the living room.

Sofa. He crashed down on the cushions, legs splayed wide, and faced Annapolis. Still there, and looking fine from this vantage point. But it wasn't. It was as rotten as the shit and puke he'd just cleaned up.

The wide windows allowed him a great view so he stayed right there, planted on the cushions, staring at the city.

Then it hit him.

"What…what if I'm the last fuckin' person on earth?" he said. "What if I'm the last? I can't be the last. The others got away. They got away. They're… somewhere. Hell yes, if not in the city then they're somewhere else. On the fringes someplace. Like here, but they're alive."

But the question came back, rattling him badly.

"The fuck am I gonna do if I am?"

At that point, if life were a movie, Gus might've said something profound, perhaps even heroic. But the reality of it was… his innards were still unsettled, and those troubling thoughts kept circling his head like hornets homing in on imaginary bullseyes. He couldn't get over seeing Tammy—undead Tammy-—being shot by a cop, along with all those other people walking around in a state of zombie-ness.

"The fuck am I gonna do?" he muttered, voice cracking.

In the silence that followed, all he heard was the washing machine performing its cycles.

And that was perhaps worse than any reply.

4

He got through the day, but the night was no better.

In fact, the night was worse.

Around the same time as the sun started its evening descent, Gus retrieved his clothing from the dryer and put them on. He wondered about the power and how long it would last, but for now, that thought didn't bother him.

Warm clothing straight from the dryer was usually a delight, but not today. The hangover only worsened his despair, and by suppertime, sundown troubled him much worse than expected. There was power, and thus light, but the sun's slow descent—and the coming darkness— almost got him drinking again.

Almost.

He picked at a meagre supper of unsalted crackers and peanut butter, then washed it all down with ginger ale. He stayed in the living room, his food and drink on the coffee table. Night deepened and the temperature dropped. The warm weather they'd all enjoyed leading up to the outbreak was over and done with, and Mom Nature was returning to regular programming.

He switched on a nearby lamp, but that made evening worse as the windows became dark mirrors. Switching off the lamp wasn't going to happen, however, as total dark—and being *alone* in the dark—would be a nightmare.

Beyond his reflection in the glass, the pre-programmed city lights winked into existence. All that illumination set the sky aglow over Annapolis, but there was nothing warm about it. Things were happening down there. Bad things. Horrors at street level. He couldn't see them, but he could sense them, as surely as one could feel another person stepping into their personal space. And it wasn't just an intrusion. It was, for lack of a better word, an infection.

One that continued to get closer, to spread. A diseased vibe radiated off the cityscape, thick and offensive, like the smell off an unclean urinal.

Gus couldn't relax. His skin turned to gooseflesh despite the heaters cutting in. His thoughts returned to the other survivors. There *had* to be other survivors, not counting the ones he'd dropped off at their rides on the Mollymart parking lot. That was a few days ago, so their names didn't come to him right away.

He remembered Anna, however, easily the most memorable of the bunch. The big woman who took no bullshit or prisoners, and drove a pink SUV. *The pinkest one in the Valley,* she'd declared. She'd driven off into the night, looking to get back to her farm in Falmouth. There were the two Mollymart employees, Rebecca and Walt, who were zombie experts. A meat guy was in there, too, but Gus couldn't remember his name, only that he'd sped off in his car. Then there was the idiot with the cellphone, recording everything. Gus couldn't remember his name, but he recalled Mel Grant and the pain in the ass she was.

Still, he hoped they'd all gotten back, wherever they were going.

They were survivors—they were *people*—so there had to be others.

Had to be.

Hopefully all this shit would blow over in a week's time. The army would come in and settle things down. Restore order. Allow whoever was left to emerge from their homes or basements or wherever they'd hidden. A week at least, Gus figured, nodding, assuring himself the zombies couldn't last any longer than that. They'd be weakened without eating anything. Bed-ridden. Crawling along the ground like… well… weakened zombies. Starving to death.

Or so he thought.

But what if it didn't blow over? What if it continued, well past what he could imagine?

Then the howitzer shell dropped.

What if it stayed this way? Forever.

"Oh Jesus." Gus couldn't allow himself to think that. Hope was better, and he would drink that by the liter. He was in a good place, with food, water, and electricity. All he had to do was sit and wait. Stay put, watch, and listen. And wait for the mechanized cavalry to show up. They would, and he suspected they would be mighty pissed.

Thoughts of Gord entered his head then. His friend and co-worker of so many years, now dead and gone. Benny as well, although it was anyone's guess if Benny and his Regional Manager date were still alive. Toby, well…Toby had been the lucky one.

Good lord, Gus smiled sadly and closed his eyes. Toby had indeed been the lucky one. Killed in one explosive moment by a guard rail bursting through the windshield. Of them all, Toby had surprised Gus the most. Toby had gone from being a fearful painter trapped in a basement to a bat-swinging killer of zombies. It was Toby who'd cleared the way for them both to get aboard the Camaro. To escape. The man had singlehandedly bludgeoned several infected citizens in that driveway.

Dull guilt rose in Gus, remembering that he'd been the one driving the muscle car. Blinded by a zombie clinging to the hood, yes, but he was still behind the wheel.

"Sorry Tobe," Gus whispered, a hot lump forming in his throat. It seemed late, but all of yesterday had been a drunken state of shock and awe.

"I'm sorry," he repeated, in the distant glow of the city lights.

It didn't ease his guilt, but it didn't hurt to say it either.

He woke with a lurch, staring at the ceiling with a blanket pulled up to his drool- soaked chin. Gus made a face at the handful he wiped off and cleaned his hand in the blanket. For a second, he wondered where the hell the blanket had come from, but remembered it was on the sofa. Given everything that had happened in the last couple of days, he barely remembered the layout of the house.

His stomach had come around, feeling much better, so that was good. He rose, stretched, and squinted at the city.

Rain. Wind. An honest-to-god late October shit-spurt of a morning that smothered Annapolis in a clump of spiderweb gray. If the city was down there, he couldn't see it. He walked over to the rain-spattered glass. Trees swayed at the edges of the property, waving their fall leaves like yellow and orange pom-poms. Leaves also tumbled along the ground, some leaping into the drained swimming pool. Everything was in motion except down in the valley, where that dismal haze obscured the city.

"Yuck," Gus said, though grateful for his safety.

He was *safe.*

He turned away from the windows and took in his refuge. Timber frame. Bright and airy, despite the shitty day. Warm too, as the heating system kicked in and hummed away in the background. There was a fireplace at one end, along with a recliner made even cozier with a few brown pillows.

Gus wandered into the kitchen and stopped at the pantry doors. Inside sat all his supplies. Maybe a dozen or so tins of various canned food and five boxes of spaghetti pasta. A box of crackers, with two long packets left. The bottle of peanut butter he'd feasted upon from the night before, half-empty——*because as you eat it, you* empty *it. Toby.* Gus snarked and smiled again, sadly, remembering the conversation of not too long ago.

A bag of Oreos, double-stuffed and unopened. Those he very much approved of. Two bottles of preserved beets—hardcore, but what the hell, he'd eat them. Half dozen chocolate bars, which was the cat's ass. No chips, go fuck a duck, but that was okay. Maybe he'd get some later.

That stopped him cold.

Maybe he'd get some later. And how the hell was he going to do that, Watson? Just run on down to the nearest Mollymart, debit card at the ready? Easy to think, but the reality was *No sir, fuck you very much.* That raised the question of how *long* he intended to be on the mountain. Well, right now, he'd just have to hunker down and wait. He wasn't equipped physically or emotionally to go looking for people. Not down there. Not yet. No, he'd leave that to the police, if they were still a thing. Or the army… if *they* were still a thing.

Which meant he had to ration himself for a bit. Maybe. Until the end of the week at least. Just to see how things shook out. Until then, he had to stay in the house. Stay safe. Wait things out. He had plenty to eat and drink until everything died down.

That sounded like a plan. One he readily accepted.

Gus drifted into the main floor washroom, undid his painter overalls and jeans and went through his morning functions yet again, this time with less explosive energy. That alone relaxed him. He sat there on the throne, his mind numb, and eventually reached for the toilet paper. After cleaning himself, he studied what was left on the roll.

A little less than half.

He looked around. Unlike his own bathroom, where he'd kept several piled in the corner, there were no nearby stacks of TP. The cabinet positioned over the crapper behind him had a single spare roll.

"All right then," he said. "One left in the breech. Rock on."

Good for a week, at least, if he was rationing himself. Which prompted him to consider the rest of the house. He'd gone through the place after he'd first arrived, before hitting the rum. Just a quick search to ensure he was indeed alone, but with everything that had gone down, he barely remembered the layout. So he pulled up his clothes and decided to familiarize himself with the place a little better.

Starting with the basement.

The main room was a den of sorts, dark from the lack of windows, looking lived in. The walls were painted brown, perhaps to enhance the movie or gamer experience, while the carpet was grey, thick and surprisingly cushy. There was a pool table in one end, with a nearby dart board. A small wood stove occupied one corner as well, away from the bookcases. A couple of bean bag chairs and a comfy-looking sofa faced a big ass television. Gus owned a regular-sized tv, but the one here was a sixty or sixty-five incher at least, resting upon a wide entertainment stand that had one of them fancy terabyte units the kids called a "T-box," or a "T." Depending on its storage capacity, the thing could potentially contain a vast library of digital content, which only mildly interested him. It would be a long time before he could sit down and watch a flick.

Bookcases stood against the walls, offering an assortment of hardcovers and paperbacks. Fluffy heads of cute stuffed animals were arranged throughout, peeking out from corners or filling open spaces. There were candles around too, a lot of them, the fat ones that would burn for a long time.

Standing there, scratching his belly, Gus took it all in. He had been in plenty of houses, even got to roll out a small in-home theatre, but this particular den looked like a hybrid of sorts. It was untidy, with a few things tossed about, but not dirty in the least—just a family cave with a small scattering of items, left in easy-to-reach places, waiting for whoever to return on the weekends.

There were two spare bedrooms down there as well, barely decorated and hardly used. No clothes in the closets. There were no extra washrooms either, which he thought strange but not a big deal. One room just off from the stairs had a small storeroom with rows of bare shelves as well as an empty stand-up freezer. On one of those shelves was a plastic container of sanitizing hand wipes and a pack of disposable masks. Nothing else, however, which only reinforced his suspicion that the owners only lived here at certain times of the year. A couple of suitcases had been stashed under the stairs, as well as Christmas decorations.

Gus didn't think about that, just yet. Halloween was only a few days away, which was weird since he was living in a horror scenario. Christmas would be harder, remembering how Annapolis did up its street lights. The annual parades. The people, good lord, the people.

Those thoughts depressed him.

He wandered through the house, taking stock of the main floor and the timber frame's bare beams crossing the ceiling. Each of the three bathrooms had toilet paper, but whoever had owned the place must've known they were in short supply. Only five rolls of butt floss remained in the whole house. Not that it bothered him too much—he'd just start using face cloths if he had to. Or towels.

That thought depressed him even more.

Stop thinking about shit, Gus told himself, but it was futile. He was *in* shit. *Unreal* shit. The deepest *kind* of shit. He picked and pulled at his overalls and realized he didn't have a change of clothing, that all of his clothes were at his place in the city.

That prompted him to check the closets. The clothing and footwear were all much too small for him, as was a collection of winter coats hung up in the mud room. Everything was for much smaller people. The largest boots were a size nine, while the few shirts and pairs of jeans were for a much slimmer guy.

The waist size for the jeans alone was an impressive thirty-two.

"Fuck me," Gus said, tossing the clothing back into the closet. "My fuckin' thigh wouldn't fit into that."

He'd always been a rather husky thirty-eight during his teens, only to increase to a hefty, present day total of forty-four. Forty-five around Christmas time. Tammy had asked him to lose weight, and he wanted to try one day, just to see her reaction. None of that was going to happen now.

Her smiling face appeared in his mind, killing him inside.

Gus returned to the kitchen, where the whiskey waited. He mixed himself a drink in a beer glass. That first mouthful was harsh around the edges, but he choked it down and added a little more ginger ale to soften the rest. His stomach didn't protest or send it back up, which he appreciated.

A drink in both hands, he drifted into the living room and faced the windows. The weather had worsened. Rain pelted the windows and softened the world for winter.

A winter like no other.

He had food, but he would need more. He had clothing, but he needed more. He had *toilet paper*, but would definitely need more. Hell, he would be out of asswipe within two weeks if things didn't start changing. Two *days* if he had another spray-and-pray episode like the one from yesterday.

Things would get better, he told himself. Things would get better. They *had* to get better. Even now, someone somewhere was working on organizing shit and taking care of the zombie plague. There had to be.

At least, that's what he told himself.

He wandered the house for the rest of the morning, staring outside whenever the mood hit him, which was often. Eventually, he sat and nursed his drink while facing the wall of windows and the fog concealing Annapolis. Rain continued its assault. The day darkened, and Gus switched on a nearby lamp. He switched it off again, then on.

Power.

He had power. So that was good.

He didn't drink to excess, just enough to shake the feeling of being left behind. And being very much on his own. He flicked on the living room television, a much smaller cousin of the one downstairs, and started channel surfing. An eerie "This channel will be available shortly" message filled every screen.

Gus turned off the set.

He skipped both lunch and supper and stuck with the whiskey instead, appreciating the buzz, however temporary. When it got dark, he lay down on the sofa and spread a blanket over himself, facing the window. Rain continued to blitz the countryside. There were plenty of beds in the place, but he still hadn't put aside that feeling that he was trespassing, that he had taken shelter in another family's house.

He stayed on the sofa, staring at the dark beyond the glass and listening to the storm. Lightning would have been suitable, all things considered, but it never happened. The wind blew harder. Rain bombarded the windows. The air cooled, and, as expected, the heating system kicked in, causing pipes to ping and heaters to hum.

Twice he thought about turning off the lamp. Both times he didn't. That little bit of light was all he had now, his only friend in the world, and it warded off any terrors waiting in the dark.

5

Gus woke, imagining he'd heard a doorbell.

Silly, sure, but still he waited for a follow up chime, listening, listening *hard*, as one might do in the dead of night. The only sound was the rain pelting the house. And the wind. He looked in the direction of Annapolis, straining to hear, and felt unwell from the earlier whiskey buzz.

There was no follow up chime. He listened for a few minutes more until finally deciding all was good. Probably a dream one might encounter in that state between sleep and consciousness. Or *waking*. He supposed he could get up and check out the front door, but a part of him, the little boy part, let off a defiant *fuck that*. Let *them* make the first move if they wanted in.

Then it hit him. He was in the dark. The lamp was no longer on.

Gus studied the nearby fixture while the pulse in his temples and ears drummed a discomforting beat. Pipes pinged around the house, every sound sharp and ominous. His night vision was fine inside, but he couldn't rightly see outdoors, where unseen things rustled, sometimes scratching at the glass. With the blanket pulled up to his nose, Gus didn't budge from the couch. He eyed the windows and saw nothing except that cold, terrible blackness swallowing the home.

The timberframe creaked. Shivered. And it did so every few seconds, just after Gus closed his eyes. It happened so often in fact, that he finally lifted his head off the pillow, as if that might improve his hearing, or better detect whatever haunted him.

It did not.

A deep void lay beyond the living room windows. The heat under his blanket made him sweat, so he pushed down the material until his arms were free. Halfway through this adjustment, he glimpsed a figure outside the window, shocking him on the spot. Sexless, adult-shaped, it stood there with hunched shoulders and faced the house.

Or so Gus thought. Truth was, he was so freaked out, he couldn't tell if the thing was actually looking inside or towards the city. The rain didn't bother it, and Gus dared not move for reasons his terror-stricken brain couldn't formulate. He remained on the sofa, unmoving, watching the thing as it, in turn, stared inwards…or so he thought. If he so much as breathed, it would start swinging at the glass. Or simply plow through it.

Even in all that wind and rain and nighttime cold, however, it didn't budge. Only the dead could maintain a pose like that. Gus watched it, his breathing fast and desperate, struggling to control his fright. Any time, he expected a flutter of movement. A flinch. Or even just the thing's arms rearing back before smashing the glass.

All the while, the soft drums in his ears kept right on beating. Still, that after-midnight visitor stood as motionless as a gunslinger, waiting for him to make the first move. The phantom would have to wait until dawn, however, because Gus wasn't moving *shit* unless it crashed through the glass.

The figure did not crash through the glass.

Nor did Gus relax. He watched it, wondering if the unknown shape outside was the same bastard who'd rung the doorbell.

And so they stayed that way, long into the night. At times, the dark spells became so impenetrable that the visitor would disappear. It would bleed into existence long seconds later, unmoved, as if a sheet had drifted over the glass.

Despite his fright, Gus's eyelids started drooping.

Until they closed entirely.

He woke to a gray morning, where the nighttime visitor no longer stood outside the window. Startled by the disappearance, Gus scanned left to right, seeing only the gloomy dawn. Being able to see lessened his fear, so he kicked off his blanket and struggled to his feet.

The lamp… still dead to the world. Gus studied it for a moment before reaching for the bulb. The damn thing flickered to life as soon as his fingers touched the eggshell glass, needing only to be tightened.

"The fuck," Gus muttered, screwing the thing in deep. "Who the hell puts a light bulb in like this? Did the antique *phone* ring or something? Christ almighty."

He snapped the lamp on and off, guaranteeing that it worked. Feeling shitty from a lack of sleep, Gus forced himself into a state of alertness that really wasn't there, then checked every window for potential lurkers.

Nothing.

"Fuck this," he declared, and went for the kitchen. A collection of knives rested on the countertop, twelve of them, in fact, all jutting from a block of wood. Gus grabbed the biggest one—a machete of a butcher's blade—and lingered there, in front of the sink, peeking out the kitchen window.

Nothing there, either. But there were so many places to hide.

That didn't sound right, however. Though his experience was limited, he suspected the undead could give a swinging monkey fuck about hiding. In his opinion, the faster they were in your face, the faster they could chew it off.

The rain had stopped. The van was parked just inside the gate, which remained closed. He'd secured it after checking out the place and before getting royally plastered. The bars of the gate weren't wide enough for a body to slip through, and the stone wall encircled the whole property, starting at a sharp rock face and ending at a cliff.

If it *was* a zombie, it was showing some goddamn ingenuity by getting inside.

All right, Gus's brain reasoned. *Here's the situation. Either he's still out there, inside the wall, or not. If he's out there and can't get in the house, that means you have a decision to make. Do you go out and get him? Or wait for him to walk away?*

Gus scoffed at that. He didn't think the thing would walk away. If anything, the undead dickhead could have walked off the cliff and gone splat––saving him the trouble of having to put him down.

There was only one way to find out.

"Fuck me," Gus muttered before running a hand over his face. He studied the knife. While it would do the job, the real trouble was in having to get close. *Real* close. And he wasn't up for getting close, not even with a bat.

Hell, right about then he *wished* he had another bat instead of a knife. Then he remembered the garage. Perhaps something useful waited there for him.

A minute later he stood in the garage. It was huge. Cavernous. Large enough for four cars and kept clean. A set of mountain bikes rested against the far end, along with a low stack of pleasant-smelling firewood, all cut and ready to go. The usual assortment of tools rested on nearby benches or hung off the walls. A grey locker near the workbench drew his attention, because it was there he spotted the axe.

It was old, with a wooden handle, but it had length and weight.

The length sold him.

The controls for the garage were on the nearby wall, while a set of remote controls rested on a bench next to the mudroom doorway. Not exactly wanting to open those big doors with the possibility of a zombie outside, he took the axe and remote and returned to the front door of the house.

Gus pulled on his sneakers, hefted the axe and paused in the porch area. He took a few seconds to inspect himself.

Jesus Christ.

Just the painter overalls. Not even a fucking coat. He was practically naked except for the one-shot axe. One shot because, if he missed, the zombie would be close enough to tackle him for a very bloody hickey.

A nervous energy sparked in his meaty calves, spreading to his chest, carbonating every ounce of juice in between. Sensing that buildup, his brain wondered if his intention was such a good idea.

"Course not," Gus replied, and quickly undid the front door locks.

He pulled that barrier open and drew back into a baseball batter's pose.

Nothing came at him.

The van was out there, with nothing else except the stone wall. Gus peeked out, eyes wide and ready to pop out if someone so much as patted him on the back. He eased outside, surveying everywhere and fearful of a heart attack before breakfast—which, he had to admit, was one way to start the morning.

The front of the house was clear. Dead leaves covered the paved walkway and the lawn on either side. A drizzle began to fall, bringing a haze with it.

Scratching his upper lip with lower teeth, Gus closed the door behind him and eased farther outside. That gap widened as he eyed the far corners of the house. The wind continued to blow, but not so bad as the night before. Rainwater quickly soaked his sneakers.

He marched for the van, ignoring the dampness in his feet and the drizzle clinging to his clothes. He left a noticeable trail in the dead foliage, but as far as he could see, his was the only one around.

The van doors were locked and he'd forgotten the keys. The water reached his socks as he circled the van, deeming the vehicle safe. The left side of the house got his attention. Gus side-stepped, broadening his field of vision, checking around the corner.

All clear.

The undisturbed carpet of leaves coating the lawn indicated nothing had crept by during the night. The lawn, maybe four inches deep, needed a mowing. Every step of his left a track.

Fear ebbing away into annoyance, Gus picked up the pace. He trudged for the corner, passed it, and rounded the rear. There he stopped and stared, planting the axe headfirst on the ground.

No one. No zombie, no person, not even a fucking garden gnome. Just more wet leaves and grass, right up to the sliding door, and not a hint of any trespassing. He checked on his own tracks to confirm and, judging by the mushy wake he'd just left behind, there was no way a zombie could have circled the house without leaving a trail. Not in that slop.

Gus exhaled with a pained grimace, placed a hand to his chest, and felt the early morning cold air on his lightly dressed person.

"Anyone fuckin' around out here?" he barked, and immediately cringed. That came out louder than he'd wanted.

A breeze rustled a few treetops. Otherwise, silence.

"I deserve to die after that," Gus whispered. He readied his axe, waiting for the inevitable stampede.

Except nothing happened.

The pool, he thought, and zeroed in on that drained backyard pit. He edged toward it, staying well in the open. The concrete cavity was empty, however, its sea-green depths drained and coated in an organic sludge of leaves.

Gus saw Annapolis then, spectral in the morning fog. The ground leading to the cliff was untouched. He checked the drop-off anyway. All clear, forty feet down. Nothing had gone splat at the bottom, and the area was clear enough of underbrush to know if someone had.

He scratched at his unshaven chin. Had he imagined the whole episode? At this point, he supposed, anything was possible.

Nerves, he told himself, the tension in his frame slacking off.

Just then the roof caught his eye, where several glassy black rectangles lay side by side, covering the entire length.

"Solar panels," he muttered. "You got solar panels on this thing? You wealthy bastard, you."

That's when he noticed the lack of power lines.

Whoa, he thought, then remembered his original purpose for being outside. He circled the back to the last side of the house. Zombie free, as before. A shed was built onto the rear of the garage, however, so he opened the unlocked door.

Car batteries. Maybe two dozen, on shelves and trailing wires to a control panel displaying red LED numbers. The set-up surprised him, but he wasn't an electrician, and refused to touch anything for fear of shagging it up. The shed was empty, and, weirdly, lacked a door to the garage. Deciding someone had screwed up the design, Gus closed the door and glanced around.

On the nearby hillside stood a small windmill, motionless despite the breeze. Nor were there any cables going to the shed. He figured they were either underground or not hooked up.

"I'm not complaining, mind you," Gus explained to himself. "Off the grid is fine with me. Must be nice having your wallet. Yep."

Much more relaxed, he strolled back to the main gate. He'd closed that gothic barrier the same day he'd arrived. An iron bar—a piece of metal the length of his arm—lay across the middle. Just as he'd left it. He supposed if the owners did return, they'd wouldn't be able to open the thing from the outside, anyway. Unless they knew something he didn't.

Leaves littered the road leading up to the gate. His feet were squishing now, soggy cold and grossing him out, but he needed to make sure.

More dead foliage plastered the road leading toward the highway below. All of it was untouched. A firm tug on the bar informed him, yep, the gate was indeed locked.

Secured, Gus deemed, slowly turning and taking it all in. *Unless they can climb the wall, nothing's getting in here.*

Which made him feel a little better

Sneakers farting, he went back to the house and locked the door.

<h1 style="text-align:center">6</h1>

He kicked off his footwear on the porch, draped his wet socks across them, and left everything in front of a heater. Barefoot, he trudged into the kitchen. His thoughts kept returning to the nightmare. The whisky bottle called to him from the cupboard, so he mixed himself a drink. Glass of sanity in hand, he returned to the living room, to the sofa, where he sat and watched the world.

The drizzle thickened to rain.

"Gotta think this through," Gus told himself. "Nothin' got over the wall last night. Nothin' got into the house. So… I imagined all that shit. Thanks brain, for the goddamn horror movie in the middle of the night. Appreciated. Say…" He held up the cocktail of ginger ale and whiskey. "How about I kill you off just a little bit more? My way of sayin' 'fuck off'."

With that, he drained half the glass.

"Maybe that'll get you onside here," he muttered through a couple soft burps. Then he rolled his head around his shoulders and checked the nearest clock.

8:47 am.

He was drinking in the morning.

"Five o'clock somewhere," he declared softly. At Annapolis, he said, "Stay right there," then got up and returned to the kitchen.

He fired up the stove and worked on a meal of spaghetti, with some frozen wieners chucked in for flavor. There was no hamburger, so he made do with what he had. He drank while he cooked, taking peeks out the window at the gate and wall before stopping and staring at them.

"Maybe you're trying to tell me something," Gus said, pasta bubbling away in a pot. "Maybe… this place isn't so safe after all."

It seemed pretty damn safe to him, however. If the zombies could beat their way through the tempered glass doorways of Mollymart, how would they fare with iron bars and stone? Not too good, in Gus's mind. Oh, they might get through eventually, probably would get through by some unseen means. If they did, what would Gus do next? What *could* he do next?

"Not fuckin' much," he admitted.

Not now. But he *could* do something over time. He could improve his defenses, make it so that anyone trying to get in would dearly pay for every inch. If he was going to stay at the house, that is.

Honestly, where else did he have to go?

He studied himself. His painter duds. He'd left his axe with his sneakers, near the front door.

"Shit," he said. He wasn't going anywhere. Not because he didn't have the gear, but because he was a hundred-and-fifty pounds overweight, and the thought of going beyond that wall, well, terrified him.

The house was a fortress, and, to put it politely, he'd have to be insane to leave it.

Droplets jumped from the boiling pot and hissed on the stove top. He switched the heat to low.

When breakfast was ready, he slopped everything into a bowl and ate standing up, leaning against the island. Some sauce landed on his overalls, which he fingered off and licked clean.

Later in the afternoon, Gus had two more drinks, just to ease into the evening. He warmed up the leftover spaghetti and wieners and placed the remainder in the fridge. He flicked on the lights to brighten the mood, and when he was finished eating, he dumped the dishes into the sink. There was an urge to do something. He thought of his brothers out west, but couldn't remember their cell numbers, and the house phone didn't work anyway.

By the time it was dark, Gus not only felt worried, helpless and alone, but consumed with that same need to do something. *Anything.*

As long as it was inside, of course.

Then something occurred to him, and he searched the kitchen. The calendar was on the wall, near the stove.

October, he thought. With a little mental accounting, he realized it was Halloween.

Halloween.

If ever there was a fucking time to be the last man on earth, now was the time. Just his goddamn luck.

That night, in morbid celebration, he drank the rest of the whiskey and passed out on the sofa—with the axe leaning against the coffee table, just in case.

For the next two days, Gus stayed inside the house.

It rained on and off during that time, which made the decision to stay inside easier. He drank cinnamon-flavored whiskey and suffered for it. After stretching out on the sofa for the second night, he had another, less frightening incident where he woke to a subtle scratching against the window. He sat up and grabbed the axe, waiting for whatever might come. Except nothing did.

The sky began lightening when Gus realized he was hearing twigs, snapped off trees and skittered across the lawn, sometimes right up to the glass. If soggy leaves weren't enough, now he had twigs. It was a goddamn deciduous dandruff going on out there. Seeing as he was wasted and wide awake, he decided to search the grounds again, just to be sure.

All good.

He killed some time in the basement, where he ignored the pool table and instead watched movies. As suspected, the terabyte unit had hundreds, perhaps even thousands of movies and completed television series. Whoever owned the place had a lot of horror flicks, but he avoided those, not needing more bad dreams.

He watched a few silly comedies to keep his morale up. He snacked on *Oh Henry* chocolate bars and double stuffed Oreos. When the temperature dropped, he pushed a button on the thermostat and made it warm. When he got thirsty, he drank water or one of the soda pops. When he was *really* thirsty, he cracked open a can of cider.

After a movie, he would rise from the basement and approach the city-facing windows. Everything seemed fine from a distance. Not a hair out of place. Maybe law and order had returned. Maybe the cops or the army had finally arrived and cleaned up the town.

Such thoughts dissolved, however, when he pulled open one of the sliding doors.

Hazy streetlights came on in Annapolis, setting the sky aglow, but there was no other activity. Not a screech of tire rubber, not a blaring horn. Nothing.

On the evening of the third day, however, Gus was in the washroom on the main floor. He was taking a leak, absorbed in that basic biological function, when he perked at distant gunfire. Not as much as before, but enough for him to pinch off the flow and stuff his junk away in a hurry. Grunting, swearing and ignoring the warm dampness in his crotch, he hurried into the living room.

A second series of *pops* echoed from the direction of the city.

Gus went to the sliding door and opened it, the icy fresh air slapping his face. The shooting had stopped, but he'd heard it all the same. Gunfire. He *hoped* it was gunfire. He stood there, leaning out the door, staring down into the valley. He waited a long time, suffering the drop in temperature, until he realized he was losing heat from inside the house.

The gunfire did not repeat, and there was no other noise.

Disappointed, he closed the door and crowded the window, his breath steaming the glass.

He hoped whoever was doing the shooting was okay. Hoped they had gotten away.

That night, he stayed off the alcoholic distractions and sat on the couch, waiting for more gunfire from the city. He skipped supper, which didn't bother him. He turned the lights off and kept the axe handy.

And there he sat, watching the city, waiting for another violent sign of life.

Until sleep took him.

Nightmares woke him twice. The second time, he stayed awake until dawn, leaving his post only when he needed to use the bathroom. In the afternoon, he brunched on Oreo cookies, finished off the pack and washed it down with water. He didn't feel like pasta, so he cracked open a bottle of preserved beets and ate half of that, wiping his mouth on his sleeve and noticing the purple streak there.

There was a bottle of prunes as well, and Gus figured what the hell. He'd never eaten any of those explosive colon bombs before, and he remembered Toby talking about how folks in Korea had no designated breakfast foods. Food was food, and they ate whatever was on hand. Gus didn't know how Toby knew that, but then that was the magic of Toby. Half his bullshit was actually true.

Thinking of the departed man, Gus cracked open the bottle of prunes, dug one out with a spoon, and sniffed it.

Smelled okay.

"This one's for you, Tobe," he said, and ate the prune. Sweet, but the texture wasn't exactly appealing. There were soft, unpleasant bits, which he spat-dribbled into the garbage can. He ate three more before placing the bottle in the fridge. Wasn't bad. Not at all.

With brunch finished, Gus went back to the sofa and continued watching the city in that shellshocked stare of someone operating on only a few hours of shut eye. The lack of sleep made him feel hollow. Fried. But he would make do, even though he wasn't sure what he was making do with. Or for.

In time, he gave up on hearing anything and dragged himself down into the basement. There, he put on a movie. A zombie movie this time—he felt strong enough to watch it. In fact, he felt oddly compelled to watch it. One by George Romero, where the people were holed up in the shopping mall.

Two hours in, as promised, the prunes hit him.

He'd known the slippery little nuggets were a source of fiber, but there should have been a warning label on the bottle. It wasn't so much the fruit that bothered him, but he'd used a surprising amount of toilet paper in cleaning up, and that concerned him. The toilet paper was a finite resource, and when it was gone, he didn't like the idea of using face cloths for wiping.

One episode later and he decided—no more prunes.

Unless he absolutely had to.

7

After another lousy night of waking up and scanning the dark for frights, Gus practically sleepwalked into the kitchen. Another grey morning greeted him, and he couldn't remember what day it was.

"Christ," he grumbled. He had to keep better track of time. The calendar stared back at him. The thing was an uninspiring office edition, with a picture of seemingly unending, interconnected pipework. He tore it down, accidently ripping out the tack and hearing it bounce off the floor.

"Fuck." Gus bent over for the tack. He flipped pages to November and stuck it to the wall. The kitchen became very quiet. The dates slowly unfocused into blurs. Gus squeezed his eyes shut for a second, found a pen and squinted at the calendar. He drew Xs through the last few days, not knowing exactly what day it was, but figured starting off on November first was close enough. Which would make the current day…the fourth.

And as he crossed off those days gone by, the clinging, ass-dragging funk of depression and sadness was slowly replaced with restless energy. Gus recognized it instantly. *Nerves*, though he wasn't one for anxiety attacks. Never had one in his life. But if he had to guess, he was on the verge of one now.

Not surprising, either, seeing as he was scratching off days, on perhaps the last calendar ever to be made. If it was a panic attack… now was as good a time as any to get one. Or a series of them, however they went about happening. Every now and again, Gord would talk about his wife, Mary, and how she would get them. She had medication for her episodes when they got really bad, but Gord reported that hour-long walks also did wonders for her.

Does real wonders, Gord had explained.

Even as Gus heard his dead friend's voice, the slow, live-wire build-up of energy in his legs extended to his crotch. His belly. It reached his sternum and

31

became a hornet's buzz of power that spun and crackled. His hands started trembling and he made a fist around the pen until his fingers and palms hurt. He dropped the pen and took a deep breath, then took several, fighting back the very urgent need to scream. To just unload whatever was in his lungs and fill that five-gallon house with ten gallons of noise. Hell, what he needed was to open the door and just shriek. Let the world know he was there. That he was still alive.

That urge swelled, threatened to crack ribs. It rustled and clawed at the back of his throat like spider-legs struggling for purchase, except Gus didn't *want* to scream. He *couldn't* let himself scream. Screaming might attract some very unwanted neighbours, even this far up in the boonies. But he had to do *something.* He had to, or he was going to fucking burst. An alien had infected him, insisting its presence against his ribs and elbowing his heart out of the way.

Unable to take much more, Gus marched double time out of the kitchen, grabbing his axe en route. In the front porch he realized he needed his sneakers, so he pulled on his socks. Using too much force, he ripped the little woolly bastards at the ends. Fuming, he threw them aside. Not bothering with replacements, he hauled on his footwear and went outside.

A long walk does wonders.

A long walk does wonders.

He slammed the door behind him. Fresh air smacked his face. He took in two lungfuls of that frosty goodness and got marching, axe held across his chest as if he were on a parade ground. After a dozen paces, he double-timed it, but that didn't cut the cheese, so he started to jog. He went all the way to the gate, where he took a sharp right and followed the wall, headed for the drop off. Somewhere along the way, Gus put his head down and charged.

A long walk does wonders.

Does wonders.

DOES REAL FUCKIN' WONDERS!

Orange and yellow leaves blurred underfoot. His chugging, gluttony gasps for breath filled his ears. He grunted. Groaned. Strained to place one foot before the other.

Gus looked up.

He was less than ten feet from the drop.

With all the grace of a sinking, one-engine tugboat gunning for safe harbor, he swerved and hit the deck. He tramped over the wood, barely missing one of the lawn chairs, and thumped onto wet ground on the other side. His feet were cold and everything between that and his brain numbed. Gus broke into a run, red-faced and jiggling all the way across the back of the house, or the front, whichever suited the owners. If anyone spotted him from afar, well, he could imagine what they saw—a fat slob on the verge of a heart attack, sprinting along the cliff. In painter duds, no less.

With an axe in his hands.

In fucking November.

Gus's breathing sputtered, became ragged as his pulmonary system quickly overloaded. He was no Donovan Bailey, to be sure. He lurched into the next turn, almost landing flat on his chest but somehow remaining upright. He switched the axe from one hand to the other. The shed with the alien car batteries that mysteriously powered the house came into view, then the grey, sour-puss underballs of the sky. The house streaked by, then the hillside fell away as he rounded the corner of the garage, whereupon he released a dying caveman bark at the sight of the stone wall.

Gus ran—well, *staggered*—across the inner grass to the wall. He put out a hand to support himself until that same hand grabbed at his ribs. There was a sharp stabbing pain in his right side. *Sweet Christ!* A goddamn *stitch*, right under his man boobs.

"Fuck me," Gus wheezed, hobbling along and wincing with every breath. Every intake knifed him straight through his diaphragm, and reminded him why he didn't exercise.

He slowed into an arthritic lurch, still pressing a hand against the pain. A stitch. Whoever named it got it right. Felt like being shoved through a sewing machine, affirmed with every breath. Sweat streamed down his face and slipped into his eyes, just to give him a little more to do.

But he didn't stop walking.

When he reached the gate again, he moved as if he'd taken a bullet to the ass cheek. All was clear beyond the bars, so he kept on walking. The stitch stuck with him, not finished with its punishing needlework. His sneakers and feet were soaked again, and water leaked from every pore of his person.

He turned at the end of the wall and continued along the drop, focusing on the far hill.

Gus reached the deck, where he stopped, gazed at the valley, and whispered in a strained voice, "Fuck this."

The needle had become a wooden shiv, and the invisible little elf who had stuck it in worked it with both arms.

As he hobbled back to the front door, Gus realized his nerves had thankfully settled down. He'd also must've shed five pounds in that short but energetic burst of activity, which somehow took the edge off.

"Thank you, Gord," Gus said as he stepped into the house.

Stripping off his soaked sneakers, Gus tread barefoot into the kitchen, leaving damp prints on the hardwood. He grabbed two cans of ginger ale and proceeded to the living room couch.

Red-faced and shoulders heaving, he plopped down.

When he was ready, he cracked open the first of those two cans, drank deeply, and came up for breath with a cannon blast of a burp.

His clothing soaked up his sweat. His feet dried. His stitch died away.

When he'd returned to a relative state of wellness, he rolled over onto the sofa, stretched out, and fell asleep.

8

After two days of anxiety-fuelled patrolling, where he marched until he damn near dropped, Gus woke on the morning of the sixth.

He got up, placed a finger to each nostril and blew his nose. No sooner did he clear his sinuses did he sniff at his arm pits. *That* opened his eyes. He hadn't bothered to shower after his patrols. To make matters a little worse, the temperature had dropped several degrees yesterday, even coating the back deck in an icy morning glaze.

Stewing in his own stink, Gus eyed the world outside. Still overcast. Still cold looking. Annapolis remained a dead and silent disc lining the base of the valley. He strained to think about what else he'd done yesterday. Nothing much, really. After the over-energetic walks, he'd been exhausted enough to sit and stare out the windows. He ate when needed, drank (no booze, just water and pop), watched movies downstairs, and tried to stay awake long enough so that when he did sleep, there were no bad dreams. Not that it worked. Twice he woke to his own petrified shrieks.

Not rested in the least, Gus watched the city. His own body odor shook him out of that morning stare.

"God almighty," he whispered. "I *reek.*"

On his to-do list for the day—a bath and a wash of clothes. It almost sounded like a regular day. He rose from a damp puddle of blankets on the sofa, and decided those needed a wash as well. The couch was okay, but maybe needed a spray of air freshener. If he had any. He'd been sleeping on the couch ever since he'd found the place. The thought of sleeping in any of the bedrooms, in a strange bed, felt wrong to him, even though he doubted the owners would ever come back.

So he shuffled into the kitchen, scratching at his balls and butt. He pulled opened the cupboards and stared at his remaining food stock.

The candy bars were all gone, as were the Oreos, which befuddled the hell out of him until he remembered he'd eaten them all. There was one packet of crackers left, as well as the last of the peanut butter. He was really going to town on that combo. Five cans of spaghetti sauce remained, as did a couple boxes of pasta. All good. He could dine on spaghetti for months if he had to. There was also a bottle of preserved beets (with one already opened in the fridge), but what got his attention, what he *really* zeroed in on, was a single can of, of all things, *You're Welcome* brand sweet green peas.

"You're welcome," he grumbled, taking the can and studying the label. *Sweet peas*, he thought, *goddamn sweet peas*. Perhaps there was a can of sweet peas at the very back of every pantry on earth. Or beans. Whatever. Both were, both *had* to be, the finish line of side fixings. The absolute *last* thing you would put on your plate, that you would want to eat, but nevertheless picked up at the grocery store.

Gus squeezed the can, hefted it, then placed the tin at the very back of the cupboard, hiding it behind the last bottle of beets. Beets and *You're Welcome* sweet peas. *Sweet Jesus*. It was like a sign warning of the cliff, just a foot away from the actual drop.

And he was staring right at it.

This is it, he thought without fear. Without nerves. *You're going to run out of food. Soon.*

The unthinkable, as improbable as a zombie invasion, overloaded him and left him at a loss. He couldn't run out of food. There was *always* food. At the grocery store. You had money, you walked in, and you bought what you needed. *Here my good man. You have food, I have money.* It was as easy as that.

Then another thought struck—*what was he doing here? What was the plan again? Had there been a plan?*

He believed so. At one point.

The sky was a grim shade of grey, making him wonder if the sun had decided to take the week off. Or the month. Maybe even the *year*.

November. It was November. The sixth.

And he hadn't seen or heard from another living soul since he'd arrived at the house.

There was no plan, he told himself. Only the hope that the zombie plague would be under control by the end of the week. That was the so-called plan. A train wreck if ever he'd heard of one. And the calendar would inform him, would *warn* him, as it had yesterday and the day before, that the end of the week… was coming.

No, the end of the week was *gone*.

And he was still self-isolating on top of a mountain. With winter coming on, of all things. The sky warned it was going to happen any day now. Any time. Snow. And when it did snow, it would be on the ground for a very long time, because there was no one to clear the roads. The department of highways and the Annapolis city council would not be assigning schedules to road-clearing crews. There would be no big machines plowing and salting the roads. That little service, taken for granted for so long… was no longer available to him.

Feeling sick, he studied his food stores. All the while, an unpleasant tingling started in his calves. Buzzing upwards through the meaty tissue, *spreading*.

Winter. Winter was coming. Hell, winter was *here*, and it was getting ready with the snow. With the *blizzards*. Any one good dumping of fifteen or more centimeters would trap him. Half a foot on the roads, and he'd be stranded in an A-frame chateau overlooking the city. Trapped without proper supplies. The first snowy wallop, and he wouldn't have to worry about zombies.

All he would have to worry about would be a slow—and no doubt painful death —by starvation.

Silence then, grim and oppressive. Gus realized he had walked back into the living room, where'd he'd essentially camped out ever since finding the place. Bleak daylight shone off the hardwood floor. Beyond that, the picturesque view of the valley and city that unquestionably added thousands to the property value. The blanket from the night before lay crumpled upon the sofa, the pillow there imprinted with his head. As gloomy as the day was, the interior was still beautiful. Peaceful. Where you could lie down and write poetry, or that great novel, or some shit.

Then the vibe changed, and Gus saw the house for what it would be.

His coffin.

A great big coffin. A *cozy* coffin. With him, too weak to move, but just enough flailing energy to tumble off the sofa during a night of horrors, where he would lay upon the floor, gasping, convulsing, and dying of hunger.

If he did nothing.

If he simply stayed up here and waited, hoping for someone to come rescue him, for someone else to deal with the undead plague of the city…

"Fuck that," Gus swore, breaking the stillness.

He decided to do something about it.

The buzz in his lower legs droned on, but thankfully didn't go any further.

Gus went back into the kitchen, opened the designated junk drawer and pulled out a notepad and pen. He needed a shopping list. Needed to take stock of everything he had and would need.

That stopped him cold, and he looked back at the near-empty pantry.

"The fuck I need this for?" he asked, and tossed the writing materials away. He needed *everything*. Food, clothes, medicine, even fucking *entertainment*. Anything he could get his goddamn mittens on. Mittens! He needed fucking *mittens*, for fuck's sake! Just his luck the house he'd holed up in belonged to a family of hobbits.

Where exactly would he get everything he needed for the winter? That made him shiver. The city was right there, but he wanted no part of that place. Annapolis was now ground zero. The very core of evil. That sounded like something out of a bad movie, but it was true. Annapolis was off-limits, which meant he'd have to get supplies elsewhere. Which meant he had to go look for them. Transportation wasn't an issue. He still had the van. *The van!* That big shitty bread box on four wheels was suddenly the second most important thing in his possession. He had a ride, and the beast could carry loads of whatever he found.

All right. He was cooking with gas now. One problem solved, and now back to the first question. Where would he get everything he needed? To survive the approaching winter?

He glanced towards Annapolis again, for another long withering stare-off.

"No fuckin' way," he declared.

But then where? The army base? Gus wasn't a hundred percent certain. Seeing how close Greenwood was to the city, however, and not hearing a peep or a rumble of any heavy machines or even a sign of troop movement, well, all that suggested Greenwood had their own problems. Greenwood might very well be offline like the rest of the valley. Thinking more on it, he hadn't even seen or heard any aircraft whatsoever. No planes, no helicopters, not even a goddamn drone. Not even as much as a residual smoke trail across the sky. Hell, he couldn't remember the last time he'd seen a seagull.

Then—the light bulb moment.

The burbs. No, not even the burbs, but the other properties like the one he was presently living in. The ones out of town, scattered all along the highways, leading down into the urban center. There were plenty of houses, all nearby, and all of them a helluva lot safer than driving down main street. That frantic tingling returned, prompting him to leave the living room and hurry upstairs to the master bedroom. The whole place was every bit as fine as below, and even though he couldn't bring himself to sleep upstairs, he'd certainly explored it.

Two pairs of thin socks were stored away in a chest of drawers. They weren't winter, but he'd double them up. He grabbed them and, planting his considerable two-pillow backside on the edge of a queen-sized bed, pulled the socks on without ripping them apart.

Time.

Jesus Christ, he mulled, feeling a calamity about to bury him alive. He returned to the main floor and saw it was a little after nine in the morning. The evening started around 3:30, and got dark 4:30. There was no way he was going to be on the road at night. He wanted to be back well before then, with all doors locked up tight.

Which meant if he was going to do something today, he had to get moving *now.*

This only added to the fire lit underneath his sizeable ass.

There was no winter clothing. No coats or gloves that fit him. Everything he owned was all back at his place, but that meant going into the city, so fuck that noise. Gus thumped downstairs, got his axe and went to the front porch, where he grabbed his sneakers and the keys to the van. He yanked open the door and stepped outside, closing up the house with a firm tug on the latch.

The van waited. Gus hoofed it over to the machine, feeling the winter in his woefully inadequate clothing, and rounded the broad rear. He got in, tossed the axe into the passenger side, and glanced over his shoulder. There was a lot of space back there in the van. Easily big enough for a pair of coffins.

"All right," he said, and gripped the wheel. "All right."

He fired up the van and fiddled with the off-kilter gears, cursing until he found Drive. He eased the machine into a wide turn until facing the gate. Locked from the inside. *Why didn't the owners get that thing automated?* he wondered. Was it a power issue? Too much of a draw? Were the missing owners preppers who left their home for whatever reason and got caught? Got killed?

Questions. Mysteries. Ones he'd never get answers to.

He parked the rig and got out. Working harder than he had all week, he shoved the bar back with a grunt and pulled open one side of the gate, then the other.

The road beckoned, covered in wet leaves and disappearing amid the forest at the far end.

Hand resting on the door handle of the beast, Gus stared at all that open space, realizing he was on the brink of heading out into a dead world—a very dead world. After a week of fear-induced, drunken isolation, God only knew what waited for him down in the valley. Colorless images formed in his mind. Dead faces and fisheye stares, protruding tongues and clawing hands, reaching for whoever was closest.

That bit of imagining caused him to take a good long look at the house. Warm. Safe. Dry. And above all… no unreal insanity of dead people walking around.

Then there were his clothes. He wasn't dressed for this. Wasn't armed, despite the axe. Wasn't *ready*. He was, in essence, a movie character, expendable, someone the audience not only knows will die from stupidity, but will probably cheer when he does croak.

And in those deciding seconds ticking away, he did the thing he was absolutely certain he should *not* do.

He put his head down and gripped the door latch. Pulled himself aboard the van and closed the door. The steering wheel became an anchor, and he held onto it as he shifted into Drive. Then, knowing he was going to die, one way or the other, Gus put his foot down on the accelerator, and eased the van through the open gate.

9

The mountain road cut through a pale forest whose sleepy calm that didn't reach Gus in the least.

The highway came into view and he braked, stopping at the base. He blinked at that single solitary strip of pavement—empty and cold-looking—realizing he had one choice.

Go right or go left.

Gus sat and fidgeted, nerves ringing and eyes wide as if he were peeing blood for the first time.

Out of habit, he flicked on the indicator and signaled a right turn, thinking himself incredibly brave for doing even that. He kept his foot on the brake, however, content to study the forest as his indicator clicked away. Seconds passed, and that soft clicking seemed to grow in volume. There was still time to go back, rethink this from the ground up. There was no need to rush into things, which he was most certainly doing. No need at all.

Instead, he took his foot off the brake and eased out into the highway. As he increased speed, he scanned through the available radio stations, letting the numbers flash across the interface. Nothing, however. Not even a public service announcement. No clue of where to go, or where to reconnect with other survivors.

So Gus drove on. He didn't drive fast, even though there was no sign of life. Not a damn thing. It wasn't often he drove along this route, so he wouldn't know just how lively it was during the day. Knowing the state of the city, however, and perhaps even the world from a TV and radio standpoint, the lack of life seemed all the more profound. More sinister. Trees went by as Gus did another scan for broadcasting radio stations. Not a one. *Goddamn* he could do with a bit of music. Just one song on repeat. Even that seemed better than nothing.

He twiddled with his nose, feeling itches even after he scratched. His jeans underneath his painter overalls pinched at his crotch, and he lifted himself this way and that to create room. Sweat oozed from his face and hands, even though the heat in the van was barely on. The forest he passed through laid no shadows across the road, and Gus found himself longing for those picturesque, sun-patterned shades.

There were smaller towns about, but the populations in those usually shopped in Annapolis. There were farms on the other side of the mountain, but Gus didn't care about those. Not at the moment, anyway. He'd turned right and let his memory do the driving.

The forest thinned on either side, becoming tattered in places, revealing a few open fields. A car came into view, stopped on the left shoulder—a blue sedan in need of a little paintwork around the edges. The driver's door hung wide open.

A nervous Gus slowed down alongside the vehicle.

Blood coated the windows, as if someone's head had exploded. Through the jagged streaks, however, the interior looked empty, but he wasn't completely sure. Gus studied that gruesome blast of red soup, thinking of what might happen to a person stuffed inside a giant microwave set on high.

No chance in hell he was going to get out and look inside that thing. No chance.

He let out his breath, realizing he was holding it, and glanced around. Bare trees with seasonal foliage stood thick on either side. There were rolling ruts in the land, but nowhere for a zombie to hide. So he took his foot off the brake and rolled on, speeding up to fifty.

It was then his stomach turned on him, still seeing all that blood inside the car. How much blood was in one person? Gus couldn't remember, but it looked like the sedan had been painted in the equivalent of a couple of full-grown bodies. Maybe even three.

He needed a drink. Water would be nice. Whiskey nicer. Then he realized, in his haste to get on the road, that he'd forgotten to bring any food or drink.

"S'all right," he said, as the forest flashed by. "S'okay. That's what I'm out here for. To get… stuff."

A black and white image of that bloody sedan revisited him.

Christ, Gus thought, and wiped his face. And that was just the beginning. He was going to see worse.

More abandoned cars along the road, in much better condition than the first. He drove by them all; each one empty, their doors opened. The trees on the left ended, and a driveway split a grassy plot of land right up the middle. At the end stood a two-story house, which faced the valley much like the place he'd taken refuge in for the past week. That home didn't have the great privacy or the view, however, but it was the first house on this rather hasty foray into civilization, so he slowed down and leaned over the steering wheel.

The paved road went some fifty meters, ending at the rear of an L-shaped house, where the broad side looked toward the city. The part facing the highway had two windows, providing all the view anyone needed of the driveway. Bare Dutch elm trees stood on the corners, their limbs like veins against the clouds. A detached garage lay at the end of the driveway. That was fine, but the door was closed.

The brakes squealed when he applied them, yet no zombie showed itself and the countryside remained empty. The van idled in the middle of the road. Gus sat and ruminated, his unease thrumming, knowing he had to do something within the next few minutes. Part of him hoped someone would appear at the front door. That would be best. Because, seriously, what he was considering…it was stealing. Looting. Just going up that driveway would be trespassing.

Shaking his head, Gus turned into the driveway, his unease growing, just a fright away from panic. He had a very bad feeling about the house. For one, it was painted a shithouse brown, a terrible color. Those looming corner windows watched his approach, and made his paranoia dance. If anyone was inside, they had already spotted him.

And maybe they already had. Maybe they were already pulling on boots, to step outside and say hello.

That got a nervous smirk from him. He should be so lucky.

Gus eased by those corner windows and glimpsed all the way through the interior, to the other side. The sight prompted him to brake. He lowered his window and caught a whiff of exhaust, but he could easily see into the kitchen, and the living room beyond that. The beast idled, waiting, and Gus waited in turn, watching for movement in his field of vision.

Except nothing did.

He placed his hand over the van's horn, wavering, wondering if he should make some noise. Rubbing his chin stubble, Gus decided to continue on, where he turned around in front of the garage, in case he needed a quick escape. He turned off the engine and pocketed the keys, in case, on the long shot, someone spied him and decided they wanted his ride.

Things got real quiet.

Still no indication of anyone having heard him.

No movement on the main drag either.

Quiet. So quiet.

Gus opened the door, the hinges groaning, not only betraying him but paralyzing him on the spot. Another short, painful wait—but no one appeared. He stayed motionless for a bit longer, holding onto the door like a shield. If there was undead around, they *had* to have heard that metallic *yark* of ungreased joints. And if they heard you, they would come looking for you. Memories came to mind of the neighbourhood across from Mollymart.

Still no reaction from inside. No screams or moaning or the sound of footwear clattering off pavement. No bodies charging the window and plunging through in an explosion of glass.

All right, Gus thought, flexing his hands, trying to control their trembling. *You know what you have to do. So you do it. Okay? You're just looking for food, so get it done. Okay? Okay then. Worst thing in there are people, and you can talk to people. Just don't stutter. That might set them off. In what way, though? Fuck off, brain, I'm handling this. So let's go and get this shit done. Shake the water lily and tuck it away. Faster we're done, faster we're outta here and back on the road.*

Dreading the next part, he eased out of the van and reached back for his axe. The garage was behind him. A single oval window dotted the upper center of a huge door. Unblinking, maybe even on the verge of his heart exploding, Gus made like a ninja and crept to the window to peek inside.

Garden shit. Shovel. Pick. A stack of winter tires and a couple of kids' bicycles. More importantly, empty. Which he knew. Already addressed that. If they heard you, they'd come charging. "They" being zombies. He hadn't figured out why people wouldn't come running. That is, if they were around and alive.

Gus bared teeth and wiped sweat from his face again, wondering what a meltdown felt like, suspecting he wasn't too far away from experiencing one firsthand. Somehow he made his legs work, and reached the front door of the house. There was a small circular window there, like a ship's porthole, and the doorbell was on the right. He stopped, wheezed as if working on one lung, and forced himself to take a breath.

Here we go, he thought. *Moment of truth.* Moment of: *Hi there—wonder if I could borrow some sugar? Oh, you survived the outbreak too? That's swell!*

His legs felt charged, ready if and when needed. All he needed to do was give the signal, a scream of pure shit-spraying terror, and his legs would do the rest. Get him right out of there. Then his only problem would be stopping.

For long seconds, he stared at that infernal doorbell before sticking out a thumb and pressing it.

Happy chimes went off, impossibly loud. They only tinkled, but to Gus, they were the swinging bells of some great cathedral, urging all to mass. Somehow, he didn't run for the van and make dust clouds for home. Instead of running, he found the courage to lean into the window and peek inside. A small, clean-looking porch area lay beyond the glass. A number of winter boots were arranged neatly in a row, right below several coats hung up in an open closet space. A hallway went left, into the kitchen, then right, going deeper into the place. Just a regular house. He regarded the door again and realized nothing had come at him, that it remained very quiet.

Knowing he was summoning his own death, Gus leaned into that hot button and rang it a second time. While he waited, the van behind him pinged as the engine cooled.

Deciding to proceed, Gus checked his flanks and grasped the doorknob. He turned that brass piece…till he heard the softest click.

Now! He urged himself. *Do it! Go, go, GO!*

But he didn't go. Not the way he wanted to, for fear of being somehow struck down or tackled. And his legs were no longer working right. They weren't legs anymore, but boneless spongy columns bent at the halfway point.

Instead of charging in, he opened the door just a few fingers—when the foulest stink smacked him full in the face. A noxious gas cloud smelling of shit and decomposing meat invaded his gullet, and his breathing, so quick to begin with, sucked all that nastiness down in one gulp.

Gus gagged, stole a polluted breath before clamping a hand over his mouth and backing away. No face mask. No scarf. Not even a fucking set of clothes pins to pinch off his nose. His stomach churned with washing-machine might.

Then he thought the worst. *What if whatever was turning people into mad raving ijits was an airborne thing?*

If that was the case, he was pretty much fucked. But then he remembered what he'd already been through, the zombies he'd already been in close contact with, and calmed somewhat.

Getting his breathing under control, he regarded the open doorway.

"Anyone—" *home?* he wanted to ask, but it came out as a loaded dry heave, sounding like an old plank being plied off a summer deck. He'd unconsciously backed up a couple of steps, to breathe better. If anyone was in there, however, they were dead and rotting. Long gone to a better place.

"Oh god almighty," Gus muttered, not appreciating how that foul air was making contact with his eyes. "Anyone hear me? Hello?"

Then everything was screaming at him to get out of there, to just boot it back to the van and leave this place. Fleeing from zombies was one thing, but willingly entering a grave? He forced every step, working those jelly legs of his, but the rest of him wanted no part of what he was doing or where he was going.

He inched into the porch area, fearful of corners and what might be hiding behind them. Sweat slipped into his eyes and he furiously dabbed them clear. His breathing was far faster than before, and that *stink*… only now did he understand how smell could incapacitate an individual. That god awful smell was *repulsive*. It was a fetid, open sewage line of meat and rot and any other decomposing filth left in the sun, producing such a scorching olfactory experience powerful enough to induce blindness.

There were boots on the floor. A size eight at least, which was too small for him. There was the kitchen, clean and thank the lord empty of people. White cupboards. A nice fridge, plastered with crayon drawings of picnic fields, sunny skies and animals playing underneath. A cast iron frying pan rested on the gas stove, reminding Gus of superwoman Anna and her pink SUV. A dishwasher stood close by, as did a nice cubby hole of a table where a family of four or five could squeeze together for breakfast.

His nasal cavity felt positively corrupted now, and his eyes watered. He lurched for a nearby dish towel hung off the stove handle, before his nose practically dissolved. He yanked it free and covered his face, grateful for the makeshift mask. The cloth stunk of soapy residue, but it was better than the carrion stink permeating the house. He mashed it to his face like an oxygen mask and sucked back liters. Anything was better than breathing in that horrible smell.

And still nothing came charging at him from around a corner.

Remembering how a pack of zombie children had chased him through a house, Gus was beginning to think the home was indeed very much empty. Past the midway of his endurance, of nerves and smell, he got moving, following the wall, glancing back every second step. Sweat continued to sting his eyes. The sweat was much sharper than his own tears, and he soaked up whatever he could with a quick dab of the dish cloth. The hallway became a smeared tunnel of potential horrors. Yet when it ended in the living room, and that picture window view of distant Annapolis (he had a better one), Gus didn't feel any relief.

The living room was an empty beige cave, so he continued deeper into the house. Along the way were a set of white carpeted stairs, leading to the basement. Into darkness.

Gus peered into that pit, imagining the absolute worst, knowing full goddamn well the stink was definitely coming from the basement.

I'm not going down there. I'm not going down there. Fuck it. There could be an undead jamboree down there and I am not going down there.

Worse, he thought he was getting a buzz off the dishrag. Like he was inhaling chemicals not meant to be inhaled.

He pressed on, leaving the stairs, going for the bedrooms first. A mouse could fart and he would jump through the nearest window, he was so on edge.

The first bedroom was for children. Two little girls, by the look of it, considering all the pink and stuffed animals spread across two separate beds. Posters of cartoon characters covered the walls. A little toy bakery lay on the carpet, along with a nearby picnic setup of dolls. The empty beds were made, crisp as if never slept in, and the room itself had been dusted at least a week earlier.

He moved on to the master.

Another empty room. Clean, with a window looking out at the valley. A queen-sized bed filled the middle of the floor, but there was enough space for a sofa chair crammed into a corner. Two chests of fine-lacquered wood flanked the bed.

No parents were present, however.

Thank Christ. Gus pressed the dish towel to his face, coughing into it before wiping his brow. He glanced down the hall, toward the stairs leading to the basement. *No,* he vowed, chewing on his lower lip and tasting soapy shit. *No way.*

No. No, no. NO.

It wasn't like he *had* to go down there, not at all. Seriously. He could search the house and take what he wanted, make like a Black Friday sale and boot. And maybe there was a one percent chance of the owners coming back to meet him in the doorway with his arms full. *Why, hello neighbors!*

He shuffled back to the stairs. His nerves weren't frazzled, but positively *crackling.* There would be serious, long lasting effects. Didn't need a shrink to tell him that. Or, at the very least, there would be dreams.

Legs weak, he leaned against a wall and peered down into that carpeted dark. He clicked a nearby switch twice, then sighed. *Course not.* Goddamn switches never worked in the movies either. Not when you needed them. All the same, he continued flicking the switch before ending with one last disgusted snap and head shake.

He dropped the dishrag for only a second, and the stink was impossibly worse. What was making that *smell?* Did the house's shit pipes explode or something? Or something similar?

What's similar to a house's shit pipes exploding y' fuckin' dummy? His brain shot back.

And that scared him a little more.

"Anyone down there?"

No answer.

"Course, not," Gus muttered. "Look. Ah. I'm a little freaked out here, okay? Just a little. To tell the truth, I'm a sneeze away from shittin' myself, okay? If you wanna know. I'm coming down, so don't get all chaotic or bent out of shape, all right? Just lettin' you know. Saw your place from the road and just checkin' in, is all. See if you're all right. If you're okay, maybe we can trade? Or, I dunno, team up or something? I… I found a place further up the highway. Up on the mountain. I got power. Water. Hot water, if you need it."

They probably didn't have any of that, judging by the light switch.

"I don't got any food," he carried on. "And that's what I need. If you got any to spare, that is. Or know where I can get some."

The grocery store, you fuckin' bum, go to the grocery store, said the voice in Gus's head, but damn if he was listening to that nut.

There was another switch nearby, for the hallway, so just to make sure, he reached out and flicked it.

Light winked on from overhead.

'Course. He tried the switch at the top of the stairs. Not a gig. That got him fuming even more and, actually, miraculously even, took the edge off his fright just a little. He needed a flashlight.

Back in the kitchen, he took the opportunity to check the cupboards, relieved to see a few food items tucked away. There was stuff in the fridge as well, but mostly perishable, about to go bad. The leftovers of a roast chicken looked greenish. In a drawer next to the fridge he found a flashlight, long and metal. It worked, too. Worked real well, in fact—he could adjust the width of the beam.

"All right," he said, and took a minute to tie the dish towel around his head.

Flashlight in one hand, axe in the other, he went back to the basement stairs. Gus didn't think himself an overly brave man, but he had guts. Yet the amount of guts it took for him to take that first step not only surprised him, but left him dizzy.

He descended, one quiet step at a time, careful not to trip, and that God-awful stink intensified. The flashlight's hard white glare showed him everything, while his improvised mask fluttered with every breath. He turned right on a landing and caused a floorboard to squeak, which caused him to become a full-on statue. Nothing jumped into his sphere of light, however, so after a few seconds, he started down again.

The bottom level was another renovated cave, and definitely the source of that toxic gas misery. He swung the shaky flashlight beam around, the fluttering in his mask coming faster, his eardrums on the verge of bursting.

Brown carpet. A heavy-duty treadmill. Bar setup. Nice. He'd have to check that out. Some shelves with assorted trophies. A few books. A poker table. Why not? Then a wood stove and some knocked over chairs and then two corpses hanging from the ceiling, a woman and man, black tongues protruding from sagging, clay-white faces. The ropes hung from bare timbers, but to get to those timbers, one of them had to hack out a jagged section of gyprock.

Which one of them obviously had.

Gus stood there, no longer breathing, staring at the hanging couple. As he processed the sight, his eyes drifted down to the couple's feet and their socks. The man wore standard sweat socks, but the woman wore polka dotted whites, which seemed truly out of place in such a scene.

Gus backed up until he hit a wall, and there he stayed. He reached back and felt the wood keeping him upright, patting it, *thanking* it, because if the wall wasn't there, he would've surely fallen on his ass. He stared at those two displays of death, horrified to the core, yet unable to tear his eyes away. There was broken glass underneath the lady, and an empty light socket near her head. She'd probably busted it herself when the rope went tight, and the instinct to save herself kicked in, whereupon she flailed and clawed at the knot overhead attempting to save herself.

Gus remembered to breathe and swung the trembling flashlight beam over the rest of the basement. On some macabre whim, he centered on an open doorway, where the light reflected in a mirror inside.

Gus studied that doorway, his every hair crawling with the knowledge he would not like what he found inside, that while the two hanging bodies may be bad they were probably nothing compared to what lurked just out of sight. He decided he didn't have to check the bathroom. The basement was a grave, and a grave it would remain, so all he needed to do was go back upstairs and grab whatever he needed, whatever was useful.

But for some headstrong reason, he went to the bathroom anyway. The light wavered in the mirror, revealing part of a shower curtain. Gus stopped. Brushes and combs and hair scrunchies covered the countertop under the mirror. Bottles of shampoos rose like the towers of a miniature kingdom, and next to them were those fluffy, curly things that helped one exfoliate.

Don't go in there, his brain warned, sounding more serious than he could ever remember. But he took a step inside that baleful side chamber anyway.

That was when the flashlight beam found the bathtub, and the two little girls, no more than eight, inside.

That's also when Gus started screaming.

10

"Jesus Christ," Gus panted, the fresh air stopping him on the threshold of the house. He walked out to the front of the van where he began to pace. His throat burned, scalded from screaming, and his shoulders ached from where he'd banged into doorways on his flight upstairs. No doubt there would be bruises.

The last few seconds, before emerging from the house, had been a nightmarish blur, where the ghosts of those two little girls and their terror-filled, vacuum-sealed shrieks filled his ears. He still saw their tiny hands behind their backs. And the clear plastic bags drawn over their heads, stealing their lives and freezing their faces.

The parents had done that, but how the hell could they? Yes, there was a plague on, where the living became dead things that ran around the neighborhood looking to bite people, but was that enough to murder one's children? And how did they get both kids in the tub? Had they killed them at the same time or in different rooms, perhaps distracting one while the other parent did that horrifying deed.

A horror show of how things might've played out ran through his head.

"Gentle Jesus," Gus wheezed and whined. "Didn't need to see that. Did not… Oh…"

He stopped pacing and planted his forehead against the cold metal hide of the van, where he steadied himself. To a point. Once he had a grip on his sanity, he turned back to the house.

"I'm sorry," he said, meaning it. "I'm so sorry."

Only the wind answered him.

The house waited for him to make his move, so he did. Gus went back to the driver's side of the van, having lost all interest in continuing. He knew he would see things. Deep down, he knew. Scenes of death that would perhaps stay with him forever. But he wrongly—*stupidly*—assumed they would all be adults for some reason. That somehow the world was merciful enough to spare the kids from such a gruesome ending.

Back aboard the van, he locked the doors and sat back.

Every place would have a scene like that.

No. Not every place. Just a few. Where people decided that the world was done, and decided to exit with it. In their own way.

And the horrible thing about it all? Despite the heartbreaking scene he'd just absorbed, there would be more. There would be *worse*. Without a doubt.

That was it for him. He'd had enough.

"God… damn," Gus whispered. He couldn't go back in there. He *wouldn't*. The house was a crime scene. All he wanted to do was leave and try and forget about what he'd just seen.

Gus was about to start up the van when he pursed his lips. The highway lay at the end of the driveway, this *morgue's* driveway. Morning was getting on.

Get moving, Gord said, not-so-long dead, from the backseat of Gus's mind. *Get moving.*

Gus looked back at the house, half-expecting to see the whole dead family standing in the doorway. They weren't. The bodies were in the basement and there they would stay, which meant he didn't have to go down there. Not at all. Everything he needed was upstairs, anyway.

Hating himself, he slumped in the seat. Then, after settling down and thinking for nearly thirty minutes, Gus got out of the van. The dish towel he'd stripped off lay on the ground. He picked it up, shook it out and once again wrapped it outlaw-style around his face. Then he returned to the house, axe in hand.

Leaving the front door open, he went to the kitchen cupboards and searched each one until he found what he was looking for.

His heart dropped.

Two cans of cream of mushroom soup. A box of spaghetti noodles, one box of breakfast cereal bran flakes (what Gus called 'extra strength colon blow'), and a small box of ice cream cones.

Evidently, someone had forgotten to go shopping.

Gus cursed himself. Feeding a family of four obviously diminished the food stores, and avoiding starvation was probably the reason mom and dad up and killed their kids before opting to hang themselves.

What a choice, Gus thought. *And what a thing to do.* Horrified at what had gone down, he regarded the cupboards once again. He took the cans first and realized he didn't have anything to carry them with.

Damn, he was really making this up on the fly.

The dish towel around his face was becoming irritating, so he took it off and tossed it into the sink. The fresh air current diluted the house smell, but it was still there.

A quick search revealed a stash of reusable grocery bags, so he shook out one and placed the meagre provisions inside.

The refrigerator was a bust, and there wasn't much in the freezer either. Feeling as if he was violating some unwritten code by taking the scraps, Gus hefted what he had and headed outside.

At the back of his van, he opened one door and put everything in, along with the rest of the reusable bags. Gus considered the garage. The side door was unlocked, so he went inside. Nothing had changed. There were a series of plastic recycling bins, as well as one for the regular trash. Gus left that. A shovel and pick hung on the wall. The pick he might find a use for, but the shovel was the old aluminum kind used for snow. He couldn't remember if he had one back at the house, so he took both items.

There was a green-handled hammer as well, cousin to the *whammer*, which Gus believed Gord used as a weapon. He didn't want to think about Gord, so he grabbed the tool. It would be a good backup to the axe.

The other items in the garage were deemed unnecessary, so he left.

Shovel, pick and hammer went into the back of the van.

Gus faced the house, knowing he was forgetting something, but damn if he could remember what. Not that it was important, since he couldn't bring himself to go back inside. He was done with the place. It was going on noon and, God help him, he would need a shitload more than a couple cans of soup and a box of spaghetti. Let alone ice cream cones.

He got back in the van, started it and rolled down the lane, the smell of the dead family clinging to his skin and memory. As he made his turn, the bags and whatever was in them shifted and slid free, rattling across the floor behind his seat. Tree tops sped past, but what Gus saw were the faces of those two little dead girls. He checked his speed, but his dashboard only showed him the choked white expressions of the parents.

That turned over his stomach.

"Oh no," Gus recognized that building, *impending*, sensation right away.

"Oh fuck me, not *now*," he wailed, glancing left and right.

Now, his stomach urged, before truly putting force on his lower colon, reminding Gus he had not taken the time to properly empty his bowels that morning. After everything he'd seen and smelled, yesterday's shit wanted out.

He clenched, clenched for all he was worth, feeling a mountain-sized mudslide coming on. Definitely no *shart* happening down there. The house of the dead family was behind him, but he wasn't going to make it in time.

He braked to a stop, knowing he had only seconds. His colon rang the warning bell again, really leaning into it. He clenched hard enough to make a diamond. He grabbed the gear stick and tried to put the van in park, but the fucked-up stick chose the worst time to be fickle. Gus nearly saw stars from the amount of willpower and exerted sphincter control. He worked the stick, got Neutral and groaned. Frantic, he doubled-down until he got Drive— whereupon he ejected a hearty "*Fuck!*"—before finally locking down Park.

He opened the door and almost fell to the shoulder of the road. The wintry air momentarily eased that relentless rectal pressure, but he knew he had no time. No time at all, and there he was, on the verge of a fucking Pompeii-sized bowel movement, right on the side of the highway.

With nowhere to squat, Gus speed-walked through a field of knee-high bushes like he had a greased jug of moonshine shoved up his ass, and his ass wanted no part of the thing.

He only got three steps when it happened.

BREACH! He had *breach*!

He didn't even think twice.

Gus undid his overalls in a second. He realized in horror he had his jeans underneath to contend with, so he undid those with a frantic level of hand speed rarely achieved. Everything got shoved to his knees, including underwear.

The caress of frigid air across bare butt cheeks failed to buy him an extra second from what was coming, from what *had* to happen. In fact, that sub-arctic breeze did the exact opposite, working more like a lit match waved over an overloaded septic system. Knee deep in bushes, with nowhere to squat, Gus dropped his well-padded bum onto the ground.

Touchdown.

He got his hands under him and hefted himself, a split second before it all came out. Somehow, he weathered the storm, finished, and on trembling arms and heels, maneuvered himself away from the blast zone. Only a few feet, when he lowered himself into the brush and rolled over.

"Thank you, baby Jesus," he panted. "Thank you."

A feeling of wellness overcame him—until he realized his current predicament.

He was lying on the cold, cold earth, surrounded by what might've been wild blueberry bushes and their assorted cousins, with a potentially shitty ass.

And nothing to clean himself with.

Gus rolled his eyes. He couldn't haul up his drawers without cleaning himself. His self-dignity simply would not allow it. The greenery around him was laughable, the leaves no where near the size or strength of the two-ply needed for the job. There were those reusable bags back in the van, but he'd have to walk back to the van, enduring every disgusting squish and rub between his cheeks. Worse, he remembered that thing he forgot to get back at the house of the dead family—that thing being toilet paper.

He'd forgotten the fucking crap wrap.

"Never again, Lord," he vowed, glancing at the heavens. One episode of being caught out on the highway was all he needed.

The memory resurfaced of him tossing the dish towel into the sink. That piece of cloth would have done the job. Gus had an idea then. He reached down and kicked off his sneakers. Off came his doubled-up socks. Pulling the fabric apart, he reckoned he had at least four solid wipes before he was out.

Socks in hand, Gus was glad—so very fucking glad—that Toby wasn't around to see what he was about to do.

11

After dealing with his unexpected emergency, Gus got dressed, pushed himself up from the ground and returned to the van. Without socks. Those would remain among the blueberry bushes. Slow walking back, he could tell there was still some cleaning to be done downtown. Not a lot, but enough to let him know he didn't have the necessary materials to finish the job. He felt dirty. Filthy. But nothing he couldn't handle until he got back to the house.

Or the nearest toilet.

Not even dropping a one-ton deuce on the side of the road made him want to return to the last place. So he started up the van, kept his butt cheeks partially spread, and drove for about two minutes.

It was a defining moment. He wasn't heading home just yet, no sir. He was going forward. To the next place.

Some hundred meters from the last.

The next house had a car parked out front, which meant the owners would be home. Gus slowed, but wasn't overly happy to see the place. That could've been because of the residual peanut butter between the pillows, though. The house was actually a renovated trailer, with a section built onto it to double its girth. The front door was left wide open. A stack of tires lay at the edge of the place. There were other tires placed around the front, filled with flowers withered by the cold.

Gus turned onto a gravel driveway. When he finally braked, his ears perked at the long, lingering sound of a can rolling across the metal floor. That wobbling startled him at a time when he really didn't need to be startled. The sound ended with a gentle tap against the base of the driver's seat.

Gus awkwardly stretched around and identified the culprit—a can of cream of mushroom soup.

"You little bastard," he hissed. "No fuckin' wonder kids hate you."

Sighing, he looked back to the trailer. A picture window covered with a flimsy gauze hid the interior. Gus waited a minute, fingers flexing on the steering wheel, waiting to see if anyone might show themselves.

No one did.

And that front door didn't move an inch.

There wasn't much space to turn the van around, but he got it done. Having the machine in position for a quick exit seemed like good planning to him. The stick shift fought him until he found Park which, coupled with the ghost dab of bacon grease between his particulars, pissed him off more than it should have.

"Remind me to get a new van," Gus grumbled. He stood and grabbed the axe and a few grocery bags. Still pissed, he kicked the can of soup further up under the chair, causing him to hate the thing even more. Leaving it, he walked to the rear doors. There he studied the trailer again. That familiar nervous energy returned, building in strength, filling him with undiluted dread. His throat went dry. He started squinting and scratching, especially his balls, unable to get them in the right spot. Jesus, he hoped no one was home, that maybe they left the door a-swingin' to get to a bus. A cab. Hell, even roller blading to safe ground sounded like a plan. *Something.* He couldn't handle more dead people. Dead people made dead by their own hand, or family relations. Goddamn he would scream long and loud if he saw more or worse than the first place.

"No one's home," he vowed. "Not a soul."

You doing this? he asked himself. *You doing this? After the last place, you actually going to do this? Remember what you saw? Remember the shit you took? The shit you're still wearing?*

Taking a deep breath, he clutched the door's latch and pulled up. Yeah, he remembered, and yeah, he was going to do this.

The right door popped open. He pushed it wide, mouthing a hateful *"fuck"* at the hinges' metallic whine. Gus hopped down and cringed at that greasy, motor oil sludge lubing his butt crack just a little more. He could've used a grocery bag, but he didn't want to toss a shitty grocery bag on the side of the road. That... would be littering.

The open trailer door beckoned, and Gus hefted the axe as he approached the low wooden deck. The wood creaked when he stepped onto it, and he paused there, waiting for a reaction. A side window offered a peek into another kitchen, with surprisingly nice cupboards. He expected a face to show itself—a grey one, with its swollen tongue sticking out and headlights for eyes. None did, however, so he stepped softly inside the trailer.

"Hello?" he croaked, and cleared his throat before asking, "Anyone home?"

An empty porch area had an assortment of footwear but also room for more, suggesting shoes or boots were missing. There were a few coats hanging off the wall. A nice winter one and a heavy, thicker coat for extreme weather. Gus glanced ahead, into a kitchen—smaller than the previous nightmare, but comfortable. A red-and-white checkered tablecloth covered the table. Artificial flowers dotted the center.

"Hello?" Gus said, strangling his axe until his knuckles ached. "Anyone here? Just, ah, passing through. Wondering if you're okay. See how you were doing. With all the shit happening."

Speaking of shit… A horrified Gus thought he could smell himself. After a moment's hesitation, he pressed on. "Anyone in here? I came down from the mountain. I feel weird… Feel weird talking to myself."

Past the kitchen, the trailer became a long corridor east to west. He shuffled one way, into a living room. The space was neat, almost impeccably so, but small, with few places to hide. A grand picture of a tropical beach hung over a well-used couch, and a nearby coffee table was, in fact, a huge cribbage board, with cup holders at the corners. Beyond the sheers hanging in the window was the open rear door of his van.

Giving everything one last lookover, Gus backed up and went the other way, where he discovered a bathroom.

And spotted a full roll of toilet paper on a wall dispenser.

The sight of it made him forget his fear, if only for a short time. He leaned inside the bathroom, searching it while flexing fingers on the axe, very much aware of the toilet paper. As much as he wanted to, he did not give into the urge to drop drawers and wipe. Not yet, anyway. He had to check out other things first.

So he walked passed a counter and cupboards, a fridge and microwave, towards a pair of saloon-style swinging doors at the end. The fridge growled, still drawing power, and he took no comfort from that background noise. A package of granulated cloves rested on the countertop, the top torn open, its contents spilled in a streak of brown powder. A scent laced the air, reminding him of Christmas.

Gus paused at the swinging doors, where he peeked over them and saw three more doorways spaced out along a hallway.

"Hello? I'm still feeling really weird here." In truth, about a hundred thousand watts of dick-shriveling fear coursed through him, right down to his ball sack.

He went into the hallway and stuck his head into the first room. A tiny office, and utterly opposite from the tidy home he'd explored thus far. There was a workstation covered in papers and binders. A couple of smiling stuffed animals filled corners and niches. The laptop on the desk was switched off. Hanging off a wall was a framed picture of a bearded guy, smiling hugely and wearing aviator goggles and sitting in the open cockpit of an old bi-plane.

That scene of happiness caused Gus to just suck it all in. He hoped the guy got out. Hoped he got his family out, or his friends.

Gus withdrew and crept to the next room—a long washroom with a bathtub, and a second throne with a pink fur warmer over the seat. That fuzzy receptacle positively radiated goodness, and next to it was yet another roll of toilet paper.

Things were looking better by the second.

The final room was the bedroom, had to be, and he hesitated halfway to its threshold. Memories of the dead family in the basement assaulted him, goosing his anxiety. The bedroom might very well be a prime place for… suicidal-minded individuals.

The doorway glowed with overcast daylight, daring him to come closer, but Gus didn't want to. Really didn't want to. In the end, though, he began creeping towards the finish line, widening his field of sight. The edge of a large bed, already made up, came into view. Six-foot-tall tiki lounge lamps, festooned with Christmas lights, stood in the corners, next to a nightstand with a kindle unit on top.

And nothing more. The place, thankfully, was empty of bodies.

"Thank you, Jesus," Gus whispered.

He stepped into the room and checked out the closet, filled with men's and women's clothing. The men's wear was all too small, which got him fuming. Being big-boned was starting to suck pink donkey cock.

"Clear," he muttered, but not entirely convinced.

He shuffled back to that first bathroom just off the kitchen, where he plopped down on the toilet next to a small shower. For the next few minutes, he finished the business he'd started roadside, dabbing toilet wads with water from the nearby wash basin.

Despite the terrible morning, the one good piece of luck was that his underwear remained untouched. That alone lifted his spirits. At one point,

Gus leaned forward and held his head, just taking it all in, while his nerves did a reset, rolling back the anxiety meter. His hands quivered, however, which bothered him. Nerves. Goddamn nerves.

He finished, flushed, got dressed and immediately grabbed the remaining TP as well as a stack under the sink. Five rolls total.

Then he went about what he originally came here to do.

As far as he could tell, whoever lived here had left in a hurry and never came back, judging by the open front door. No one went outside without locking up, not in this day and age, and if someone did return in the next little while, Gus would explain his purpose in full.

And hope they were the understanding sort.

And that they didn't have guns.

The fridge had the usual perishables. The milk had gone bad, but it kept company with a nearby jug of orange juice. There was margarine, assorted jars of jams, ketchup as well as other condiments—including a squeeze bottle of Maritime Madness—a hot sauce produced in nearby PEI. A bag of Macintosh apples in the bottom drawer. A loaf of bread was a little stale, but he took it anyway, knowing he had a toaster back at the house. A pack of pizza buns, or "poor man's pizza" as he called it, was on the bottom shelf. He immediately nuked two of the little bastards for twenty seconds in the microwave.

While waiting on the pizza buns, he stuffed all the food into his grocery bags. When the microwave dinged, he dropped everything and went for the good stuff. Good lord, there was a hint of mold there, just in one spot, but those two slabs of bread, sauce and cheese tasted so good. He washed it all down with the juice from the fridge.

Gus belched and checked himself for crumbs. Once brunch was done, he searched the cupboards. Tin peaches and fruit cocktail. More soup. Various cans of pasta goodies, including some exceptionally high-quality ravioli. There were bags and boxes of spaghetti and macaroni, as well as the flat pasta he couldn't rightly name. Three cans of mixed vegetables. He nabbed an untouched six-pack of Pepsi, including a can of hot chocolate with marshmallows. Two Halloween boxes of bite sized chocolates, where one box had already been opened and sampled. Everything went into a bag. In all, he filled three bags, enough to keep him going for a week if he really buckled down on the rationing.

Once finished, Gus pushed through the swinging saloon doors and checked the second bathroom. Along with what was on the dispenser, another six rolls of satiny wonder wipe waited for him under the sink.

"Thank you, lord," he said, appreciating the good fortune. There was toothpaste, mouthwash, and dental floss, which he took, as well as the bathroom cleaners.

The clothing wasn't his size and, upon further checking, neither was any of the footwear, so he left all that. There were no weapons to speak of in the place, except regular kitchen knives, but he had plenty of those back at the house. The books and movies present didn't interest him either, being mostly romance or cold war fiction.

He went through the place one last time, finding a money belt stuffed full of hundreds and fifties in a chest of drawers. Gus stared at the cash before counting it, figuring what the hell. Three-thousand-four-hundred dollars had been tucked away in there, but he didn't take it. He was ninety-nine percent sure the owners weren't coming back, that *no* one was coming back, but he left the money, anyway. It wasn't his. If Gus returned to the house for whatever reason in the future, all he needed to do was check the top drawer, to see if the cash was still there.

He wasn't after riches. Only the necessities.

Including the bum wipe.

After he loaded everything into the van, Gus returned to the kitchen and found a pen and paper.

He wrote:

Thank you for the food and drink and toilet paper. You weren't home when I got here, and honestly I figure you're dead. Sorry if I'm mistaken. I'll be driving along this main road again every so often, in a van. If you need anything, stand on the side of the road and wave me down. I'll give back what I owe, and share whatever I have.

Regards and thank you again, Gus B.

He read over the note, approved and folded the paper before placing it on the table. The pen went into the pocket of his overalls.

"All right," Gus said and, feeling better, walked out the door. Two for two, except that first one was a bitch. He still wasn't entirely comfortable about stealing supplies, but figured the recent note explained himself well enough. No dead families either, which was a certified bonus. The very thought doused his rising spirits.

Once aboard the van, he thumped around, arranging items and tying off the bags so that he wouldn't have another rolling can episode. When everything was packed away, Gus plopped down behind the wheel and started up the engine.

It was 11:44 AM.

No one came running out of the trailer. No one emerged from the surrounding woods.

Gus struggled with the gears, got the right one and drove to the highway. There, he indicated a right turn, and took his time doing so. Time. He still had quite a bit, despite a very real desire to head back to his upscale rat-hole.

The clouds continued to darken, threatening to snow. That worry pushed him to keep going, even though the dead family episode still frazzled him in the worst way.

Another thing popped into his head. No zombies.

That got him hoping. Maybe the great Annapolis outbreak was over and done with. Maybe the monsters dropped dead again after a few days, from a lack of food or water or whatever. Maybe they were croaking right this instant, and the raging epidemic was finally over.

Those were all good thoughts.

A bright sign on the left got his attention. Hanging off the front of a wire fence, the sign advertised "Suzie's Pet Spa!", along with a phone number. Behind that, at the end of a long driveway, a sporty black SUV sat parked before a white bungalow with green shutters.

Gus slowed to a crawl, inspecting the house. Those feelings of dread returned, flaring up in his calves like a mild electrical current. There was no question about what the zombie bug did to the people of Annapolis, but what about wildlife? He didn't want to see any zombie animal, but hated to think of any abandoned or trapped cats or dogs, waiting for owners who would never return.

His hands trembled, and he balled them into tight fists. It didn't help much, and Suzie's Pet Spa, and what potentially might be waiting for him, wasn't helping either. He didn't have to go in there—could just drive on to the next one, a *safer* one, because he *knew* he was going to hate what he was going to see.

Instead, in a surprising display of willpower, he turned into the driveway and headed for the house.

All seemed quiet enough. Gus turned his rig around and backed up to a side entrance, where Suzie had hung a second sign, just like the one on the fence.

He switched off the motor and wiped his hands in his overalls. His clothes were damp, his throat suddenly dry. Gus pushed himself back into the seat and took a deep breath, which did little to calm him. Still, he remained in that crash position and listened, very much aware of the silence, and the alarming uptick in his own heartbeat.

Nothing. No action in the least. The spa stayed quiet, even though he expected a zombie's face to slam against his window.

Nothing of the sort happened, however.

"Fuck," Gus suddenly blurted. *Is this how cops or soldiers feel?* he thought. When they're about to charge through the front door of someplace dangerous?

He wondered how they dealt with the tension, the fear of the unknown, then the downtime afterwards, when all was said, seen, and done. Those questions went through his mind, and he realized he was wasting time. The thought of the timer entered his head, like the one he and Gord and Toby used on the job to increase productivity. He needed one of those.

Somehow, he got a shaking hand around the axe. Then the hammer.

He sized up the house again, and that side door.

"I'm gonna die here," he whispered, and knew it.

He exited through the rear of the van, dropping to the ground, shocking his feet and knees.

A smaller "Suzie's Pet Spa" sign hung to the right of the entrance. The door was locked, however, which meant someone was probably home. Gus knocked and waited. The window had a shade drawn, so he couldn't see inside. A fenced-off backyard had all sorts of small steps and platforms for dogs or cats to go up over, or crawl under.

He knocked again.

No answer.

There was a front door, the private entrance, so Gus walked around the house, past a couple of hedges as he sized up the paint job on the shutters. The drapes inside had been pulled together. That detail slowed him, but he kept going to the front door.

He knocked and waited, watching the windows. If there was someone barricaded inside and they were peeking out, he figured carrying the axe wasn't going to convey any goodwill.

But then again, at least he was human. Scared shitless, but human.

He leaned in close to the door. "Anyone in there?"

No answer.

"Hello?" he asked.

No reply. Hesitantly, he tried the doorknob.

Locked.

"All right," Gus nodded. "I'll leave you alone. I just wanted to see if you were okay. That's all. I mean… you know what's going on. Times are dangerous."

He backed off, watching the windows and unable to tell if anyone was inside or not. Walking into a place with its doors open was one thing, but he wasn't so keen on breaking into a place.

Still… he wandered back to his van, kicking at dead leaves near the foundation. There was a window down there, which suggested a basement.

Gus went to the gate in the fenced off backyard. That was open. He stepped inside and eyed the back windows, which weren't as curtained-off as the front. There was a rundown porch area back there, in need of repair, along with a clothesline strung up away from the pen.

I'm gonna get shot here, Gus knew it. *For trespassing.*

He went to the door, the old porch creaking as it took his weight. Gus expected a scream, a shout of warning, or a dead face appearing in the window.

He knocked again.

As before, no answer. He gripped the doorknob and wavered on the next part, fighting down the impulse to get the hell out of there.

He tried the knob and it turned.

Holding it, and surprised that the owner had forgotten to lock it, Gus exhaled, swallowed and pushed inward.

The smell smacked him hard, not unlike the one coming from the family of corpses.

"Shit," he groaned, failing to escape the stink. Again he considered getting the hell out of there. Instead, he asked, "Anyone home? Anyone?"

He stood in a kitchen, which seemed weird since it meant Suzie had her animals go through it to get to the backyard. Not the set-up he would have, but whatever. The nearby sink held at least a day's worth of dirty dishes. Everything else looked spotless. A table had plain place mats on it, and a tablecloth neatly folded over one chair. The walls were cringeworthy sunflower-yellow with white baseboards. He went to the stove where a dish towel hung, grabbed the cloth and held it to his face.

"You okay in here?" he asked, taking the towel away and rushing his words. "Hello?"

The living room was dark and ordinary looking. There was a climbing tree thingy for cats, three sleeping pads for animals set out by an electric fireplace, but nothing much else. Gus wandered through, towel mashed to his face, his eyes beginning to water.

A set of red carpeted steps led to the basement. Gus rolled his eyes, unwilling to commit, and shuffled down the hall. He passed a long bathroom, complete with a tub. Then the bedrooms. The first one might've belonged to a teenager, considering the assortment of action movie posters covering the wall. The closet was open and stuffed with kid's clothing.

Gus went to the other bedroom, finding it difficult to get his breath.

The smell got stronger.

He suddenly wasn't so worried about the basement anymore.

Taking a step further, his pulse started that ominous drumming in his temples, where each hammer blow wanted him to turn and flee. The doors were locked for a reason, and he was about to discover what that reason was. The last bedroom was a dark rectangle, a portal to something he knew he would have a hard time dealing with, and that stopped him. His shoulders sagged as his imagination flexed. Zombies. Goblins. All forms of twisted, evil night-hags eager to hook his eyes and jerk them from his screaming face.

"Hello," Gus asked warily, lifting his axe.

He went forward, slowly widening his view, seeing the foot of maybe a twin-sized bed draped in shadow. Blankets covered two feet and legs, then a torso.

Gus stood in the doorway. He remained there for a while, transfixed by what lay before him, suffering in both sight and smell.

It was a woman, probably Suzie herself, her head resting on a pillow. Her rifle was positioned to shoot herself under her chin, which she'd done to great effect. Her lower jaw hung open, as if waiting for a dentist to peer inside. Tar doused the front of her pajamas and pillow. There was a small amount of matter dried on the bed board, a dank speckling of tissue that resembled lawn clippings and divots. There was some lumpy grey stuff in there as well, but Gus tried hard not to look at that.

Suzie was dead and gone. Her final act before shooting herself was skipping the dishes, pulling all the curtains and cozying up in bed in her favorite pajamas. On a night table sat an ash tray, next to a lighter and a small nub of maybe a joint.

Gus wondered if that had helped her pull the trigger. Though he didn't know her, his throat constricted hard until it hurt.

"I'm sorry, Suzie," he choked out. "I'm sorry."

Thankfully, she didn't answer.

Gus suddenly wasn't so scared anymore, but he felt sick all the same.

He retreated to the bathroom, found the sink and got there in time before the pizza buns left his stomach in one heaving gush.

12

It took him fifteen minutes to declare the place empty of people and animals. It was a sloppy search, because Gus didn't want to be in that grave, didn't want to be breathing in Suzy's very messy death. After a lifetime of not seeing any corpses besides that of his parents, the body count was stacking up pretty damn fast.

He left the house out the back way and just sagged to that weathered step, where he held his head. The cold air was purifying and very good to breathe. Just that act of taking a deep breath, holding it, and letting it out in a hiss, helped clear his system. The image of poor Suzie in her bed, however, with that gun resting on her gore-saturated shoulder, would stay with him for a while.

"And that's just this morning," Gus winced. "Just this morning. Jesus, Jesus … I can't take this. I can't take this. Is the rest of the city gonna be like this? Huh?"

He glanced over his shoulder at the door. Suzie was gone, so there would be no guilt in taking what he needed. That meant going back inside. Which he seriously did not want to do.

But he had to.

Because Suzy had a gun.

He stood up, took a couple of deep breaths, and went back to the bedroom.

The gun was a small wood stock .22. Gus cleaned it off with the dishtowel and some water from the bathroom sink. After that, he closed the bedroom door and left Suzie where she lay, not bothering to go back in there, for fear her eyes might open and she'd start screaming.

The .22 was a single shot, bolt action. Gus wasn't an expert with firearms, but he knew he was clumsy with such a weapon. And even though it had done the job on Suzie, he wasn't sure it would do the job on a zombie. A moving zombie.

He took it anyway, but there were no more shells in the house.

Checking the cupboards, he found a collection of sugary powdered juices and teas. No coffee, but that was fine. There was a single loaf of what appeared to be raisin bread, but mold had overwhelmed it. Four tins of sausages which Gus enjoyed back in the day, as well as your usual condiments. There were baking supplies—flour, little packages of yeast, and chocolate chips—so he took all of that. Seasoned crackers of a brand he remembered seeing at Mollymart being on sale. And in one cupboard was a case of twenty-four plastic bottles filled with water. There wasn't much in the fridge, as most items had spoiled.

He rummaged through the rest of the kitchen, taking whatever food and other supplies deemed necessary or useful. Two full packages of toilet paper, sixteen rolls each, were stuffed into the bottom of the bathroom closet. Gus was glad to take them. He ventured down into the basement, holding onto the empty rifle and the axe, as if paranoid about putting down either weapon. The downstairs had a laundry room, as well as the actual pet spa itself, filled with grooming materials and tools for use on visiting animals. There were no cats or dogs, which was a relief. He didn't want to see any dead animals.

There were no extra bullets for the gun, and he went through the house twice, skipping over Suzie's final resting place. There were stores in the city he could visit if he really needed shells.

Which meant going into the city.

After the morning he'd just had? Fuck that noise.

Even though the room with Suzie's body had been closed, the back door left open, the smell lingered, debilitating him with every whiff. It was nearly 1:15 in the afternoon by the time he finished scavenging and fired up the beast.

When he reached the end of the driveway, Gus stopped and sized up the highway leading to the city, which was perhaps twenty or thirty minutes away, depending on how cluttered the road was. The van idled as he stared, lost in the moment. Time. He had time to check out another house, but who knows what he might find. And he'd certainly found enough this day. More than he cared to think about.

His mouth went dry, so he reached down for one of the bottled waters. He drank a third and placed the bottle in the cup holder.

Then he turned onto the road, heading back to his mountain hideaway.

He'd had enough for one day. For the rest of his life, really. All he wanted was to get back, despite the fear of winter dumping a foot of snow on him anytime. And truthfully, the way he was relaxing just by heading back, the way all the tension just leaked out and left him exhausted—that proved his choice was the right one.

I'll need more, though, he knew. Much more food and supplies. *Prepare for the worst and all that.*

The faces of the dead haunted him all the lonely drive back. The clouds darkened, and a light rain fell by the time he got back to the walled house. He climbed out and opened the gate, seeing nothing to suggest anyone else had been there. Once inside, he secured the gate, and, with one last look at the road behind him, he returned to the van.

He drove right up to the front door.

"Anyone here?" he asked on entering the house.

No one answered, which meant squat to him. He kicked off his sneakers, lifted the axe, and went searching.

"Look, all's good," he said quietly. "I just found the place and decided to stay. I… I'm not sick or anything. Come out and let's talk. I got stuff for us. Lots of stuff. Just… just don't wait until I'm relaxed and scare the shit outta me. It's all good. All safe. Really."

That last assurance made him stop and frown at the axe he carried.

Deeming the place empty, Gus returned to the kitchen and his little supply of booze. He cracked open the bottle of cherry brandy, found it sweet, not needing any mix to help it down. He drank two mouthfuls while steadying himself against the kitchen island, facing the window. He downed three more shots, taking his mind off what he'd done that day. What he'd seen.

That made him take a couple more mouthfuls.

Then it was back to work, parking the van inside the garage and unloading everything on board. Some of those bags had rolled over and spilled their contents, which irritated Gus, but the cherry brandy was telling him it was okay. So he picked up what had fallen out, packed up the bags again, and lugged everything inside the house.

He distributed the toilet paper throughout the three bathrooms. Then he locked the front door and went upstairs. He drifted from room to room, double checking that he was indeed alone. There was a bathtub in the main bedroom's en suite, so he turned on the hot water and inspected the available shampoo and soap.

Gus realized he needed one last thing, so he went back downstairs, got the bottle of cherry brandy and returned to the bathroom.

Steam billowed, and Gus, feeling the weight of the day, stripped. His fatigue, mental and physical, grew with every article removed. When he got down to the gritty, he flung his sweat damp underwear into the sink and vowed to deal with it later.

After the tub was full, he slid into the water. The temperature was a shade too hot, but Gus didn't dare turn on the cold. Instead, he opened the bottle of cherry brandy, flicked the plastic stopper across the room, and drank.

All the while taking the scalding heat.

"*Ooo*," he panted, "Eeee-*yew*!"

He boiled and tried not to close his eyes for too long at a time.

The en suite had a window, situated just right to see the clouds outside. The bathtub water swished with every little movement.

Wet and gleaming, the water up to his chin, Gus watched the sky.

"Thank you," he said, remembering the dead family.

"Thank you, too," he said, for the empty trailer. "And you too, Suzie."

Gus drank and stared, listening. To the house. To the water.

"Fuckin' end of the world," he whispered. "I'm at… the end… of the world. And I could be the last fuckin' guy around. Holy… shit."

There had to be other people. Had to be.

But what if there wasn't?

He thought, long and hard. And when he got to the hard parts, the really disturbing parts, he raised the bottle and got through that way. By the time he finished his bath, it was growing dark outside. The cherry brandy worked its magic, taking the edge off completely. He stepped out of the tub and dried off, his skin prickling with the change in temperature. Having no extra underwear, he washed his sweat-soaked drawers in the bathroom sink and slapped them over the door to dry. Not wanting to put on his clothes, he selected a fluffy bathrobe, not caring that it barely closed in the front. Though, with his luck, the owners would return while he walked around with his junk hanging out.

He went to the kitchen, intent on the pizza buns he'd recovered, despite yarking up the previous meal. The cherry brandy was gone, but that was fine. He didn't want to drink, anyway. His supply of alcohol was taking a beating. The whiskey was long departed, as was the rum. There was a pint of vodka left, and that sinister bottle of gin, which he knew goddamn well he'd get into eventually.

He ate half a pizza bun and washed it down with water. Perhaps it was the hot bath, or maybe just being behind locked doors, and the safety of the wall, but he was exhausted. Spent. Done and done. He wasn't averse to hard work, but the day wore him out in ways he identified right away. Nerves. Straight up nerves. Being constantly on edge. And that level of alertness, where his eyes and ears were set at eleven, well, he'd never been that way before.

The question returned—did soldiers operating in a combat zone feel the same way? He was physically, mentally, and spiritually drained.

And because he was so tired, he placed the remainder of his meal in the fridge, drank a little more water, and considered sleep. Plenty of bedrooms upstairs, but he had a thing for the sofa. He shook out the blanket, took off his robe and stretched out on those cushions facing the front windows before covering himself up.

Nighttime outside.

Overall, he'd done good. No nervous breakdowns, so that was great. Oh, there was that thing about taking a dump on the side of the road, but that wasn't shitting yourself, so he mentally patted himself for a job well done.

Thoughts of the dead family returned, and their meagre food supplies. Was that the final nail? When the mother or father opened the cupboards, and realized they were nearing the end of everything they had to eat? To get fresh groceries meant going all the way into the valley, to one of the supermarkets, and risk encountering the undead? Or, in the grips of despair, end it the only way available to them.

What a choice, Gus thought. *What a fucking choice.* And that same choice was his, now. While he did well for the day, he didn't have near enough to survive a winter. He'd have to pick through more houses, which meant seeing and smelling more dead people. In essence, graverobbing.

Not robbing. Not if they're dead. Mercifully, his brain didn't argue the point.

Sleep wasn't far away, and his thinking slowed.

Clothes. He'd need clothes, too. His only pair of underwear was hanging off a door. He had a gun, but no ammunition. Everything he needed was in Annapolis, especially his clothing. All he needed to do was give his balls a flick and go into the city. That put a sleepy smirk on his face. *Go down into the city.* That was all he needed to do. That would make it all right.

Darkness pressed against the windows, a lightless pitch that suggested a fog had drifted in. Dark. So very dark. The place could have been twenty thousand leagues under the sea. The cushiony softness of the sofa and the blanket helped him retain body heat. His eyes focused on one point in the window, and, in his sleepy senselessness, he didn't really understand or comprehend why he was fixated on that one point, even when heavy feet stomped across the deck outside.

Gus lurched to a sitting position, whipping the blanket off himself as a figure crashed through the glass in a spray of shards. A rush of jagged pieces reached the base of the sofa. The thing only got a step inside when it slipped on one of those greasy slivers and crashed to the floor, flailing all the way and moaning.

Gus stood, slicing both heels to the bone on the glass, sending twin bolts of agony up his legs. He hopped off-balance, the glass embedded in the bottoms of his feet, screaming when those same hateful pieces sunk even deeper.

He whirled, fell, and landed on the sofa's still-warm cushions.

But that wasn't the worse of it.

Coming in behind that first undead thing, rounding the smashed edges of the frame, were the rest of the family. The wife, with her head twisted at a harsh angle, an angle Gus knew was because of her husband's crude noose. The wife was the fastest, and she sprinted across the floor, reaching for him. Then came the little girls, scampering after their mother, their blue grey faces attempting to chew through the clear plastic bags still trying to suffocate them.

Gus didn't have time to breathe. His feet oozed great black flows, and when he grabbed the back of the sofa to hoist himself up, two cold hands clamped about his ankles.

The father.

Blue grey face sneering, leaking oily filth. Empty eye cavities alive with worms.

Gus screamed himself awake. He thrashed, flailing at apparitions no longer there. His hands passed through empty space and he fell off the sofa, and onto a heated floor. He kicked out, slamming the coffee table and sending it skidding a short distance away. That connection brought him back and he saw the windows were intact, his floor cleared of glass, his feet uncut. Although his right foot ached from kicking the coffee table.

Gus staggered to his feet, checking both as he rose, and scanned the night beyond the deck windows.

A dream. A goddamn *nightmare*.

The glass remained unbroken, and there certainly was no dead family coming to get him. Relieved, he reached around and felt his ass and sighed.

All dry back there, thank you Joseph and Mary for that small mercy.

He searched the shadows of the dark house but found nothing. Heard nothing. Feeling a quick patrol was in order, he walked around and eventually stopped in the kitchen. The oven clock said 3:47 AM. A good five minutes later, Gus returned to the living room and sat back down. He let his breath out in one long hiss.

Goddamn nightmare.

He planted elbows to knees and held his head, and on impulse, pinched one of his nipples.

"*Ow* fuck!" he hollered, but got what he wanted, which was the assurance he *was* awake, and not trapped in a nightmare-within-a-nightmare.

Settling back, he covered himself again, divided on whether to go back to sleep. So there he stayed, replaying the horrors his treacherous brain had concocted without permission. Just cause. Just to scare the living shit out of him, which it had. Mission accomplished.

Gus got up, retrieved his axe, and returned to the couch. He placed the weapon against the armrest, where his imprinted pillow lay.

He did not lie down.

It took a long time, but perhaps a little after five in the morning, Gus fell asleep sitting up.

13

The next morning, he woke—sleepy, depressed, and perhaps a touch hungover. It wasn't a debilitating hangover, just a minor headache and his body complaints about being dehydrated. The morning function on the toilet took longer than usual, but Gus didn't care. Not with all the toilet paper he'd scored the day before. He could make like a sick elephant and not worry in the least.

Parts of the nightmare came back to him. In hindsight, it had been a pretty damn good one, as far as nightmares go. He didn't feel overly tired, however, and figured getting to bed so damn early was the reason.

Which left him with the next question.

Was he going to search more houses today?

Good question. He wandered from room to room, weighing the pros and cons of heading back out there. There was no desire to go, not one squirt, and that was putting it mildly. The thought of winter making itself officially known any day convinced him otherwise. Any day he could wake up to a raging blizzard and twenty centimeters on the ground. And if snow came tomorrow, it would stay until spring.

As good as he'd done the day before, he did not have enough food to make it to spring.

Not quite as urgent, but up there, he also didn't have any extra underwear.

Still clad in a bathrobe, Gus climbed the stairs and located his drawers hanging off the bathroom door. He felt the cloth, gave it a good squeeze, even a curious sniff. Clean, but damp.

He hated wearing damp drawers.

He took them downstairs to the laundry room and threw them inside the dryer. While that was going, he visited the kitchen and had a modest breakfast of pizza buns, an apple, and a glass of powdered purple juice, which might've been grape, but sure as hell didn't taste like it.

The dryer chugged in the background.

Gus had a choice to make.

It was November the seventh. Food was necessary for survival, but he needed clothing, and he doubted he was going to find anything his size in the houses that he searched. Not in time for winter, anyway. The way he saw things, he had two choices. Go into town and hit up one of the clothing stores, risking a confrontation with a whole lot of dead assholes, or… go home to his own apartment. Make a straight line to his place, brave the surprises no doubt lurking therein, and raid his own home. Both choices had him going into town. His apartment was on the third floor of a twelve-unit complex, but it was in the city, and the city was potentially infested. If he could reach his building and get inside his place, he could lock the door, seal himself in, and get everything he needed.

All he would have to worry about then was getting back, and avoiding the undead degenerates looking for a hearty meal.

There was a third choice… keep on searching houses on the main road like yesterday, and scavenge whatever might be inside while hoping to find someone who enjoyed cheeseburgers and ice cream as much as he did. Even then, there was no guarantee he'd find clothes to fit him. And it could take days, depending on the amount of zombie resistance he encountered, and every day brought a greater chance for snow. In December, the chance doubled, and all bets were off come January.

"Christ almighty," Gus whispered.

There was more risk going into town, but it was all there and waiting. Forget the stores and the malls, just head straight for home. A quick and nasty in and out. There was always the chance that all that zombie-ness had petered out. It was awfully quiet down there.

That sunk it for him.

He'd chance it and go back to his place for his winter clothes.

"Okay," he let out softly, his nerves tingling.

Some twenty minutes later, he retrieved his undershorts from the dryer, and very much enjoyed their toasty goodness.

Then he proceeded to get ready.

He dressed—with the painter overalls on the outside again—and double-timed it through the house. Axe in hand, he went to the garage and the waiting van. Bags were in the back. The hammer got tossed on the passenger seat.

The pick and shovel he'd found the day before got split up—the pick went into the garage while the shovel stayed in the beast. The .22 was there, but without bullets, it was just an awkward club. Still, he would take it along in case he came across some ammunition. There were plenty of hunters and gun nuts in the valley. Just a question of whether they were still around.

That got him thinking. Where could he find guns? Honest to Christ firearms? The police came to mind. And the police that saved his ass just a week ago, where Tammy had been gunned down.

That killed him, sticking a knife deep into his heart. He hadn't forgotten her. Probably never would, but the thing the police had shot wasn't Tammy. It was a thing… *wearing* Tammy. Gus didn't want to go there, but the images came anyway—the barricade, and several cruisers and cops making a failed stand. Several of them had died, and brought Gus full circle. Their guns were just lying around. That part of the city was an hour or two drive away, depending on the road. And whether there were zombies. It sounded like a plan.

Prepping complete, he stood in the garage and pressed one of a series of buttons located on the wall.

A garage door went up, opening on an absolute shitter of a day. Rain crashed down at an angle, puddling and soaking the ground. Treetops whipped back and forth over the stone walls, while a despondent fog hid the rest of the world.

Gus stared at the rainstorm, heard and saw the ferocious gusts whipping around the trees. With the weather reflecting his mood, he got aboard the van. Started it up and backed out, winning another bout with the gear stick.

As he drove towards the main gate, a strange thing happened.

That unwanted tingling started in his chest. As soon as he recognized that unpleasant vibe, it spread into his lower parts and his anxiety spiked.

"What the hell?" he whispered, feeling that unexpected surge followed by something even worse. The not-so-familiar, but recognizable, sensation of an approaching loss of consciousness. He started to sweat. Sparkling motes of black and purple filled his vision.

*Passing, I'm passing…*he realized, and sought the brake with a foot dipped in cement. His hands were already disconnected, falling from the steering wheel.

He slumped forward, entering a warping tunnel, then blackness.

All was quiet. For a time.

The wind blew outside the van.

Rain spattered the windshield and the metal hide.

That constant spattering brought Gus back. He woke, and discovered he'd passed out on his steering wheel because he wasn't wearing his seat belt. With a groan, he leaned back and wiped the drool from his budding beard.

The stone wall filled the windshield.

In the last few seconds before passing out, and *realizing* he was going under, Gus had managed to get one heavy foot on the brakes—but not enough to stop the vehicle. When he finally lost consciousness, his slumping weight against the steering wheel turned it, enough that the van came to a stop against the outer wall.

Instead of the gate.

"Sweet Jesus," Gus whispered. He checked his feet, realizing what might've happened if he had kept his foot on the gas. The van might've smashed through the gate or crumpled against the wall. The thought shook him. Hitting a stone wall while passed out at the wheel, and all because of goddamn nerves.

"Work with me, here," he said, rubbing his face. "I got no time for this shit. No time at all."

Even as he spoke, trying to rev himself up to the day's task, he knew he wasn't going anywhere. Not if he was passing out at the wheel, despite the urgency.

And truthfully, that was all the reason Gus needed to *not* go.

Exhaling, he worked the gear stick and found Reverse, then backed away from the wall.

No damage to the barrier itself, but he wondered how the van looked.

To a soundtrack of wind and rain, he returned to the garage and closed it up for the day. The front of the van wasn't in bad shape, so that was a little good luck. It could have been much worse.

Gus left the axe in the kitchen and went to the pantry. He picked out the box of Halloween chocolate bars, the last of the pizza buns, and a few cans of Pepsi. There were no potato chips, which was a shame, but he'd make do. The dwindling booze supply reminded him of the house with the dead family, who also had a bar in the basement. That thought gave him the shivers. Anything could stay there, as he wasn't going back. So he settled on the remaining cinnamon whiskey. A few cans of generic lemon lime joined the group. Medicine gathered, he made two trips to the den in the basement as he transported everything below.

There, he dragged an end table next to the recliner, which was a better choice for the afternoon instead of the bean bag chairs. Unloading everything on the table, Gus settled in and powered up the home entertainment center, which was in direct line of the recliner.

His nerves were still twitchy. Still on edge. Needed to forget about reality for a while. *Just a day*, he promised himself. *Just one day. Try and put everything from your mind. You can't go down there and be a breath away from passing out on the spot. That shit won't do. Reset and get back out there in the morning. First break of day. No more thinking of winter or any other shit until then. Okay?*

All right, then.

With that, he took a deep breath and let his worries go. He flicked through the sizeable selection of movies, and clicked on a title that caught his attention.

As the opening credits began for *On Golden Pond*, Gus poured himself a drink.

*

"Watched *On Golden Pond* last night," Gord said, placing his roller in a tray and adjusting one shoulder of his white overalls.

"Any good?" Gus asked.

"Yeah. It was."

"Never heard of it," Toby said, squinting at his paint lines and looking for runs.

"Before your time," Gord said. "Classic film."

"Lost me already," Toby declared from the other side of the bedroom where the crew worked. He held onto his brush as if it were a pointer. Two slashes of white latex paint decorated each cheek, underneath his eyes.

Gord got all squinty-eyed. "Why's that? You know the story?"

"*Phhst.* Course not."

"Well, maybe if——"

"Don't care so you can stop right there, Mister movie critic. You said the f-word, that's all I need to know."

That crossed Gord's wires even more. "I did not say the f-word."

"Oh yes you did," Toby said, inspecting the ceiling even though that was done yesterday. "Big old f-bomb. Lost me right away. You said it and you didn't even know you let it go. That's sad, Gordus. Real sad."

The two other men exchanged looks. Swearing on a job site was taboo. No one wanted a mouthy crew painting in their house, and the boys knew it.

Gus decided to step in. "He didn't swear, Tobe."

"I didn't say he did."

A hostile-looking Gord hooked his thumbs into his overalls. "You havin' a moment there, butterballs?"

"'Course I am," Toby said. He faced them both, who were on the other side of the covered bed. "You said *film*. That's the f-bomb. For me, anyway. You lost me right there. When anyone uses that word to describe a regular old *movie*, I get all twitchy around the eyes."

"Well, what do you call it?"

"I don't call it *film. Blah.*"

"That's what it is," Gord insisted.

"Little pretentious sounding, ain't it?" a wincing Toby asked. "*Film.* I watched a *film* last night. We're making a *film.* We're heading down to the emporium to take in a *film.* Seriously? Where's your monocle? Where's your ascot? You smoke ciggies with those fancy filters? Which does shit, you know. You're still fuckin' up your lungs."

Gus raised a warning finger at that, but Toby waved him off. "Ah, ease up Timmy. The Dunphys went out fifteen minutes ago. Least I thought that's what she said. She said something when I went for a leak."

"I didn't hear anything," Gus said, looking at the closed door.

"You were working over there," Toby said. "And you zone out when you work."

"Wish I could zone you out."

"That hurts," Toby frowned. "Really. I'm inclined to let you wallow in your own ignorance after that one."

"He asked the question." Gus pointed at Gord.

"Doesn't matter," Toby said. "That last one was a little too close to the bone, Gussy old man. Little too close to the bone. And I had your Christmas present all picked out, too. Had the order all ready to go on Amazon. Gift wrapped on site, too. To show I spared no expense. And just to be clear, I'm certain Mrs. Dunphy left with her husband a little while ago."

"You sure about that?" Gord asked, glancing at a nearby window where one could see the driveway.

"Lemme check…*ETHEL!*"

That blast ripped through the two men. Gus matched Gord's startled expression before both men glared at Toby.

Who held up one finger, invoking silence, then… "*ETHEL!*"

A disbelieving Gord—or at least as close to looking like he was disbelieving—glared at the bellowing painter. The only thing that would scare

Gus more would be Mrs. Dunphy bawling back an answer. And then the game would truly be afoot.

"Goddamnit woman." An impatient Toby shook his head.

"Her name's Edna," a disapproving Gord quietly corrected.

"Right. Well. No wonder she didn't answer. Anyway, she's not home."

Gord planted hands to hips and stared at his younger co-worker.

Gus placed a hand over his own racing heart. It did appear, however, that the Dunphys had indeed crept out and were well removed from the painters' conversation.

"All right." Toby reared up. "What was that question again?"

Gord scowled and crossed his arms.

"Right," Toby said. "'What do you call it?' I think you said. Well, mister, I use the commonly used term for it. *Movie.* Short for moving pictures. Which is what it is. A stream of moving pictures. Recorded images. Without lecturing you at length about Movies 101, I'll paraphrase. Back in *your* days, I know they would shoot their blockbusters or their indie productions on film. Actual *film.* What do they shoot it on, now?"

Gord wasn't backing down. "S'all on digital now."

"Thank you," Toby pounced. "So, why don't they call it a recording? Hm? Or a hard drive? Or, or, a *digi?* Hm? Or some other catchy name. No. They gotta call it *film,* when it's no longer a film at all. No film is ever used, it's all recorded on hard drive. Little more that a really long memory. They simply use the term because it's more artsy-sounding. *We* make home movies, *they* make films."

Gord squinted one eye at him. "I know what a goddamn film is, dickhat. Spare the lecture. We only got a five- minute break. Which we're almost done with, and I don't feel as if I took one."

Toby squinted back. "That's *mister* dickhat to you. And let me finish my thought next time. *Film,*" Toby huffed and pinched at empty air, "encapsulates the... *zeitgeist.*"

"The what now?" Gus asked.

"That word, that thing... that's uh, reflective of what's in style."

"I don't know that thing."

"Yeah," Toby admitted. "I might've stretched it with that one. Gonna haveta look up the definition. Shit. Hate it when I do that. Anyway. That's film. Now, *movie? Pah!* I spit on your movie, commoner. I spit on your popcorn as well. And if I still have spit, I'll lob a long one at your wide screens."

Gus sniffed at his brush. It was latex, and nothing oil-based. So in theory, Toby *should* be sounding much more lucid.

"Goddamn, I knew we were overdue one of his episodes," Gord said to Gus, who shrugged his eyebrows. Gord looked back to Toby. "Next time you feel one coming on, just stay home."

"What, and not come to work?" Toby asked.

"You hate work," Gus answered.

"But I love quitting time."

"Look…" Gord said, and Gus knew right away he was about to fire back on full auto. "I say *film*, because that's what people in the industry say, and I happen to respect those people. We *paint*. They make *films*, and that's the term they use, because it's their business and they want to put out a quality product. So, aside from you thinking it's snobby, and shitting on the professional filmmakers and their hard work, there's no difference."

Toby went silent, mulling things over. "S'pose not."

Gus stepped in. "I get 'film' because it's from the film stock shit they used back in the thirties. And I get 'movies' because we're talking about moving pictures. Or *motion* pictures, even."

"Yeah, well," Gord said. "People who make films, who are in the business of making films, call them films, because they have pride in what they do. I'm a house painter, specializing in interior and exterior applications. I don't slap on a coat of whatever when it's needed."

"Not all filmmakers use hard drives." Gus pointed out. "They use clouds, too."

"Clouds?" Toby asked dubiously.

"Oh yeah. Uploads them right away. Right after they got the shot. Same as saving shit. I mean, backing it up."

"Anyone still use film?" Gord asked.

"Fuck if I know," Gus answered. "Seems old-fashioned to me."

"And expensive as fuck." Toby added.

"You sure about that?"

"Well, not really."

"You best know these things if you're gonna talk about it," Gus said.

"I *do* know," Gord stated. "Just the other month there was one lady who released a flick done on film. Art house release. Down in Texas."

A disarmed Toby raised a hand, silencing them both. "Break's over."

The two painters regarded him for a second, then went right back to their conversation.

"Funny," Gus went on, "you think they would've come up with something for movies done in digital."

Gord nodded. "Been long enough."

"Probably because of hard drive."

"Why's that?"

"Kinda sexual."

Toby went over and picked up the timer, which he then held up to the others.

"It *is* kinda sexual," Gord smirked.

"We're gonna see a 'hard one,'" Gus tried out.

"We're gonna see a 'hard one'?" Gord scoffed. "Try again."

"How about 'hardie'?"

"No."

"Just thinking out loud," Gus said, rubbing his chin with the back of one hand. "Something like that, anyway."

Toby started the timer, and that commencing beep silenced the two men. They all shared a look before picking up their brushes and rollers.

And work started again for the next thirty minutes.

*

Gus opened his eyes and stared at a black screen.

Black screen. The *film* had finished. The last one he'd been watching before falling asleep was *The Three Amigos*.

He stayed in the recliner, seeing the discarded candy wrappers and the empty pop cans. The screen remained black but for a few options at the bottom, suggesting what else he might want to watch.

Gus sat quietly, remembering the smell of the paint from his dream, which surprised him. He didn't think that could happen. *Gord and Toby*, now. He smiled fondly. A guy couldn't ask for anyone better on a crew. They were the best, and even though Gus loved painting anyway, he had to admit, half that love came from the people he worked with. Even Benny, when he got right down to it.

They were his crew. His friends.

That got him, got him hard. He sniffed, feeling his throat tighten, and looked around for tissue. Finding none, he snorted it back and swallowed.

He reached for the cinnamon flavour whiskey.

That shit wasn't bad in the least.

14

Despite being visited by Gord and Toby in his dreams, and finishing off the cinnamon whiskey, Gus suffered through another night of nightmares. As soon as he closed his eyes, it seemed, he was either being jumped by that dead family or replaying his descent into the basement, where he would interrupt the mother and father suffocating their children with plastic bags.

So he woke up around three in the morning, and stayed awake until daylight.

Whereupon he fell asleep for a couple of restless hours, woke, and drank roughly two liters of water. The morning had almost become afternoon by then, and the rainstorm from yesterday had petered out into a miserable mist. Feeling in no condition to venture outside, let alone head back to Port Williams to look for police weapons, Gus once again spent the day downstairs, watching movies, eating, and drinking water or pop. No alcohol, however, as he was down to a quart of gin and a pint of vodka, and not really keen on either one. Supper was a meatless spaghetti, with a jug of powdered fruit juice that tasted like cherry.

That night, the nightmares returned, worse than before. The dead family were full- on zombified, popping out at him at every corner and taking him down in big, gushing bites. In fact, after waking and remembering the dreams, he was amazed blood could… *spray* like it did, like a whale spout after a really deep dive.

At daybreak, a dark-eyed, grim faced Gus looked like he'd spent the entire night in a very loud rock club. Maybe up underneath the stage, where the drummer was pounding out war hymns. In any case, he breakfasted on leftovers, again scoffed at the notion of heading out into that plague-ridden world, and retired downstairs to watch more movies. He stuck with 80s and

90s comedies mostly, enjoying those best. And he stayed away from the gin and vodka, shivering at the very thought.

When night came, and he felt the need for sleep, he resisted, getting up and pacing, splashing water across his face. Anything to stay awake.

Sleep meant nightmares.

The rain stopped the next morning. Even though Gus wasn't operating at full capacity, he couldn't wait any longer. No excuses—there was a job to do. If he put it off another day, he'd probably have a nervous breakdown just from *not* going. The scavenged supplies weren't going to last forever.

He still didn't want to go.

Not after what he'd seen.

He was scared. Terrified even. There was no denying it. He stopped and argued with himself several times while getting ready, anything to convince himself not to go. To not leave the house. He fumed. He swore. He paced, alternating between stopping in the living room and returning to inspect the pantry.

It was insane to go down there.

Maybe he could get by on strict rationing. Maybe this morning a plane or helicopter would fly over. Maybe he'd hear a voice on the radio, or one of the television channels would broadcast a message to all survivors. Maybe, maybe…

Or maybe, he told himself, *you could end it now. Save yourself a slow and painful death starving up here, because that will happen for certain if you sit back and do absolutely squat.*

Gus didn't want to die. Not by starvation or zombies… but one seemed a better chance of happening if he didn't do anything about it.

And after a couple of hours of internal struggle and ass dragging, he got as ready as he could with the clothes he had. The lack of gear and proper protection was another reason not to go. He felt like he was a walking pork chop for the undead if they got their hands on him.

Unprepared. Out of his element. Depressed.

At the very end of his mental moaning, however, he somehow found himself behind the wheel of the van, driving up to the main gate. It took only a few minutes to clear the gate, and in less than three hours of waking up, he was on the highway.

The pavement was not dried out from the dousing of the previous days.

The countryside raced by, thinner and paler in the colder weather. He turned up the heat, because he wouldn't make it with how he was dressed. As he drove, he choked the steering wheel, glancing left and right, scanning those early winter treelines and seeing nothing.

"The fuck am I doing out here?" he muttered, the words barely audible above the engine. The plan this morning—which should have happened a day ago—was weapons. His clothing could wait and, really, it was a shitty idea anyway. He'd make do with what he had or could find. Finding the empty .22, however, that got him thinking about the police barricade, after the cops had pulled him free of the car he and Toby…

The memory stabbed him. He'd been driving when he hit the guard rail that took Toby's head clear off.

"Sorry Tobe," Gus said softly. "I'm sorry."

It was all he could do, so he switched back to the day's mission.

He passed the first three homes he'd looted, even slowed to a crawl when driving by the trailer where he'd left the note. No one came out to greet him, and the front door remained as open as he'd found—and left—it.

The house after Suzie's place was on the left. A dirt driveway led to a large bungalow set upon a slope, overlooking a yellow lawn. A pair of small cars were parked beside the place.

No sooner did he see it, when his brain posed the question, *But what if there was something in there? To save you the trip?*

That was something to think about.

"Goddamnit," Gus muttered, pursing his lips as if he'd tasted poison. "Just… Goddamnit."

It was this kind of indecision that was going to either kill him or drive him batshit crazy. What if, what if, what the fuck *if.*

He braked and turned around in the middle of the road, the scenery whipping past. Not a minute later, he was driving back to the big bungalow on the slope with the two cars parked out front. Potholes pitted the driveway, all filled with mud water, bouncing him along and forcing Gus to drive more cautiously.

It was during one of those jarring trampoline-dips when a figure came around the corner of the bungalow, from the back of the house. Leaning to the left and walking as if he'd been shot in the kidney, the figure took one halting step after another toward the van. Gus slammed on the brakes and watched.

Only one, and with every step, the details came into better view. A zombie, wearing muddied jeans and a shirt. The shirt tails hung out and its buttons were half undone, exposing a patch of white moss clinging to a blue-grey chest. The zombie's bare feet alone were horrifying, the same corpse-color and visibly bloated, as if the thing had inflated them with an air hose.

The face was something else. It was no longer human, but a bloody caricature of humanity, where the eyes appeared blowtorched and ruined. And the mouth…

Gus covered his own.

The jaw of the zombie had been pulled off, leaving shredded cords of black muscle, the ends rattling against its throat. Worse still, the upper jaw gleamed in places, revealing a few golden teeth.

And that ruined abomination hobbled forward in a quickening gait, sensing visitors and eager to greet them.

Gus checked his door and his windows. Everything was locked.

The zombie got within ten feet. That was close enough. He clutched the gearstick and worked it, searching for Reverse.

"Fucking *gears*," he blurted.

The zombie stepped closer.

Gus reversed, hitting the gas a little harder than he should and sending the beast backwards in a jaw-rattling straight line, over the potholes. The van bucked and jumped, flinging him against his window despite the seatbelt.

He braked, fearful of leaving an axle in the road.

The zombie continued marching after him. There were no others between the van and the house. The axe was nearby, but that would mean getting out and taking a swing at the thing with a gimpy walk.

Then—a moment of clarity.

No axe was needed. Not for this infected pedestrian. He had the van, and he'd used it before.

Aware he was moaning, Gus struggled with the stick again, searching for Drive until locking it in. He accelerated, bouncing back over that moon crater surface until the van practically *leaped* at its target.

The gimp lifted an arm just as the beast bashed into it—a solid connection of man-on-machine. The zombie dropped from sight and the van's left side rose and crashed down. Gus drove over the undead, stomped on the brakes and almost ripped the gearstick out to get Reverse. The van rolled backwards, flattening zombie ass once again.

Gus kept reversing until the gimp came into view.

A tire tread ran *through* the chest cavity, crushing the middle like a can of mushy diced tomatoes way past the expiry date. He'd squished both legs as well. Gus put the van in Drive. He lined up the head and raced for it, hitting a pothole before connecting with the skull. That little bounce provided a little extra *oomph* a split second before the sensation of a crumpling aluminum can, which Gus felt all the way up through the steering column.

Goddamn, he thought, cringing at the impact.

He turned the van around so that the rear doors faced the house, and he had a clear view of the gimp, wet-looking and mashed into the ground. Surprisingly, that flattened beer can of a body didn't bother Gus. He didn't barf or feel sick, but he was breathing hard, and he took a second to glare at the gear stick and its screwed-up labelling.

Then the moment passed.

The beast rumbled, perhaps wanting more. Gus scoped out the area, ensuring there weren't any other gimps coming at him.

Gimps. *Good name.* At least for that one. Gripping his axe, he parked the van and got out, the air chilly after the heat of the interior.

The squashed thing in the driveway didn't budge.

Keeping an eye on the zombie, Gus came around the front of the van and eventually studied the house. No sooner than he did, a second shadow appeared behind the window of the main door. It bumped against the barrier, then pawed at it clumsily.

Gus gripped his axe across his pelvis. It was too cold for this shit, so he walked to the front deck and slowed upon reaching the door.

His stomach sank.

The zombie behind the glass faced him, its grey-clouded eyes ogling, yet not quite seeing. Its mouth was a crooked buzzsaw of enamel shards. Black blood caked her face—as well as the front of the shirt she wore. A huge gash split her forehead to the bone, dousing everything below it. If he didn't know better, he would've sworn she had dipped herself into one of those mud spas.... just before trying to rip out the throat of anyone nearby.

With those fucked-up teeth.

The more likely scenario, though, was that someone had hit her in the face with something. Or, remembering the siege at Mollymart, maybe she'd smashed her face against a wall or a door. Repeatedly. Whoever she was, she lifted two discolored hands and clawed at the window, the glass squealing under her fingertips.

Gus reared up the axe, sighted where she was, and hesitated, half-hating himself for what he was about to do. There was no other threat, so he placed himself directly before the door.

The zombie bared those horrific teeth in an anger fueled hiss, perhaps sensing him, and pressed its face against the glass. That got him thinking: *How the hell could she make that sound if she was really dead?*

A second later, Gus drove the axe through the glass and into the thing's forehead. The zombie flopped backwards and landed out of sight. The axe stopped at the windowsill, but the falling weight pulled the gimp's head off the blade.

Gus stood there, transfixed, until his senses returned. He hadn't killed, or *re*killed—or whatever the fuck you called it when you put down a zombie—since… he had to think about it. The biker mom and her husband, back when he and Toby had decided to make a run for it, in that Camaro. He'd killed both those people—those zombified people—in a short but intense struggle that almost killed him, but he got it done. Oh, he'd run over plenty with the *van*, but that wasn't like doing it with an axe. Or a bat. He didn't like it then, and he certainly didn't like it now, but… this one… wasn't near as bad as those first two.

Also, he wasn't anywhere near passing out.

He checked himself and found no injuries, though his right shoulder ached from putting everything he had into that one tree-felling swing. Nothing came around the corners of the house, and nothing more appeared beyond the smashed-out window.

He leaned into the windowsill. The zombie lay flat on her back, the gash across her forehead now a meaty, if not lopsided, cross, exposing things best kept inside the skull.

"Sweet Jesus," Gus moaned. After a second to recover, he checked his surroundings and tried to enter the house.

Though dead and gone, the zombie's legs jammed up against the door, and Gus found himself in a pushing match, making like a bulldozer to gain entry. The old girl didn't move easy, not until he lowered his head and really put some effort into it. When he'd widened a big enough gap, he squirmed through, trying hard not to look at the fucked-up yoga pose of the zombie at his feet.

Sweating, Gus moved into the house. As careful as he might be, he had to step onto a floor glazed with blood. Blood, and there was enough of it, had saturated the carpet then *dried,* creating a stiff, crunchy sensation underfoot.

Axe ready, he proceeded down a short, surreal hall, where someone had taken a full can of maroon paint and simply released their inner artist. Except that inner artist must've had jumper cables attached to its pink parts. Color splashed and ruined the walls. Then there was the smell. As always, that full-on, gag-inducing stink that felt like disease with every intake of breath.

Gus realized he wasn't covering his face and mouth. Too late now, he'd been breathing it all in for seconds. He looked to the right, at a living room with nice furniture, except for the bloody foot and handprints tracking across a not-so-white carpet into a kitchen. There were great splotches of black in places as well. The place was empty, so Gus went into a hall, where a left turn led to bedrooms, and a right straight into the kitchen.

He checked the bedrooms first.

They were empty, as was a nearby home office. There were no other stairs, so he ruled against a basement, which was fine by him. Clothes and footwear abounded; the men's sneakers and shoes actually fit him, so he took the sneakers into the kitchen. A duffel bag hung from a closet hook, so he grabbed it and opened the bag over the kitchen table. His spirits rose at finding a pair of winter boots and two sets of insulated gloves. In one closet was a large blue container marked *Ed's*, another marked *Chrissy's*.

Winter clothing, all finely folded away. Ed was a big guy, but not so portly as Gus. He pulled out a large sweater and still couldn't get into the thing, despite stretching. Still, he was grateful for two sets of warm gloves. Nothing else fit him, so he went back to the kitchen.

Canned fruit, canned corn, and even tuna and salmon. Pasta. Stir fry noodles. Some tomato soup. There was leftover Halloween candy as well. A bag of chocolate chips for baking. What really lifted his spirits, however, were three family-sized bags of potato chips.

"Thank you Ed and Chrissy," Gus said, snatching the bags of Ketchup, Smoky Bacon, and All Dressed. There was also a Halloween box of thirty little bags of plain chips.

In the freezer was an assortment of frozen meat, mostly hamburger, but also some processed food. As much as Gus rejoiced upon finding all that, he was doubly happy to discover a tub of bubble gum ice cream way in the back, unopened, and a half-empty tub of double chocolate.

He could've eaten both right there.

He didn't, however, and continued searching and dumping his loot into the duffel bag.

There were two bathrooms, and he took a total of fifteen rolls of toilet tissue. All that cushy booty made him even more relieved that he stopped and explored the place. There was no alcohol of any kind in the house, which Gus thought strange. The other places didn't have any either, and he wondered if people who lived along this strip were religious or something. Nor were there any guns besides the .22, but that didn't surprise him as much as the lack of booze.

When the bag was almost full, he lifted it, grunted at the considerable weight, and regarded the main entrance.

His shoulders slumped.

A minute later, he finished dragging Chrissy's dead-again ass into the center of the living room, where he dropped her.

There was too much to carry in the bag, so he unloaded some stuff, and returned for it later. Once all was settled away, he did one last look-around the property, and followed a dirt road going up behind the home.

To a shed.

Or really a two-door garage, except the wooden doors were padlocked. Gus went around the side of the building, where he found an unlocked door. Ready with the axe, he entered.

Inside, propped up by a kick stand, was a glorious Harley Davidson motorcycle. Gold painted gas tank, black leather, and blazing chrome. It was a big machine. A road bull. A two-seater bronco adorned with leather saddlebags with the dangly bits underneath. A work bench sat nearby, next to a hanging pair of leather jackets.

But what really caught his eye were the helmets on the workbench. His and hers for sure, as Chrissy and Eddie were obviously a couple of summertime hog riders. Maybe even the fall. He would never know, but he liked the look of the helmets.

Gus picked up one, turned it around, and approved of the thick sun visor, which, when pulled down, pretty much protected the entire head. He tried it on and found it too tight, so he put it back. That one had to be Chrissy's, which left Ed's, so he picked that one up.

Gus sized up the features, admiring the stout weight and the glossy shine. He flicked the visor up and down twice, making little automated noises the second time. Then came the moment of truth. He hoisted that black potholder over his head and pulled it on. The helmet was snug, mostly because of his fat cheeks, but Gus liked the fit. It felt good. Secure. He knocked on the visor and its toughness impressed him. He supposed if you were going to ride a crotch rocket, the visor had to be able to withstand a drop and roll on the pavement.

Still wearing the helmet, Gus wandered over to the leather jackets. Both were too small for him. Eddie's was tight across his back, and he couldn't pull the front together at all.

"All right," he said, and flipped up the visor. "No coat. No guns either, for that matter. But this, this fuckin' rocks."

There was an inside piece that fit over his nose perfectly. Impressed with the equipment, he rapped the axe head off the helmet.

Didn't feel a thing.

"Oh yeah," Gus said with approval. "This works."

Heavy, but not uncomfortably so. He'd get used to it.

The motorcycle, though in great condition, would stay. He would only break his neck riding the thing. In these times, where the undead might mob a highway, he still preferred the size and power of the van.

He left the shed and, on the way back, nodded at the house. "Thanks Chrissy," he said, and meant it. "You too, Ed." He aimed at the zombie in the driveway.

After packing everything away inside the van, he removed the helmet, and secured himself in the driver's seat.

What next? he thought.

Well, you could stay the course. Search the houses. One at a time. You got a motorcycle helmet here. Maybe you'll come across a place belonging to a gun nut who's got a small arsenal tucked away in a shed. Or a basement. No need to go to the police barricade then.

Something to hope for, Gus figured.

Or you could go for the sure thing. The police barricade and all them guns. No time wasted there, and no fighting off dead people still in their homes. Save that for when you have a gun.

"But… I have ice cream," Gus stated weakly.

His brain went silent, then. *So put it back in the freezer. Putz.*

Gus fumed at that, and reluctantly, made his decision.

He dug out the tubs of ice cream, along with the rest of the frozen food, and brought them back inside the house. Left them in the freezer.

"I'll be back," he said to all of it, before closing the door.

Then he was back in the van, driving along the outer ring roads circling the city, aiming for the Port Williams area—and the police barricade that had both saved him, and…

He stopped thinking about the other part, where he saw his undead Tammy gunned down.

After a time, the houses appeared in ones and twos. The lots drew closer together.

Gus drove by them all, coming up around the city, using more of the back streets, entering the edge of the suburbs and recognizing where he was. The houses became more numerous, the lots smaller, closer. That made him nervous. He much preferred the mountain highlands and the more rural setting. At the very worst, he could turn around and head back.

No, he shook that off. Port Williams was close. He was practically there, and he was driving the van… which had proved itself to be a tank.

Ahead, the suburbs beckoned, their miss-match rooftops dark under that grey November sky. Abandoned cars became commonplace, turning the road into a snaky obstacle course. He weaved around the more troublesome knots, slowing to do so, which got his nerves tingling again. More homes appeared on either side of the street, bungalows, split levels, and striking two-stories, all in surprisingly good condition. The lots became even more closer together, at times divided by neat wooden fences. Front lawns and decks with chairs drifted by. A couple of kids' bicycles lay discarded near an elm tree. A green garbage bin had been knocked over, its contents strewn on the sidewalk. One house had scaffolding set up to redo the siding, which would never be completed. Cars and trucks sat in driveways and cluttered the streets.

He slowed down, driving with greater care.

Not a zombie in sight.

No sooner did he think it, however, when things turned for the worse.

It was the van. The powerful chugging of its eight-cylinder engine woke them. Attracted them.

From the shadows, poor infected souls lifted their heads and lurched into sight. At first they appeared in his peripheral vision, shambling forth from their wide-open homes. But then they were everywhere—in open doorways and driveways, crawling out from behind hedges, rising from destroyed flower beds. One figure, splayed out behind a tree, jerked its bare head up as if hooked on a lure.

Gimps. Zombies.

No longer stampeding, they shambled forth as if their joints were poorly fused together. Dozens of them, emerging as if all was just rosy with the world.

So much for the infection burning out.

Gus's nerves revved, cold sweats already rising to the surface. There was no going back, however. One quick peek in a side mirror showed them spilling into the road behind him. So he drove onward, and nearly choked when he saw what lay ahead.

The road narrowed into a bottleneck of cars and trucks, with a few even driven onto lawns. The uneven spread of machines prevented him from speeding through that gauntlet. Front and back ends jutted into the open road, which had to be carefully navigated. Car doors were open and hanging and he clipped one with a metallic slap, a noise that might as well have been a call to war.

And, like a drugged army, the zombies answered.

"Holy shit," Gus whispered, checking his mirrors and windows.

Inside a stopped pick-up truck, a set of colorless hands slammed against the driver's side window just as Gus drove by the vehicle. Dried blood stained the glass as a face mashed a grey ear into the surface. As the van passed, the gimp shifted its mass to the windshield.

Then it was gone from sight.

Others moved closer to the road, however. Zombies rose from between the stopped traffic, their postures crooked and painful-looking. Heads turned, tracking the moving van before lurching into pursuit. Zombies stiffly converged on the street up ahead, seeking to meet the van head on. The maze of abandoned vehicles caused them difficulty, however. Some banged into engines or trunks and stumbled out of sight. Others walked straight into the vehicles and struggled to get around, going one way before sliding the other. One corpse limped into the rear of a street bench, flipped over it, and crashed face first to the sidewalk.

There weren't enough pitfalls to stop them all, however.

Figures of all shapes and sizes sought to navigate the surrounding maze, closing in from both sides of the van.

"*Shit*," Gus spat—and he was only in the burbs.

Undead continued to appear, hobbling down driveways as if drawn to a parade. A few pointed arms. Others flailed, no where near the van, but trying to connect anyway. A man—a *big* man—ball-shaped and showered in blood, stood out from the others. His bald-head swivelled on red-soaked shoulders.

Gus knew right away he would be a problem.

Twenty feet away and the fat zombie seemingly ghost-walked through a pair of full-sized sedans, one arm raised like a traffic cop.

Except there was no hand at the end of that arm, just a chewed upon stump.

Gus accelerated, unable to avoid that bulbous mass without smashing into another stopped car. The oversized zombie stepped into the road, still pointing that ravaged stump, walking on stubby legs and wearing equally saturated cargo shorts. The mouth opened in an opera singer's scream. All that was missing was the horned helmet.

That mutilated arm hit the van's windshield and smashed it aside. The impact spun the ball-shaped bastard around, where he disappeared between the cars. That riled up the others, as more corpses waded out into the open. The stopped vehicles blocked some, but the rest kept on moving, probing, pressing themselves against those vehicles, at times hooked by side mirrors or tripping over things unseen. And for each one impeded, another took its place.

They lurched into the street as the van passed by.

One of them struck the right side, the impact loud enough for Gus to flinch. The corner of the van tapped another zombie, a thin woman, shoving her arm back until the joint locked, hyper-extended, and twisted her off her feet. More zombies waded into the narrowing road. Blood caked features and shadowed blank expressions. Some smiled, while others' mouths hung open. A few waved at him, and it took him a second to realize they weren't really waving, but had broken their wrists, resulting in pom-poms of rotten meat they swung about.

Another zombie slapped the driver's side but Gus dared not rush, for fear of clipping a car or worse. Two more strikes as he sped up, threading the channel at a wretched thirty klicks an hour, which felt like he was worming his way through an overcrowded parking lot. Zombies, trapped in their vehicles, watched with undead expressions of dismay. Other cars had their windows smashed out, the interiors empty, again displaying a brutal strength the freshly turned possessed.

More cars up ahead, partially blocking the way like a sloppy jigsaw puzzle. The sight of them nearly caused Gus to go into cardiac arrest, so when another hand cracked into the van, his head nearly came off his shoulders from the fright.

Gus had no choice but to slow down.

Zombies found holes in that shoddy barrier of vehicles and plodded through, filling the road. The banging upon the van became more insistent, and the zombie-speak—that moaning, wailing nonsense—grew louder.

Then came the worse, and Gus could not take his eyes off it.

The road ahead curved, but the cars jammed along it formed an elbow of a turn, a near impossible fifty-degree angle that he would have to slow to a crawl to get around. Worse, and adding to his dismay, the lawns just beyond that killer turn were practically empty, as if everyone simply drove their cars into the street for whatever reason and then left them there.

The sight of that narrow channel chilled him to his balls.

All because he wanted to search for guns.

All because maybe, just maybe, he'd hoped the plague had run its course, that things were somehow safer.

He was wrong.

In his side mirror, the road behind became a quivering mesh of dead people big and small, limping and trailing after him like the meal on wheels he was. The closer undead continued slapping the van in a tuneless beat.

The turn loomed directly ahead, and Gus had no choice.

He braked while turning, easing the van into that wicked switchback, where a pack of gimps massed.

Gus braced for impact.

The zombies, a few taller than others, walked right into the grill. The van mashed into them, pushing them back and aside. Arms and faces flattened over the hood and windshield. Hands splayed against the glass. Bodies faltered and the front tires rolled over them, giving Gus the tooth-rattling sensation of driving over logs. The zombies behind him caught up, slapping the metal hide with even greater fury, nearly melding into a single noise rivaling those scenes out of old prison movies, where the inmates voiced their displeasure by rattling their cages.

A set of hands latched onto the driver's side mirror, and Gus screamed when those flesh-mitts switched to his window before falling away. On the passenger side, blue and grey faces mashed the glass with alarming thuds before rolling away. One fat-lipped zombie attempted to bite through the window and shattered all of its bloodied teeth upon contact. The same zombie then *smeared* its lips across the glass until they popped sludge. Another gimp grabbed onto the passenger side mirror and held on, pulling itself along for a heartbeat before it dropped from sight.

The van huffed and pushed through the mass of flesh and bone impeding its turn. Gus was halfway through, with only feet to clear the front of a pickup truck. A thick row of walking corpses blocked him. He gave the beast shots of gas, spiking the engine, which pushed into the zombies with warning eight-cylinder huffs. They pawed at the windshield, pulling off one wiper, then the other.

A zombie got an arm over the hood as if he were adrift at sea and the van was a lifeboat. The lower half of that monster's face was hidden behind a bicep, but its rotting eyes glared at Gus. There was a frightening *whump* from the rear of the van, and when he glanced back he saw a worrying crack down the middle of the window in the right rear door. A spidery hand then *plastered* the windshield up front, jerking Gus's attention back to the fray. Corpses stumbled and fell under the van, as if being fed to a wood chipper, and the beast rolled over them in sickening lifts and falls.

Cringing and distracted by multiple points of contact, Gus hunched forward. He gripped the steering wheel like the anchor it was, trying to keep his shit together, trying to keep pressure on the accelerator without going full throttle, which would only launch him into cars and bodies. The van continued turning—an agonizing slow arc, enduring the undead assault from all quarters. At one point Gus thought he heard hands *hammering at the floor underfoot.* That freaked him out all the more, to the point where he couldn't breathe, couldn't *see* straight, and all that was ahead of him was the fucking undead neighborhood watch.

Then he was around the turn, and the only thing between him and a relatively straight stretch of road were more dead people.

Gus hit the gas.

The beast reared up on the last carcass going underneath it, and that sudden lift shook free the zombies clinging to its mass. The van crashed down, bouncing away limbs and bodies.

"*GAH!*" Gus cried when the tires hit level pavement and got traction, launching him up the street. A child's tricycle was the only obstruction and the beast smashed it aside. Gus cleared that road, forced himself to slow down, and drove through a part of town where zombies aimlessly strolled.

A sign ahead displayed the words PORT WILLIAMS.

He was close. Closer than he thought. In fact, as he steamed down a straight strip, glimpses of dykes and marshland could be seen ahead, flickering between the residences.

Zombies filled the lower section of the road. Out in the open, like ugly mannequins released from retail zoos, becoming animate as he approached.

Arms came up. Some broke into swaying, atrophied trots. Two charged the van like low flying missiles, looking to tackle the machine, but Gus hit the gas and bounced them off the grill, leaving their twisted forms in the dust.

Up ahead, splayed across that one road where he'd crashed the Camaro, were the remnants of the police blockade. Except it wasn't like he remembered. Driving up behind that defensive line and seeing the battlefield from the police side forced him to slow down the rig. The row of white and red roadblocks, the kind that resembled wooden sawhorses, had been shunted aside or knocked over entirely. Bodies draped the ones still standing. Bodies draped the ones knocked over. In fact, there were bodies hanging off pretty much everything in sight.

They covered the ground too, two and three layers deep, and clumped higher in places, stretching far back from where the police had started gunning them down. A black sap coated the streets, leaked from the toxic heaps of fallen undead. Bodies were torn asunder. Heads were face down and up, stricken or blasted away.

It wasn't so long ago, but seeing the scale and scope of all that carnage, of people who once lived and breathed and worked within Annapolis, stunned Gus.

Three police cruisers were parked behind the fallen barricade, but they were covered in decomposing carcases and sun-dried bodily fluids. Gus wasn't about to search those rigs, not without a biohazard suit. There were no police among the corpses, so they had either escaped or, worse, been killed and turned.

Brakes squealed as the van stopped. Gus leaned forward, horrified at the scale of destruction.

He located the long barrel of what might've been an automatic rifle, peeking up over a gimp that had its head blown off. The rest of the rifle lay beneath the dried-out husk of another zombie, one that had taken a full shredding burst to the face and body.

Gus gawked, hopeful but also horrified, while the screams of outraged undead grew. He checked his side mirrors, saw a charging wall bearing down on him, and deemed he had time. Back to the rifle. He wasn't even sure of how to shoot the thing properly, but it was a weapon. A *firearm*.

Thing was, the gun barrel was some twenty feet away from clear road, and he'd have to roll over mounds of dead people to get it. The alternative wasn't appealing either, because it meant him getting out and walking over that decomposing mess. He thought he'd be able to find weapons, but he didn't think he'd be digging them out from a veritable chum bucket left to putrefy in the open.

Which was right about when two runners caught up to the van and slammed into the rear.

The sudden two-punch impact jolted Gus, and he twisted around to see the dead bastards clawing at the rear doors and windows. Only two, but there were others on their way, walking as a solid mass towards him.

That broke him. There was simply too much heat. Too many of them, coming out from everywhere, not giving him a chance to breathe.

Gus hit the gas and left the two runners behind in the dirt.

He concentrated on the road as gimps marched over lawns.

They're fucking everywhere, he thought, the panic rising.

It was a good plan in theory. He just didn't expect so many of them, so soon. In the burbs, of all places.

He aborted and drove north, knowing he could loop around and escape another way. He shot up one street, climbing a slope, when he spotted the rear end of a police cruiser driven nose first into a ditch. Unlike the massacre back at the barricade, this car didn't have a corpse on it.

Gus slowed to a stop beside it. The cruiser was empty.

Placing the van in park took time, and the stick shift felt as stubborn as the gears on a rusted-out tractor, but he was getting faster. Gus checked his surroundings and jumped out. Seconds. He was working with seconds.

The zombies were already converging, staggering out from behind houses, rearing back in ghastly surprise at the two-legged dinner before advancing.

Gus rushed the stricken cruiser, where he saw two dead-again corpses in the ditch. Another pair of unmoving gimps lay pinned underneath the car, one facedown with a front tire parked on its lower spine, the head of the other resembling a flattened melon long gone bad.

When Gus got close enough, the one with the tire across its back twitched.

The car was otherwise empty. Not a weapon in sight.

Pissed off at the lack of firepower, he remembered something. He opened the driver's door and located the trunk release. He popped the lever and went for the rear.

The hunting party behind him was closer now, at least a dozen, but even as he took note of them, the *runners*, the same two energetic ass munchers, overtook the hunting party and shoved past them.

Horrified by the Olympic-level speedsters gunning for him, Gus opened the trunk.

Angels could have sung.

There, on the floor, a shotgun waited in a foam-filled slot. Twelve gauge. Gleaming. A second empty slot was below the full one, suggesting another boom stick was out there somewhere. Not that it mattered. One was enough.

Aware of a furious flapping of sneakers on pavement, Gus grabbed the gun but didn't see any shells.

The runners were closer now, less than fifty meters—not even half a football field.

Gus hoofed it back to the van, glimpsing the incoming sprinters. Those undead sonsabitches were making the rest of the pack look bad. He reached the driver's door and hauled himself inside. The stick caught, but he got the machine in gear and hit the gas. Gus didn't bother looking back, sensing, *knowing* the pair of heat-seeking zombies were somewhere behind him, perhaps a foot away from slamming into the van as it picked up speed.

Then he was leaving them in the dust once again, their reaching hands only inches away.

Putting some distance between them, Gus exhaled, knowing he was lucky, knowing he had come close, yet elated that he had an honest to Christ *gun*, tossed barrel down into the passenger side.

The road remained straight as more of Annapolis's undead populace crept from their hiding places. They were no where near the street, however, so he passed them by. In short time, he found a turn-off, which would bring him back onto the outer ring road.

He'd had enough of the city for one day.

15

All that terrifying excitement caught up to him after the fact.

First it was the shakes, which he controlled by holding onto the steering wheel all the more. Then a lightheaded giddiness gathered behind his eyes, creeping up on him, bordering on tunnel vision. That's when he knew he was in trouble, and searched for a place to pull over. Tethers of motion sickness latched onto his guts by then, hooking them, gently twist-turning in an evil, off-kilter agitator kinda way.

It was coming on, and Gus didn't need it. So, checking his sides and seeing he was relatively in the clear, he pulled over onto the shoulder not too far out of town, where the forest was just starting to thicken on either side of the road. Once stationary, the tunnel vision really started to come on, and he alternated between leaning on the steering wheel and back in his seat, taking in deep, soulful breaths.

Which didn't do shit for him. So he cracked open his window as much as he dared. A gush of air streamed in, and that helped settle his innards.

"Oh sweet Jesus," he groaned at the ceiling. "Is it gonna be like this from now on? Huh? Is it? 'Cause if it is… I don't think I can do it. I don't think I can do it at all."

The engine idled, filling the silence. He stared down his nose at the long curving strip leading up the mountain. The side mirrors framed the outer edges of the city. A segmented series of buildings rose above the treetops. Gus again focused on the road, relaxing his eyes while his internal clockwork sorted matters out. He hoped he wouldn't get a stomach cramp. Oh lord above, he didn't need another episode on the side of the road. If the urge did overtake him, however, he remembered there was plenty of prime taint cleaner in the rear.

After a short time, he studied the side mirror. He was on the north side of Annapolis, and he realized he wasn't that far away from his apartment building. In fact, he could be there in twenty minutes, depending on how jammed the roads were. He could be inside his apartment in twenty-five.

Gus gnawed on his upper lip as that knowledge sunk in.

And he had the shotgun—but with no shells. On that mental note, he checked on the weapon. The thought that he probably should not have an unsecured firearm in his front seat, business end down, occurred to him. He didn't care. Thing wasn't even loaded.

Or was it?

That caused him to size up the weapon.

He knew a little about shotguns. Not a lot, but a little. His dad had one, and every year, his father and two brothers would go hunting deer. There were no shells in the rear of that cruiser, but what if the officer loaded the weapon beforehand, knowing that there were zombies on the loose? Maybe, during the last stand, the officer had a better weapon, with a larger magazine capacity, and left the shotgun but gave any extra shells to someone who could use them?

Gus leaned over and pulled up the twelve gauge. He fumbled a bit until he opened the action, and a red shell popped out and clattered onto the floor.

"Holy shit," he whispered.

He didn't know if officers were permitted to carry loaded weapons around in their trunks, but he supposed if you needed it, ready and loaded was how you wanted it to be.

He tilted the shotgun and started plucking out rounds. One fell to the floor, but Gus didn't swear. He was too happy to swear. There were five shells total. Five rounds. Not nearly enough, not for the potential shitstorm he'd be walking into if he tried to get home. Five shots and then he'd have a club, because he couldn't use the shotgun while carrying an axe. It was either one or the other.

"One or the other," he repeated softly, inspecting the weapon.

Good news was, there were plenty of twelve-gauge shotguns in the valley. All he had to do was find them. Or head on down to the nearest sporting goods shop, like Stanley's, and grab all the shells he needed.

That was a risk, too, as Stanley's was zombie ground zero. More of what he'd just escaped from.

Same with any other place selling, or once selling ammunition in the city.

The knowledge made his head hurt, so he decided for the second time that day that he was done. He reloaded the gun, slapped it back into the front seat, barrel down, and situated himself behind the wheel. The drive back was a long, reflective one, where his nerves settled down. To a point. Along the way, he stopped in at Ed and Chrissy's place and grabbed the frozen food from the freezer. No way he was gonna forget any of that. Especially the ice cream.

Upon returning to the house (whoever owned the place still hadn't shown up), he secured himself away with the serious intent of celebrating still being alive.

The party consisted of cracking open that bottle of gin. As far as booze went, the gin was the lesser of the two evils, and he had more gin than vodka.

After the day he had, it felt like a gin night.

So he drank, mixing that medicine-smelling stuff with cola, then ginger ale, finding neither one very good. Didn't matter. He wasn't drinking for the flavor, but mostly for still being alive. And the buzz.

He thawed out a slab of hamburger and fired up the stove. When the hamburger was ready, he doused it with salt, pepper, onion and garlic powder, along with a dash of barbeque sauce. Those condiments were at the heart of several magical dishes Gus could produce, and the kitchen became redolent with them. He rolled out a dozen meatballs and dropped them in the frying pan. When they were ready, he tossed in the leftover spaghetti. Unable to wait, he opened two bags of potato chips, and munched while he cooked.

It was dark when supper was ready. By that time, he was halfway through the quart of gin, ignoring all warning signs to slow down. No way he was slowing down. Tonight he was on the alcoholic autobahn, where there were no limits. The secret, he realized, was mixing the drinks one ounce gin and seven ounces pop—in the beginning—before gradually increasing the doses. The three-finger shot went down just as pleasant as sticking his own fat fingers down his gullet, and produced a gag and shiver every time.

He ate in front of the television downstairs, watching old episodes of *Battle of the Planets* before switching over to movies. The drinking continued, and his grasp on reality warped and stretched. Funny thing, he missed commercials. He wasn't a big watcher of television to begin with. Certainly didn't care for ads back in the day, but in their absence he longed to see a few. Just a few. Maybe fast food commercials. Anything to do with hamburgers. Or cars. Any of the new models coming out. Just hearing that super excited voice describing Black Friday or Christmas sales would be wonderful. If he saw any of them now, it would maybe mean the world was all right, that he would get up in the morning, listen to the road and weather reports like before, and drive out to a worksite, where the guys would be waiting.

There weren't any commercials however, so he switched over to one recorded channel called "Relaxation," where the screen flowed through various tropical beach settings for minutes at a time.

Relaxation. He was all about that. Had to relax as much as possible. To forget. The gin went to work on him, and watching and hearing waves lap against a white sand beach filled the silence.

Eventually, the memories came back.

Zombies. Gimpy, days old dead bastards and bitches. A good-sized crowd of them.

Gus reached over to the end table, poured himself a three-finger shell of gin, added Pepsi, and choked down a mouthful. The gin worked as an emotional anesthetic, and left him dreamy. There would be nightmares, make no mistake, but drunk as he was, it didn't worry him so much.

All them zombies. Worse, they were wandering around like free floating tripwires, and if you disturbed them, *alerted* them, not only did they come after you, but they brought others. Attracted others. Which was why there were zombies appearing out of nowhere, it seemed.

He'd have to remember that.

Flashbacks to Mollymart then, where they had piled up in front of the locked doors of the main entrance, bashing away at the glass until it shattered, wrecking themselves in the process.

Today, however, they were slower, with the exception of the two runners that came after him. He supposed they were freshly turned. The slower ones had been dead much longer. That wasn't a bad theory, so he'd keep it.

The troubling thing was, the truly terrible thing, was that he didn't even go that far into the city. He was only traveling the back roads around Annapolis, what he thought of as suburbs but maybe wasn't even that. All those zombies. He wondered what was waiting for him in a real residential zone. Hell, if he drove *by* a residential zone, thus alerting just one of those walking, shitty ass bastards?

The swarm at the police barricade, came to mind.

Times *ten*.

Gus drunkenly scoffed at that. It wouldn't be that bad, would it? Seriously? The population of Annapolis was what? Three hundred thousand? Give or take a hundred grand. Whatever it was, he only needed to drive into a crowd of a few hundred to get stuck.

Even though the city population had slowed down, they were still… walking around. Sooner or later, he would have to go down there. There was simply too much to leave on the table. Clothing. Food. Weapons and ammo. Medicine. *Entertainment.*

He drank more gin.

He needed to be smarter. Needed to get better organized. But however smart and organized he could be, the *fear* would still there. That eight-cylinder, pedal-down surging, caught-in neutral-sensation where all that nervous energy was revved up and demanding he run. Just bolt. And running was the easy part. Puking, shitting himself, or just passing out were all possible. Worse still, a combination of the three, or all at once.

Maybe he'd get used to it.

Gus stared at the television screen. A single palm tree. Cloudy, flat-line horizon with a setting sun. The south Pacific water, flat as a sheet of polished glass.

To get used to it, he'd have to do *more* of it. Which circled back to getting his ass in gear. Tomorrow was the eleventh of November. Gus corrected himself. He assumed it was the eleventh, but he might be a day or two early or even later. Not that it mattered. Snow would come down any day. Any day. And when it did, he was stuck here with whatever he had up until that point.

He had the shotgun now, and that would help. The hammer as a backup. The axe would stay behind. And he had the motorcycle helmet. He needed more shit like that. Armor. Body armor. *Leather* body armor. The kind bikers wore while on their rides. Leather strong enough to protect against road rash sounded like it would do the trick. Against the clawing and the pulling and the biting. He remembered a shop in town that had a selection of leather goods. Knew exactly where it was.

All he needed to do was go down there and get it.

Another teeth-clenching drink of gin, a grinding of the jaw, and the cold stare of the determined.

Tomorrow, Gus told himself.

He'd go there tomorrow.

16

The next morning, Gus was too hungover to do squat.

After an hour of intermitted sitting on the shitter, he decided to stay home.

Which he did.

And watched movies.

17

The morning after that, Gus got up, dressed, and went through his morning routine. He felt rested. The nightmares had stayed away the last two nights, and he wondered about that while on the toilet. The gin had probably helped. A ghost of a smirk played on his features. All he needed was a reason to pick up drinking. A reason? *Another* reason?

Clouds blanketed the sky yet again, pulling a cold, dreary calmness over the land. There was no sign of snow, so Gus decided once more to attempt a supply hunt. He prepared the van, and, upon starting the machine, realized he'd need gas as well.

"Anything else?" he asked aloud. "I should put together a goddamn shopping list."

Except at the very top of that list would be the word…. *Everything*, and he remembered having the same conversation with himself days earlier.

Twenty minutes later, after opening and then closing the main gate, he was back on the mountain highway and driving into the city. The houses he'd searched still had their doors open. No one waited for him along the road.

After Chrissy's and Ed's house, those now familiar vibes started to take hold. In the lower legs first, always the lower legs, then extending to his chest.

After everything he'd gone through, seeing the next house on the road didn't seem so bad at all. *Keep it simple*, he thought, wanting no part of the city. Fuck the city. The city was *alive* with them. Maybe in a few days, things might be different down there, but he wasn't counting on it.

One house at a time was the way to go.

The property was a lovely one, some hundred meters or so past Chrissy's and Ed's house, at the end of a long, picturesque driveway. An overgrown lawn lay beside the place, while a wall of fir trees shielded the property from passing traffic. Yellow painted bungalow, eavestrough, and a double-door main entrance with plenty of flowerpots out front. The concrete driveway was a straight run to a two-door garage, where a blue Ford F150 pickup waited to be let inside. A satellite dish stuck off the far corner, appearing like a little quarter moon jammed into the house's shoulder. A pup tent had been set up on the lawn, near a good amount of firewood that had been cut and readied for the winter.

Gus stopped just behind the pickup and inspected the stacked row of wood. He had a fireplace. And a downstairs wood stove. If he lost power, he'd need to burn wood and he was looking at enough of it to last the winter, if needed. Not only that, he could haul everything away in the pickup if he didn't want to use the van. It would take time to collect all that firewood, he figured.

A force slammed into the van. Gus jumped, kept in place by his seatbelt. An elderly woman staggered into view on the passenger side. She reared back, dripping putrid muck. The zombie wore a shirt that might've been dipped in years' old motor oil. She withdrew with a frazzled look of crazy and a whole lot of monster. Grey hair hung in thick tatters over her face, falling just above her mouth and the remains of her smashed out teeth.

She hit the glass with the flat of her palm.

Gus fumbled with the gearstick as the gimp recovered from the forceful, open- palm death strike. He reversed and roared out of the driveway, as if chained to a launched rocket. The zombie stumbled after him, spitting, dripping things best not thought about. He braked in the middle of the driveway, squealed in boyish terror, shifted and hit the right gear on the first try.

He floored the pedal and the concrete driveway flashed past, instantly collapsing the space between his front bumper and the zombie.

The gimp walked right into the van and the greater mass knocked its reanimated carcass back twenty feet at least, where she plastered the spot right between the two garage doors. The impact spattered her arms and legs wide an instant before she crumpled to the concrete.

Still tasting his heart and one foot on the brake, Gus glared at her, daring her to get back up.

"Stay down, sister," he warned, strangling the steering wheel. "Stay the fuck down. I don't wanna hurt you…"

Which was absurd. He was going to have to crush the thing's skull to get at the house.

On cue, the gimp pushed itself up on one arm. The other arm hung off the shoulder like a meaty pendulum. Gore dripped from the face and neck, pattering the concrete, which was right about when Gus got a better look at the thing's legs. She wore shorts and her lower legs were grotesquely swollen, the size of prize-winning watermelons. Just looking at those two chunks of ham horrified him.

Taking advantage of his distraction, the zombie stood on those bulging lower legs.

And shambled toward him.

Gus reversed some twenty feet back down the driveway, moaning as he navigated the straight run by side mirrors alone.

When she covered half that distance, he shifted into drive and charged again.

The collision was loud, dense, with the heavy, tactile quality of hitting the broadside of a well-fed cow, or so Gus thought.

The zombie flew back, arms flailing—the broken one really whipping around—and spattered onto its back.

Setting his jaw, Gus leaned over his steering wheel and drove forward.

Bones snapped and crackled under the tires.

That wasn't the worst. The worst came when his front right tire rolled over the eggshell of the thing's head. There was a brief resistance, just a split second, then that jug-like clatter of cranium bursting under the weight.

"Oh…," Gus groaned. "That did not go down well. Not *at all*."

There was enough room to clear the pickup and the garage, so he made the turn and faced the stored firewood. A quick reverse placed the van right over the corpse he'd just flattened. Nothing else charged him. Nothing else slapped itself up against a window. For that, Gus was happy.

He still had to get out of the machine, however.

So he did.

"Oh Jesus," he said, because he saw that, in running down the zombie, he'd unintentionally run over one of those oversized legs—bursting it. A vile, semi-black jelly splashed the concrete in a considerable pressurized spray, staining a sizeable portion of the once-untouched driveway. The weight of the van rolling over the leg had burst open a foot-long gash in the meat, and everything inside had spewed forth. A white hand, the veins ink gorged and spidery looking, rested on the concrete just above that rancid spew of body sludge.

Gus looked away before he spotted the head. That, he didn't need to see.

It would probably resemble a deflated basketball with hair and tire treads. One look at something like that and he would puke. Puke with authority.

So he stuck the hammer into a side pocket and readied the shotgun. He also pulled on the helmet and flipped up the visor. It wasn't much. Matter of fact, it felt goddamn flimsy, but it was all he had.

Thus armed, he went around the van, very much aware of the body beneath his vehicle. The main entrance of the house was not open, so he checked his corners before heading for the back. Nothing tried charging him, so he wondered where the hell undead granny had come from.

Besides the woods.

He stopped before the home's large picture window, facing the road. No drapes or curtains hung there, so he could see straight inside. Empty, but devastated, as if a small tornado had pitched down right in the center and tossed the living shit out of everything. Paintings hung askew on walls spray-painted with bodily fluids and tissue. Lamps had been knocked over and monster mashed into the carpet. A glass coffee table had been likewise sasquatched into the carpet. A dining area lay beyond all that destruction, along with an opened patio door aglow with daylight.

Gus gave the first corner a wide berth as he went around it. Everything remained civil, all-clear except for a propane tank. The owners had a sizeable backyard with some lawn furniture set up, no doubt enjoying the little heatwave the valley enjoyed leading up to the whole zombie shitstorm. A large garden was also back there, studded with foot high gnomes sporting pointed hats and smug smiles. Gus didn't like the little ceramic bastards, but granny and whoever else lived here obviously had a major chubby for the things. Dozens of them dotted the backyard, near the trees or on the lawn. Some of those little clay shits stood in the garden's bare dirt, while others were on their sides as if kicked over.

One section of the garden was raised and had a cross at the head.

Took him a second to realize it was a grave.

The sight of that final resting place drew him in, mindful of the open back door. A small shovel and pickaxe lay alongside the grave, and a wreath of pulled-up flowers were scattered in clumps around it.

Gus wasn't sure what might've happened. Maybe her husband had died. Maybe he'd become a zombie and she put him down. Whatever the reason, she buried him out back, in the company of gnomes. Being so far out of town, and knowing funeral services were a thing of the past, maybe she opted for the only thing she could do, and that was placing him to rest in the garden.

Maybe. Didn't explain how granny got turned. Maybe it was someone else in the grave.

He wasn't about to dig it up to find out.

The place was quiet, but he supposed the helmet had something to do with that. A quick check told him he was still alone.

Gus moved to the deck and faced the open door. There he stopped, a guy wearing winter boots, painter overalls, and a motorcycle helmet. Carrying a shotgun.

He cleared his throat. "Hello?" he asked. "Anyone home?"

Again, no answer.

The next part was hard, because it meant going inside.

Knowing full well what might be lurking, Gus almost didn't go. His guts were churning, becoming a buttery mass of hot eels. The helmet was heavy on his head, but the fresh air helped. Broken coffee mugs covered the floor just past the threshold.

"Gonna fuckin' die here, I know it," he muttered and, reluctantly, entered the dining room.

A fat house fly buzzed by, bloated on filth and stunned by the cold. On the wall leading to the kitchen, a wooden rack had a number of keys hanging from it. Gus glanced into the living room and saw the curtains pulled off the rods and puddled on the floor. The smell wasn't so bad, and he guessed the open back door had something to do with that.

Then he was walking through the house.

Three bedrooms, all empty. Two bathrooms including an en suite. All empty. Closets. Empty as well except for clothing and shoes.

There was a downstairs area, and Gus found the light switch (which worked!) and cautiously proceeded down, hating every squeaking step, until he entered a comfortable den and a spare bedroom. There was also a storage room, filled with all manner of dry food.

Jackpot.

Thank you Lord.

It took less than fifteen minutes to check the place, but at the end, he leaned against a dining room wall, clutching the shotgun like a protective totem, and decided on his next move.

A speedwalk later, he was back at the van, grabbing the duffel bag.

Like the previous places, there was only a limited amount of food in the kitchen, but he took everything. There was a small freezer with a nice pack of pork chops and three trays of hamburger meat, extra lean. A box of ice cream sandwiches were stashed in there as well. He left the frozen food and loaded up on everything else. A quick search of the cupboards produced a coffee mug with something written on the side.

Love you.

Always and Forever.

If anyone tries to take you away from me…

I'll find them, and punch them in the nuts.

Words of endearment if Gus ever saw them. He almost took the thing, because it was something he would say to Tammy.

A moment of depression followed that thought.

He put the mug back and looked around. Not ten minutes later, he lugged a full duffel bag out to the van.

Next trip was the storeroom in the basement, along with the freezer. The storeroom had a good amount of everything, from tin milk to canned fruit, canned ravioli, soups and stew. Even little *Joe Louis* cakes stuffed with sweet cream. The freezer had bags of fish, three frozen pizzas with the stuffed cheese crust, a couple of roasts, as well as a box of chicken wings and two full chickens.

"Holy shit," Gus said, sizing up the frozen pizzas.

He'd just found supper.

Everything got transferred to the van.

From there he went to the front porch area, where an open closet held several coats and jackets. One jacket in particular got his attention. A heavy blue one, with a fur lined hood. He pulled it out, sized it up, and pulled the thing on.

It was a little tight with the coveralls, but it fit.

"Oh my, oh my," he let out. "I'm warm. I am *warm*. Put some butter on me I am *warm*."

The coat had a thick lining, and was a good one. In addition, he found two cloth bags stuffed with winter hats and gloves.

"God love ya," Gus said, going through each bag and trying everything on.

A second search of the house turned up five sweaters, less than a dozen pairs of socks, as well as two pairs of jeans that also barely fit. There was even underwear his size. A dozen pairs in all. He hesitated with those, however, not exactly thrilled about wearing another guy's drawers. They were obviously clean, so he got over his qualms and took them all, even the lighter shades, because who knew when he would get to his own apartment. The sweaters were tight but warm and he'd need them, going into winter.

"Suck it in," he said, which he did, and held it. He let it out with avalanche force.

"I'm on a roll here," Gus said, stuffing everything into a brown suitcase he'd found in the master bedroom closet.

Food. Clothes. Winter gear. Household cleaning supplies. Two full packs of ass crack cleaner, sixteen rolls apiece, and in glorious two-ply. He was a little disappointed with the lack of booze, but all in all, he was happy.

And he still hadn't checked out the garage.

It took a while to stash everything into the van. He sized up the interior at one point, including the crack splitting the rear door window. There wasn't much he could do with that, not now anyway, but the van could use some shelves or something to keep things better organized, as well as stopping everything from sliding all over the floor.

After loading the van, he stopped, felt the sweat underneath his layers, and checked on the time. 11:20 in the morning, which surprised him. He didn't think it was that late.

"You were busy," Gus told himself. "Just like the job. You get moving and the time flies by. Only problem now is space and…" he looked at the sky. "Daylight."

It seemed like forever since he saw the sun. It was up there, hidden behind a mass of nasty cotton.

He got back to work.

The garage held a rugged all terrain vehicle mounted on a trailer, and he considered taking it. Truthfully, he'd rather have a snow machine for the coming winter, because once the snow was down, he wasn't planning on doing much about it.

Snowshoes and ice augers hung off the walls. Booster cables and a well-stocked work bench had everything a person needed if they were into that sorta thing. Hand power drills, wrenches, and screwdrivers. Boxes full of screws, bolts, washers and nails. An electric chain saw lay nearby. There were a pair of milk crates, which Gus immediately grabbed for the van. Another surprise were two large plastic bins for recycling, both of which contained empty bottles. He upended the works onto the floor, noticing several wine bottles in the mix. The bins went into the van, shoved against the wall and solving his problem with shit sliding around. All he needed to do was drill and bolt together.

A golf bag lay in a corner, and an assortment of putters and clubs were inside. That got his attention. Gus pulled one putter free and hefted it, deemed it light but liked the range. He swung the thing, inspected the scratched head, and put it back. The club was heavier, but he wasn't exactly sure how the thing would hold up if he met any zombies. Sure it was metal, and had a greater weight, but that long neck just didn't instill confidence.

In the end, he left it. The chainsaw interested him for only a few seconds.

If he needed either one, he knew where they were.

Once he was all packed up and ready to move, Gus returned and got the last of the frozen food. Then he sized up the van's interior and all the supplies gathered. The firewood would have to wait for another day.

He stopped and studied the one hand and leg sticking out from under the van. "Ah… sorry, this, ah, happened to you," he said. "Thank you. For everything. I'll put it to good use."

Back at the house, and once everything was washed and stashed away, he went into the kitchen and threw on a frozen pizza. Pepperoni and cheese with a cheese stuffed crust. While he waited, he munched on an ice cream sandwich, wishing he'd gotten the ones with the chocolate chips.

With the outer gate closed, and the afternoon feeling old, Gus decided he had no intention of heading back out. The day had been fruitful. He would eat his pizza, maybe watch something on TV while getting a pleasant buzz on, and forget about the undead lady he ran over.

Around quarter to three, Gus sat down, still wearing overalls, and placed a paper towel beside the cutting board. He clapped his hands, rubbed them quickly, and studied the bounty before him.

"Not bad," he said with a little smile. "Not bad at all."

Pizza at the end of the world.

All he had to do was run over zombies. Monsters that were once people. Then invade their home under the pretense of checking for survivors and taking whatever he deemed essential, right down to the just his size underwear.

In the vast silence of the empty house, Gus stared at the food as the smile on his face drooped and faded away. The depression returned, sullen and deep. He placed one elbow down, then the other, and held his head.

"Graverobbing," he said through his fingers. "I'm graverobbing. Christ."

18

There were nightmares.

Horrible dreams, where the owners of the last house weren't dead at all, where Gus tied them down, looted the place, and left them screaming as a zombie army burst through the surrounding forest.

That got him up around 3:00am, and he didn't go back to sleep, so he watched *The 40 Year Old Virgin*, instead, staring with dead eyes at the movie. Whenever it finished, he switched on the old gameshow *Switch-off*, only to switch it off some ten minutes in, remembering how much he hated the over-excited contestants. He wondered why there were gameshows on the box at all, but ultimately didn't care.

At some point, he rose from the couch and wandered upstairs, wearing a t-shirt and boxer briefs. He wanted water, to pour into his mildly sour guts. Vodka wasn't his drink, and he'd only gotten down a single glass before leaving the rest.

When he shuffled into the living room, he stopped and stared.

"Why… good morning Mister Sun," he whispered.

The smothering cloud cover of the last week had moved off, revealing an orange dawn outlining the distant mountains. It was awesome. Nuclear. Cosmic, even. He basked in those strengthening rays, realizing how much he'd missed a sunny morning. There was no sound inside the house or out. No bird song. No smoke trails of airplanes marred the sky, and Annapolis itself looked even deader than usual.

"What a day," he said. "What a day, what a day."

One where a person got things done.

Gus headed for the kitchen.

Breakfast was leftover pizza. It went down better than last night, when he choked down only half the pie. He then went through the rest of his morning routine and got dressed in a pair of newly acquired jeans and a sweater.

Work—his one, driving thought. It was time to work.

The sun had lifted his spirits in ways the vodka from the night before could not.

He got moving.

Around 8:30am, Gus pulled into the driveway of the house he'd cleared out the day before. The dead person was still there, and he spared it only a glance before getting out of the van. Wearing a pair of disposable latex gloves and flipping the visor down on his helmet, he dragged the crushed zombie by the ankles around the back, into the flower garden. There, with the nearby tools, he dug up the other end of the garden, dragged the body into it and covered the corpse with dirt.

It took a little over an hour, but he was glad to do it, and the sweat rolling off his face and soaking his clothes felt…clean. Honest. That alone made the time it took worth it.

When he finished, he returned to the house and grabbed the keys to the pickup truck. The machine had a half tank of gas, so he started tossing firewood into the boxbed. If he was sweating before, that grinding stoop, grab, and release, where the wood would clatter across the metal floor, got him melting. All that motion made more of a racket than he liked, but he had the shotgun nearby, and constantly checked to ensure nothing crept up on him.

Once the truck was loaded, he climbed into the cab, started up the machine and drove back up the mountain. Back to the place that wasn't his, but might very well become his if the owners didn't return. The thought of them never coming back crossed his mind.

Back at the house, he unloaded the firewood on the front lawn, across from the last garage door. *Water weight*. The way he was sweating, he must have lost ten pounds already. When he cleared out the box bed, he wiped his face with a towel, saddled up and drove back down the mountain for more.

He got in two runs, back and forth, unloading the wood onto his lawn.

For lunch, he ate the last of his leftover spaghetti and meatballs, wishing he had some garlic bread to go with it. After lunch, he went back to the house with the firewood, got two more boxloads, and brought them back.

A little after three in the afternoon, with the shadows lengthening across the lawn, he returned the truck to the little bungalow. He left the machine in the driveway and took his van back to home base.

All the while on the road, every trip back and forth, he watched the trees, looking for anyone. Anything. The last nightmare he'd suffered stayed with him, and he remembered how the undead had charged through the forest.

Back at the house, he went through the motions of securing the gate. After he parked the van in the garage, Gus inspected all that firewood and decided to stack the whole load on the side of the house facing the mountain.

But that was tomorrow's job.

After locking the front door, he proceeded upstairs, where he started a bath. He stripped, peeling away the clingy layers, and tossed them into a nearby bin. A hot bath was his reward, and he dunked himself up to his chin and relaxed.

He woke up in the dark, in much cooler water, and nearly broke his neck getting out of the tub.

Supper was spaghetti from a can, which he heated and later devoured.

It was only after seven, but the labors of the day, the hot bath, and the previous sleepless night had drained him. He threw his dirty clothes into the washer, retired to the living room, and prepared his bed on the sofa. While the machine chugged away in the background, he switched off the nearby lamp and stood in the dark.

Before he dropped into bed, he looked at the window. The night sparkled, full of stars, the city lights clearly visible in the valley below, still switching on at preprogrammed times.

And for whatever reason, Gus knew, just *knew*, that despite burying the dead lady in her garden, in the shadow of the cross, *despite* not seeing a zombie all day and the hard physical work… *despite* the bath…

The moment he closed his eyes, the nightmares would gather.

But he was too tired to try and stay awake.

So he crawled into his bed, hoisted the blanket to his chin, and sighed.

He stared at that far-off glow of what was once civilization, until his eyes closed.

"Would you like to check yourself out at one of our self-check counters?" the Well-Shop lady asked, wearing a red vest over her regular clothes. She had to be in her sixties, at least, but supercharged by at least three cappuccinos. Her smile suggested her cheeks ached the way she was contorting her mouth. She was far too chipper for the super store, the hated competitor of Mollymart East.

Gus glanced down at the contents in his shopping cart. Thrown in there were a half dozen paintbrushes of various sizes, empty roller trays, and a new scraper. The scraper was the important bit. He'd worn down his old one to a respectable nub. His left foot itched, right in the arch, in a place he knew he couldn't access without taking his sneaker off. That would not do in current company.

And when he glanced down, Toby, wearing a mask of calm that Gus knew was a complete lie, stepped up. He didn't really step up, but rather piped up.

"Do we get a discount?" he asked the Well Shop lady.

Her smile became sympathetic. "No, I'm sorry, you don't."

"So what do we get?"

Well-Shop lady had prepared for the question. "You do get a Well-Shop shopper's point card, and every purchase you make here goes toward earning points, which you can later redeem on the company's website, or here with your next purchase."

Toby nodded, agreeing it was quite the deal. "So I don't get a discount on anything?"

"No sir. Except the points."

"And I still have to check my stuff out by myself?"

"That's correct."

"And bag it."

The Well-Shop lady's smile became just a touch frosty around the corners. "You have to bag your own items, sir, yes."

"I see, I see," Toby matched her smile, nodding all the while. "So, no discount, bag my own shit, in my own bags, and I get points. To use back here again."

Well-Shop lady's jaw tightened.

"I do have a question," Toby started.

"Just drop it," Gus said.

"Huh?"

"We'll go to a regular checkout, thank you," Gus said to the Well-Shop lady.

"This way is faster," she said, gesturing at the full corral where shoppers plopped, pushed, and bagged all by themselves. There were a dozen terminals. All full, without a line.

There were also a dozen regular checkouts, but only two people working them, and a line-up of at least a dozen.

"We're good, thanks," Gus said, and pushed his cart toward the line-up while guiding Toby with a hand. Toby didn't want to go, clearly sensing he had a righteous upper hand to play. Gus insisted, though, smelling smoke before the fire broke out.

"I was winning that one," he said to Gus.

"You were being a pain in the ass."

"She was pushing the self-checkout!" Toby stressed in a lowered voice and leaned in. "I mean, doesn't she *know* about the self-checkout? Every person she steers into that pit of retail death takes work away from not only *her* but the regulars *working* the checkout."

"I'm sure she knows."

"Then why does she do it?"

"Because it's her job?" Gus ventured. "And if she doesn't, this place will get someone who will."

"Fuck," Toby said in that same low tone, glancing around as if in hostile territory.

Gus stopped at the back of the lineup.

"I like to sit in on one of those mucky-muck meetings," Toby said. "Just be a fly on the wall, taking a dump."

Gus widened his eyes as if forcing himself awake. Toby didn't notice, standing with his hands in his pockets, looking around and shaking his head in scorn.

"Whatta job," he continued. "Whatta place. Seriously."

Gus exhaled, knowing it was about to start, knowing the word *seriously* was Toby's verbal equivalent of a starter's pistol.

And Toby didn't disappoint.

"I mean, think about it. Just think. A dozen suits all around a big ass table, in a big ass room, maybe with a big ass view of a big ass downtown. Right? And Teddy looks over at Bobby and says, Bobby, how's this quarter's numbers looking, old chum? And Bobby, still sore from taking it up the ass from bossman Sammy—"

"Bossman Sammy?" Gus asked dubiously.

"Bobby says," Toby went on, ignoring both look and question. "Looks good Teddy. Looks good. How good? Asks Teddy. *Real* good. Yup. Reeeeal good."

Gus rolled a hand, indicating Toby get on with it. Ahead, the other customers stood with their backs to the conversation, their expressions hidden. One guy shifted from one leg to another.

But that was all fine with Gus, because he was listening to Toby.

"How good, Teddy asks again, and Bobby, still tasting salty tapioca from lunch—"

Gus held up a hand. "Is Bobby a man or a woman?"

"Whoever you want him or her to be, Gussy. So anyway, Bobby says real good. With authority, y'know. Like he—"

"So it's a he?"

"Or a she. Bobby says, really *really* good."

The line proceeded two steps, and Gus and Toby advanced with it.

"She gives them a number," Toby continued. "And, as televised, they are good numbers. Those are some real good numbers there, Bobby, says Billy, all smiles as if he's getting a sloppy one right under the table."

Gus winced. "You're in a public place, here."

"S'okay, s'only Well-Shop. Billy likes public places, anyway. So yeah, he's getting his chubby chuffed and buffed and Bobby says, you better keep that thing under the table, mister. Just kidding, she doesn't say that. She says— you bet, but they could be much better, y'know? And that gets everyone's attention, 'cause those *were* good numbers, but everyone there only wants one thing, and that's *better* numbers. Always better numbers. So they're all hooked and lean in for the gobble gobble. Right? For the thigh meat. The dark and greasy. To which Bobby goes, I've been thinking how we could do better. Like, really better. Not only reduce payroll and increase our profit margins, but actually have the sheeple do the work we would otherwise *pay* someone to do, and have them willingly *choose* to do it, like *like it*, right down to bagging their own shit."

Gus shook his head as the line proceeded another two steps. He and Toby did the same. Something in that line squeaked suspiciously, sounding like a wet tire puncture. Gus glanced around for the source, but Toby kept right on talking.

"How do we accomplish such a magical thing? asks grandaddy Terry, combing out his beard with his fingers. Well, granddaddy Terry, Bobby says, we give them one of these, and she flashes a piece of plastic with the corporate logo on it. Y'know? The edges all shiny and shit. Give 'em one of these and the dopamine points."

"What's dopamine?"

"That's a feel-good chemical in your brain. You play video games?"

"No."

"Hm. Well, you're not a sheeple. I knew I liked hangin' out with you for some reason."

"Still not sure what dopamine is."

"It's a chemical that the brain ejaculates whenever it gains something it thinks is totally great, but really is shit."

Sounded harsh to Gus.

"The greater the thing," Toby continued, "the more ejaculate in your brain."

Sounded *gross* to Gus.

They moved two more steps. Almost to the checkout counter. And the faces were still unseen, looking this way or that but never quite visible.

"All right," Toby goes on. "So anyway, the card? Earn points! The greatest scam ever."

"But… you get free stuff."

"You what who now?"

"You get free stuff. Those points. You can redeem them."

"You can not."

"Sure you can. I got a point card."

"For here?"

They both took another step, placing them next in line for checkout.

"Not here. For gas. I earned enough points for a fill-up at the gas place."

Toby looked at him with a cartoonish expression of horror.

"I knew I should've stop hanging out with you. Get your fix there, Jude. And don't forget to sanitize your hands afterwards. Lord knows what's on 'em."

Gus did a confused double take before shaking his head. He started placing gear on the counter. The checkout guy was slouched over, long hair hiding his features. A smell of mildew, of unwashed surfaces, drifted from him. Gus stared as the checkout guy robotically dragged things under a scanner one by one, placing them on the far side.

With each item, the scanner flashed red, each flash more intense than the last.

Then Gus blinked, breaking the spell, and looked around.

The Well-Shop was dark, as if a major fuse had blown. The only light came from the entrance, where a waning shard slowly retreated.

"Point card?" asked the checkout guy, his voice eerie in that empty flight hanger expanse of a retail store.

Gus handed it over, not remembering how it had gotten into his hand and missing a chance to see the guy's face, who had already turned away.

Toby was missing, too.

But that didn't bother Gus. He picked up his green reusable bags and walked toward daylight. His sneakers squeaked. He noticed a distinct lack of people. The once-busy corral of the self-checkout station was empty and coated in cobwebs. The wide aisles just beyond faded away into absolute dark. He had no idea were everyone was, but they weren't here.

He glanced back, but the checkout guy was gone. In fact, darkness engulfed that whole section of the store.

And as he walked, he became aware of something else.

A sound, coming from within those darkened aisles. Organic, but in an insect kind of way. It wasn't the sound of flies. It was worse than that. It was a ravenous chittering of dried teeth, or doubled-up mandibles, biting, *gnashing*, storming for the entrance. A dark swell rushed forward, the floor flickering in a charred brass kind of hue.

Carapaces. More specifically, *shells*.

And whatever they were, they not only surged along the floor, but along the shelving units in an evil wave. An oily rush of millions of hard, lustrous shells, growing louder with every passing second.

Daylight washed over Gus then, as he stepped through the entrance.

Weirdly enough, the sky was polished brass, an alien heaven under which he did not belong. The van waited for him under all that shine, the only vehicle on the parking lot, way at the back, under a pole touting a huge W. The rig looked rusted out and battered, in much need of a touch-up. Gus walked across the lot, his footsteps ominous in his ears, but that awful chittering didn't follow him into the light. Matter of fact, he didn't hear that at all anymore.

Then he was at the rear of the van and opening the doors.

"Gus?"

Toby. It was Toby. Standing at the driver's window and looking concerned.

"Yeah?" Gus asked, but he was checking out the interior. All his purchases were aboard and accounted for, including a lot of food and clothing, as if he were running a retail store out of the rear of his van.

"Hey."

Gus met the face of his friend.

"You be careful," Toby told him in an uncharacteristically stern voice. "You be careful out here. And don't you worry about points. Don't you worry about anything. Just be smart. Be careful. You hear me?"

For some reason unknown to him, Toby reached out and clasped Gus's shoulder. "It'll be bad at times. Real bad. But don't worry about the points. Okay, buddy?"

His grip was warm and strong and totally comforting. Toby held on, held on far longer than Gus might've been comfortable with if he were awake. He was dreaming, however, and he was with a friend whom he missed very much, and wasn't ashamed to say so.

"Hey… Tobe," Gus said, his throat tightening, his eyes on the cusp of watering.

At that point, Toby smiled with all the power of the sun.

Before Gus could ask forgiveness, he woke, and saw it was morning.

19

Gas. He needed gas for the van.

The road curved as he drove along, heading for a service station outside a place further south on route 12. The little town of New Cross was on the other side of the mountain and heading in the direction of Halifax. Gus had no intention of going anywhere near Halifax. He wasn't keen on heading to New Cross, either, but chances were the little gas station on the edge of town might very well still have fuel. It also would be nowhere near as infested as Annapolis or Halifax. The town only had about five hundred people scattered over an area of mostly farmland.

Five hundred people.

Christ. Gus studied the road, hoping his plan was a safe play. He wore his newly acquired winter coat, as well as a pair of jeans and boots. His helmet was on the seat next to him, along with the twelve-gauge barrel down. The hammer was on the floor, and the axe in the back. Frankly, he was outfitted for war.

Houses dotted the road, but he'd search them later. Gas was his priority this day. Some of those places belonged to commuters working in the cities. Several farms were also along the strip, as marked by the lack of trees in places and the unobstructed view. At one point he glimpsed horses in the middle of a pretty big field. Even a few cows.

He didn't stop for them. Felt bad. Wondered if Anna had made it back to her own farm.

No other signs of life, besides the farm animals. If anyone saw him, they did not attempt to flag him down. By this point, if no one was trying to get his attention, they were probably dead.

Or planning to rob him.

Gus had seen plenty of post-apocalyptic movies, wild westerns and action flicks. He never expected to be living one. Just be careful and take no more chances. Simple. That, and don't do anything stupid. Easy.

He'd been relatively relaxed that morning as he ate breakfast, still thinking about his dream and Toby's message to him.

Don't worry about the points, he'd said. Gus had no idea what the hell he meant, but he *thought* it meant... don't try and grab everything, which was comforting in a way, and totally Toby.

As the morning progressed, however, as he got ready to head out on the road, his nervousness increased. He even did a couple of quick marches around the house to get the blood going, to try and burn off that building energy. It worked, but as he drove through a deserted countryside, the nerves came back.

In the lower legs first, as if they were marinating in a vat of ginger ale.

"Just awake," Gus said, trying to convince himself otherwise. "That's all. Just awake. And, really, I *want* to be awake out here. No falling asleep at the wheel. Fuck that noise."

He passed two cars along the way—a jeep and a little pickup, both pulled over onto the narrow shoulders. The occupants were still in the car, strapped down by their seatbelts. One zombified driver turned its head and tracked him as the van went by. Gus accelerated to eighty, the speed limit, and kept watchful. All he needed was to hit a deer or an escaped horse. Or a herd of wandering cows.

The sign for New Cross appeared. A transport truck was stopped just behind it, the driver's door opened.

Gus didn't stop.

New Cross was a small, scenic town that struck him as a lovely little retirement community. He doubted the people living there ever expected to be roaming their farmlands in an unliving state of decay.

Huge front lawns drifted by, beautiful pieces of property. Everywhere Gus looked, zombies stood or staggered around, like folks afflicted with extreme dementia—except with pieces missing. A few of them turned upon seeing or hearing the van. A few more started walking toward him.

Gus whipped by them all.

Five minutes later, the gas station appeared.

Mountain Gas Works, the sign said, still hanging from its post. A pair of cars were stopped around the two pump stations, but they would not stop him from refueling.

The problem was the zombies.

A dozen or so of them wandered the refueling area, and the station itself. Three zombies lurked within the garage bay, where the door was lifted completely up and out of sight. The desiccated blue-grey features of the undead didn't change as they watched Gus pass. Across from the station stood a *We Got It* convenience shop as well as something that caught Gus's eye completely.

A liquor store.

Then he was past the little section of town, driving on south.

Gus slowed when he reached a hillside driveway. He pulled in and turned around, meaning to go back to the station. When the van righted itself, zombies filled the road, hobbling toward him in a rusty clockwork of motion.

"Fuck knuckles," Gus said and accelerated, aiming for the middle of them. His anxiety level steadily rose as the distance between him and the group shrunk.

The zombies didn't get out of the way.

He hit the first one dead center, bouncing the head off the hood before it rattled under the van, an instant before the other zombies hit. Meat and bone flew across the front of the vehicle. Several zombies got hung up on the van's front, clawing for purchase but failing and tumbling off at various angles. Zombies on the edges of the charging van reached out and had their hands slapped away.

Gus shook and fell in the seat as the van rumbled over the fallen undead. One deformed gimp held on where the wipers once were, his grip weakened by two missing fingers. Gus noticed the stumps just as the thing dropped from sight.

Then he was through.

Handprints and grime spattered the windshield, but Gus hunkered down and turned the van around. His field of vision shifted, from gas station to woods to the pavement littered with corpses. Two zombies stood on the opposite edges, however, spared by that initial charge. They hurried toward the vehicle.

They were too far apart to get both at once.

So Gus ran over one, turned around on the gas station lot, and ran over the second.

Just to make sure, he rolled over the others as well, in a jumpy ride that didn't bother him as much as he thought. It didn't take long to finish the job, not in his mind, and he wanted to make sure he got them all. Crush the legs, at the very least, if only to rob them of mobility.

After a rocky minute, he stopped on the station's lot and popped the lid for the van's gas tank.

Armed with his shotgun, Gus walked to the rear doors and readied himself. Once again, his breathing quickened. He pushed the rear doors open and jumped out, boots hitting the pavement.

The carnage shocked him, all done by his hand.

"Jesus," he whispered, and lifted his helmet's visor to see better. "Absolutely no fear of nothin'."

He'd just run down a dozen people or so, dressed in summer clothing. *A dozen deadheads*, he corrected, then warned himself not to forget it ever again.

His boots clicked as he walked over to the gas lid, eyeing the crushed zombies, not entirely trusting his own handiwork. Gus took the regular fuel hose, saw that it was a dollar seventy-eight for a litre, and grabbed the nozzle. He inserted it into the tank and squeezed.

The gas pump surged into operation.

The numbers flickered as gas flowed into the thirsty van, and Gus realized he didn't have to pay anyone for the fuel. The noise of all that pedestrian destruction might attract others, so he stood on guard, shotgun in arm. Sizing up the nearby buildings, he guessed he was in the center of town.

Gus studied the pump's display. *The fuck was taking so long?* The Brush-it truck didn't take so long to fill.

The beast did, however.

Every passing second got on his nerves. He started fidgeting, leaning this way and that to make sure nothing was creeping up on him. Feeling dangerously exposed, he wanted to get going, then he started thinking about the gas. He'd found *gas* for his van. It was a huge question mark, how much fuel was left in the station's tanks, but the empty cars around suggested there was a massive fuel-up at some point.

He would need fuel for the days to come, and it was too risky to leave any of it at the station. Another person could take it, or he might be cut off from refueling by snow or anything else.

It would be smarter to take what he could. Hoard it. He didn't worry so much about it going bad, knowing there were additives galore in the mixture to keep octane levels up for months. Maybe even years.

He sized up the garage. The front door was closed and the windows were intact. Only the one garage bay door was up. Across the street was that *We Got It* convenience shop and the liquor store.

The pump cut off. Gus squeezed off a few more drops before returning the nozzle to its perch. Taking a two-hand grip on the twelve gauge, he went around the rear of the van, tried one of the doors and realized he'd locked it. Other than the oily massacre he'd left behind on the pavement, no zombies were in sight.

Though the garage bay door was open, the smell of motor oil, grease, and spilled engine fluids lingered. Gus entered and saw that it was empty. Tools and equipment lay scattered everywhere, but he didn't see what he wanted.

He found a door to an office. Inside were computers on desks and retail slips and invoices pinned to a note board, as well as a place to sit down and eat. A little microwave and coffee machine were positioned in the back, with a calendar flipped to October. The photo showed, of all things, a sunny New Brunswick river, and a half naked fly fisherman casting out into the water. Butt cheeks bare for all to see.

Gus went back into the garage. A second open doorway stood near the back. Taking a beat to listen yet getting nothing, he went over and looked inside. Tires. Many tires. Stacked and labeled.

But there were also two red five-gallon gas cans tucked into a corner. *Five gallons*, Gus thought as he took them. That was what? Fifteen liters? Twenty?

He lugged both containers back to the pumps.

He had his hand on the nozzle when he saw it—the last zombie he'd clipped on the road, forty feet out from the station. The thing pulled itself along by one arm, one slow, agonizing drag after another. Its shadowed head and shoulders lifted and dropped as it slid over pieces of its unmoving companions.

"Oh, you unlucky bastard," Gus whispered.

Keeping his eyes on that piece of moving meat, he went about filling the gas cans. The fuel rushing inside the container masked the sound of the zombie's halting advance. Every now and again Gus would check the pump gauge, glance around, then return to the last gimp coming his way.

"That's it," he quietly urged. "Come on over. You're doing me a favor here. Really."

The zombie's face came into greater clarity, scorched to the bone as if left on a BBQ grill. A film of gravel coated its features.

Gus tightened the plastic cap on the first can, then got started on the other one.

While he filled it, he studied the thing worming its way toward him. His nerves were zinging, but not nearly as bad as before. Probably because the zombie was the only one, dragging broken legs.

The gas cans were filled so he let them be, and shouldered the shotgun. Remembering Rebecca's words, he aimed at the head and hoped for buckshot.

But he didn't pull the trigger.

It wasn't about killing a dead thing. He felt he'd moved past that point. He *was* nervous, but more about missing at that range. And nervous about the noise. Would it draw more zombies? Goddamn right it would, if they were around.

Then there was the thing about the shells. He only had five.

Gus lowered the shotgun. He flipped down his visor and walked over to the crawler. There were plenty of heavy things in the garage, to smash in a skull, but he didn't think about using any of them.

He stopped just a step away from the groping dead hand.

As expected, both the crawler's lower legs had been crunched and stained. One of the van's tires had mashed the thing's knee, as well, judging by the tread marks across the back of its beige pants. It was a young man. Maybe someone who lived out here, but who'd commuted into one of the cities for work. He had short hair, a narrow, fricasseed face covered in gravel, and all his teeth. Every visible inch of his skin—other than his face—was that nasty shadow of hypothermic blue.

The thing greeted Gus with a soft expulsion of gibberish, and reached for his ankle.

Gus jerked his boot back and, in a flash of fight or flight, considered stomping the crawler's head. He avoided another slow-motion grab for his ankle and mentally considered the best way to dispatch the gimp. Then he remembered—the shoulder stock of his twelve-gauge was solid wood.

He retreated another two steps while reversing the weapon, and got into a stance as if about to rake leaves.

The crawler swung its arm wide, still searching for an ankle but only dusting off the concrete.

Gus clocked its forehead with an awkward thrust, lifting the skull back on the shoulders before it crashed down. The strike failed to stop the zombie, however, and it lashed out, weakly, fingers skittering across the ground.

A dangerous combo of frustration and impatience welled up in Gus. Holding the shotgun like a baseball bat, he reared up for an over-the shoulder strongman-swing and brought the gun crashing down on the crawler's head.

The head broke open and the twelve gauge went off.

Heat blasted Gus's left side and it took him a split second to realize the gun had fired. Cold air struck his ribs, and he immediately pawed at the wound, checking for blood. There was none, but his vision narrowed. His breath left him and his legs felt funky. He dropped the weapon onto the unmoving zombie before flipping up his visor and staggering back. Black ooze seeped from the sizeable dent in the crawler's hairline, all the way down into the thing's evil smirk.

Gus pressed a hand to his side, on the verge of passing out, and checked his hand again, fully expecting to see blood and bone fragments.

But the glove was clean.

He stopped, swayed, sucking in air and staying upright while he patted and pulled on material, checking himself. A child-like squeak of horror left him. The shotgun had effectively shredded his winter coat, part of his overalls, and the sweater underneath. The blast had ripped everything away right down to dark red skin, as if a shark had chomped into him, taking away a good chunk of the first few layers.

But that was *all* it got.

The rest of him, the important parts, were fine.

In shock, Gus continued to pull the ruined coat this way and that, checking the extent of the blast radius. He patted himself down one last time and found no blood, just the sting of cold air on tenderized skin.

Whereupon he straightened, exhaled and collapsed against the van. He pulled the helmet from his head, needing air. That wasn't fast enough, however, and he clutched his knees and barfed breakfast onto the ground.

"Guh," he hitched and loosed again, letting it drain out of him. "*Guhhh.*"

He dropped to a knee and continued retching, until all that remained were wet, dribbling hitches. He spat, tasting puke but breathing clean air. The land tilted. Black sparkling motes flickered before his eyes. Before he knew any more, the ground rushed up to catch him.

The wind rustled his ears, cold and pure. Pressure eased from the back of his head and his face. There was no sound, and Gus did nothing until he essentially rebooted, realizing, on some distant plane of consciousness, that he'd just clubbed a zombie with a loaded shotgun.

Luckily enough, he'd only lost his breakfast, not his life.

"Jesus Christ," he whispered and feebly checked left and right. He turned over with all the grace of a beached whale and stayed there. After a while, he rose to a knee.

Still alone. Still alive.

Even though he had no right to be.

"You fuckin' mope," he softly swore, before checking on the crawler—whose grimace was no longer so smirky. "Awww… even fucked up my favourite overalls. And my new coat. God… *dammit.*"

Moaning, Gus stood. He checked the blasted opening in his coat and clothes one more time before letting it go.

"Need a smoke after that one," he said, regarding the crawler again. "Got any?"

The zombie didn't answer.

"Fine." Gus said. "I don't smoke anyway. Might be a good day to start, though."

He looked around and saw the liquor store.

"Or not," he finished.

The coast remained zombie-free, despite the blast and near-death experience. The want for that drink increased tenfold. *Any* drink. If there ever was a time in his life where he needed a drink, *now* was that time.

Leaving the van behind, a stunned and stupefied Gus marched over to the liquor store and went inside.

"Anyone in here can get the fuck out now," he said weakly, clenching his shaking hands.

Right there, beside a single checkout, was an assortment of various brands and flavors in one-ounce shot bottles and pocket flasks.

Gus grabbed one of the small flasks and cracked it open.

Rum.

Captain Morgan, to be exact.

Not that Gus cared. He choked down half a mouthful, swished and spat out another, then guzzled down a third.

When he realized he'd left his shotgun across the street.

You fuckin' idiot.

He wasn't going to survive the next *minute* at this complete and utter state of breakdown.

"Sweet fuck and rosemary," Gus seethed and lurched to the door. The roads remained empty, which was great—but the zombie cavalry might very well be on the march. Or trot. Or whatever.

Rum flask in hand, Gus walked back to the van and located his shotgun. He picked up his helmet too. Two more drinks stabilized him during that time—quick, almost furtive gulps, and a third one for luck after he'd picked up the helmet.

Still no zombies.

His throat was telling him no more undiluted rum, *pleading* no more, but his brain was saying *fuck that*. So Gus took another mouthful, checked the wreckage of his coat again, and decided to leave.

He froze in mid-step and swung his red-eyed attention back to the liquor store. The front counter was pretty much untouched. Gus shook the flask, gauging the last few swallows in there, then studied the liquor store, then the van.

He took two more swallows, grimacing both times, growling at the end. Medication out of the way, he stuffed the flask into his remaining good pocket. He climbed aboard the van, got it rolling and backed up to the liquor store. Checking the coast one last time, he got up and nearly tripped climbing into the rear, but steadied himself and made it to the doors.

Gus flung them wide open and hopped down. With two steps he was back in liquor heaven—or at least an outlet—and eyeing what was available.

Pretty much everything.

Rum.

Whiskey.

Scotch.

Vodka.

Gin.

Gus went to the rum section first, four shelves high. Rubbing his chin and knowing the clock was ticking, he didn't dicker on the brands.

"Uh." Gus suddenly wavered, and glanced into the deeper sections of the store. It was darker back there, since the only light came from the front. The overhead lights remained off. There was a solid, one-way window in the back, behind which was probably the office and the storage area.

"Anyone in here?" he asked and got no answer. "I can…"

Pay? Was he actually about to say that? After taking food and shit from those other houses? Well, god*damn*. Gus fumed and went to the back.

"Hello?" he asked, after pushing through the swinging door. Not a peep. As empty as the front. Whoever had worked here had left in a hurry, switching off the lights but not bothering to lock anything up. Like Mollymart, the storage room was a lightless cave of full shelves, and he wasn't about to root through it all.

The only light came from the office to his left, so he checked that out. Empty, just a nest of papers, pens, and files scattered over a closed notebook and a computer terminal. A large filing cabinet stood near the side wall, so he checked that, finding nothing of interest. He also glanced behind the door, found a broom and dustpan, and swung his attention back to the store, seeing it through the one-way window. From this perch, he could see the entrance and the van parked before it.

Feeling less guilty and more than a little hammered, he returned to the main floor and didn't know where to start.

Before him was a section of wine.

"Fuck it," he said, and grabbed a nearby cart.

Twenty bottles of Moscato went in there, and when it was full, he pushed the cart back to the van.

No zombies waited to ambush him.

He loaded those bottles into one of the recycling bins, wavered when he was done, and listened. Scanned the roads.

Not a damn thing.

Gus went back inside.

The rum section was right there so he grabbed whatever he could, jamming plastic forty-ounce bottles into the cart. Amber rum, spiced, white and dark…it all went in, piled on top. Brand didn't matter to him. It was all the same. When the cart was full he steered it outside and speed-loaded two dozen bottles into the van. Sweating, swearing, and constantly checking for dead people, Gus felt a little more exposed with every trip. And also a little more plastered.

Fast acting, he thought, but he had close to a flask's worth in him already. Quite a bit, but he didn't get sick, despite the flurry of activity. And it would be a long winter. A *long* fucking winter. Hell, the snow might never *leave*, so best to prepare for that.

With feverish enthusiasm—tweaked by booze—Gus went back inside and loaded up another two dozen bottles. All rum. There was plenty of it. The rum motherlode lay before him. On the third trip back, he saw he'd cleared out a small section of the shelves, but the shelves were *wall* length. Practically *store* length. He didn't want *all* rum, not when the place had so much more. So he whipped the cart over to the whiskey aisle and made like a liquor bandit, grabbing forty ouncers by their necks.

Two trips later, his danger sense started ringing.

The racing back and forth was exercise, and he was chugging and sweating when he stopped to listen.

No one. Not a sound, and the rum wasn't hitting him that hard. He'd spent perhaps forty or so minutes at the store, however, and that was probably pushing matters. He'd already gotten lucky once that day.

No way he was going to die over booze.

He shoved away the empty cart and climbed aboard the van. Seconds later, he trudged back to the driver's seat, minding his footing all the way. The front seat squeaked when he landed in it, and he nearly gave himself whiplash from tossing his head back.

Hands on the steering wheel, Gus glanced around. The zombies he'd killed stayed dead, and everything else looked clear. Those warning tingles were a vibe now, one that warned of burning too much daylight here. He'd gotten his fuel and then some, and to add to that, landed quite a haul of fun juice.

Get in, get out, said Gus's pickled brain.

So he started up the van, put it in gear, and drove away.

20

The rum helped.

What was a pleasant buzz became *more* of a pleasant buzz, and after his near-death moment—by his own hand, no less—Gus needed a little chemical calmness. In fact, he welcomed it. Deserved it.

During the drive home, he slowed but didn't stop, and pulled out that little flask.

Distracted driving, he thought, sneaking peeks at the road while he opened the bottle. With that done, he one-handed the wheel and tipped the flask back, sucking down whatever was left. That last gulp produced a shiver and a cough.

Gus frowned. Tammy would *not* be impressed. She hated drunk drivers. And here he was, doing shots behind the wheel, with a load of stolen booze in the rear. *Appropriated booze*, which sorta meant the same thing. If the cops pulled him over now, he wondered if they would arrest him or simply take what he had for themselves. Another shiver ripped through his oversized frame, more of a spasm, forcing him to concentrate on the road.

Sorry Tammy, he projected. The world was different now, so he hoped she would understand. He'd already run down dozens of once-living people and, to make it worse, did it all while sober. And if the cops did pull him over, he would probably celebrate by doing a couple of whiskey bullets.

His spirits had improved, though. Nothing like clubbing a corpse's head and nearly blasting yourself in half to slow down time. And that's what Gus was doing now, slowing down time. Like driving forty in an eighty zone. Or something like that.

That episode of near-death stupidity gnawed on his mind, however, despite the flask of rum in him. The drink took most of the edge off, thankfully. Hell, with the load he had in back, he could keep the edge off for a while, by gum.

That got him thinking.

It was stupid. Probably the rum talking, but it made sense.

He was a wreck before going out to pick through houses. A cargo ship-sized bundle of nerves, and today, in one momentary lapse of reason, pushed by a building powder keg of anxiousness, he'd almost cut himself in half with his own shotgun.

Just to save a shell.

No doubt he could've been smarter about it. Could have used the axe. The hammer too, for that matter. He'd rushed into executing that corpse because his nerves were popping. He'd *have* to be smarter, but he also had to take the edge *off*. Take down the fear factor a few notches. Constantly being on the verge of shitting yourself wasn't helping and, as recent history would show, doing the opposite would probably, eventually, kill him.

He approached the junction turn that would take him back up the mountain, and he took it with a little more speed than usual, causing a considerable amount of rattling in the back. Forest streaked by, and Gus checked on the time.

1:34 pm.

Was it that early still?

He had plenty of time. *Plenty.* He could unload and head right back for more, no sweat.

I almost shot myself, came his inner voice. *Almost gave myself a brand new asshole without the fancy plumbing.*

The clock changed to 1:35.

No, he said to himself. *I'm done for today.*

And he was.

Those thoughts remained for the rest of the drive home. They stayed, too, when he was finally behind the stone wall, with the gate secured, and the van parked in the garage.

He lowered the garage door, and during that clatter of descending panels, he took off the winter coat.

The sight amazed him.

The ragged hole there was the size of a large pie, burnt around the edges.

Just a few millimeters more, and Gus would have gone splat himself.

He threw the ruined coat over a nearby garbage bin, which was stuffed with the last two weeks or so of his refuse, and that got him despairing. Another problem. Never before had he appreciated the city force of garbage collectors. With them gone, he had to figure out what to do with his trash.

"One thing at a time, buddy," Gus said, and dismissed it.

The sweater was likewise ruined, but his overalls were even more disappointing. They were his favourite. Sure, they made him look like he was selling ice cream out of a horror truck, but they were his uniform.

"Well damn," he whispered, knowing there was no way he could fix them. Unless he found some similar fabric and sewed on a super-sized patch.

Maybe.

Gus went to the rear of the van and pulled open the doors. There was plenty of daylight left. He could stack that wood. He most certainly could unload the truck and make ready for the next trip out there. Not today, mind you. Fuck that. But next time.

After the day he had, all he wanted to do was take a few of those bottles of liquid merriment into the house and forget.

Rough day at work? Tammy asked him.

Gus answered that with a series of smirking grunts.

Go on inside, get cleaned up, and I'll give you a back rub.

Her voice stopped him and the sadness returned.

"I miss you, babe." He rubbed his nose, staring at the bottles. "I miss you something fierce. But…as much as I miss you… I'm so glad you aren't around for this shit. I'm so glad."

He grabbed one forty ouncer of rum and one of whiskey.

Everything else he left behind.

In the laundry room, he placed the bottles aside while stripping everything off. Socks and underwear got tossed into a hamper, overalls hung on a rack, and a sweater chucked at a garbage bin. He might manage a needle and thread for the overalls, but the sweater was beyond him.

Then the nerves came back. Thick and heavy and squeezed from the devil's accordion itself.

"Not again," he groaned. "Sweet fuck. Can't I have a moment for myself?"

In the kitchen, his hands quivered just a little as he dug out the cola and ginger ale. He set up the biggest glass he could find, a beer mug, and poured in about four shaky fingers of rum. Four fingers didn't look like a lot to him. Not in the mug. So he poured another shot.

There was an ice machine in the freezer, but he ignored it. Gus cracked open a can of cola, and topped off the drink with that, slurping at the fizzy excess when it threatened to overflow. He drank half in roughly three seconds, taking it down in long pulls, and gasped when he lowered the mug.

"Needed that." Gus studied what remained. "Good stuff, Henry."

A thunderous belch followed.

There was no cringing. No guts on fire. And certainly no spasms that accompanied a straight shot from the bottle, so Gus knew he'd found the right dosage. He stood there, gripping the counter edge and staring out the window.

He stayed there until he got all that first drink down.

Whereupon he mixed himself a second.

And after that… a third.

The next morning wasn't kind to him.

He rolled off the couch, kicking at the blankets. The nearest bathroom was a marathon crawl in shocking slow motion, and when he bumped into the toilet, he gripped it with both arms and lowered his head like a horse at a trough.

Except he wasn't feeding. Not in the least.

The subsequent caveman sounds echoed in that porcelain chamber pot, but he did what needed to be done and got cleaned up as best as possible. As expected, last night's binge rendered him unable to go down into the city. Or New Cross. Or any of the houses dotting the road.

Gus didn't care.

The good news: he had no nightmares. Not a one. The fact that he woke at daylight surprised him, despite feeling like the inside of a moose's shitbag after a meal of salt and water lilies.

Heavy clouds blanketed the sky, resembling the underbelly of some great serpent. One look at that and he turned back to the living room. He spent most of his morning in the bathroom but managed to get down some canned peaches and crackers for breakfast, drinking only water. He dressed in his skimpy bathrobe, the one that didn't completely close in front, and eventually wandered downstairs, into the den.

The afternoon was different.

Around one o'clock he watched a movie, still favoring the comedies, but eyeing the selection of zombie movies as well. Around five he queued up *Undead Isle*, which had a few good reviews. It wasn't a George Romero movie.

Undead Isle was a typical zombie story, taking place somewhere in the South Pacific. The plot was mildly interesting, about a tribal hunter who goes into a forbidden cave, gets infected by zombie worms crawling around in zombie batshit, then spreads the zombie disease to the rest of the tribe. From there the blight spread outward, to the nearest corner of civilization, until the whole island was crawling with zombies…which was right about when a yacht of pleasure seekers and party goers dropped anchor unknowingly off the coast, near a popular resort.

Gus should have turned it off when the tribal hunter walked ankle-deep through infected piles of guano, but he kept watching, watching, staring at the screen in hungover fascination. When the main characters of the yacht started fighting zombies, things got somewhat interesting, only because of the weapons they used. The undead died from head shots, which was fine, but when one guy needed to go to the townhall to save his girlfriend, things got silly, especially when the idiot decided to do it while wearing only flip flops, his bathing suit, and brandishing a fish gaff.

Gus switched the movie off and sighed.

Holy shit.

"How the hell does slop like this get made in the first place?" he wondered aloud. "You need… *something* covering your ass, dummy. I mean… *Christ.*"

At some point after, he wandered back to the kitchen, took out a box of frozen fish fillets—all breaded—as well as two handfuls of string fries. He couldn't remember what freezer he'd taken it from, but he'd gotten it from somewhere. A bottle of ketchup and tartar sauce were readied as well, along with an entire bottle of wine, which he uncorked and allowed to air. Tammy taught him that.

When supper was ready, he ate, drank the whole bottle, and cracked open two more.

You were hungover this morning, his brain reminded him.

"I almost shot myself yesterday." Gus said. "And this stuff? It's wine. Practically grape juice. Who gets plastered off grape juice?"

No answer to that, so he went back downstairs.

He turned on the George Romero movies and hunkered down for the evening.

21

It was the twenty second of November when he decided to go out again, mostly because he was running low on food. The good food. Frozen pizza, breaded fish sticks, and ice cream. Stuff like that. The tubs of ice cream and ice cream sandwiches he'd found didn't last at all and seemed to go faster—and better—after a night of drinking.

For about a week he'd stayed inside his mountain retreat, shuffling around the house in his undershorts and undersized bathrobe, watching movies with his hairy belly hanging out and eating whenever the urge hit him.

Drinking, too, whenever the urge hit him.

And at the rate he was going, the urge was *pommelling* him, *repeatedly*, about the head and shoulders.

He needed the break. Needed time to reset. The near-death moment by shotgun had done it for him. It wasn't that he was scared of heading back out there. Oh no. He was simply recuperating, gambling that the snow would not fall until December. It was a risky call, he knew. Every bit as risky as heading out and going through dead people's homes for supplies.

He did do a few things outside.

He stacked a good portion of firewood outside the house and inside the garage, along the wall of the farthest bay. The garage was perhaps one of the best things he liked about the house. Press a button and the door went up. Press the same button and the door went down. So simple, but it delighted him every time. He wasn't sure how long those motors would last, the wonderful machines that got everything moving. Even if something did happen, though, he could still open the doors manually.

He hosed off the van and its front grill, which was a nasty piece of business that required more than a couple of drinks. It wasn't so bad once he told himself he'd only run over a couple of squirrels. Or raccoons. All wearing people sized dentures. The van itself would need repairs. Maybe even some reinforcing. The rear window was looking especially vulnerable with that crack. Gus supposed all the windows were vulnerable, but only with the strong zombies. The freshly turned ones. They seemed to weaken as time went on.

Which was another reason to stay the fuck out of Dodge. Every passing minute, they got weaker.

During that week off, he discovered something else, as well. He'd realized he didn't have nightmares when he went to sleep hammered, passed out on the couch. That was some serious beneficial side effects of having one or two tipples before bed. And if it worked at bedtime, there was no reason it wouldn't work during the day. The hangovers were killer, but he used aspirin to get him by, as well as water, which got him thinking about the well situation.

The house had to have a well in addition to the nearby cistern, and he wondered how big it was. A cistern might have a five or ten thousand litre capacity, and even then, he wasn't sure about keeping it purified. The well was different. It could potentially go dry if he used a lot of water. So, he used the dishwasher only, washed his clothes only when absolutely needed, and became increasingly paranoid about flushing the toilet.

Which made the hangovers worse, in a way, and made him worry about using so much water.

He'd have to look into finding an alternative crapper. Maybe one of those portable toilets for work sites. One of those blue thrones. Set it up outside, away from the cistern, and use it as an outhouse. He could drop pipe all day long then, without fear or guilt of using too much water. Find some sawdust to take care of the smell. If the water stopped running anytime, he would at least have a blue shit shack as a back-up. Finding one of those, or something close, would be a project for the spring. If he got through the winter, that is.

Which brought him back to the present.

He'd been home all week, eating his finite stores of food, drinking his finite quantities of spirits. He'd watched a lot of movies. A lot of zombie movies, just to brush up on the subject. The movies were survival guides, really. Fictional, yes, but he learned from them without having to actually put himself at risk.

And he realized several things.

Body armor. He needed some, and since he had the motorcycle helmet, he returned to the idea of more leather. The real tough stuff that covered a person from neck to toe. Motorcycle rider tough. He knew he'd decided on finding leather duds days ago, but things had changed since his twelve-gauge moment. Yes, he was procrastinating, but only when it involved heading out beyond the stone walls.

There was time. Plenty of time, really. Even if the snow fell tomorrow, he was sure the all-seasonals on the van could get through five to ten centimeters *easy* as long as he drove slow.

So…tomorrow, then, he told himself, standing with his gut hanging out of his too-small bath robe, sizing up his dwindling pantry and studying his lunch options. He could sure go for a frozen pizza, but he'd chewed through the last of them a few days ago.

That was okay. That was fine.

Plans were already made. He was ready. All systems go. He'd go out tomorrow and get whatever he could. He'd make a couple of runs. He had the means and the willpower to do it. And he'd get everything on his shopping list. Everything and more. Tomorrow. That would be the day.

In and out.

No one would realize he'd ever been there at all.

Just like a fucking ninja.

<h1 style="text-align:center">22</h1>

Five days later, under grey clouds, Gus gathered up everything he needed for a scavenging run. The duffel bag was in the back, along with the bins for storing supplies. The winter coat was gone, so he doubled up on sweaters, very much aware of the straining fibres. The shotgun was in the passenger side, pointed down as usual, and the hammer on the seat. The axe lay in the back.

A full forty ouncer of whiskey filled the co-pilot seat.

A forty ouncer of straight up water sat next to it.

The fizzy mix had run out a day ago, which was another reason he needed to make the run today. There was water, however, so he filled an empty forty with just that. Whiskey and water wasn't his drink, but it would work in a pinch. There was still plenty of wine, but he would save that for a *victorious return* sort of thing.

Gus eyed the van, black and bruised and scarred and waiting for him to take the steering wheel. He studied those dents, those lines, and admired the machine. He'd done the same little thing for the past two mornings, intent on going out then, but backing out before he could even raise the garage bay door.

This morning was different.

As he studied the van, that debilitating wave of nerves returned with a vengeance: a growing, paralyzing pins and needles gush that screamed at him to stay right where he was.

Fear kept him back, and though he was well-aware the feeling was a defense mechanism to keep him alive, he was also going to suffer a long and horrible death by starvation. *If* he gave into his fear and stayed on the mountain, stayed in the house.

Took him four days to figure that out.

Only took him a few minutes, however, to figure out the solution.

His hands twitched. He squirmed and swallowed, already feeling the unpleasant roll of his guts. But before that dreadful white noise could once again scare him into not venturing forth, before his fear could sway him into doing nothing for another day, like it had done so many times over…

Gus turned to a workbench.

And the bottle of Jack Daniels sour mash waiting there, which he'd placed the evening before.

He poured himself a four-finger poke to the eye (said so because, with a water mix, the drink often left him squinting). He raised that bombshell in a beer mug, winked at the van, and drank. And drank. And *drank*. And when that drink of oh-so-desperately-needed courage was gone, well, Gus went and poured himself a second round.

That one took longer to get down. He wrestled with that watery under-taste, unable to decide if it tasted shitty or simply okay. Not that it mattered. He didn't need it to taste good.

Like any medicine, he only needed it to work.

By the time he'd downed the second liquid rocket and readied a third, the first missile to the liver was already delivering results. The whiskey napalmed the light breakfast of crackers and peanut butter he'd had an hour earlier.

He drank the third one within ten minutes, slammed the empty vessel down with authority (and a touch of ornery spite) on the nearby bench. The impact rattled the two bottles of Moscato waiting for his return, but they did not fall over. A good sign.

Gus glared at the van, the three heat seekers consumed in roughly thirty minutes taking effect. A slow burn of self-awareness ignited, like a match struck off boot leather and tossed into a cocktail vat of gasoline. A sense of not giving a rattlesnake fuck ensued, candy-coated by invulnerability—with just a dash of being pissed off.

"All right," he said and burped, staring hard at the vehicle. "We doin' this, this morning or what? I know you're ready. And goddamn, I'm *feelin'* ready. This is the one. Right now. We're doin' this. We need a shit ton of everything and it's all down the mountain. All down there. And today? Today we go *get* it. And if any of those meateaters come at us?"

Gus punched one hand into the other. A little too hard, but fuck it.

The van waited.

"You good with that?" he asked.

The van did not reply.

"All right, then." Gus was even more vulcanized by the prairie fire ripping through him. "Let's fuckin' *do* this."

He climbed aboard the machine and tapped the remote for the garage door. One of these days the thing's batteries would die, but not today. The garage door cranked open. Gus worked the stick, located Drive, and hit the accelerator. The van roared into the open air, startling him enough to slam on the brakes. Breathing hard, he looked into his side mirrors and sized up the skid marks through the lawn and leaves.

"Christ," he whispered. The gas was a lot touchier than he remembered, so he warned himself to drive carefully.

Which he did, all the way to the gates. The bar never felt lighter, he never felt stronger, and he yanked open the gates with a caveman's enthusiasm. A few minutes later, he was riding down the mountain, the road knobbier than usual. Another hard impact and he took the hint and slowed down. Just as well. The speed he was going, his ass would've looked like a squished raspberry by the time he made it to the highway.

Which appeared ahead, the junction coming into sight. He slowed to a stop at the base, sizing up the dirt road and thinking about doing something to hide it. Some camouflage, if he could manage it. One day.

Signaling right, Gus turned and leaned over the wheel, grimacing at the road. He felt good. Determined. Fired up with a sense of renewed purpose.

Nerves?

Not one tingle.

"Fuckin' called it," Gus said, and wished he had some music.

In what seemed like no time, he reached the first house belonging to the dead family. As much as he pitied them, Gus would no longer think about those people. Or any other deceased or turned folks he had encountered. It was better that way. Those thoughts sailed through his inebriated mind, and the first half-dozen houses went with them.

In time, five bungalows appeared on the right, and Gus hit the gas with a calmness that made his brain chirp: *That's right, you undead fudge lickers. Daddy's found his balls. Daddy's found his balls right here.*

Daddy's also got no fuckin' coat, his mind said after a beat, but he ignored that. Such negativity had no place in this dojo.

A few shallow potholes forced him to slow down, but that was fine. He turned toward the first of those five houses. A smashed picture window greeted him. Broken shards lined its frame, while glass fragments covered the lawn.

Gus parked and sat back. The van continued to clear its throat, rumbling, idling, and that was noise enough.

Nothing approached him.

"Five houses," he said, keeping an eye out. "No more of this one house, two house pre-school shittery. We're going all in today, boys. All fuckin' in. A quick pick and flick. Balls in and balls deep."

Somehow, hearing his own voice rallied him even more.

He tried getting up from his seat twice, before realizing the seatbelt was preventing him. After a quick search for the release, Gus whipped the hindrance away and rose. The walls supported him as he thumped his way to the rear, tangling one foot in the duffel bag and kicking the nuisance away. He stopped, took a breath and pulled on his helmet. He then grabbed the twelve gauge and flicked off the safety.

"All right," he said, feeling positively manly.

Nerves weren't an issue now. Not in the least. Gus opened the right door.

Christ it was a long way down. Had it always been that way? Not that it mattered. He got down on one leg and lowered the other over the edge, probing for the ground. When he got both feet down, he sighed, straightened, and turned just as a gimp lurched out from the corner of the van, shocking Gus all the way down to his curly cakes.

The zombie rushed him and, in doing so, clipped its shoulder off the corner of the vehicle. The impact staggered the undead—a tall rotted man wearing a t-shirt and cargo shorts—and spun him off the once sure line of attack.

That was all Gus needed.

Going full on infantry mode, he stepped into the gimp and cracked the wooden butt of the twelve gauge across the face of the monster.

The zombie fell.

No nerves, all reflex, Gus stepped back, took aim at a lowered head, and fired.

The corpse's face exploded in an angry puff of bone, grit and teeth, spattering the crushed stone driveway. The zombie's entire frame collapsed and didn't move again. The head, or half of it, was destroyed, splayed across the driveway like two liters of curdled milk.

Gus tried to scratch his nose and hit visor.

The nerves were back. Back big time, striking electric guitar power chords through his chest, sending bad vibrations into his calves.

The shotgun blast was as good as a dinner bell.

Zombies emerged from behind trees and bushes, as if an entire god forsaken family had camped on the front lawn. Six of them at least, of various sizes. A regular civilian line-up of people you might see at the grocery store. Except for the missing parts and pieces and the horrible, fire-hydrant dousing of blood splattered across their persons. They moaned, spoke gibberish. They pointed pulverized hands that swung from broken wrists. Bare feet slapped the pavement as the whole pack trotted across the road.

Gus turned to get back into the van, when he spotted two *more* undead frights running at him from the next house over. One of them made an absolutely wretched sound—a smoker's death-rattle of a wheeze that stunned Gus.

He backed into the rear door, the edge digging into his ass. He shoved the shotgun across the floor, where it got tangled in the duffel bag. Not caring, Gus pulled himself inside in a kicking scamper of legs and feet. He rolled over, hauled himself up to his knees and reached for the rear door. A pained grunt left him as he pulled on that hunk of steel and closed it. Wheezing, sweating, he rose and glanced out the windshield, where indistinct figures charged the driveway. He was halfway to the steering wheel when someone slammed into the side.

A woman with short, blood-crusted bangs pressed her face against the driver's window a second after Gus landed in the seat. She dragged her profile left and right over the glass, the ragged hole in her cheek flat and stretching, exposing her entire upper rack of teeth.

Nerves. Every fiber, every gangly *neuron* within Gus was singing and hitting the high notes.

But the nerves didn't rattle him. And, surprisingly, the alcohol didn't impair him.

Something far more interesting happened.

The booze met the nerves head-on, like water engulfing live wires, and, in that snap crackle of opposing forces, a balance was somehow reached. The nerves sobered Gus enough to function with clarity, while the whisky insulated him against the debilitating jitters.

He'd reached equilibrium.

And in that zone of total, destructive Zen, Gus worked the gearstick as if he'd owned the machine for years.

He locked in Reverse without the slightest hitch. With an eight-cylinder huff of might, he *hammered* the zombies at the rear doors, splitting their ranks like drooping corn stalks. Hands, arms and torsos slapped against the reversing van, while ahead, a few undead flailed at a vehicle no longer there.

Gus turned the wheel, whipping the machine around and onto the road and exposing a few late stragglers to the party. More hard impacts across the van's metallic rump, and he glimpsed one gimp sailing backwards, to land feet up in a ditch.

A trio of zombies charged his grill.

Gus cranked the van into Drive and charged. He hit the three runners in a spatter of faces, torsos, and hands, once again experiencing that awful whump, thump and crackle underneath his wheels. He steered up onto a front lawn, did a slow turn and saw the zombies he'd just steamrolled, as well as a few more wading into the fray.

Grimacing, Gus hit the gas.

It only took a couple of minutes, but he eventually crushed them all… and rolled to a stop in the first driveway.

Breathing hard, but not gasping like before, Gus glared at the house with the broken picture window. Even though he was still three parts drunk, he'd realized what he had just done, and he still wasn't happy about it. In fact, he felt miserable. They were zombies, yes. Monsters, yes. But once upon a time, they were people.

He reached over to the passenger side, picked up the bottle and, shaking his head the whole time, sipped. Water be damned.

A minute later, he slid out of the van, righted himself, and winced. Black goop and hair stained the front of his ride. The black shit was probably blood. Zombie blood. Or whatever the scientific name would *be* for zombie blood.

Dents covered the sides and hood. Sizing up the grill, he knew he was going to have to either reinforce or replace. One day.

The undead that had landed in the ditch had found a friend, and both corpses crawled onto even ground. Gus climbed aboard the van, made his way to the rear, and hopped out the back.

Axe in hand.

He killed them both with one chop to their heads, and that kinda grossed him out. No matter how much he knew what they were now, he didn't think he would ever get use to the sight, or the *noise* of dispatching the already-dead.

Once they were gone, Gus surveyed the extent of the battleground.

Battleground.

He'd just run over at least five houses' worth of people and finished off two more crawling out of the ditch. What was worse, if he was going to get through all this, if he was going to survive… he would probably have to do it all again. Probably a lot.

It was… going to take time to get used to it.

Fuck me. Gus suddenly no longer felt quite so high. The nerves and alcohol continued to neutralize each other, however, allowing him to do what he needed to get done.

Trying not to dwell on what he'd just done, the… *unlives* he'd just taken, Gus swapped out the axe for the shotgun and proceeded to the first house.

He didn't walk with purpose. Nor with determination. Gus walked like a guy half in the bag and trying hard to deal with it.

Thankfully, there weren't any more dead people looking to eat him. All five houses were clear, but a semi-sloshed Gus went through the paces of checking each place and loading up whatever he could find before moving to the next one. It took time, energy, and every time he got back to the van to unload any food and essential supplies, he would stop, mix up a water and whiskey, and drink it down.

It was dirty work. Especially in his state, but he was practically *fearless*.

And badly needing to pee. Which he did once, swaying in front of a hedge. All the while, he believed the area was cleared of zombies, though he did expect to see blue and pink birds circling his head at any moment.

Clothes.

Maybe there were some extra-extra large clothes in there. Or something very stretchy.

There were no clothes his size, but upon walking through one bedroom (where the floor tilted and rolled like a dinghy at sea), there were plenty of bedsheets and pillowcases, blankets and comforters. He took them all. There was a rechargeable hand drill in a work shed, so he took that and an assortment of screws. The same shed had a six pack of ginger ale on a shelf, and a pile of treated lumber along the side. He grabbed the pop and eyed the large two-by-four planks just waiting to be used for some home renovation project.

He lugged the wood back to the van, teeter-tottering all the way. The planks slid along the floor, right up under the seat, in an almost perfect fit which pleased Gus mightily. It took him three trips to load everything, and on the fourth trip he grabbed a hand saw and returned to the van. It was there that, in a head scratcher of a moment, he couldn't remember where he'd put the drill and screws.

Unable to locate the tool after a short search, he pulled himself into the back of the van, and, much to his chagrin, discovered that he'd dumped the drill and screws into one bin… where it had rained down onto the food items already in there, creating a pain in the ass salad he'd have to paw through and separate.

Gus sighed, staring at that mess.

Did I do that? 'Course he'd done that. There was no one else, but damn if he could *remember* doing that.

That got him to do a self-check—everything in place and no damage taken. Good stuff. Wicked, even. He was redder than a baboon's ass and streaming sweat but otherwise, he was, at a guess, approaching a hundred-percent medicated. The whiskey was a grab away but he decided to lay off the juice for a little while, for fear of tipping the balance and sliding into complete drunken bastard mode.

And hurting himself in the process.

Although he was feeling pretty damn invincible at the moment.

He shifted from one foot to the other, huffing and puffing, and hunched to see what he'd brought back to the van.

Holy shit.

He was ready to open shop. It looked like he was moving in somewhere. Or moving out. Or whatever.

Gus waved his hands, shooing away such particulars, and that little motion nearly toppled him.

He'd gone through the houses and taken pretty much everything he believed he needed. Food, bottled water, bum wad, blankets. There was even a load of wood jammed in the rear of the van, and it took him a second to remember moving it. Then another second to ask: *the fuck did he want with a load of treated wood?*

Gus wobbled for the rear doors and almost fell out while closing them. He turned around and saw that, to get back to the driver's seat, he'd have to climb over all that stuff.

Fuck that.

The rear doors opened again and he almost went plop getting out. He didn't however, and closed one door with a shoulder before slamming the other. Good thing the van was stationary, and he slid along its length back to the driver's door. Got in with a tired groan. Tossed the helmet, got settled away with a tug at the boys, and started up the machine.

2:36 in the afternoon. The numbers rippling before him.

Plenty of time to get back.

The booze was in the nearby seat. He mixed two parts whiskey and the rest water. Strong, but he was Gustopher. He was Gus-o-*matic*.

He was also completely pickled.

He gripped the wheel. *Too much* came the flickering, short-circuiting sign in his mind, on the verge of going out. Gus leaned forward and took a few deep breaths, his senses bordering on a watery numbness. A different sweat broke out, cold and sparkling, and he stared at the line where the windshield met the dash. He'd gone overboard on the drinking. Too much. *Way* too much. He was blasted. Wasted. One part petrified and three parts ossified. In an effort to control his nerves, he'd pretty much scorched them.

"S'all right," Gus said, leaning back with a *thud* and clenching the steering wheel. "I'll just… drive sober. Sober as can be. Think sober, dive sober. I mean drive sober. Not a problem. Just in case the cops have road shits. Road *checks*. Haha. Not… not shits."

Gus smirked.

He put the machine in Drive, lurched forward when he discovered he really had Reverse, and nearly hit the house before he found the brake. Gus got Drive. The *real* Drive, the forward moving one, and eased out of the driveway. The van's tires rumbled over carcasses in a deflated, bouncy castle kinda way.

None of that bothered him in the least.

Houses passed by as he followed the road. Each one a different shape or size, but not always colors.

Gus leaned into the wheel, narrow-eyed and focused.

God above he wished he had some music.

After a time, two figures standing on a sidewalk turned as he rolled by. Gus didn't see their faces. Didn't need to. If they were outside and in the wide open, they were probably dead. What was more perplexing were the residential lots. They were becoming more numerous, which was weird.

Another gas station whisked by, but he dare not stop. A *Lucy's* burger place. A *Needs* convenience store. A two-story school with wire fences surrounding its grounds. The road became increasingly tangled with cars, some empty, some not. Those vehicles were unclean fishbowls where things moved around inside.

Then there were the *zombies*. The free moving ones. Always on the periphery.

Gus had been focusing too much on weaving in and out of traffic, but he saw them.

Zombies ambled all over the place. All various shapes and sizes, height and width, young and old. The sheer diversity of them was staggering, from being untouched (in a purely undead sort of way) to looking as if they'd pulled themselves out from an adult-sized blender. They walked and crawled. Some lurched, swinging their arms like hundred-pound pendulums, while others moved as if ruined by rust. A few merely stood and swiveled. Some startled at the van, while others lifted limbs and pointed with bright expressions of *there's one!*

All the while, Gus drove on, the horror unable to reach him, powerless to stop him.

The sights confused him as he glanced around, sizing up the houses and streets growing around him. Doubt furrowed his brow with every passing second.

Waitaminute… he thought, squinting at his surroundings.

Did I make a wrong turn?

Jesus Christ and *Mary.*

He was in the city.

That got the tingles going, just a smidgen. Right behind the ball sack, too.

Undead wandered the streets, oozing from alleyways, from behind corners. They emerged from open doorways and those smashed out. A few even turned in windows and even flipped over knee high sills.

Gus hit a straight stretch of road and sped up, leaving them all behind in a growling surge of engine.

"Chuck you, Farley," he slurred, "Buncha fugly uckers. Go buck a fuffalo."

Thing was, there were more up ahead. Many more. Perhaps hundreds of the flesh- eating amoebic mass that was Annapolis's populace, alerted by the sound, drawn to his movement. Their voices—those haunting, breathless sounds coming from things that should not be able to make any sounds at all—reached him through the van's walls. A pitiful wailing of both anger and pain, announcing there was a living among them. A growing rallying cry that sounded like them alerting others to pinch off all means of escape.

"You ain't gettin' me," Gus slurred, recognizing where he was. "No fuckin' way."

He swerved into a side street and raced through, bashing through a series of reaching hands and arms. The van clipped two upright corpses and spun them to pavement, then nailed a third gimp side on, its head clacking hard against the hood and releasing a jet of black pudding before whipping out of sight.

A street party filled the road ahead, but Gus spotted an escape route—an empty driveway ending in a wooden fence. He turned hard, avoiding the mob, and barreled up the driveway. The van smashed through the wood, sending fragments in every direction.

Backyard. No pool this time, thank the Lord, but a small garden with little signs dotting the lawn. The van thundered over that patch of toiled earth, hard enough to make Gus's teeth ache.

"Je-ee-sus- Chri-ii-ist."

He crashed through a hedge, whipped through another backyard and ended up on another street.

Bypassing the zombie crowd entirely.

He barked a laugh and hit the gas, speeding away from the undead.

The mountains behind the city rose up, and Gus recognized them. One solitary building stood before them, and he knew it was the main hospital. Probably some cool medicine shit in there. He'd have to go there sometime. Not *now*, of course, but some time.

He didn't give it another thought, concentrating on driving sober, searching for intersections and right turns, looping back in the direction that he should've gone before. The roads sloped to higher elevations, and the residential areas tapered away to a few houses along an unobstructed strip of pavement. It wasn't the way directly back to his place, but on some level of understanding, he knew it was the right direction. Property lots became bigger, with the forest thickening the farther up he drove.

"Freedom," Gus announced. "That's right you undead fucks. I'm slick. Slicker n' snake shit."

Or something like that.

Which was about when he saw the tree.

From one front lawn rose a huge weeping willow. It wasn't the tree that got his attention, however, but rather the red sedan smashed into the tree's substantial base. That car freed a memory, and Gus slowed down until he was next to the crash site. The engine block had mashed itself into the tree trunk. Pinned against it were three gimps, which became animated upon his arrival. The car was pretty much accordioned, the front flattened into the sedan's interior, squishing its two occupants. One of them even twisted its neck to see who had stopped by.

Gus looked around. The only other zombies on site were the ones crushed against the tree, waving at him. The rest of the area was clear. For now.

He locked onto the sedan again, dread overriding his alcoholic high. Those people inside the car turned as well, as much as their crushed bodies would allow. He parked the van, grabbed the shotgun, and got out. Checking his surroundings, he proceeded to the car. The sedan looked familiar, but that didn't mean anything. He had to know, however. Had to make sure. Of course, there were dozens of identical models around the valley.

As he crept closer, the tingles flared up again, but this time, they were mixed with sadness.

The impact had crushed the sedan's two occupants, between the dash and their seats. The one on the passenger side had short, platinum-colored hair in which a good part was soaked in tar. Glasses were lodged onto the dash in a sprinkle of crystals.

Even though she was missing an eye and half her face, Gus still recognized Rebecca, the cashier from Mollymart East. The resident expert on zombies. Next to her was her man, Walt. His sunken cheeks appeared even more concave, and part of his thin moustache had been ripped away along with his upper lip and nose. The Mollymart man's throat had either been torn or bitten out. It was hard to tell which.

The sight stopped Gus cold. He stared at the two co-workers, ignoring the horrible threesome up front, pinched between car and tree.

The windshield had been pulled asunder, opening the interior to the living inside. From what he could figure, Rebecca and Walt had been driving along the road, maybe attempting to escape a pack of undead, or maybe they'd got caught in a mob and a few latched on, blinding Walt—much like what had happened to Gus, when he hit the guard rail and killed Toby. Except it was a tree that had stopped Walt's little sedan, and stopped it with authority. After that, with the windshield's integrity damaged, it would have taken little for a zombie—a fresh zombie, with its zombie strength, to peel away that protective barrier.

All the while, the two Mollymart employees, trapped and unable to free themselves, could only sit and scream as the zombies slowly worked their way inside. Maybe they'd hit the tree, pinned themselves, their lower legs broken as the zombies closed in. Maybe they'd died upon impact, but he wasn't sure about that, not with the way they were worming about now.

The sight of them, the thought of what they went through in their final moments… that was too much for him to process. He staggered back, mesmerized, their undead mewling loud and very much aware of him.

Then, he lifted the shotgun, his hands trembling again. At such a range however, a little trembling would not matter much. Walt and Rebecca moaned and watched him, imploring him to come closer. Walt's exposed jaws flexed, demonstrating his bite power, while Rebecca's mouth was open to the fullest—a ready and waiting bear trap.

Gus lined up their faces, hoping to get both with one shell.

And squeezed the trigger.

23

The ride home was a lonely, wretched one.

After closing and securing the gate, Gus backed the van into the garage, but didn't have the will to unload the thing. Then he remembered the frozen food he'd taken, and the ice cream and various other treats, and that moved him into action.

Not before taking several swigs off his whiskey, to honor the memory of a pair of decent people trying to get home.

He carried in all the frozen food, barely aware of doing so, and filled his freezers to capacity. Ordinarily that would lift his spirits, but discovering the fate of Rebecca and Walt had hit him hard—much harder than he would have expected.

When he had all the perishables packed away, he went into the kitchen and dealt with the grim discovery the only way possible.

He got drunk.

Really drunk.

So incredibly crossed-eyed stupefied in fact, that at one point during the night, his senses surfaced enough for him to realize he'd opened up a tin of beans in tomato sauce and had eaten half the can's contents without knowing it. There was plenty of grub in the house, certainly enough choices in the fridge, but for reasons unknown to him, he got the hankering for beans in tomato sauce. No bread (there wasn't any, anyway) and no crackers. Just the beans.

Then all conscious thought left him a second time, and he knew no more until morning.

That was the beginning of a fog of depression that lasted a week. Rebecca and Walt had been the experts, and of them all, with all their knowledge about the zombie epidemic, they should have escaped everything going down. They didn't however, their fate sealed by taking one wrong turn, executing one fatal move. And if they couldn't survive with all their zombie smarts, what hope did he have?

That thought plagued Gus through the week, where he dressed only in underwear, tight t-shirt, and bathrobe, and roamed the house in a daze. He drank heavily, going through half a forty ouncer bottle a day, mixing in cola or ginger ale, and watching movies. Mostly comedies, but failing to laugh at any of them.

One morning he rose, a living corpse himself, and went to the washroom, where he stood before the mirror. His eyes resembled a pair of clenched, crusty bung holes, and when he drew a brush through his hair, a great clump of it came away. Gus studied his substantial hair loss, dropped it into the sink, and immediately raked the brush through his remaining moss.

"Oh fuck." He pulled away strands and let them drop. "Oh… oh *fuck*!"

Stress. It had to be stress. Working its unholy magic upon him, drying out follicle after follicle with frightening speed. The departed hair filled up the wash basin and a horrified Gus stared at it. He was losing it, anyway, but the zombie outbreak had accelerated genetics.

That only got him drinking more.

Several mornings he woke in a pool of his own drool, with dreamy recollections of barfing with violence into a receptacle, then not knowing what exactly that receptacle was. It might've been a toilet. Might've been a waste bucket. Hell, at that point, Gus got up and checked his boots for fear of filling them, then forgetting.

Thankfully, however, that wasn't the case.

There were other physical oddities happening to him as well, besides the hair loss.

He itched. Badly. And all over. Worse, the itching seemed to be concentrated around his crotch and testicles, for some goddamn mysterious reason. His entire groin crawled at times, as if he'd doused his shorts in itching powder or some other irritant. He clawed at himself, above and below the belt, luxuriating in the fleeting comfort, reddening his rolls and scrotal skin and half-expecting to pull back bloody fingers. For the most part, only red streaks covered him where he'd raked himself. Hot baths didn't help, and he took more than a few during that time, seeking relief and not caring about water conservation.

Skin lotion came to mind, but that meant traveling down into the valley, and fuck if he knew what to look for. Which was his way of saying, fuck all of it. Old man winter could up and shit a month-long blizzard tomorrow and that still wouldn't move him into heading back down into the city. Venturing into Annapolis, or even just driving along the outer ring roads, ran the risk of encountering more people that he knew. Maybe even knew well.

No way was he doing that to himself. No fucking way.

So he stayed home, under mental lockdown.

On the fourth of December, a much-hungover Gus woke on his favourite sofa and saw snow falling outside his windows. The whole of Annapolis, usually dreary but visible in the distance, was blotted out by a foggy greyness shedding snow upon the land. As that snow fell, Gus rose, blankets falling off his shoulders, his hands straying to his crotch.

Holy shit. Winter was here. The day he'd been dreading had finally arrived, and it was coming down in great cottony chunks that covered everything in sight. Judging by the accumulation on the railings, at least five centimeters was down, transforming the landscape into a lumpy white mattress. And considering the deep haze, the snow didn't appear to be slacking off anytime soon. Gus stood with his house robe open, gawking at all that wonder coming down. He stayed that way for maybe all of thirty seconds.

Which was right about when the panic took hold.

He stampeded for the main entrance, undid the locks and yanked the door open. The framework clipped his shoulder as he rushed through, but he barely felt it. A single horrified croak left him upon seeing all that precipitation filling up his front yard. He held his face, then covered his mouth before clasping both hands over his head and spreading elbows wide like a set of antennas. *Snow.* Holy fucking snow fell, gathering in that breathless silence of a world halfway into hibernation.

Gus Berry, however, was wide awake.

He didn't scream, which was admirable, considering the lightning crackling through his veins. In a minute he was clothed in jeans, no socks, and a too tight t-shirt. He charged into the mudroom, where he stopped to haul on boots and a coat. Then he was in the garage, the door rattling upwards as he commandeered a blue snow scoop. There was a wide shovel, but anyone who knew anything knew those things were shit for shovelling. You needed the scoop for the big jobs, and the square shovel for the finer touches.

This was not a job requiring a fine touch. This was full scale, fire truck emergency requiring the biggest plow he had available.

In short time, he had the pavement uncovered and the snow shoved aside, then made the first cut, all the way to the closed gate. He dumped often, every ten feet as he hit deeper sections. In no time his breathing became hoarse, ragged wheezes punctuated by wet coughs. His hands turned red. Sweat streamed down his face, his back, and stung his eyes.

When he reached the gates, he stopped, entire frame shaking, and turned around.

"Sweet *fuck!*"

Snow already dusted that first cut, showing no signs of stopping.

"Come on," Gus barked, often glancing overhead. "Just come the fuck *on!*"

He retraced his steps, not collecting anything near what he scooped in that initial charge. When he reached the front step of the main entrance, he whirled around and attacked the driveway again, widening his path. His heart pounded, red-lining, but he barely slowed down.

Until he reached the gates a second time.

Barely a third cleared, and the snow sprinkled the pavement again.

Gus wanted to scream, needed to scream, just *shriek.*

Instead, he swallowed it all down.

All that inner angst compressed for a single fate deciding second… then detonated. He stumbled back, arms flopping, and landed on his ass, discovering the hard way just how much snow five centimeters actually was— —which was nowhere near the pillowy softness needed to cushion his fall.

Not that it mattered. When he hit the ground, Gus let off a boiler load of steam in one great huff and toppled onto his side. There he stayed, his cheek squished and freezing to the ground, one eye staring while his brain sought to reboot the entire system.

The cold helped.

Around the third minute, Gus rolled over onto his back, as if gut shot and left for dead. He spread his arms and legs wide. Snow dappled his face, made him blink, until he closed his eyes. His breathing became less harsh and more even, returning to normal. A minute later, he got to his knees and eventually stood. The scoop waited nearby, so he picked it up and lumbered back to the garage.

Where he lowered the door behind him.

Gus retreated to the living room. He stood over the couch when his knees buckled, landing him deep in the cushions. His foraging runs were over.

Everything that he had gathered up to this point was going to be all he would have to see him through the winter. If he tried getting down into the city now, with lowly all-seasonals on the van, he chanced getting stuck, and then…

Slack jawed and on the brink of catatonia, he stared out at the world. At times, he wondered how he would die. Trapped like poor Rebecca and Walt in their car or, if he was smart, just sitting down in the bathtub upstairs and blowing his own head off, after leaving a suicide note of course. Maybe he'd stick that note on the front door, to prepare anyone stumbling upon the house and the mess he would leave behind. At least he would be in the tub.

He drank heavily, chain drank, really. Mixing a fresh one right after emptying his mug.

By late afternoon, he'd passed out, sliding off the couch and onto the floor.

When it started to rain, he didn't even hear the patter on the glass.

24

When he woke, he struggled to sit up, and once again gawked at the weather.

Rain. Coming down hard, steady sheets pouring over the lip of an overwhelmed eavestrough nearby, creating a waterfall that was at once surprising, calming, and oh so pretty.

Rain.

Gus stood and walked over to the sliding door, pulled it open, and shivered. It was cold outside, but certainly not freezing, and the snow from the day before had been reduced to a mangy slush. If he wasn't sick to his stomach, Gus would have thought he was dreaming.

Instead, he realized that he'd been thrown a bone.

"Thank you, Lord," he whispered. He wasn't religious, not by a long shot, but he was starting to believe there was someone up there fucking around with him. Scaring the shit out of him one day before hitting him with… this.

Thrown a bone, indeed.

He intended to make the most of it.

His plumbing however, reminded him differently, and he spent a good chunk of the morning on a toilet, letting his body purify itself. While that was happening, he got in some serious thinking. Snow cometh, and snow goeth away. A warm front, just a few degrees above freezing, just enough to switch everything over to rain. All that snow was enough of a fright to motivate him.

He would stay off the sauce for the day and hit the city tomorrow at first light. A couple of things he had to keep in mind. The booze worked. It smothered his nerves and allowed him to function. The bad news was, if he drank too much, he would drift dangerously close to being utterly useless, which was totally counterproductive. He would have to strive to hit that perfect balance like before and *maintain* it, rather than sliding into dangerous levels of plasterfication.

In summary, booze good, even essential—just not too much.

The other thing was, in taking a wrong turn thanks to downing too much liquid courage, he'd driven into a zombie populated suburb. He'd escaped, but that little bit of reconnaissance had proven helpful. The gimps were slower now, and maybe becoming even slower as time went on, but there was still the danger of clusters, of getting trapped by them. A cluster, a *pack,* had perhaps resulted in poor Rebecca and Walt's death.

He had to never directly engage to the point of risking… what was the word he was looking for… *mobility.* Mobility was life, the chance to retreat and scrounge again another day.

He couldn't think of anything else, except that he had to be a hundred percent recovered before heading back out, whereupon he'd become three parts fried yet again. Gus wondered if he had a Catch-22 there, and decided he did. Sorta. Kinda. Maybe.

This would be a recovery day. There was plenty to do around the old homestead, around the old ranch. He realized with a start that he didn't even unload the van from the last haul. Oh, he'd brought in the frozen goodies, but the rest was still in the van.

Shaking his head, he finished his morning deposit, wiped and flushed.

Right after breakfast, Gus finished unloading the van, surprised he had packed in so much. The treated wood landed on the garage floor, and he quickly overloaded his pantry and the storeroom in the basement. Everything else went into the spare bedrooms downstairs. They didn't have shelves like the storeroom, but perhaps, since he had the planks, maybe he could do a little basic carpentry using the storeroom shelves as a guide. At the very worse, he would grab a bunch of milk crates and lay the planks on top.

At one point he paused, thinking he would need a lot of shelves.

Yesterday's snowfall had scared the shit out of him. He would not be caught like that again. Not if he could help it. If he got the amount right, he'd be going into town only half-sloshed, just enough to get past the fear factor, and get shit done. To keep him from breaking down into a gibbering mindless mess.

So he worked for the rest of the day, packing things away and getting things done. Not a drop of alcohol passed his lips. Supper was a Strongman's frozen TV dinner, with a pair of chicken cutlets guaranteed to contain at least twenty five percent protein. Gus ate it all and damn well enjoyed the meal, but could hear Tammy *tsk*-ing in his mind. She didn't eat frozen dinners.

Gus did, and he knew, one day soon, they'd be all gone. Then he'd be dreaming of them.

While he ate, he thought about tomorrow. Food and supplies were on the list, but he'd need armor as well. And his regular clothes. His apartment building would probably be the most dangerous, potentially having a small army of gimpified residents just waiting for his fat ass. He could just resupply himself with new clothes, if he could find his sizes. Armor was needed first, and the best place to start was an outdoor shop specializing in sporting goods.

He knew just the place. Like Stanley's in the mall, but bigger, much more specialized, carrying not only the equipment but the clothing. Hunting camos, that sort of thing. He also knew the place had a selection of leather goods, for the motorcycle crowd.

All right. He had a plan. For better or for worse.

Rain, shine or even a little snow—but only just a little—Gus intended on heading into the city and getting his armor.

On the morning of the sixth, Gus rose just before dawn, alert and determined.

He went through his morning routine, ending it all with a light breakfast of canned Chunky soup, the chicken noodle kind, and threw in a handful of crushed crackers as well. After breakfast he went to the garage, where the van waited, already prepped and gassed up from the day before.

With everything he needed already aboard, he walked over to a locker and pulled out a bottle of Captain Morgan white rum. He poured himself three fingers in a beer mug before topping it off with a shot of sweet lime juice and a can of ginger ale. That all went down in five mouthfuls, where he allowed it to settle before loading the mug again. He had filled a bag for the road, with another bottle of rum, so refilling and maintaining a buzz would not be a problem. The challenge would be pacing himself, to keep from getting full-on shitfaced.

"The things we do," Gus muttered and finished off the second drink.

His stomach clenched at one point but otherwise took it well. Gus patted his gut for cooperating. He considered returning the forty ouncer to the locker, but decided to leave it on the workbench. As an afterthought, he left a can of ginger ale there as well.

If he made it back, chances were he would need that drink. To celebrate making it back in one piece.

Then he got aboard the machine. Powered it up and opened the garage bay door.

Predawn light revealed a wet lawn.

"Okay buddy," Gus said, and patted the steering wheel. "We got a job to do. An important one. They're down there, waiting for us. Waiting for us to fuck up. But we're not gonna fuck up. And they're not gonna get us. No sir. Fuck that. We're gonna go, do what we gotta do, get what we gotta *get*, and then get the *fuck* outta dead city. Full impulse power and all that. You hear me?"

The van idled.

"Good. Glad to hear it."

He shoved the stick, getting Drive on the first try.

"Here we go…"

25

He linked up with a direct route into the city. Vehicles cluttered the highway, and though Gus could maneuver around the various knots and drive through the narrow channels, he had to slow down to do so. The idea of getting out and moving those cars and trucks appealed to him, but as before, the owners were still trapped inside some of them.

Another idea popped into his half-sloshed mind: if the zombies slowed over time, he could, in theory, open a car door and just yank the corpse out. Without much risk to himself.

Placing you under citizen's arrest. Fuckin' A. Wasn't a bad idea at all. No wonder creative types liked to tipple while working. He tucked that away for a later time. Then another … If the cold could kill an exposed person wandering around outside, what might happen to a walking deadhead after three months of Nova Scotian winter?

Deadhead.

Gus approved of that one. That was a keeper. He was coming up with some quality material. He glanced over at the bottle of Captain Morgan in a ruck sack. Maybe, if he was lucky, he could hit Mollymart and get some cola. Or any other supermarket.

But first things first.

A charred skeleton of a truck loomed ahead. A semi lay dead just past that, driven through a roadside billboard, its empty trailer busted open and scoured clean of whatever it had contained. A motorcycle lay on its side, its seat gutted, yellow foam fluttering. More cars then, one unmoveable mass, their doors hanging open and their windshields smashed.

Then the houses, coming into view on both sides of the road.

He slowed, taking in the sheer volume of traffic sprawled across four lanes. The rum in his system didn't feel like it was doing its job. Gus glanced over at the bottle, then the road, and squinted in dismay.

Bodies lay across squared lawns and didn't move.

The corpses' clothing appeared stiff, frozen. It was a cold morning, the dashboard thermostat reported it was minus four Celsius, which would freeze water. It certainly had been colder during the night.

A few of those bodies had their heads smashed open, and Gus found that he could look at them just a little longer than before.

Trash bins were overturned. A couple of houses had been ravaged by fire, leaving only blackened framework and scorched remnants of walls. More corpses, splayed out and staying dead. One house had a chair out front, right beside the open door. An old woman sat on that chair, wearing an untucked shirt and knee length shorts. Like so many others, the front of her looked like an ink bomb had gone off in her hands. When Gus got closer, she turned her head and stood.

The chair actually stuck to her behind.

A flabby arm rose as Gus drove by, then she was gone. Still, the sight of that half-frozen deadhead, with a chair hanging off its butt, made him shiver. He reached for the heat controls and turned a knob.

More people came into view.

Most stood like mannequins, their dead skin shimmering with frozen moisture. Some were walking, staggering along in that rusty gait suggesting wicked arthritis. He saw three children zombies—two little girls and a boy—all wearing pajamas and needing to be back home in bed somewhere. All three turned and tracked the van as it drove by, and Gus didn't give them a second glance, feeling the tingles yet again.

But not as bad as before. Not near as bad.

A smile crept across his face. At least that part of the plan was working. And it seemed like his itching problem wasn't so bad this morning, either. Maybe the fortifying of the nerves had lessened that, as well. Or maybe the itching came and went as it pleased. Maybe he needed a new detergent. He hadn't thought of possibly being allergic…

The zombie population thickened. The undead willed themselves into movement, shambling across lawns as if searching for the morning newspaper. They cluttered the street like oversized meat pylons. Blood covered some of them, while others appeared just as clean and cool as the day they died and rose again. They were everywhere, and growing awareness of all those dead people did nothing for Gus's morale.

But the magic of Captain Morgan didn't leave him, and for that he was grateful.

He drove through a main intersection without slowing, leaving the clump of dead citizens behind, and turned right. There were still plenty of vehicles around, but the lanes were clear enough for Gus to increase speed to fifty.

Even better, he didn't have to hit anyone along the way.

Going good, going good, he thought, eyes darting left and right.

A large square building came into sight, its unlit sign displaying the words *IO Marine*—where "IO" stood for Indoor and Outdoor recreational goods. The parking lot was huge and relatively empty, on the edge of a large commercial part of town.

Not empty, he corrected himself, as he approached the turn off for the store.

Perhaps a dozen zombies patrolled the parking lot. Certainly no more. But they would come at him once he parked. He leaned forward, seeing a few houses in the distance, but nothing more. It was still a problem. If they knew he was around, they would hunt him down.

Not hunt, he told himself, turning onto the big store's parking lot. They didn't have the brains to hunt. If they saw or heard you, they came after you. He wondered, however, once they started moving, how far would they go before something *else* distracted them.

The clouds split and fragmented, allowing daylight to shine down on the remaining three cars in the parking lot. The pavement was glossy in places, suggesting black ice. Gus aimed for the nearest cadaver walking straight for him.

"Tag," he said, and stiffened his arms for impact. "You're *it.*"

The grill smashed the gimp in a burst of black sludge. The head snapped forward, stamping its face into the hood and sending teeth flying, before the body dropped to the pavement.

The rear tire rolled over something, jostling Gus in his seat.

"Now you're it," he said and drove at the next target.

Nine. There were nine deadheads roaming the parking lot. Gus ran them all down. They didn't bother with dodging the oncoming freight van. In fact, they did mostly nothing just before impact. A few raised their arms, for all the good it did them. Some had more juice in them than others. One wore only shorts, exposing a set of those positively gross bloated calves.

He looped back for secondary passes, lining up front tires with skulls and crushing them like hard candy shells. Those were the finishing touches. The killing blows.

After dealing with the parking lot threat, Gus backed up to the main entrance and parked the van.

Wind slammed into him when he swung open the rear doors, much colder than expected. Gus flicked his visor down, checked his corners, and jumped to the ground. Shotgun in hand, he approached IO Marine's entrance.

Which did not open.

Figures. He studied the sensor overhead. Someone had locked the doors, and it should not have surprised him. He would have to find another way in.

Gus eyed the cars on the lot and had an idea.

"Why not," he said. "No cops around."

Five minutes later, he stopped the van at the nearest sedan and got out. The car door was locked and the interior empty. The next one was a larger model but contained a zombie, trapped by a seatbelt. A key fob rested in the spare change cup, right next to the dead thing's leg. The zombie regarded Gus as if awaiting further instructions.

Gus left that one alone.

The third car was also locked and empty.

He studied the machine with the zombie inside. "The win-nah," he announced, and returned to the vehicle. He brought the hammer with him for the job. He wore gloves and made sure he was covered, but if the thing got a hold of him, if it was stronger than it looked, it would have little trouble biting through the two sweaters he wore.

Gus readied himself and yanked open the door.

The zombie regarded him with a pissy snarl.

Gus slapped away a half-frozen arm and pushed the head aside. He then grabbed a shirt collar and attempted to pull the zombie out, as if extracting a stubborn garden snake from a hole. The seatbelt kept the thing in place. The zombie clawed for him, awkwardly, missing the mark as Gus shoved the head down.

Whereupon he nailed it with the hammer.

The zombie slumped, and things got awkward.

The hammer penetrated the skull and got stuck in there. A frantic Gus pulled one way and then the other, unable to root the tool free, before realizing the zombie was dead and gone. Stepping away from the corpse and getting himself under control, he left the body hanging halfway out of the car, still held in place by its seatbelt.

"Out of the car," Gus commanded, and fumbled with the belt's release button. It snapped free in a hiss of fabric. "Out of the car, goddamnit." He again pulled on the hammer. "Out of the fuckin—"

It tumbled out, and Gus jerked back a step. When it failed to rise, he gave it a dirty look and kicked its chest. He extracted the hammer from the skull. Spoiled brain dripped from the steel, and a clump of jam he didn't look twice at. Gus checked on his surroundings, just to avoid looking at the dewy gobs dripping off the tool.

"Ew," he said, cleaning the hammer in the gimp's shirt.

As luck would have it, some of the organic foulness had lodged onto his sleeve.

"Oh you dirty bastard, you dirty, *dirty* bastard."

He grabbed a leg and pulled the entire thing away from the car. Once done, he pinched part of the zombie's shirt, and dry-scrubbed his sleeve. A few good rubs got it as clean as it was going to get.

"All right," he said and climbed aboard.

And almost puked.

The smell wasn't so bad with the door open, but when Gus closed it, all that rotten, shitty ass foulness enveloped him. He cracked open the door once more before it killed his buzz.

"Goddamn you stink," he aimed at the dead zombie nearby.

There was no comparison, simply a brain dissolving effluence, a killer combo of plant and animal decay probably rotting every hair in his nose. Even though he had his helmet on, he still breathed in that noxious, cancer-repelling stench, sickening him.

He started up the car. Lowered all windows.

The main entrance loomed, and he drove straight for it before slowing and swinging wide. There, he reversed (appreciating how the labeling actually matched up with the gears) until the rear camera showed the trunk in line with the glass doors.

"Tempered glass," Gus whispered. He heard Walt's voice, explaining the front doors of Mollymart. Sadness followed the memory.

He shifted gears and hit the gas.

Drove out some twenty feet and stopped. He did up his seatbelt, exhaled, and knew he was going to have a drink if this worked.

Gus shoved the gearstick into reverse and hit the gas again.

The car charged the main doors with demolition derby enthusiasm—the rearview camera displaying just how quickly the space shrunk between the two—and just before impact, the sensors chirped the equivalent warnings of *NO! NO! NO!*

There was a clap of exploding glass and crumpling metal. The airbag deployed, punching him into the seat, dazing him. As the airbag deflated, he pushed the thing aside and checked both the entrance and the parking lot.

"That was kinda fun," he groaned, and drove the car out of the wrecked face of the shop. Tempered glass fell in his wake. He left the machine and jogged back to the van.

Still no sign of any deadheads.

He couldn't believe his luck. Decided he would have to be careful.

Within minutes, he had the van parked and its rear doors thrown wide, right in front of the smashed entrance. He hopped to the ground, taking the jolt and knowing he couldn't do that too many times in a row. Things crinkled underfoot as Gus walked inside. He couldn't see shit, so he flicked up the visor and studied the interior.

Oh my.

He'd found a winter wonderland.

Aisles upon aisles, stocked with all manner of outer clothing. Thick winter coats and pants. Gloves. Hats and helmets. Boots. Boots that looked like shoes, and even thick socks. And that was only within the radius of daylight from the entrance. The place had more, much more, and he squinted at the deeper, darker sections of the store, where his eyes failed him.

He lifted the shotgun.

"Anyone in here?" he called out. No answer.

If drunken memory served him correctly, the leather goods were near the back of the store. Along the way, he stopped by the checkout area, scouring all the last-minute knick-knacks a person could buy. Fishhooks, lens, gear, and poles, but also… flashlights.

Gus grabbed one and switched it on, producing light.

"Anyone in here *now*?" he asked, swinging that beam around.

Again, not a sound.

He headed for the leather goods section, and stopped upon seeing an aisle of winter coats.

A dark navy-blue job with fur lining the hood greatly appealed to him. Then another without a hood. He put the twelve gauge down and tried on the coats. Smiled at the comfortable fit. And the warmth. He didn't know how cold it was until he wore the coat.

Shopping cart.

He needed one so he returned to the front, grabbed a cart and wheeled it back. The two coats got thrown in there, along with a few more pairs of gloves and woolly socks. There were more boots, and he tossed in an extra pair of those as well. The cart filled up quickly, but Gus didn't care. He dashed through the store, grabbing things off racks and checking sizes.

Minutes later he hit the leather section, a corner devoted to the motorcycle enthusiasts and road hogs of the open highway. Brand names festooned the walls. All manner of designer equipment hung from racks or covered shelves. A large, loose-fitting coat caught his eye. He pulled the leather coat on over the winter one. It fit. More than that, it was *tight*. He lifted his helmet, brought his forearm up, and bit hard into the material, then relaxed.

Just a deep imprint, but that piece of rawhide didn't break or tear.

He kept it on, enjoying the weight and the warmth, and picked out another coat that was more his regular size. For springtime.

Which was right about when he heard the click of a hammer being drawn back.

"Freeze, fat ass."

26

Despite the goodly sum of rum in his veins, his asshole puckered tight at the command. Gus held up his hands, still holding the coat, and dared not turn around. A flashlight beam lit up the aisle.

"Drop the coat," the voice commanded.

He did, unable to see the speaker.

Boots shuffled across the floor. The shopping cart rattled as whoever had the drop on him pulled it back.

"What're you doing?" the voice asked.

Gus swallowed. "Shopping."

"You're alone?"

"Uh-huh."

All quiet then, and, as the silence stretched on, Gus's arms started to ache.

"All right," the guy said. Then, in a much more jovial tone: "Aw, I can't keep this shit up. You can turn around."

An uncertain Gus slowly turned, squinting under the flashlight's powerful glare.

"Oh shit, sorry about that," the speaker said, and turned the light away. He placed it on a nearby shelf. He wasn't tall, a couple inches shorter than Gus, and certainly wasn't overweight. Fair complexion, unshaven, narrow of face.

"Yeah, anyway, sorry again," the speaker said. "Just making sure you wouldn't shoot me. Everything's pretty much lawless these days. And I didn't mean what I said about fat ass. I dunno what happened to me there. Felt like being tough. Didn't mean to offend. Hell, I can't talk. Got a gut myself."

The guy chuckled, ending it with a hoggish snort.

"So…" Gus drew out. "I can put my hands down?"

"Oh sure, go ahead."

He did, thankful to do so. He made the mistake of glancing at his shopping cart, however, and the shotgun laid across the top.

"Ah," the guy said, waving off the look with a dismissive hand—the same hand holding a respectable sidearm. "Don't worry about it. You can go back to shopping. I was out back there. Stocking up, like you."

"You were out back?"

"Yeah. Got my rig parked outside. Loading bay area. Wanted to pick up a few things before I hit the road. Never got past the storage room."

He chuckled again. Gus actually smiled too, somewhat uncertainly.

"So, you weren't lying?" the guy asked. "It's just you?"

"Yeah, just me. You?"

"Just me. What's your name?"

"Gus Berry."

"Raymond Ray."

And the guy actually held out a hand. Gus hesitated before reaching out and taking it. "Wait…" he said. "Your name's Raymond Ray?"

"Yeah."

"*Ray* Ray?"

Another smile. "Yeah. That's me. My mom thought it was cute, apparently. And my dad didn't disagree so, yeah. Too bad everyone in the schoolyard didn't think that way. Aw, that's a lie. It wasn't that bad."

"Ray Ray," Gus repeated and chuckled. "Why not? That's a good name."

"Ray Ray, rah-rah. That's what they used to say when I was playing soccer here. Run, run, Ray Ray, run, run. Anyway… that a twelve gauge?"

"Uh, yeah."

"You got shells for it?"

"Well, no."

"Well, damn son, you came to the right spot. This way." Ray stopped in his tracks and peered at Gus with a different scrutiny, a much harder, more lethal expression. "You're not going to shoot me, right?"

"What? No. No! 'Course not."

"Especially not in the back."

"*What?* No!"

Ray's face was a stern thing for all of three seconds, before softening. "Figured. You don't look the type. Had to ask, though. Things are pretty messed up, right? I mean, damn. *Damn.* And really, after the week I've been having, getting shot in the face is better than having your ass eaten out. By a zombie, that is. Anyway, c'mon. I'll show you were everything is."

He waved the gun in the direction he meant to go. Gus grabbed his shopping cart and flashlight, keeping his hands off the shotgun, and followed Ray through the store. After so long, it was a little weird to be talking to a person, especially one who pointed a gun at him, and was now leading him off to… ammunition.

It was more than a little weird, and a lot to process, all in a very small window of time.

"Uh, wait," Gus said, his mind a rush of noise. "Before we do that, I need to find some padding. Elbows and knees. That sorta thing."

"Like armor? To protect against bites?"

"Yeah."

"Not a bad idea. You were right next to it. Right over here."

Ray led him to it.

Gus stopped and stared. "Holy shit," he whispered.

He'd found the holy land of all leather accessories. For bikers anyway. One aisle over from the coats were pants, shorts, boots, gloves, and helmets. There were stylized inner vests and body airbags (which Gus never even knew was a thing). There were gloves, elbow pads, knee pads, shin pads, knee and connected shin pads. Neck braces, back protectors, *lumbar* protectors, and chest protectors. There were coverings that to Gus didn't look like coats, more like form fitting superhero physiques modeled after a body builder. There were even protective cups.

"Holy shit," he whispered.

Ray Ray nodded agreement. "Something, ain't it?"

"You bet it's something."

"All quality merchandise too. Made right in Ontario. We only carry the good stuff."

"You work here or something?" Gus asked, while reaching for a pair of gloves.

"Actually, I do," Ray replied in a wistful tone. "Or did. Assistant manager. Twelve years, five months. Had the key codes for the front door. Parked my rig out back, just to keep it out of sight. There are some crazy individuals around."

That got Gus's attention.

"Yeah," Ray said, seeing his reaction. "Crazy. Insane. Bug shit *nuts*. Don't know if it's the zombies or the lack of law but some people are… yeah. Probably some mental issues going on, or they ran out of meds. All exacerbated by the end of everything. Exacerbated. What a word. Just means made worse. Much easier to say. Two syllables. Anyway. I mean, all this… it's not the end of everything. It just isn't. Things will get back to normal. It'll just take some time."

Gus chose not to comment on that, but he did hope Ray was right.

"Anyway," the assistant manager continued, "I was loading stuff out back there and heard you come through the doors. You crazy guy, you. Gave me a heart attack."

"Sorry about that."

"Oh no," Ray assured him. "I don't care. Not like I work here anymore. Was gonna happen sooner or later. Didn't expect you bashing in the front doors, though. Another time I would've called the cops, but now? Fuck it. I'll probably do the same if I have to. Scare whoever's inside. Ha! Yeah, you made me jump. Damn near sharted myself. I mean, usually people hit the grocery stores first. If they could get past the zombies, that is. After that it's gas. I mean, this isn't even third. More like… I dunno. Bottom of the line stuff. Or advanced level prepping, after the fact."

Gus held up a hand. "Groceries went first?"

"Yeah. 'Course."

"How'd you know?"

"I saw things, man. A *lot* of things."

Gus watched him.

Ray studied him back. "Where've you been, anyway?"

"Up on a mountain," Gus replied, and immediately winced.

"Ah, don't worry. You don't have to tell me. I don't mind. Security and all, especially now. Don't know who you're meeting these days. Psychos be hiding once upon a time but now, those nut bars are swinging from lamp posts. You know I met the Redeemer a few weeks back? Well, I did. Least that's what he called himself. Funny thing, back before all this went down, he was just called Burt. And all Burt wanted me to do was bow down to him. Yeah. Like that. I was like, nuh-uh. Get outta here crazy ass Burt. You smell like cheap glue. Anyway. So, yeah. I'm heading out west. I won't be around to bother you. This was my last stop before I hit the road. Say, you wanna head out with me?"

The question hit like a straight jab to the chin, cutting through the barrage of information and leaving Gus momentarily speechless.

Until he asked, "Where you goin'?"

"Ontario. Then straight up north, where there's not many people. Place called Bearskin Lake. Real isolated but self-sufficient, you know? Do things the old way. Spent a couple summers up there. Got to know a few people. Beautiful part of the country. People are super nice."

"How you gettin' there?"

"Driving."

"Drivin'?"

"Yeah, driving." Ray nodded and glanced around. "That's why I'm here, like I said. Picking up the last few essentials before I head out. Tent, sleeping bag. Coleman stove. I won't be back this way until all this blows over. And when it does, not sure if I'll be back. We'll see."

The rum didn't seem so strong anymore to Gus. He stared at Ray—he really didn't know the guy, though he seemed friendly enough. "Well, it's a good idea, but not now. I think I'll stick around here."

"You sure?"

Gus thought about his brothers. From what he'd seen and experienced, odds were they were dead and gone. Alberta was a long road trip. Too far, really. Hell, Ontario was a long road trip, and even if he got that far, he was doubtful anyone would go with him all the way to Alberta. He'd have to do that alone, driving across a part of the country unknown to him. Too many dangers. Too many unknowns. And frankly, when it came to isolation, the place he had up on the mountain was just as good as any little place on the edge of nowhere. Plus, it was next to home, what he still considered home.

Home was best.

"Yeah, I'm sure. Maybe… I dunno. Maybe I'll head up to Greenwood."

"Best stay away from there. I met a couple who worked on the base. They were driving to Yarmouth, of all places. Yarmouth. Well, they can hide in the fog, I guess. Anyway. They said the base and town were overrun. Very dangerous."

That stunned Gus. "No shit."

"None." Ray shook his head and glanced towards the entrance. "They could've been lying, but I don't think so. Word of advice, stay away from the populated places, if you can help it."

Gus glanced towards the entrance as well. "Something wrong?"

"We're yakking a lot here when we should be working. We just don't have much time."

"I cleared the parking lot before I came in."

A wry smile hitched up half of Ray's face. "I cleared the parking lot before *I* came in, and that was almost an hour ago. I actually drove around to lead them away. If *you* killed any, they were probably ones following *me* first, who lost the scent."

Gus looked to the front doors and back to Ray again.

"Yep," the man said. "It's like that."

"You mean *more* will be coming here?"

"Oh fuck yeah. Be surprised if they don't. They just walk around until something gets their attention. Then they go after that until the *next* thing gets their attention."

Gus quieted as his nerves began acting up again, pushing against his rum armor.

"We better speed this up," Ray said. He hurried off, brought back another cart, then stood by as Gus tried things on and sized up matters. It took an anxious ten minutes, but he got the sizes he wanted. Even a bitchin' pair of leather pants which he could wear over his jeans.

All the while, Ray watched him and the front door, while informing him of the finer points of the equipment.

"All great quality. Made right in Ontario. Nothing but the best here at IO. Extremely durable. Double stitched. Hand made and quality assured. I actually know the lady in charge of QA. Great lady. Hope she made it. See those holes? Allows air through. Real comfortable, too. And strong. Real strong. Perfect for any impacts or abrasions, commonly known as road rash. But for what you want? What you really want? Anything that gets a hold of you…well, they better have teeth of steel to get through that. I mean some titanium choppers. See how that fits? Quality, right?"

"Right." The nerves were done testing Gus's rum armor—now they were poking holes through it.

"Don't mind the front doors," Ray said. "Not yet. Let's finish this."

Gus refocused. "Will do. Thanks Ray."

"Don't mention it. And remember, if you decide to lose some pounds, this is all here. Come on back and get a smaller size. Can't see anyone trying to carry off all this. Oh, wait, shells. You wanted shells. You done here?"

Gus nodded.

"This way." Ray hurried off, leading Gus to the firearms section, where they inspected an impressive selection of shotguns.

"Nothing heavy here," Ray said as he went around the counter and stooped to unlock a display cabinet. "We're on a clock here now. You'll have to come back if you want another shotgun, or a replacement."

He placed a gun cleaning kit on the table. "You know how to clean a weapon?"

"Yeah," Gus answered.

"There you go. And oh yeah."

Ray dug out the shells.

Boxes upon boxes of twelve-gauge ammunition. Ray stacked them high on the glass countertop, creating a little wall. "All buck shot. This'll stop a zombie. You know about them, right? How to put them down?"

"I do."

Ray shook his head. "Shame how all this got started."

"How did this all get started?"

"You don't know?"

"I dunno," Gus admitted, while transferring the shells into a shopping cart. "Virus, I figure. Got into the air."

Ray scowled, eyeing the distant entrance, then started speaking as he brought up more ammunition. "No, not at all. That's what they *want* you to believe. It was in our *food*. All that processed goodness. All the chemical additives the companies would sprinkle in there like fairy dust, to get us to eat more, crave more, and buy more. Ultra-preservatives. Emulsifiers. Flavour enhancers. All done by the big six. Chemicals just building up in our bodies, reacting with other chemicals and meds, to a point where they couldn't be naturally voided and just took over. And by that, I mean switched people over. Just like that."

"Not a bug?"

"Not a bug." Ray said, dropping a flat of shells onto the counter. "I did some reading online before it all went to hell. Scary what we're eating. What we *were* eating. Anyway, sorry. Don't mean to bore you. What's done is done, right? The clock's been reset."

Oh, Gus thought, *it's been reset all right*.

"You good?" Ray asked, taking a breath.

Gus sized up what he had. The assistant manager had supplied him with four flats worth of shells. Each flat contained ten boxes of twenty-five rounds, or two hundred and fifty rounds per flat.

A thousand shells right there, on the counter.

Then there were at least another four dozen loose boxes of various brands, for another twelve hundred rounds or so.

"Oh yeah, just wonderful," Gus told him. "But what about you?"

"I loaded up on everything out back. Got everything I can carry and more. Not going off to war or anything. Just trying to get to Bearskin Lake. I was heading out when you came through the front doors."

Gus winced. "Sorry, man."

"For what? S'okay. I don't work here no more. And like I said, I got plenty. And there'll be stores along the way. I'm good."

Gus adjusted one flat in the cart. "This place is an armory."

Ray looked around the shop again, but this time in fondness. "We got a lotta business when this place was open. A *lot*. It was a good place to work. Good people. *Great* people, to be honest. Great times. Yeah. Wow. Anyway. Anything else I can get you while I'm here?"

The question was just another shocker that left Gus mush-mouthed, simply from talking with another person.

"This is… a lot. Really. Thank you so much, man. Is there anything I can do for you?"

Ray pursed his lips. "If you can get away, that'll be enough. Us leaving together, in different directions, might confuse whatever's coming. And *something's* coming. Just a matter of how many. Anyway. I'm leaving town so, remember, the shop is here. Whatever you need should be still here. Come back anytime. Just be careful when you do. Zombies. And crazies. What a combo, huh? Anyway. I'm glad to help you out before I go. It… feels good to help out with, well, what's left of the community."

That further stunned Gus, but then he thought of something more. "Before you go. Ah, there is one more thing."

"Name it. I'll save you the time looking for it."

"You got any baseball bats?"

27

"How's that?" Ray asked.

After a rush back to the entrance, they slammed on the brakes in a sports section Gus had completely missed. Standing in the aisle, among baseball gloves, rubber bases and an impressive selection of other sporting supplies, he glanced at Ray and nodded, much approving of the brand new aluminum bat in his hands.

"Oh, this is good."

"What were you using before?" Ray asked, visibly anxious.

"Axe. And a hammer."

"Gotta get in close for that. The bat's got less of a chance of getting stuck. Hold on." He hurried a little further back in the aisle, grabbed what looked like a sack off a shelf and returned.

"For the bat," he said, and laid a bat bag atop everything else. "You can sling that over your shoulder. It's like a golf bag, except for bats."

"Nice."

"And really well made," Ray pointed out, unable to help himself. "Double stitched. High quality material. Made right in Ontario. We sold a lot of those."

The two men regarded each other.

"Time's getting short," Gus said, sobering by the second. His nerves jingled, like wind chimes caught in a hurricane.

"Yeah, I'll help you roll that out to your truck."

"Van."

"Oh, cool."

And true to his word, Ray steered a full cart back to the main entrance. He grew a little more cautious as they drew closer to the outside, checking corners and peering into the parking lot.

He faced Gus. "We don't have much time."

"What?"

"Don't look," Ray said, and jammed the cart up against the van's bumper. "Get in there and start taking this shit."

That unlocked Gus. He did as told, hauling himself into the van perhaps the fastest he'd ever done. He got to his feet, grabbed his helmet off the ceiling and glanced out the front windshield.

A line of figures advanced on the parking lot.

"Gus!" Ray whisper-yelled.

Gus whipped around and stooped to grab one of the flats of shotgun shells. They were the heaviest, but the loose boxes were the worse. Ray practically threw them in the back. Once that was done, he started in on the remainder of the shopping spree, tossing everything into the rear while Gus shoved and jammed it everywhere to make room.

He checked on the front.

That dark search party line of indistinct forms drew closer.

Even worse, second and third ranks followed.

"You say you got a place here?" Ray asked, distracting him again.

"Huh? Yeah."

"Nice set-up?"

"Yeah, nice set-up. Found it a few days after the shit hit the fan. I just walked right on in. Whoever owned the place wasn't home when I got there, and never came back. Or at least haven't come back."

"Never came back," Ray said and tossed in the last of the leather gear. "Bet that's a familiar story. Look, you seem all right to me, so I believe you. But a word of advice? Anyone asks you how and when you found the place? You tell them it took longer. Weeks or even months. Just so it doesn't sound like you moved right in. Like, you were watching the place or something. Sounds like you're a looter instead of a survivor. Or worse."

Gus hadn't thought of that.

Ray grabbed one door and slammed it shut. He then grabbed the other door and, before closing that one, smiled. "Nice meeting you, Gus Berry."

"Same back at'cha, Ray Ray."

"Sure you don't want to head up to Bearskin Lake? The more the merrier."

There it was, one final offer.

"I'm good here," Gus said. "Thanks again, though. Really. For everything."

Ray nodded understanding, then got serious, and glanced out at the parking lot. "Get moving."

He slammed the door. The man darted back into the gloom of the store when a loud bang sounded. Gus turned.

A zombie had slapped the windshield and was dragging his hand across it. Others were surrounding the front. One did a chest bump against the grill.

Whimpering and barely noticing he was doing so, Gus checked on Ray and saw he'd already disappeared.

Get moving, he thought.

The gimps advanced along the sides of the van, closing in on the gaping wreckage of the entrance.

Gus stumbled for the driver's seat. He plopped down and ignored the face trying to bite through the window. A zombie duo landed blows across the hood, as if they were free-style swimming. Gus didn't look at their blue-gray expressions. He clawed at his seatbelt, fumbled with it, and yanked it across his waist. It got twisted. A fist slammed against the driver's window, scaring him close enough to squirt. Gus struggled to fasten the seatbelt, ignoring the twist in the material, hearing his own growing growl of panic. He missed it on the first attempt, reset, and missed again.

At least a dozen deadheads stood before the van, pawing at metal and glass.

Others moved past, perhaps in pursuit of Ray.

Gus slipped the seatbelt into place and fired up the engine. The dashboard flared to life in a back-lit flash of white, red, and blue. He glanced at the bottle of Captain Morgan in the passenger side.

"Buckle up," he ordered.

And hit the gas.

The van shoved the zombies in front, knocking them into those behind them. A handful collapsed and the van rolled over the whole bunch, resulting in the most violent, mechanical bull ride Gus had ever been a part of. The beast rose and dropped over the still-writhing logs and, as God as his witness, Gus felt skulls being crushed through the steering column. His foot came off the accelerator, so he stomped on it a second time, resulting in that angry gush of power he was beginning to love.

The van charged forward, bashing away hands and arms, flattening bodies and sparing no one.

The parking lot was full of them.

In a demonstration of undead unity, zombies marched on the building. All shapes and sizes. All manner of bloody horrors. A ravenous protest where, if you weren't with the group, you would be eaten. Right down to the bone.

They could not stop the van, however. Could not grab on. And the undead were spaced out enough that they couldn't impede it.

The beast picked up speed. Gus hunkered over the wheel, splitting the undead ranks, splattering them across the pavement. And through all those horrible faces, near the exit of the parking lot, a zombie missile sprinted into the fold, arms and legs pumping as if about to take a running jump into a pool.

Except that pool was the van.

But another thing distracted Gus then, rapidly coming up on his *left*, and the sight of it surprised him.

A zombie.

A bloody, brutalized *wreck* of a zombie, missing one arm but holding up a *cellphone* with the other, as if recording the very head-on collision seconds away from happening. And as that moment-capturing zombie flashed by the driver's window, in a second where time seemingly *stopped*...Gus recognized him, *remembered* him.

It was the same pudgy dick from Mollymart, the one insisting on recording everything on his cellphone.

Perry.

Fuckhead Perry.

The undead had gotten at that considerable paunch of his, having ripped it open and scooped out everything in there. Whatever was left hung over his gore-stained waistline, the unfrozen bits fluttering like gelatinous tubing.

Which was right about the time the runner, still charging the van, hit the front head-on with all the force of a cruse missile. There was an explosion of meat and bone and rancid chunky stew and a horrific instant where the thing's face flattened itself against the windshield but failed to break through. A super-imposed snarl of shattered teeth and blood for all of a split second.

Then, like before, the whole mess flopped off the hood.

Gus screamed the second the zombie sprinter hit the van. He *continued* screaming because he couldn't see *shit* through the rotten slop covering the windshield. And the undead had pulled off the wipers long ago.

He braked, getting a fishtail, glimpsing, in a surreal moment of panic, fuckhead Perry actually *smiling* as he tracked the whole attempted escape with his bloodied cellphone.

Then the undead twat was gone, and Gus pumped the brakes, exerting control over the van.

There were two parts of the windshield not splattered in congealed slop.

One was at the base of the glass, between the vents. The other was the upper right side, just under the sun blocker.

Picking his poison, Gus hoisted himself up, straining against the seatbelt, and peered through the higher slot. Part of him insisted he was no good at this stuff. That he was close to breaking. He released a wheezy grunt.

Upper torsos zipped in and out of view.

And driving through the mob further out, on the actual road, was a large blue pickup truck hauling a black cargo trailer.

Ray?

Ray Ray?

Who else could it be?

As Ray plowed through the zombies in the street, the undead near Gus turned at the commotion.

Then the blue pickup with the cargo trailer was gone, and Gus glimpsed a red exit sign with an arrow pointing through it.

Ray Ray, God bless him—if it *was* Ray Ray—had reached his rig and driven around the IO store to the road, distracting Annapolis's population from swarming him.

It was the last thing the assistant manager did for Gus.

Should've shopped here more often, he thought, just before he slammed into a series of zombies and ran them down like nasty road pylons. He clipped the red exit sign, tearing it from the post and sending it spinning. He crashed through another knot of bodies, cringing as each torso rattled off the vehicle. Each one was a hammer to the front of the van, and each one left a dent of love. He didn't have time to wonder how many bruises the machine could take when a zombie's decapitated head *bounced* off the windshield, clearing away a melon-sized portal in the glass. Gus was too busy keeping his shit in and his foot on the gas to doing anything more but freeze, blink, then drop back in his seat, once again able to see where he was going.

"*FUCK!*" he shrieked. He turned the wheel, narrowly avoiding the flag mast of a power pole. The van savagely bounded over a curb and continued on. There was a hill, but it was crawling with zombies. Gus spotted a lane and turned for it, blasting down an alley and aiming for a rapidly approaching opening onto another street.

Three zombies stepped into that same opening, already turned to meet him.

Gus ran them down, almost biting off his own tongue upon impact. Foul organic matter splashed across the windshield again, obscuring much of it, making his job that much more difficult.

Space. He needed space. Somewhere to stop or slow down and at least clear off the goddamn windshield, but how could he do that when the entire fucking *city* was after his chunky ass?

So he drove, turning right and left, gunning down straight sections of road and slamming on the brakes. He hit zombies, spun them round or knocked them flat and drove over them.

Everywhere. They were everywhere.

Gotta get out of here. Gotta get out of here.

Parking lot up ahead.

Of a Canadian Tire store.

With no time to enter the right way, the van rolled up and over a curb, tossing Gus against his seat belt and clotheslining him when the four wheels once again touched pavement.

The ride evened out.

Surprisingly, there weren't many zombies on the lot.

Gus sped by them all. He drove around the corner of the building and got out of sight. There, he braked hard and, taking a deep breath…

Got out.

28

He had to see.

Cold air flash-chilled his face and he sucked in a chestful, hoping it might clear his mind, wake him up. It didn't. The windshield resembled a pizza heavy on the sauce and meat. He had nothing to clear that shit off, except...

He stripped off his new coats, took off his outer sweater and, without a second thought, used that to scrub off what he could. The sweater quickly absorbed its fill and Gus, disgusted, threw it away, mindful of his hands.

Done.

He glanced around.

Zombies. Of course. Already lumbering toward him. All woefully dressed for the winter weather. Uncaring. Unflinching. *Unrelenting.*

Stick and jab, Gus remembered. He still had the van. Still had his wheels. But he was near the city's heart, a city that knew he was there, and banging the dinner bell. Gus winced, realizing he was scratching at his nutsack as if there was a brushfire down there.

"God...*damn*," he let out. Had to be the detergent. An allergic reaction of some kind. Hard to believe the stress was making him claw his own balls off.

Mobility, he thought, forcing himself to focus. He had mobility, and he had speed, but speed wasn't going to free him from the inner web of the city.

He had to be smarter than *them,* and they didn't have the goddamn smarts to get out of the way of a van.

But there was so *many.*

Gus hauled himself aboard the van and slammed the door. If he got the chance, he'd have to find and replace the lost wipers. If he got out of this rotten pickle alive.

Perry whasisface, entered his head again. That undead moose-knuckle had somehow managed to keep a hold of his cellphone. A true pain-in-the-peehole if there ever was one, even in death. *Karma*, Gus thought, and wouldn't lose any sleep over the guy.

The bottle of Captain Morgan had fallen on the floor. Grunting, he reached over and grabbed it by the neck while the van idled. The zombies were closer, but Gus needed equilibrium. Needed his medicine. Hell, he needed the whole goddamn *prescription* is what he needed. His nerves felt amplified to ten. He twisted the cap off the bottle, got in a mouthful, and swallowed.

"*Gah!*" he gasped, making a war face before resetting and taking in more. Another blowtorch huff of breath. Cringing, Gus eyed the advancing dead, plodding toward him as if they wore cement shoes.

He choked down a third shot.

Then, one final rum bullet before shaking himself and screwing the lid back on the bottle. Red-eyed and gasping, Gus gripped the steering wheel and grimaced at the collapsing circle of undead surrounding him.

"Fuck you guys," he spat. "I'm going home."

He shifted, and the view slid away to the right. Gus increased speed and crashed through four gimps.

Everywhere. They're everywhere.

If it wasn't traffic blocking him, it was the reanimated dead.

Worse, every impact he took speckled the windshield just a little bit more. Long seconds later, he got clear and wound his way down to the reclaimed dyke lands, where he turned left then right, remembering the layout of the streets, hoping he could get clear. One turn of the wheel, in a downtown area, and he barreled through an empty alleyway. Near the midpoint was a junction, another alley—a one lane hangman's noose, between a pair of taller buildings.

And that alley was clear.

Against his better judgement, he slowed and turned into it, and abruptly stopped the van in a squeal of brakes. Ahead about fifty feet was an empty street. Two lanes, with a small two-door car right across the way.

Gus kept his foot on the brakes and watched that opening. Watched the space behind him. Every fibre within him screamed to keep moving, but instead he stick-shifted into Park and switched off the van. His nose itched, so he picked at it.

Relax now, he ordered himself, and sat there. Vigilant. Staring at the open street ahead and, at times, checking his side mirrors.

The fuck you doing? his brain finally asked, realizing its orders weren't being followed to the letter.

As a reply, Gus reached for that forty-ouncer bomb of courage on the passenger seat. He held the rum bottle with both hands and sipped as if it were superheated coffee. Didn't help. He shivered and stuck his tongue out in an expression of *blah*, but he didn't drop the bottle.

I said, the fuck you doing?

Ignoring the voice, Gus fidgeted and clutched the bottle tighter.

And in that beat of time, a zombie sashayed into view, working its hips as if the thing had taken a direct hit to the ass. The gimp looked relatively intact, so Gus figured it was one that had picked up the infection naturally instead of being bitten.

The zombie kept right on walking, moving out of sight, not even glancing his way.

Get us out of here, his brain ordered, fully aware of the corpse. *Now.*

Fuck that, Gus sent back. *Run silent. Run deep.*

Those things didn't think. They just reacted. And Gus was in a tin can, covered in zombie guts. As far as he was concerned, he was suddenly just part of the landscape. All he had to do was make like a tree. Or a building. An *empty* building.

Then the horror show.

Following the first zombie was an unholy procession of undead—a collection of blood-caked frights and stomach-turning spectacles. They dragged their mobile carcasses along the pavement, their forms missing chunks or trailing streamers of matter. There were broken arms and ruptured throats. Torn away scalps and necks with killer gashes colored grey black. Some had their clothing ripped off, displaying rotten skin and finger-clawed lacerations. Racks of teeth gleamed through missing cheeks. Missing eyes. Missing noses. Mouths hung open or were lock-jawed in place. One poor man had an entire section of his chest clawed away, right down to a gravel-speckled rib cage. A woman stared ahead with fish-eyed amazement while swinging arms missing everything below the elbows.

Then came the children.

Gus looked down when they limped into view. That was his limit. He'd seen enough, anyway. The sheer variety of death scrolling past that alley mouth shocked and silenced him.

Not one entered the alley, from either end.

Oblivious to him, they kept right on marching, going *past* the alley. Maybe it was because of the muck coating the van. Maybe it was the silence. Maybe because they were pulled in one direction by the last lingering stimuli, seeking whatever it was that had drawn them.

He couldn't stay there, in the alley. He drank more, needing clarity, to stamp out those freezing flareups of panic. Meanwhile, the zombie stream became a river.

A flooding river.

Gus stopped drinking, lowering the bottle slowly, for fear it might attract unwanted attention. He could hear them in that silence, talking zombie talk, a bingo hall's worth of gibberish. Movement in his side mirror drew his eye. A second morbid flow of torsos and body parts. A few of them actually stumbled into the lane behind him. One even collided with the corner of the building, but kept on following the leader. All marched right on by with decomposing grace.

The bottle touched Gus's lips without him even realizing it, as if the good captain himself were saying *Here, take this.* Gus did exactly that, drinking very slowly before lowering his hands.

The procession continued, thickened even, impossibly so, until Gus reminded himself that Annapolis was a city with a population of a few hundred thousand. If he ever wondered how many a few hundred thousand would look like in a street, he was getting a damn fine idea of it now. It seemed like the entirety of Annapolis's citizens participated in that march of unlife, before and behind him. Young. Old. Children. Those disturbed him the most, despite looking away. They waded into sight and were impossible to miss, walking alongside either parents or complete strangers, their mouths biting or hanging open.

Gus clutched the bottle and grew very still. All it would take was one to walk down the alley. Just one, and he was certain others would follow. Judging by the hundreds in the street, there was no way he would be able to force his way through.

He sat and stared, no longer daring a drink for fear of discovery. His nose itched again, and his balls decided they didn't want to be left out. The clock read 11:30, and every minute after that was a painful countdown of seconds. That feeling of being trapped swallowed him whole…he clutched the bottle closer. At least he had weapons aboard.

The rum crept in, calming him. He glanced at the clock and rolled his eyes. 11:33.

Christ Almighty. It felt like a *year.*

With every passing second, however, the rum lessened the claustrophobic weight of it all.

11:35…37…39.

Forty.

Gus's eyes narrowed as he studied the undead force. He leaned forward just a little in his seat, causing fabric to squeak. At times, he glimpsed the other side of the road.

They were thinning out.

Thinning out at perhaps the same rate as the numbness of the rum rushing in, to dilute the horror of it all. In recognition of that, he drank another mouthful and muted the after sputter with a hand.

Straight up rum or whiskey wasn't his thing.

But the buzz was. That tilting, detached sailor-walk trip across a tipping world was everything.

He glanced around the alley. Where the fuck was he, anyway? Maybe somewhere in Upper Kentville. It took him a little bit to realize the location. Behind the multiplex and the little group of clothing stores all under the same roof. The more he sized up his surroundings, the more he knew it, and knew how to get onto an outer ring road in less than ten minutes. Ten minutes in traffic, that was. It could take a lot longer with all the meat-blocks walking around. *Meat-blocks*, he thought numbly, not bad, but not quite on the mark. Gimps fit. Deadheads, too. Same with dead fuckers.

Then it happened.

One of those zombies stopped on the fifty-foot point of the alley, right on the line marking the border, and looked straight at the van.

Even worse, it was a kid. A little boy, no more than ten, wearing a filthy T-shirt and blue track pants. The facial features were indistinct, except for the black patches where the eyes should be, and the hanging, flexing lower jaw. It stopped and stared with all the venomous intent of a king cobra, while its unfaltering kin continued past him.

Gus stared back, his spine pressed hard into the driver's seat.

The little undead bastard at the end of the alley didn't move, didn't flinch. As if he'd gotten just the barest scent of something, and waited for more.

Even worse, Gus's treacherous crotch still itched, with all the rabid force of a lice infestation. His hand well below the dash, he slid his fingers over and rooted around down there, quelling the uprising.

The child zombie remained, unwavering, until a much larger deadhead walked by, swinging its arms, and clipped the little toe biter across the back of the head. That roused the child, and it staggered, turned, and walked away.

Gus let off fifty pounds of pressure in one mighty sigh of relief.

The clock changed to 11:45.

At 11:50 he was feeling much better. He placed the bottle back in the passenger seat. The zombies had thinned out to stragglers and were totally unaware of him. Those stragglers were the slowest of the bunch, taking baby steps because of some unseen injury or advanced joint rust. A few were missing feet, so they dragged themselves along the pavement, their knees and elbows reduced to dull grey knobs and shreds of skin.

Some people are gone crazy, he remembered Ray saying.

Some more so than others, Gus thought, and started up the van.

That mechanical rush of life alerted the dozen shaky figures in the road, who turned their dead and frozen faces.

"Peek-a-boo," Gus whispered and stomped on the gas.

Tires smoking and screeching, the van blasted through the mass, violently scattering the rear guard like wobbly ten pins. Gus braked and turned hard away from the horde, clipping two more gimps. He straightened out the van and accelerated, weaving in and out of stopped cars.

He spotted another mob up ahead, blocking the avenue. He turned at an intersection. A uniformed zombie—a police officer—stood on the corner, partially protected by a street post. Gus drove around the undead lawman, ignoring the raised hands ordering him to stop. Then he was on another street, one that curved to the left, across a two-lane bridge.

Gus knew the bridge, knew the area, having worked on several houses just one road over.

Zombies stepped out from between cars and behind trees. They closed in, seeking to head off the van. He drove by them all without making contact, their faces whipping by.

Tires thumped as the van sped over the bridge. The rum was in full force now, enabling him to function.

Then he saw the *other* side of the bridge.

A pickup, parked on a slant and blocking part of Gus's lane. And in that narrow space, already turning at his approach, was a thick cluster of deadheads, forming up like a carnivorous defensive line. A street full of brick stores appeared in the background, completing the picture.

Gus wasn't going back.

"Ramming *speed!*" he screamed, and plowed into the masses.

Torsos and faces rattled off the front of the van, bent over and beaten. Hands, arms, and even heads banged off the hood in a frightening cadence. A face splattered the windshield in a burst of ink and a dice-toss of teeth, flattening a pasty-looking ear before the whole zombie rolled away. One went up and *over* the van in a rubber-chicken shiver of limbs before tumbling off. The rest were hurled back into those behind them.

The van steamed through a meat and bone jungle. The world went lopsided, and the seatbelt kept Gus in place as his foot slipped off the accelerator. He held on to the steering wheel as the beast's greater mass and momentum bounced the machine over the meaty ruts in the road. One zombie appeared on the right and stepped *into* the moving vehicle, pawing at it—only to have its arm snapped at the joint in a gruesome hyper-extension.

"God *damn*." Gus cringed as another head cracked open on the hood, right on the edge, launching a diseased brain at the windshield that burst apart on impact.

The van slowed but Gus drove it through, trying hard to look past the grisly headcheese sliding down the glass.

Then he was clear, his rig a gore-spattered mess.

And he'd only just cleaned the thing, too.

An intersection loomed, one jammed with vehicles and a nightmarish field of zombies.

The sidewalk was wide open.

Gus rattled up over the curb and slammed into a full garbage bin, sending it flying. All manner of refuse clattered off the van, but none of it stuck. It fell away just as a zombie flung itself out of nowhere and chest-bumped the broadside of the vehicle with a clack that scared Gus badly. He bit his tongue and tasted blood. The van turned, partially because of him chowing down on his own tongue. He regained control and zeroed in on a nearby alley.

One filled with zombies. And metal garbage bins.

Gus pushed himself back in his seat, held the wheel at arms' length, slowed to thirty and went through.

In ones and twos, he struck down the undead, smacking them off the grill and sides as they didn't bother getting out of the way. They tumbled off the van and slammed into the walls. One zombie hit the front dead-on, his arms splayed across the width of the moving vehicle. There, with a positively unnerving slow-motion poise, the undead lifted its ruined face and *smiled*. The thing only had five teeth, and all five had been reduced to yellow shards.

Because of that one sly look, that undead bastard clinging to the front of Gus's ride struck him as perhaps the evillest of them all.

We see you, it said.

And that chilled Gus from head to toes and balls in between. Then he was out of the alley and into the next street over.

The entire episode had become more like drive and pound. A straight-up wedding of rodeo-riding and demolition derby, where he was the only one with a rig. The zombies in the street weren't close enough to grab for the van, nor were they fast enough to chase it. Gus motored by them all and reached the ramp for the outer ring road. Trees appeared, backed by forest and hills, and Annapolis fell away.

Minutes later, there were no more mobs of undead might, and only a few cars on the shoulders of the road. There were two lanes, and Gus weaved between both. He read the signs and, eventually, after a twenty-minute run, linked up with the twelve and the way back home. Well, *someone's* home, he supposed.

"Freedom," he whispered, hoping it was true. He rubbed his head. His hand came away coated in sweat and he realized he was practically oozing, and not from the warm interior or the leather he wore. He cleaned his hand on his leg and wiped again. And again. Until he decided to pull over onto a gravel shoulder. There was a house nearby. Not thirty feet away. Untouched.

"Holy shit," Gus whispered, feeling the rum in his system and knowing it had just held the line during his escape. He cracked opened the door and slid from the seat, discovering he barely had ankle support when he touched the ground. There he stood, careful not to lean against the van, grossed out by the filth dripping from its dented shell. He paced, taking in the fresh air, peering at the overcast sky and, always, keeping an eye out for any nearby dead fuckers.

At one point, he stopped and stared back in dismay at what he'd just come through.

The city was alive with them.

Gus sized up the mess that was the van, wincing at a section of bloody scalp stuck to his door. No way he was going to clean that off with his hand. No fucking way. And it was going to take more than one roll of paper towels.

Leaving it, he got back behind the wheel and drove up the mountain, trying with all his drunken might to stay on the road. He drove slow to better navigate that rolling highway, and somehow managed to avoid ending up in a ditch. He passed the unmarked driveway that led back to the house—his adopted home. The driveway bothered him. If he continued staying there, he'd have to do something about that open road. Some flowers would be nice.

New Cross came into sight, and he eventually rumbled through town, leaning hard on the steering wheel. Decomposing bodies stained the pavement and he avoided those, scanning for the ones still walking.

"C'mon out," Gus muttered. "Zero fucks given. C'mon out. See what happens."

None did.

He stopped in front of the garage and got out of the van, careful not to touch its polluted hide. He stumbled inside the open bay and found a water hose that worked. It took ten minutes, but he hosed off all the zombie gunk covering the van. That nasty scalp skidded to the ground in a stop-and-go motion that almost turned his stomach. The wet, clingy *splut* when it dropped didn't help matters either.

Once the machine was clean and dripping, Gus filled the tank with whatever was left in the pumps. Realizing the van was not filled to capacity, he climbed aboard, stumbled around, but managed to stow some things. When he was better organized, he dropped back down into the driver's seat, nearly swooned upon touch-down, then revisited the liquor store.

Driving at a blistering twenty klicks an hour.

"Smashed." He slurred, glassy-eyed and numb of mouth. "Fuckin' smashed here. I'm… cross-eyed and blinkin'. Cross… Fuckin' fuck. Gotta slobber. Slobber? Ha*haaa*! *Sober.* Y'fuckin' mushed mouth tit. Gotta *sober.* Up. Gotta get. There."

It took twenty minutes, but he loaded up the van with the last few cases of Captain Morgan, Bacardi, and Jack Daniels. All the while, he stopped every five steps, looked around, and listened, just to be sure he was safe. The fact that he was able to *do* that in his condition amazed him. The rum was still in control, still moving him, but that tank was approaching empty. So he refilled it when he needed, just to keep up morale.

Until it was time to get back to the house.

At 3:40, with the sky growing dark and still blasted out of his gourd, Gus returned to home base. He opened and closed the main gate, swaying left to right as if caught in a dryer's tumbler mode, and he was a big-soaked sheet. His next amazing feat was parking the van in the garage, which he did successfully, making beeping noises as he backed in.

Once he was out of the van, he took deep gulps of air and sank to his knees.

"Land," he whispered, tapping his head against the concrete. "Land ho. *Arrrr.* Oh… *arr.* God…"

Gus swallowed and breathed through his nose. He straightened, and that alone puffed his cheeks. Somehow he got to his feet, his entire digestive tract rolling at the lopsided motion, and made it to the workbench.

There, waiting for him, was the smiling face of Captain Morgan.

"Hello dear," Gus said, taking the bottle in hand. "I'm back. Little banged up. Little more runny, but nothing serious. Nothing a coat of paint can't cover up. You have a good day? Huh? Hope it was better than… than mine. The *city-ots* almost got me. Oh fuck did they ever. Maybe not almost, but… there were times. Oh ho, there were times. Road rage is a real thing. Some people's children, I tell ya. Fuckin' city-ots. Hate 'em. I swear I'll use the fire-rod next time. The boom-stick. The twelve-gauge ticket puncher. Just you… just you wait."

As he spoke, he poured himself a drink—three fingers and the rest water. He cobbled it together with no spillage and deemed it a smashing success. He slobbered it all down, and it went down much better than expected.

"Goodness," he said to the bottle, and fixed himself another. "I was so thirsty. So, so thirsty."

Then came the victory shot, for surviving the day. Then a third, because it felt like the right thing to do. When that one was ready, he raised it at the van and held his tongue in a moment's silence. She'd gotten him through, through the thickest shit ever. Sure, there was some dead guy's scalp on the door at one point, but that washed right off. There were a few extra dents, too, but nothing to keep her wheels from turning. The love taps gave the machine character. Attitude. Then Gus toasted Raymond Ray—helpful Ray Ray himself—and hoped that the assistant manager made it all the way to Foreskin Lake.

"Bearskin," Gus corrected himself. "Haha. Not… you know. That other thing. Silly."

He dismissed the moment and sampled the latest drink. The inside of the garage interested him then, and he inspected the lockers, the work bench, and the few tools there.

"Gotta get organized here," he said. "And gotta stop talking to myself. Jesus."

Then again, he figured, it was better than hearing nothing at all when he did stop talking. Anything to fill that hole. That… void of no-sound. Toby would understand. Hell, Tobe would be all for it. Tammy too. Not Gord though. Gord would tell him to shut the fuck up.

Thoughts of Ray Ray then, and whether he made the wisest decision in not staying behind. He regarded the bottle of Captain Morgan.

"Wait 'til you see what I got for you…"

With that, he finished off the drink, and proceeded to unload the van.

29

The unloading process took a little longer than he expected, mostly because he was seeing dead people throw themselves at the van when he closed his eyes. As a result, he kept right on drinking as he worked. It was dark when he finished and stumbled back into the house, thanking each and every helping wall along the way.

Walls. He thought. *Every good house needed them. Without 'em, we'd... we'd all be living in attics. God bless 'em. Every one.*

At the finish line, the kitchen, he poured himself another rum and water.

"Put that down," he said in a nagging voice. "You're gonna piss the bed later. Just piss the bed. You'll be swimming in lemon juice you pissed the bed so much."

He held up the drink. "Let the relaxation begin."

He took a mouthful, held it like the bomb it was, and let it drop. With a shiver, Gus grabbed the bottle and ping-pong-walked into the living room. There, he landed on his favourite couch and stared out at that magnificent view. Simply magnificent. It was dark out there, but it *was* out there, and he could imagine it. God, he'd lucked out with this place. Truly lucked out. And he lucked out with this couch too, *God* he lucked out. He took a moment to quietly appreciate that piece of furniture.

"Don't worry," he said quietly, while stroking the fabric of the couch. "I won't... I won't let Toby fuck you. Have... have no fear. That's... that's Toby's thing. Not mine."

All was quiet then, save for his own breathing, and the odd noise when he shifted. The day darkened, pulling shadows over the city, transforming it all into a great featureless disk with jagged edges.

"You didn't get me, fuckers," he whispered, his throat clicking when he swallowed. "Oh, you tried. You tried hard. But you didn't get me. You didn't. So… fuck you."

Whereupon he drank. Drank deeply. Reinforcing the rum already percolating in his system. And as the rum took over, in sync with the creeping of night, Gus became aware of how nice Annapolis looked from up here. How peaceful. The valley truly was a lovely place to live. And a stunner when the city lights came on, only outdone by Christmas lights. He only wished he'd brought Tammy up for a look.

He stopped himself before the misery set in. He didn't want to be miserable. Not any more than he already was. Thoughts of what to do tomorrow entered his mind.

And, just as quickly, left.

Then they entered again.

Winter was holding off, but the snow would come. Make no mistake. He'd gotten his armor, but clothing was still an issue, as was food. The big scores were still the grocery stores. Ray Ray might've known about them, but Gus didn't get a chance to ask for details. Didn't think about it really, as they were on a clock, and truthfully, Gus was kind of shocked to meet another living person. The bombshell being when Ray asked if he wanted to come along to Ontario. That would be a decision Gus might regret later, but right now, he felt better off on the mountain, in his own backyard rather than an unfamiliar one.

Grocery stores, he thought again. Big risk for a big reward. Any noise created down there would bring a mob, so anywhere he went, he would be on a clock. A great big no-nonsense clock until the first zombies arrived on scene. And where there was a dozen, there would be hundreds bearing down. Like streams of water worming its way through tributaries, finding the paths of least resistance in the cityscape.

How many zombies could he run over, before the van finally conked out on him? He'd kept his speed around forty to fifty, but even then, when they hit the front of the machine, they *hit*, and the van had the taps to prove it. Hell, the van had taken a *schlacking.*

The van was also the best weapon he had.

"Do I go down there tomorrow?" he asked, and after a time, shook his head. "Fuck, I don't want to. I *really* don't want to. But…what choice do I have?" He turned the rum bottle so as to study the decal's smiling face. "You know how long winter is? Huh? Could be… three or four months long. That's… *real* time. And it's *cold.* I need to do a walk around the house again. Make sure everything is working. Even… I even got to get a shitter started on. An outhouse of some kind. If the pipes freeze up here… I'm stuck… shitting in a bucket. I can't shit in a bucket. Too goddamn heavy to shit in a bucket. Hell, I mean… I don't even know how long those *solar panels* are good for. Or if I gotta change those batteries or whatever. Or how much… how much water I got in the well or cistern. I mean, every time I flush… I'm flushing away *fresh* water."

Gus slapped a hand to his face, feeling the real beginnings of a beard there. Not just a chin rug, but a full-fledged eagles' nest. Tammy didn't approve of them, but he didn't think she'd mind now, given the circumstances.

Busy times. He had to get busy. Part of him wished he had a timer, like the one he and the boys would use on a job. Get his ass motivated. *More* motivated. Get shit *done*.

He drank on that question, finishing off his current, and burped. His glass was empty, his guts polluted, but he got another drink anyway and went back to deep foggy thoughts.

"City's a risk," he said aloud, taking another shot and smacking his lips. "Too risky. Ris—kay. Risky risk… Maybe risky's not quite right. Deathtrap?"

He screwed up his face at the word, then shrugged.

"Yeah. S'pose that's… more like it. A god… damn deathtrap. You saw them. They were everywhere. Every-fucking-*where*. I bet… I bet if I so much as … as open a goddamn *cupboard* down there …a zombie would pop out. Right out. Little, fuckin' cupboard-dwellin' zombie. And I bet… I bet the *deeper* I go… the thicker they get. Well. Only thing I can think of… is to… is to… stick to the houses. Stick to them houses. Not the burbs, oh no, but the fringes. Of the burbs. Fuckin' family of five is easier to do than a city of thousands, right? Am I right? Goddamn right I'm right."

His eyes slunk right and left, taking in the last of the greys and the blacks of the disappearing city into the deepening night.

"Three months of winter, Katrina. Ninety days of snow. Count on four, just to be safe. That's three meals a day. Plus snacks and drinks." He winked at the Captain. "Three meals. Three times thirty. That's ninety. Ninety meals. Times four. That's… three-sixty. Three hundred… and sixty meals. For twelve months that's… fuck I hate math. Well. Anyway, point is…if I have more days like today, damn well sure I won't be eating much."

He let that sink in and lifted his drink.

"Three sixty. That's four months. Doesn't sound too bad. To start, anyway, just to see me through winter. Then… after that, it's everything else. Until… whatever."

He didn't know what that might be, but it was probably better not to plan too far ahead. Three hundred and sixty meals. He might already have that in the house. Or at least half of that in the house. Half of three sixty was… a hundred and eighty. If he had to really ration himself, it was certainly doable. He could find that in the houses, for sure. All them homes leading up to the city. Or even the ones in New Cross. He didn't have to go into Annapolis ever again this winter if he didn't want to. Fuck going down there.

Gus exhaled.

He felt better, having thought it all through. Planned out. By rights, he should have sat down and done all this "figuring" beforehand. Maybe he had, and just forgot. He'd got his armor, though. And his ammunition. A lot of ammunition. Thanks again to Ray Ray.

"To Ray… Ray." Gus toasted and drank. "May you get to… that place. Bare back… lake."

Tomorrow was another day. Hit the houses. Stick to the houses. Best to get that last hundred and eighty cans of soup or whatever and hunker down. Before the snow came. Before he reached for the can of green peas lurking in the back of the pantry.

Gus took another drink.

He'd get to work tomorrow.

Of course… that did not happen.

Under yet another overcast sky, Gus woke up sick. He stayed close to the bathroom the entire day, at times spraying and praying while still buzzing from the epic monster drunk from the evening before. He promised himself to get moving in the morning. Vowed to get moving.

Twenty-four hours later, Gus opened his eyes, snarled at the depressing clouds covering the sky, and wondered if the sun had up and left for Tijuana.

He rose from the couch and shuffled barefoot across a warm floor into the kitchen. Heating systems were still working, and that alone made his morning. Luxury, really. In-floor heating. Couldn't be beat. He could sit bare-assed all day on it.

The kitchen island seemed larger. Gus avoided its granite corners and dug out a bottle of cranberry juice from the fridge. Picked that up from one of them houses in a cluster, fuck if he remembered which, though. He wandered over to the sink and window, undid the lid and drank straight from the bottle.

"Oh baby," Gus said between breaths and drank again. Dribbles soaked his beard. He lowered the drink and wiped at his face—when he saw movement at the front gate.

He squinted.

A person… right on the doorstep of his main defense. Arms spread wide, as if a cop was frisking him down.

Except Gus knew it wasn't a person. Not a real one.

Replacing the lid on the juice bottle, he dropped the container into the sink and ran.

He dressed in a minute, then pulled on his leather coat and boots. The last bits were the helmet and the twelve gauge. He didn't bother with the rest, and jammed a thumb at the garage controls.

How many more are out there?

When the garage door was high enough, he ducked under and marched for the gate.

On spotting him, the zombie grew even more animated. It even said something, the undead equivalent of *mornin'* that went on and on and wouldn't stop.

That got Gus moving faster.

"The fuck you doin' here?" he said, checking for others before concentrating on the single unexpected visitor.

It was a man, perhaps middle-aged. He wore a summer's shirt that might've been pulled from a full septic tank. Short sleeves exposed skinny arms blotched with ink patches. The dead man had a missing eye, and a sprinkling of what appeared to be skin tags around the mouth. Light pants covered his legs, but the edges of his bare, frostbitten feet were ragged, visibly worn down around the soles.

The zombie lanced an arm through the gate, clawing for Gus even though he was twenty feet away. The zombie was alone, but seeing it so close to Gus's secret base of solitude alarmed him right down to the peanuts and cheese.

He aimed the twelve gauge. "How'd you get up here?"

Unfazed by the weapon, the zombie attempted to squeeze his face through the iron bars. Filth dripped from its fingers. Goop dribbled from its eyes.

"Just you?" Gus demanded.

The corpse extended his other hand through the gate and clutched air.

"Yeah," Gus sighed and continued aiming. He stood that way for seconds before lowering the shotgun. Where there was one, there might be others, and a twelve-gauge blast might bring them running. He raised the visor and glared at the unwanted presence before him. No way it was getting in. The thing didn't have the mind to figure out the way in, but Gus was still uneasy at its attempts. The gimp kept right on reaching for him, showing no clue or inclination to fiddle with the lock. Gus decided he would have to do something about the bars. Some planks or wood and screw the entire works together. Board up those gaps and make it into a wall. One day.

The zombie bit the air, jaws and skin working. At one point, it wrapped its mouth around one of the bars and bit, the force shattering its front teeth.

Gus cringed at that. Another sight he didn't need to remember.

"What am I gonna do with you?" he asked, staring at that horrible face.

Then he had it.

He returned to the garage, got the weapon he wanted, and went back to the gate. Upon closing the distance, he flipped down the visor.

The zombie pressed its face between the bars, its outstretched arms and hands barely an inch away.

Gus lifted his axe, lined up the hateful face, and chopped.

He struck the iron bar, creating sparks and staggering him back on his heels.

The zombie kept on reaching for him, heedless of the attempted murder.

"You bastard," Gus whispered.

He reset, gauged his aim and chopped once more.

Another sparkling connection that echoed throughout the mountain retreat.

"Jesus *Christ!*"

The bars prevented the zombie from coming through, but also were spaced close enough to grant some degree of protection from a head shot. Angry and growing angrier, Gus took three more whacks. He missed with the first and hacked into a weirdly spongy bicep on the second. On the third attempt, he split open the forehead. This unleashed a stream of muck that covered the thing's face… but failed to penetrate the brain.

A *fourth* swing split the monster's shoulder, which started a gut-twisting tug-o- war that Gus almost lost. His temper flared as he freed the axe head. The tussle not only drained him, but *infuriated* him—not from his inability to kill the gimp, but from making so much noise.

"You undead *shitpouch* you," Gus said, wavering, unsure of trying to whack the zombie again or try something else.

Fuck it, he thought, and marched back to the garage.

Retrieved the shotgun.

He huffed it back to the gate and, not sparing a second, blasted the zombie through the bars.

The shot disintegrated the monster's head and it collapsed. Black slop dribbled from the meat crater of its neck. Though the gimp was truly dead, the whole encounter pissed Gus off. He stepped up to the gate and emptied the shotgun into the carcass, each blast kicking against his shoulder, the sound deafening and echoing across the landscape.

Then it was done.

Gus inspected the messy corpse before scanning the wilderness, listening for any other approaching zombies. His furious breathing hindered that effort, so he just stood there and waited for signs.

None appeared. After a time he backed off, forgetting the gimp at his feet. If there were any others, he'd deal with them as well.

Each and every one.

30

After calming down enough to eat breakfast, Gus found himself at the island with two processed ham and cheese croissants, taken from a box saying they'd be *Ready In Minutes*!

He remembered what Ray Ray said about the food, how the chemicals were responsible. That theory sounded a little far-fetched to Gus. He'd eaten food both naturally grown and processed, and he turned out fine. Least in his mind.

Gus ate while standing guard at the sink, shotgun resting on the counter. The zombie he'd gunned down earlier stayed gunned down. No other reanimated visitors approached the gate.

He washed his food down with cranberry juice, and Gus swallowed it in great gulps and savored the tangy goodness. It wasn't lost on him that the croissants and the juice might be the last he'd ever get to enjoy, but he tried not to think about that.

After breakfast, he took a twenty-minute pit stop in the toilet. While on the throne, he counted the leaning tower of toilet paper stacked in one corner. Two sixteen packs still in its plastic, with three loose rolls on top.

Food. Water. Anal scrub. Especially the anal scrub. Who knew?

"What has two thumbs and knows TP's the shit?" Gus asked, while perched on the can. He aimed both digits at his chest. "This guy. Right here."

He finished up, got his shotgun, and went to the garage.

Morning wasn't over, and the early exercise had invigorated him. New Cross was just on the other side of the mountain and there were plenty of houses along the road going toward Halifax. He imagined there were some good pickings to be found, maybe even great pickings. There might even be a chance of making contact with someone still alive. His encounter with Ray

Ray had encouraged him that there were folks out there. Just had to be careful.

So, without further delay, he threw open the locker and stared at the gear.

And stared.

And stared.

"What is it, then?" he asked. "You stayin' or goin'? Make up your mind, because there are only so many hours in a day, and just standin' here ain't gettin' shit done."

No sir, he informed himself. *It wasn't getting shit done at all.*

Then he considered his magic potion of bravery, his liquid courage, and held back a moment.

"All right, note to self. Cut back on the medication a few ounces. Just a few. The shit works, but you can't be driving cross-eyed all over the valley. Can't be doing twenty klicks when you should be doing fifty. Or whatever. You hear me?"

As an answer, he opened a bottle of Bacardi white rum, because, what the hell? He drank it quickly.

"Good for gussy," he said, and loaded up another.

Halfway through the second dose, he started pulling on gear.

Leather pants. Neck brace. Coat. Elbow and knee pads. Then the helmet, which, when he hauled it over his head, amplified his own breathing and promised to drive him nuts. He burped as well—a great, foul smelling rip that happened with the visor down. He flipped it up and that improved things, but he would have to look for mouthwash, just so he didn't gross himself out.

The last thing he pulled on were his gloves.

Twenty-five minutes later, he had already closed the gate and was pulling the dead gimp away by its skinny ankles. The rum was taking effect, armoring him for whatever came next. It was cold, but Gus worked up some considerable heat by hauling the body over to one side of the driveway and dropping it.

"Aw fuck, I don't have to bury your ass, do I?" he panted at the dead thing. "Goddamnit. I don't have time for this shit. No time. Later, buddy."

Puffing, he walked back to the van.

He strapped himself into his seat and drove down the mountain, toward the main road. With every kilometer travelled, the morning shots of rum landed like a salvo of battleship shells, blasting his beach, numbing him all the more.

The sky remained grey, but not a stormy shade. More of the same lousy color he'd been dealing with for weeks.

"Don't you snow," Gus warned the heavens. "Don't you dare. I'm on a run down here, so don't fuck things up. Hear me?"

No answer, so he considered that a yes. Yes, it heard him, and there would be no snow.

At the end of his mountain road, he stopped and looked towards Annapolis. There, he remembered the wrong turn he made, and remembered the shitstorm he drove through getting out of the city. Pure dread gripped him, too strong even for the rum. The memories came back in a rush—all those dead people, walking or crawling. Even Perry what's-his-face, risen from the dead and still recording shit on his phone.

"Not today," Gus said in the direction of the city. "Thanks anyway."

He drove for New Cross. After Annapolis, the little mountain town was without a doubt the safer choice, its residents nowhere near as dense as the city's populace. While he drove, Gus also warned himself to be smarter. Less stupidity, less impulse, more thought. As much as he could muster while drunk.

"I'll finish off the town," he said. "Search the houses. Maybe… maybe there'll be someone around in the same boat, right? Better odds there than in the city. Doors and windows boarded up and waiting for the cops to show up. Or anyone else for that matter. That's what I'd do, by Christ."

Some twenty minutes later, broken by him adjusting the heat in the van, Gus noticed the day was getting darker. Grimmer. To the point where he snuck looks at the sky and the dreary mattress of cloud covering.

Snowflakes spattered the windshield. Just occasionally at first, then doubling up. Then tripling. Until flakes started coating the entire surface.

"Oh no," Gus whispered. "Don't… don't you dare. Don't you… you *said* it wasn't going to snow today. You *said*. You… you *promised* you overcast cloudy fuckchops. You *promised*."

More flakes hit the windshield, sinister in their portent of bad weather.

"All right, just don't get any worse, okay?" Gus bargained. "This is nothing. I can deal with this. Few flakes on the road. No big deal. Just don't get any worse, is all I'm askin'."

The storm clouds continued dropping snow on the van. The individual flakes thickened to a flurry. Worse, with a lack of windshield wipers, the snow stuck to the glass, collected, and took its sweet time sliding out of the way.

"Can't fuckin' believe this…" Gus muttered, and slowed to a stop. The flurry continued, coating the van, while the surrounding trees moved in the growing wind. He reached behind the passenger seat and grabbed a snowbrush, a black one taken from his garage, just in case. 'Just in case' had become a sure thing in a very short time. He cracked open the door, surprised at the force of the wind pressing back. With effort, he pushed it wide and climbed out, landing on white pavement.

"Oh Jesus," Gus said, sizing up the ground and not quite drunk enough to ignore the warnings. Snow blew into his face and eyes, making him squint. It obscured the curvy road ahead, cutting down visibility to a hundred feet and no more.

And it was intensifying.

The snowbrush was three feet long. Gus stretched his bulky self and wiped his side of the windshield clear. He cleared off the hood as well, hoofed it to the other side and cleared off the snow there. On the way back, he noticed his footprints.

Snow was quickly filling them.

"Well, *shit*." The van had all seasonals, and all seasonals weren't true winter tires. They were fine in flurries and light snow, but if shit got real—and it was getting mighty real with every passing second—all seasonals would be as good as skis on snowy roads.

"So much for that," Gus said, already missing the valley's road crews. "Mission aborted."

He scrubbed the new snow off his side of the windshield before climbing aboard. With grim concentration, Gus did a careful three-point turn and whipped the van around. He sped for home, seeing the faint prints his tires had already made. Daylight got darker still and the snow continued to fall.

During that drive back, Gus got out twice more to clear off the windshield. He drove at a cautious fifty, eyeing the whitening terrain, very much aware of his all seasonal tires and his semi-drunken state.

Some fifteen kilometers away from the mountain turn off, the snow eased off to a few mere flakes. Gus continued on, expecting the snow to catch up to him. It did not, however. Not by the time he reached his driveway, and not when he closed the gate behind him.

After parking the van in the garage, Gus stepped back outside. The temperature was below zero and the storm clouds thickened. A winter haze hid the far-off treetops, heralding the arrival of Old Man Winter and the great white dumping Gus knew would come. The cold got to him, but didn't force him inside, not right away. He watched the approaching front and wondered how many centimetres it would bring.

Three hundred and sixty meals, he thought.

He wondered if he'd had enough.

Should've been out there more, Gus scolded himself. *Should've had this place stocked to the rafters and winterized. But no. You had to get shitfaced every other day, then spend the next on the can. Well, you can think long and hard about it when the roads are fucking blocked with snow and the food starts running out. You'll be wishing for a goddamn pair of snowshoes then.*

Defeated, Gus retreated into his garage and lowered the door. He paced, hating himself for procrastinating up to this point, but also knowing the risk he took going beyond the stone walls. After the things he'd seen and experienced, the last trip alone was enough to keep him out of the city.

Now, however, he might not have a choice. New Cross was cut off from him.

He was half out of his zombie gear when he stopped and stared at the bottle of Captain Morgan on the workbench, meant to greet him after a successful day of scavenging.

"All right," he said. "Get a hold of yourself. You did the right thing. Sure, you could've gotten more shit, but it is what it is. And this could be only ten centimeters. Maybe twenty. Maybe *five*. Who knows? Let it all play out and get back out there tomorrow, see how bad the roads are. At the very worse, you got a shovel. You sure as fuck can use the exercise, so there's that. Don't worry. Don't. Worry will kill you. Would you rather have gone to New Cross and get stuck *there* for the night? Huh? Or just putting along, getting out every five minutes just to wipe off the windshield? Hm? You did right coming back. You did right."

He drank his rum, stopping halfway when he realized he didn't even remember pouring the drink.

"It's not going to snow for forty days and forty nights," he told himself. "The sun will come out again. I'll be on the move when it does. Back to work. This is just—just a setback. That's all. I'll be good. See what's on the ground in the morning and deal with it then. I'll be good. I'll be better than good."

With that, he left the rum bottle on the bench and walked into the house. He stopped in the living room before the windows, eyeing the gloomy clouds and the darkness they brought. Beneath all that, the jagged plate that was the city itself. Gus took a hard sip off his drink every so often and kept right on watching. At one point he checked the time, saw it was almost three o'clock, and that he'd finished his drink. Not wanting an empty glass, Gus went back to the kitchen, gathered up the necessities, and wandered back to the living room.

Where he placed everything he carried on the coffee table.

Flakes dotted the window.

He plopped down on the couch, feeling his stomach clench at the sight of the snow.

The flakes became a steadier flurry.

The city lights eventually flared to life, but even that once-uplifting sight was dimmed by snowfall. In time, night smothered even that. Winter in the valley had always been a hard thing. Snow would fall often and clog the streets, and Gus remembered wishing for those storms and the resulting school closures.

One storm in particular, a savage nor'easter, paralyzed the city and province by dumping something like three feet of snow on everyone, resulting in a province wide state of emergency. That was good for three days worth of no school, which started on a Wednesday and made for an extra long weekend. Fun times. And it wasn't until he was in his late twenties that he realized teachers were just as excited for snow days.

There, sunk deep in a couch that served as both perch and bed, Gus didn't bother switching on the lights. There wasn't any need. He could see outside better in the dark. When he needed one, he would reach for the whiskey on the coffee table and quietly pour a drink. There was no forecast to check on now, to see when all this might end, and he wondered if he was watching another nor'easter bury the world like the monster from his youth. All that falling snow stole his appetite, which wasn't a bad thing. Three hundred and sixty meals. Maybe he could make do on less. Instead of three meals a day, maybe just two.

Or one.

There, in the quiet dark, Gus sat and watched the snow fall.

31

He woke, flinched, and wiped the drool from his face. He rolled onto his side and squinted at the white morning beyond his window.

"Holy shit," he said in quiet awe.

Snow.

Long majestic crests of white formed a low wall across the back of the house, obscuring the pool and the deck. Snow covered the furniture and piled about the bases. White clumps weighed down the trees. *Snow.* Enough to turn everything into an almost dreamy marshmallow world.

Gus sat up and steadied himself with his hands.

"Well, well, here at last," he said in a defeated tone. "That's it then. All over. What I got is what I got."

Gus rose and dragged himself over to the windows. Maybe a foot had fallen thus far, enough to strand him on the mountain. There was no way he was driving anywhere with a foot of snow on the roads. His days of scavenging had come to an early end. While he could maybe stretch his supplies out to last the winter, he would still need more to stay alive. Winter was only the beginning.

"Beginning to what, though?" he asked his sizeable, dishevelled reflection. "I mean, really? When's this gonna end? Seriously? When is this *all* gonna end? Okay, I'm trapped up here. And ordinarily that wouldn't bother me, especially if I had Tammy with me or one of the boys but I don't. And I can't get off this mountain. I'm stuck here."

He looked left and right. "Which means… they can't get up here either, I guess. Which means… what?"

Make the best of it, his brain suggested.

"Yeah," Gus reluctantly agreed. "You would say that."

He went to the toilet and sat. *Make the best of it*, he repeated, ruminating over the thought. It stayed with him until he later went to the front door and pulled it open.

A foot of snow crumpled inside, breaking off a peak nearly a third of the way up the door—practically knee high. All that white extended into his yard, where it blanketed everything inside the wall, even drifting up in one long crest that snaked around the house. There was a hollow around the far corner of the garage, where the wind worked its magic, merely icing over the ground instead of burying it.

Gus bent over and scooped a handful before tossing it back. It was cold, but a mild cold, where you could feel the moisture trapped in the air.

"Just around zero," he guessed. "Wet shit. The worst."

A real workout to shovel it all. The first dumping, to which more would be added later. Guaranteed. It wasn't a blizzard that had hit, however. Not a nor'easter. Just a left jab, fired straight from the shoulder of Old Man Winter. A good, solid shot to the face, to let you know *I'm here*.

Gus closed the door.

He was hung over from the day before, so no way he was doing anything heavy. If the snow was down, it was down. At least he was home with something in the pantry. And the booze. In fact, he was very happy about that. He had enough alcohol to do him for a year. He wasn't a drinker, but he was learning real fast. On that note, Gus retreated to the kitchen.

Breakfast called.

An hour later, after frying up some bacon and hash browns, Gus plopped down on his couch. He stayed there for almost thirty minutes, watching the snow, wondering if there would be more that day or not. Eventually he got up and busied himself with arranging his food in the rooms downstairs, so that everything with the earlier expiry dates would be used first. After an hour of doing that, he checked on the weather again, saw it remained the same, and he withdrew to the downstairs den.

There he loaded up a study fest of zombie movies.

As much as he didn't want to watch them, he forced himself to. He had all the classic George Romero movies, as well as a dozen or so that were from overseas that he'd never heard of. At the first hour mark, he paused *Trails of the Dead*, and went looking for snacks. He brought back a dozen or so of the little Halloween bags of potato chips and settled in.

By the end of the third movie, a little indie number called "Dead Santa," he noticed a pattern. Zombie outbreak. Group of people band together and try to get somewhere safe. Half the movie was following that group. And among them was at least one dick you just wanted to strangle. Three movies in, different stories but all zombie flicks, there was always a dick, either lurking in the background or right up in your face. Always.

This got Gus thinking. In one way, he had it good on the mountain. Real good. It was just him and no dicks, so if anything stupid happened, it was all on him. The property was as safe as anything, being far removed from the city. It wasn't a bunker, but it was practically the next best thing.

Except, in the movies, the zombies still got in. They *always* found a way in, and they always got to the last few survivors, despite all best intentions. Always. And chaos ensued because of it.

He fell asleep on that.

And dreamed. Dreamed he was back in Annapolis, driving the beast along snow clogged streets. Zombies were everywhere, their faces partially frosted over. They struggled to reach the van racing by, and Gus left them behind in a whorl of powder.

But every turn he made, every street, they were there.

Worse, they were even more numerous. No longer on the sidewalks, they were in the lanes, forcing Gus to stay in the center. The space on the road shrunk, or rather, the ranks of zombies were becoming thicker, edging further out into the street until he was driving down a writhing, collapsing tunnel.

Even worse, Gus realized he was stone cold sober.

Hands reached for the van, slapping and clawing at the sides. The handling became sloppy, the road a trampoline, but Gus saw an intersection up ahead marked by a flashing red arrow.

He turned left.

And drove headlong into a solid mass of zombies.

The van smashed into them and stalled out. The undead splattered the front and stuck there. The more energetic gimps climbed up and over and proceeded to stomp on the roof. Grey blue faces pressed into the windows, biting, licking the surfaces, leaving rabid trails of froth. Gus turned on the radio but the only tune was that of his slowing heartbeat. He couldn't go forward. Couldn't reverse. He gazed out at the undead swarming his van when the sound of collapsing metal twisted him around in his seat.

Gus woke with a gasp.

And stared at Tammy's bare back. Her soft snoring the only sound in the bedroom. Her bare shoulders white and unblemished. Gus nuzzled up against her, the smell of vanilla shampoo and conditioner damn near irresistible.

Their bed. Their bedroom. He lifted his head, just enough to see the clock. Tammy's snoring ceased and she stirred. Gus hoped he didn't wake her, but he wanted to see the time.

Red numbers said 88:88.

Which was weird.

Gus studied the display for seconds before turning back to Tammy, whose skeletal face waited with bloody mouth wide open. She latched onto his cheek and eye with an adder's speed, chomping deep, and Gus—

Woke—flailing, springing from the couch and toppling onto the warm floor of the downstairs rec room. He grabbed for his face and pressed flesh––still there—and whimpered because of it.

"Oh *Jesus*," Gus croaked, wide awake and staring in the dark. The television had switched itself off. He panted, his heart settling back in his chest. This time, he knew he was awake for certain. Remembering the smell of vanilla, he got to his feet, shivered, and lurched up the stairs to the main floor.

Flicking on lights as he went.

In the kitchen, Uncle Jack was there, right on the island. Gus didn't remember placing the bottle there, but whatever. He needed to get medicated. Especially after the double midnight showing that wrecked his sleep.

Gus poured a third of whiskey into a tall glass. Filled the rest with water and drank half almost right away. When he paused to catch his breath, he checked the dark places of the kitchen, in case anything was lurking. Nothing. Heard nothing except his own wet breathing.

Gus finished the drink and fixed himself another.

He didn't sleep for the rest of the night.

*

The silence was the worst.

That total lack of sound, any sound. When he held his breath, only the odd creak or ping from the electric heaters broke the spell. Sometimes he could hear the wind outside, but it was faint and eerie and never more pitiful to the lonely ear. Gus sought to fill the silence, or at least ease it, so he drank. It helped his nerves.

After two more days of watching movies—mostly zombie flicks—he started watching comedies. Anything to lighten the mood, to break that forbidding lack of noise. When Gus paused a movie, he listened and realized, perhaps for the first time, his was the only real voice left.

And that bothered him.

"Hello," he asked one evening, and waited for a reply. "No, 'eh? Then it's just me? Just me."

Wonderful.

When he felt the need for noise, he watched movies, and when he got sick of watching movies, he read books. Action thrillers. Military high tech. Tom Clancy stories of intrigue and espionage, or straight up warfare. There was no bible, but Gus discovered he wanted to read it, to scratch that off his bucket list. Just to say he read it and had an opinion. Maybe even take something from it.

The arrangement of various bottles on the kitchen counter resembled a glass castle. He designated that area of various alcoholic beverages as the bar. The fridge had an ice maker in the freezer, if he so desired, but he was preferring his drinks warm.

During that time, it snowed on and off, adding a few more centimeters atop what was already there. Gus watched it at times, during breaks from his movies and reading. There was peace in that falling snow and he soaked it all in while sipping on whatever was in hand.

On the third day, he was still on the sauce, just because it was there. The alcohol helped ease his mind, and certainly kept the nightmares at bay. He even talked to himself, just to hear an unscripted voice. No problem in that. Not in the least. He was his own best company. No truer words had ever been spoken, nor would be again.

After four days, Old Man Winter showed up once again and struck with two more jabs. One in the morning, and the other four hours later. The snow kept piling up well into the night. A snowpack waited for Gus when he opened the front door, as high as his waist, while icicles hung from the upper frame.

It was enough to close the door and keep him inside, in the warm.

Winter. It finally arrived.

To celebrate, Gus decided to cook a chicken. Problem was, when he took out one of the little frozen cluckers, he suddenly didn't want to go through the effort of cooking the damn thing. A box of chicken wings attracted him, instead. Ten pounds worth of spicy Sister Claire's chicken wings, the box label exclaiming, in a starburst of light, "*Just too good to stop!*"

He fired up the oven and took a mouthful of rum and water as he removed the packaging. Chicken wings. Goddamn that sounded fine, and, as cliché as it sounded, his mouth watered at the thought. There was a cookie sheet in the bottom of the stove, so he got that out, covered it in aluminum foil wrap, and placed a grill rack on top.

Some sixty minutes later, Gus feasted, and was glad he wore only his bath robe. He drank wine with the chicken, just to give his liver a break, or at least by his thinking. There were a lot of wings and he couldn't eat them all, but what the hell, he gave it his best go. Frozen food. He'd got lucky during the last few houses he raided, but that got him thinking again. If the rest of the houses had power, and if they had freezers, there might very well be plenty of frozen treats like chicken wings waiting for him. As long as the power didn't go off. If he lost power here, he could throw everything in his freezers into a snowbank and that would work out just fine.

At least until spring.

"To spring," Gus toasted, and drank Moscato straight from the bottle. "That's some sweet shit right there. And spicy? Shame on you Sister Claire. A kids' movie is spicier than your wings."

Still, he ate two thirds of the food before stopping.

"Ate too much," Gus remarked. "I'll probably fire a fuckin' chicken at the wall if I bend over. Oh help me Lord."

He waddled back downstairs and loaded up some children's cartoons, just to take the edge off. Silence. Solitude. *No problem*, Gus thought. No problem at all. Cabin fever. He scoffed at the idea. Probably no such thing, anyway. Real men didn't get cabin fever.

"I can do this," he said, waiting for the cartoon to play. "I can do this all day and twice on Sunday."

The cartoon started.

32

Gus glared at the calendar and saw it was January.

The fifteenth.

Somehow, and it was unquestionably because of the drinking, he'd lost track of the days. No, he'd kept track of the days, scratching them off with his pen every morning or second morning, but he'd lost all sense of *time*. All sense of what a day really represented. When you were the sole person left alive, in the dead of winter, no less, with nothing to do but eat, shit, and sleep… well, one day was no different from the other. The same glass waiting to be filled and emptied. With whatever Gus deemed appropriate.

Somehow, he'd missed Christmas. Just a little. Had no recollection of the holiday at all, in fact. And while that bothered him a little, he would make up for it today. Today would be Christmas, and he would celebrate it just the same.

Visiting the bathroom made him pause, however.

His beard had thickened considerably, and he continued to lose it on top. It was like he was staring at a time-lapsed migration from his crown to his face. No doubt stress related, but Gus didn't feel that stressed out anymore. Not really. Still, he'd been losing his hair over the past few weeks, as evidenced by the alarming strands he discovered all over the place. On his pillow. In the shower and the bathtub (when he took one of either). He was losing hair like… well… *a lot*.

Then there were his eyes.

He was only in his forties, but Gus's eyes belonged to a man in his sixties. Sunken. Puffy underneath. Bloodshot.

"Heat packs," he said, studying them. "Need some heat. That's all. I know how to do that. Feel fine otherwise. Just fine."

Except he wasn't.

He'd been drinking everyday since he could remember. Alcoholic. He would have never thought. Stopping wasn't an option, not when the nightmares were waiting for him. The rum and whiskey, taken repeatedly at levels that would drop a hockey player, eased him into deep sleep where the bad dreams couldn't reach. It was either drink to excess and sleep, or not and wake up flailing at phantoms while falling off the couch. His face looked bad. Looked awful, really, but his liver probably looked worse.

So he smiled. Chuckled at the face in the mirror. Because, really, that was all he could do. Was willing to do. He poked at one bag hanging underneath an eye, pulled down the lid and stared at the redness within. What he saw wiped the smile off his face.

"Been sitting on my ass too long," he growled at his reflection. "Too damn long."

And it was true. When he wasn't drinking, he was eating, and doing very little in between. In fact, the majority of his day was spent chewing through his food stores while entertaining himself with books, movies, or staring out the window. While drinking, of course. But he was safe, though. One hundred percent safe. Secure. There had been no other undead dingdongs at his front gate, and that pleased him immensely.

He imagined his jeans would be a tight fit when he put them on, but that was a problem for another day. Who wore jeans in the house, anyway? Not this slob. No sir. Just the boxer briefs and the bathrobe. Sometimes he wore a t-shirt under there, but not often. Those were getting tight as well.

"Gotta exercise," Gus said, rubbing his face. Fat and flabby. Excess skin that sagged like an old man's scrotum. Well, maybe not that bad. The beard did hide the folds under his chin, so that was a win, but he knew his lifestyle had to change.

"Gotta exercise," he repeated with a nod, as if that sealed the deal. "And I mean it. Damn right I do. Maybe not today. Today … I'll dry out a bit. Get ready for tomorrow. See what's what. Then… I'll get busy."

Doing what, though? he asked himself.

Good fucking question.

But he would get up and start doing something tomorrow. Back when everything was fine, he would say he could whip himself into shape if he had the time to do so. If he didn't have to work, he'd be in great shape. *Superb* shape.

He had that time now. All the time in the world, really.

Tomorrow it would be, then. Exercise.

But when tomorrow came, he looked out at the snow, shook his head, and let lethargy drag him down, down into the basement. That didn't just happen one day, but the day after that, and the one after that. Usually, a bottle or two of his favourites accompanied him.

There, he would plant himself in front of the television and watch whatever caught his interest, but eventually he would get around to watching a zombie flick. That felt productive, studying up on the enemy. During those movies, he saw one thing the makers got right. The undead, such as they were, weren't that bright. In fact, there was no intelligence there at all. Worse, the survivors were, at times, idiots.

Well, they were *scripted* like idiots, to be fair. A few displayed some intelligence, but most others… idiots. Freaking out, panicky-assed dummies failing to adapt to their new zombie-infested world, and usually dying in the end. Sometimes alone, which was fine, but other times they would unintentionally—or, even worse— intentionally do something that resulted in many characters dying. Some fucked up so bad that it made Gus thankful he was operating by himself. If *he* fucked up, it was all on him.

But holy shit, why didn't people wear protection? Anything that could protect them against a bite? It drove him crazy. People knew they were dealing with zombies, even fighting them, and with a little foraging one could locate thicker clothing. Anything that wouldn't tear when grabbed. Anything that could prevent a bite. He started switching off movies when the characters were armed to the teeth and about to knowingly enter a zombie nest …while wearing only jeans and t-shirts.

Like… *seriously?*

It wasn't all movies and booze. Books were in there as well. Exercise? Well, he was usually too hungover to exercise. No way around it though, as he needed his sleep, and the only way he could sleep without nightmares was to get sloshed to the point of near pissing himself.

If it wasn't one thing, it was another.

And so, the days passed.

January twenty-third.

After another week of cold, freezing weather, where perhaps another ten or fifteen centimeters fell on top of the five feet already down, the cloud cover broke in places and the sun made a rare and limited appearance. It didn't reveal itself entirely, but rather hid behind the remaining clouds, and touched the earth in broad sweeping bands where the snow sparkled.

Standing in the living room and even more sluggish than ever, with his beard resembling some mangy pelt ripped from a grizzly bear's ass, Gus stared at the sunlight. His bathrobe needed to be cleaned, but he was becoming increasingly aware of his water situation and not knowing how much he had remaining. As nice as the house was, Gus couldn't believe that the owners didn't have a gauge or meter of some sort to alert them to low water levels. If there was such an instrument, he hadn't found it yet.

As such, it had been almost two weeks since he did a wash. Wasn't like he was sweating everyday, and a morning smell test determined if he could get another day out of whatever he was wearing at the time.

Gus scratched his beard, in the process pulling up the lower bit of his too tight t-shirt, exposing a fleshy (and hairy) navel. When he finished with his chin whisker, he reached down and tugged the shirt back into place. His t-shirt stretched over his meaty frame, to the point of being obscene, really. Considering it was all he had, though, it would have to do.

As an afterthought, he sniffed at an armpit. Wash day might be approaching sooner rather than later. There would be no washing of clothes or body parts today, however, not with Mister Sun out and strutting his stuff.

Annapolis could be seen in the distance, and he stared at the city.

He'd been doing that a lot in the last couple of days, for longer periods of time. Sitting (or standing) and staring off into space. It would be fine if he was thinking about something, but he wasn't. His mind was a blank. A sheet of black paper. He just slipped into these morning long stare sessions that happened any time of the day.

The sunlight was something fine. It hypnotised him.

At one point he discovered he was scratching at his mid-riff, because his finger had sunk deep into the flesh cavern that was his belly button. He extracted a dust weasel, partially comprised of fluff and dead skin. He stared at it as if it were a newly discovered nebula.

"Jesus Christ," Gus whispered. "The fuck's happening to me? Seriously?"

He went into the kitchen, where he chucked the dust galaxy into the garbage bucket. Which needed to be emptied. Badly.

There were days where he would ration himself to a meal or two, but then the following day, he would pig out, eat whatever he'd skipped and three besides, and then sit around bloated. Not only would he hate himself for doing so the next morning, but it would start a vicious cycle he couldn't quite seem to control. He knew he had to do better.

And all that food he consumed came in packaging, which had to be disposed of. That caused him greater appreciation for something else gone missing in the world. A proper system of waste collection and management.

Gus bent over the bucket and pulled out the near-bursting garbage bag. The lid of a tin can (he no longer saw the need to separate recyclables) had sliced through the side of the bag. As a result, a good portion of crumpled up wrappers, used paper towels, and empty cans, bulged from the slit.

"Shit." He clamped the cut with a hand. "Don't you give me a hard time now, you cheap ass… cheap ass plastic bag."

He swung left and right, holding the bag aloft, and carried it to the garage. The far end, over near the wood. A little over a dozen garbage bags filled that section of the bay, piled up against the wood and left to stink. In all honesty, he could have found it by smell alone.

Gus shuffled barefoot across the cold floor and, one handed, selected a fresh bag from an open package. Shook the bag open and inserted the ruptured one. Then, he tied it off and swung the doubled-bagged offering onto the pile. He sighed at the accumulated refuse. Everything was from one guy. One fucking guy.

That brought back a memory—a chat with one of the boys who worked the local garbage truck. That guy, named Art, would confide in him the woes and worries of the people working in urban waste management. Namely, where to put the damn stuff. It was becoming more than just a challenge. It was becoming a serious problem. With the ban on incinerators and the valley being a farm belt, there were only three designated land fills in the whole province, and all three were filled to capacity. To better appreciate the situation, Art had asked Gus to picture a gully, some twenty acres square, roughly a hundred feet deep. Then flash forward some forty years, and picture that gully level with the surrounding landscape. *Then* picture hills of garbage piled on top of that mass of plastic, cloth, metal, and God only knew what else, because not everyone separated their trash. In fact, some just heaved it all into the one bag, which fueled the daily debate of whether regular garbage bags should be transparent blue like the recyclables.

Gus couldn't picture that overfull gulley, but he believed Art.

Then Art dropped the bomb, and told him about the rat population, and how they were no longer allowed to poison the rodents. Art even related a story of a co-worker, a bulldozer operator who was once walking through hills of filth, surveying where he could safely push fresh trash up against

Mother Nature's treeline. During that walk, the guy came across a cardboard box on its side, so he up and kicked it like a soccer ball, with the intent to send it flying.

Which wasn't what happened.

Instead, he put his foot through the rotten cardboard and scared the shit out of the rats nesting inside. Perhaps three dozen of the little bastards fled the scene, dragging dirty white tails behind them. Art's buddy could only stagger back with a rotten cardboard box hanging of his boot. The rats disappeared beneath well-trodden cracks and crevices that Art had never really thought about before, but realized were hiding places for the vermin. Worse, they were *entry-ways*, into a network of burrows and tunnels.

Perhaps even leading to a vast underground domain.

Art had chuckled back then, in the way he did, only to get serious. The rats were the dirty little secret of the dumping area. Probably gone levels deep, cutting through overturned washing machines and refrigerators, buried sofas and sofa chairs. Layer upon layer, reaching depths Art didn't want to think about, creating a subterranean empire. A plague-ridden *honeycomb* populated by rats, even expanded upon, where the rats—and this was where Art really pushed home the dagger—where the rats could reproduce over and over, pumping out entire *litters* without fear of man or natural predators, year after year. A pair of rats could pump out on average a dozen babies, Art told him. Those babies would grow to maturity in a month and would be able to reproduce, starting the process all over again. And a normal rat could have *four* or *five* litters in a *year*, maybe even more in a perfect environment.

And at that, Art cocked his eyebrow in an expression of *See what I'm sayin'?*

At the time, Gus remembered his own dismay, and confided that, if it was *him*, he'd probably be running back to the supervisor, demanding a whole team of exterminators be brought in to deal with the situation. That led Art to revealing confidential discussions about waste management plans and the future of the existing landfills, and how the province was looking at Alberta as a model.

Plans that never came into existence.

The conversation with Art seemed like a long time ago.

Gus studied the garbage. Thankfully, he didn't have that problem. Not yet, anyway. He did have to get rid of his trash eventually, but that was a problem for another day. For now, if worse came to worse, he would keep storing his trash in the garage until the spring, then load it up and stash it away in someone else's garage. Better that than, say, taking it to a landfill site. And much better than dumping it over the nearby cliff, where it would no doubt stink in the summer months.

If he made it to the summer months.

Gus scowled. 'Course he would make it to the summer months. Why wouldn't he?

The shotgun, cleaned and loaded, lay on the workbench. He regarded the weapon for long seconds… and forgot what he was thinking about.

He went to the garage's side door and peered out the window. Snowdrifts everywhere. Big ones. Big enough to make a person wish for snowshoes. The wind raged across their crests, sharpening them, and that made Gus even colder.

For whatever reason, the solar panels popped into his head. The juice was still flowing, but if the snow covered the panels, would he have to get up there and clean the bastards off? Surely not. The designers had to have considered that problem. As long as he could still flick on the lights and TV, there was no way he was hauling his chunky soup ass up an aluminum ladder in the middle of winter. No way.

Exercise. He remembered his last attempt, how he'd crashed and burned. That had been his first time to shovel snow in a while, and he failed with flying colors. This time would be different. Maybe he could just go outside and start shoveling. Just around the house, so it wouldn't feel claustrophobic. Being out in the fresh air would do him some good.

Gus sized up the winter's bounty. Shouldn't he leave it, he thought, since it might hamper anyone coming up here?

"I'm not saying dig down to the goddamn highway, Gus." He raised a hand as if he had half a mind to smack himself.

He stormed off to get dressed.

Thirty minutes later—in which it took five to pull on a pair of socks and get them just right—Gus, fully dressed, waddled back to the garage and retrieved the aluminum shovel.

The plan was simple.

Clear a path all around the house. Especially the important places where he might need emergency access. Get that done and get his snow-clearing ass back inside before nightfall.

The wind smacked him when he opened the side door, forcing him back a step. He steadied himself and faced five feet of snow gathered at the base. That was his first bit of shoveling, and he stayed in the garage all the while.

"Shit." He felt not only his arms and shoulders, but also his back. Right above the waistline. "Holy *shit*."

Pathetic. He was ready to drop after a minute. It took thirty to clear the snow from the front of one garage door. Then, when he had some room, he chose one corner and started chucking with the wind.

"Pansy," he croaked, his back tormenting him. "This is nothin'. Noth-thing."

Maybe another ten minutes later, he swapped the shovel for the scoop.

The air energized him, and he puffed out great white plumes. The snow, now that he was out in it, wasn't wet but more like chunky powder, much easier to move. Within two hours, he cleared a narrow channel around the back of the house, scooping and dumping at intervals and taking more and more breaks.

"Oh Jesus," Gus panted, clutching at his chest. "Oh Jesus Murphy. I didn't sign up for this."

He coughed. Hoarked. Spat streamers and repeated. At times he held his knees as if on the cusp of barfing. His heartrate dropped in time, and his breath evened out enough that he settled down. After a while, a buzzing grew in his ears.

Which got him to lean over the trench he'd made, and look to the hill.

The windmill stood strong, visible in the haze and producing a low whirling sound. The thing was spinning so fast, Gus figured he could feed it a tree and watch woodchips fly. At least his ears were fine.

Breaktime over, he got back to work. When he reached the shed, he cleared the entrance and stuck the scoop into the snow. There was no lock on the door. Inside, the batteries and all that wonderous, sanity-preserving technology did its thing. Nothing looked amiss, so he left it alone.

The solar panels on the roof gleamed like black mirrors, but no snow collected on their faces. Gus squinted at the things, wondering how much power they were collecting. The windmill was working overtime, but he didn't know if the panels were doing anything at all or not. And he sure as shit wasn't going up there to find out.

He turned towards Annapolis and could not see anything resembling a city, just a smoky curtain streaming across the cliff and treetops. He went back to pushing snow. The only tracks he saw were his own. That lifted his spirits just a little. No deadhead could move around the place without him knowing about it.

His snow clearing efforts returned him to the front of his house, where he spent a little more time on the step area and the walkway. Every now and again he'd stop and glance at the main gate. Each time, the coast remained clear.

"Need a coke, a smoke, and a raisin square," he said, on the brink of exhaustion. He stopped, swayed, and surveyed what he'd done.

One circuit. One path. That was all he did. Anyone who cleared the wall would be up to their waist and wishing for a shovel.

He staggered back to the side entrance of the garage, knowing he'd earned a deep hot bath, when he noticed the area in front of the doors. An inch of fresh snow had already coated the concrete.

There was no need to clear it. None at all.

But he did, anyway.

Exhausted and ten pounds lighter, Gus shook out the scoop and closed the garage door. Arms and legs red and aching, he kicked his boots off and stripped. Shivering, sniffing, he gathered up his soaked clothing and plodded to the washer, leaving a trail of sweat in his wake. When he finally reached the tub, he started it up and sat, bare-cheeked and shaking, on the toilet. With his head in his hands, he waited for the thing to fill.

He was going to be stiff tomorrow. Real stiff.

Water roared into the tub. Working outside had done something good for him. He could feel it. That warm glow of productivity, despite the pain and discomfort.

Breathing in steam, Gus regarded the filling tub for long seconds before finally standing.

He lowered himself into the water.

33

January 28th.

Gus woke up on the couch and realized it was a lot darker than usual.

Then he heard it. Snow smacking the glass. Or ice pellets. Maybe both. A frozen sprinkling, like uncooked rice falling to the floor. He lifted his head and sighed at the sight. Or rather, the lack of one. Nothing existed beyond the glass. The skies had been cloudy all week, with more snow falling, filling the trenches he'd cut out earlier.

This morning, however, a storm had arrived. A smoky grey shit-flinger, whipping up frigid party-streamers and howling a ball-shriveling tune. Snow spattered the glass, which trembled under the force of the wind.

Gus closed his eyes.

He'd been digging. Every second day, when he recovered. Just getting outside and chucking whatever had fallen. The exercise helped his frame of mind. He'd even dug right up to the gate and back again, keeping a clear lane there and around the house. It took him four hours to clear everything away, with frequent breaks in between, but he didn't mind. The snow-clearing had worked up a powerful sweat, and he used that as an excuse to take a hot bath after each session. As hot as he could stand them. They were every bit as therapeutic as the snow clearing, and they helped him sleep. Along with the booze.

Today he would have dug. Had *wanted* to dig.

There would be no such thing, however. Not while the storm raged.

The warmth of his blankets stopped him from rising, so he lay there, on his side, peeking out at the powder pelting the glass. He fell back to sleep and when he woke a second time, he stayed that way, curled up underneath the layers of blankets, enjoying the trapped warmth.

After rising for a bathroom break, he checked on what had fallen at his front door. Maybe it wasn't as bad back there. Maybe it was worse.

It was worse. Much worse.

The wind wasn't so bad at the main entrance, but it still screamed when Gus pulled open the door. Waist-high snow greeted him. Imprints of the door's grooves and protrusions lined that wicked accumulation, each one a fine display of craftsmanship.

"Holy shit," he whispered, as the cold pushed him back a step.

Solidly packed, the snow didn't fall into the house, but more than a few flakes blew inside. In disbelief, he leaned over the barrier for a peek beyond.

"Holy…*shit.*"

The pathways he'd cleared had been filled again. The trench around the house was smothered in sections. In fact, all his work had pretty much been undone. The forest was barely visible.

Squinting, Gus realized he was on the verge of being buried in his own house.

Anyone else might have panicked. Panicked hard. To the point of doing something stupid.

But he wasn't anyone else.

"Fuck it." He slammed the door. "I don't need you. I'm not trapped on the road somewhere freezing my ass off. I'm *inside.* I have full cupboards. Or at least half full. And I have all the wine, whiskey, and whatever else there is to get a buzz on *in here.* So fuck ya. F-U-C-K-Y-A. I'm fucking *fine* HERE until spring."

On that note, he locked the door and went into the kitchen.

Breakfast occupied his mind. Then a movie.

January 30th.

He'd been moping around the house, slowly transforming, his hair continuing to thin on top while the rest of him sprouted. *Only molds grew faster,* he thought. The storm had moved off after dumping maybe three feet of snow. The sight of it all killed him inside, brought back those vibes of claustrophobia. Only when he looked out a window, however. And he was eating. Really eating. Probably because of all the recent exercise he was getting. What was the number? Of meals until spring? Three hundred and sixty. Well, Gus was a big man by any standards, with a healthy appetite, and he was fortunate enough that he worked regularly, and was able to put food on the table. He never missed a meal and ate well. The point being, he never had any *reason* to ration himself, never *needed* to, and that's where things became a problem. He wasn't rationing. He wasn't holding back. In fact, he was chowing down just as much as he did back in the day.

"Gotta control this better," he told himself at the kitchen island, while snacking on a couple of butterscotch pudding cups. He finished the food, disposed of the plastic cups (more garbage for the garage) and ruffled the folds of his open bath robe. On impulse, he pulled open the cupboard doors.

About half of what he had before, but there was less downstairs, because as he emptied the cupboards upstairs, he refilled them from his reserves. Still, he could make it to the spring.

"Okay, so then what? Well, you're going to have to pull on your big boy boots again and do that thing. You know. The one where you go through people's houses again. Or..."

Or you head into the city and clear out a grocery store. Or even a convenience store. Get whatever you can.

"Until what? Until you're *rescued?* But what if you aren't. What if... what if this is it? This is all there is, and there's no more. And once it's all gone, if you aren't growing it, if you aren't hunting it..."

That thought depressed him. "That's it, then. Isn't it?"

He shook his head.

"Fuck me. What a way to go." He couldn't think of a better reason to get drunk.

With a bottle of Uncle Jack in one fist and a couple bottles of water in the other, Gus descended to the den, in the insulated under chambers of the house.

And get drunk he did. By noon, he was utterly smashed. By one, he was sitting up before the coffee table, behind a makeshift battlement of empty or full bottles. Not all from this session, mind you, but over time, from earlier binges he never got around to cleaning up after. He finished pouring another whiskey and water in a beer mug and sampled it for taste.

It was fine. Better than fine.

"Gettin' good at this," he announced to the television screen.

There was no movie this time, just a recorded piece of a tropical beach, the sand white and hot looking, massaged by creamy surf. The beach, that beautiful sunny beach, helped keep the depression away, as well as the mid-winter malaise. In times like these, Gus figured every bit of mirth, however brief or fake, was needed.

He thought of Tammy and he forced it away. Another drink and swallow. "Let it snow, let it snow, let it—" at which point he burped. "Snow…. Yeeeeeah. Thank you, Sammy. Thank you, Dean. And thank you, Delores, you beauty you."

Gus sat back with knees spread wide. He stared at that beach, concentrated on it. Some place in Thailand, maybe. Or the Philippines. He'd never been to either place, but imagined they were all good.

Gus sat and watched, mentally teleporting himself to that beach, if only for seconds at a time. It wasn't as warm there as he thought, but maybe, on the next trip to the bathroom, he would turn up the heat and lose the elastic band around his waist. Get some sweat going. To work, to *immerse* himself, in that illusionary world. When his latest drink was gone. On that thought, Gus held up the mug.

"Empty again? There a hole in this thing?"

He overturned the mug, and the last few drops fell into his lap.

"Goddamn," he moaned, inspecting the damage with a drunk's sensibilities. That wasn't smart. He put the mug down and leaned forward, pulling away the bathrobe to better check his underwear. Yep. Direct hits all.

"Depth charges. All damage in the forward compartments. Couldn't have done better if I tried," he said, and sucked in his gut while pinching some fabric away. "Fuck that's wetter than I thought. We're takin' on water, Capt'n. We're takin' on water." He scowled at the empty mug. "Didn't I just finish you? I mean, weren't you empty? Don't tell me I need fuckin' glasses. I can't need fuckin' glasses. You know it's gonna be a long time before I get fuckin' glasses. Or even see an eye doctor. A long fuckin' time."

He sat and stewed in his own damp shorts, caught between the urge to change them or keep them on.

"Nope," he finally let out, and stood.

The climb upstairs was long and wobbly, where he swore the entire house was afloat on a savage sea. The walls were his friends as always. The second climb to the bedroom was even wobblier, but he made that as well. A ponderous ten minutes later, Gus stooped and swapped out his wet drawers for a dry pair, and lurched back to the stairs. Wet shorts in hand.

That first step was unsteady, and reality did a little loop-de-loo that wasn't helpful at all. Gus clutched at the railing. Everything became extra wobbly, rolling left to right and then repeating. He looked over his shoulder, where the second floor was still well within reach. Just that little motion felt like rebounding off a trampoline.

"Oh no, you don't." Gus whispered, foreseeing the impending wipeout. "No, you don't. Not this way. You ain't gettin' me this way. No sir."

With that, he plopped down on the nearest step and slid, one herky-jerky drop at a time, all the way to the bottom. There, he rested, and acknowledged his aching lower back. As an afterthought, he pinched the underwear from his ass crack.

"Second verse," Gus said, getting to his feet. "Same as—"

Whereupon a mighty belch ripped free of him, almost toppling him. He faced the steps to the rec room, where a soft, unseen light lit the way, and water lapped against a shoreline.

"Gonna walk down these things," Gus muttered.

Tammy's voice barged into his mind.

Don't you dare go down there, she said. *Don't you dare.*

"Awww Tam, I'm okay."

But she didn't repeat herself.

"Tam?" he asked, suddenly still and eyeing the walls. "Tammy?"

Nothing.

That stopped him cold. He waited, knowing it was the booze talking, but hoping for something *more*. Some divine intervention. When none came, he nodded and turned away from the steps.

"Could've just slid down them steps," he said, half to himself, half to Tam's ghost. "Did it just then. Didn't hurt. Too bad. Plenty of padding back there."

No internal voices.

"Could've just slid," he repeated, before landing on the living room couch and pitching over onto his side. He snuggled into the worn cushions, feeling the smooth grain of the material. It was fine enough.

He gazed out at the darkening winter scene beyond his windows.

And passed out.

34

Time went on.

His hair got thinner, while his beard became thicker.

Winter kept dropping snow on him, and he kept the pathways inside the walls clear. The snow shoveling was his best release. Any anxiety he couldn't remove by drinking he did so by taking it out on heavy snow. When there was no snow, he would attack whatever he'd heaped up, take it to the cliff side and dump it over the edge.

He didn't seem to be losing much weight, as all that exercise only strengthened his appetite. It was nothing for him to towel off after a snow slinging session, to settle down for a meal, and have two. Eating problem aside, he did notice an improvement in his endurance. At first he was taking breaks after every minute, then every second minute, then every five…

Now, he could shovel for fifteen minutes at a time before stopping for a five-minute breather. If he was just pushing the scoop, he could last up to fifty minutes. He was getting stronger, and that was a good thing. He'd deal with the chunky ass later.

As his food stores declined, Gus knew he'd have to go out and look for more. And soon. *Three hundred and sixty meals*, he once figured. Well, he didn't take into account double portions and snacks, and that was his downfall. He ate for two. Stress eating, really, or so he told himself. Same with the bouts of ball scratching.

Itching aside, it was only last week the little can of *You're Welcome* green peas peeked out at him from way back of his pantry. The red line was in sight, warning him. He covered up that little can with the last of the tin food from below.

Gus studied the grub in his cupboards. When it was gone, there was no more to bring up from downstairs. And the frozen stuff had been gone for weeks.

Winter would be over soon, and with it, the roads would clear, and he'd be able to go into town and look for food.

He wondered what would be waiting for him when he did.

The ninth of March. Or so he figured. Give or take a day or two, considering it was only an estimate from the time he started marking the days.

Water dripped off the house. Rain fell plenty over the last three days. A cold relentless belting that shrunk the white hills piled up around the property. Slush clogged the edges of the asphalt. A fog, supernatural in density and scope, obscured the cliffside and Annapolis in a screen of cobweb grey.

Gus leaned against the doorframe of the main entrance, taking in the melting snow and thickening fogbanks. The spring thaw had arrived, earlier than expected, shoving off winter and lifting the temperature above zero and into the single digits. Even the air tasted warmer.

"Goddamn," he whispered, taking in that fresh air, and wondering how a bear felt after hibernating. "Did I make it?"

As an answer, water dripped off the house

"I think I did," he said and smiled.

Imagine that.

And throughout that arctic nebula, where only the steady pattering of water reached his ears, Gus breathed a cautious sigh of relief.

All through the winter, he'd had only the one visitor, and that was before the heaviest snow. He had it easy, thinking back on it. Just get up, get out, and make sure the snow didn't overwhelm him or his house. There'd been no issues with the water (his greatest fear) or the power (his second greatest fear). He'd maintained his little temperate oasis behind the stone wall. His food was almost gone (his other greatest fear), but when he first calculated how many meals he needed to survive the winter, he figured on four months of harsh weather.

He didn't factor in the chance of an early spring.

Now, with everything melting, his food all but gone and his booze supplies taking a beating, he wondered. And wondered hard.

How did all those dead people do during the winter months? Did they keep moving during the coldest nights of the year, when the sun left the sky far too early and the night seemed forever? Or did they slow to a creaking stop, unable to wade through snowdrifts knee or even thigh deep, whereupon any additional snow might hold them in place, until the spring?

Even then, the zombies were once people. Still flesh and bone. Neither one held up too well to the elements. The exposure alone might do funky things to them, but the cold…

The harsh cold would slow them down. It *had* to. Maybe freeze them, to the point where limbs snapped off when they tried to move. Snapping off, landing in drifts and forgotten about.

Jesus, that was a great thought. If it happened.

"Snow would still be on the roads," he reasoned. "Slushy, though. Maybe not so bad."

It was worth checking out. Not that he had a choice. He wasn't going to live for long on what he had left in the pantry. He took another deep whiff of fresh air and listened to the patter of snow melt all around.

"Tomorrow," Gus said. "Today… I shovel."

And he did.

After dressing for the weather and stockpiling a collection of water and wine bottles just inside the garage door, Gus headed out with a scoop in one hand and shovel in the other. The snow mushed underfoot. Gus harpooned one white whale of a drift with his shovel, and got the scoop in place. Spring had made an early appearance. Only right he helped things along a bit.

It took him most of the morning, and the lane he cleared wasn't the widest, but he reached the gate and stared out between the bars as if he were a prisoner in solitary confinement. Nothing waited for him, and the surrounding trees were barely visible through the fog. Nothing moved. The zombie he'd shot and hauled off to one side was visible, just a lump really, covered in a soft looking shell of white.

Gus undid the gate, struggling with the bar, but he got it. The clicking of metal stopped him, and he watched the fog. Waited. Waited some more.

Then, satisfied nothing was out there, he opened the gate.

The road was snowy, slushy, down to perhaps five or six inches deep, but he didn't think it would be a problem. He'd just drive slow, like anyone facing winter conditions. Not today, however, not after the morning workout. He was done, but by tomorrow, he figured the road would be even better, if the temperature didn't pull a fast one and drop.

"You hear me?" Gus aimed at the sky. "Don't you dare pull a fast one. Not like before. Hear me? Don't you dare. Don't you fuckin' *dare.*"

No reply.

He took that as a *yes*.

"Tomorrow," he repeated.

With that, he went back to the house, pushing the scoop before him, eventually tossing the shovel aboard the van.

That evening, Gus stood in the kitchen, before his diminished pantry, and hefted the can of green peas.

"Little green can of peas," he said, screwing up his mouth as he spoke. "That could be the title for a song."

Maybe he would write it one day. Give him something to do.

It had been close. Very close. Besides the peas, he was down to a half box of Honeycomb breakfast cereal, three packets of instant oatmeal, and two cans of vegetable soup. After that, early spring or not, he figured he would've had to dig his way to the nearest house.

He placed the can back in the pantry, gave it a wink, and closed the door. A bottle of Captain Morgan and Jack Daniels waited for him on the island. He took the whiskey but gave the nod to the rum. "You're up tomorrow. Feel like explorin' some houses?"

The bottle did not answer him.

Gus opened the whiskey and wondered if he would actually go himself. So many mornings he'd woken up with good intentions, only to blow the whole day off.

"Well, I'm going tomorrow." He poured himself four fingers into a glass. "'Cause I don't have a choice."

There was no mix except water, but for the last little bit he'd been drinking it straight. It wasn't so bad, and, after a while, he could take a mouthful and not even make a face. Even scarier, he was starting to like it.

That first mouthful brought everything into focus, and he watched the fading day. Even the evenings were longer.

Later that night, he made a round of switching off the lights before climbing the stairs to the master bedroom. It was much nicer than his own, and though he hadn't slept in the bed, he'd checked on it plenty of times. Bouncy queen-sized mattress, comfortable, and with a place to stash books. Nearby reading lamp. Matching end tables and a cabinet thingy he couldn't remember the name for. The carpeting was a bluish grey with a soft underlay, and walking barefoot across it felt nice.

"All right," Gus said in a defeated tone. "I'm talking to a bed now. Wonderful. Look… whoever owns this place ain't coming back. And while I'm happy with the couch downstairs… tonight I'm gonna sleep here. I'm heading back out there tomorrow, and… and God only knows if I'll make it back. So, one night ain't gonna hurt."

He paused then, expecting a voice to object, but no one did.

"All right, then."

The comforter was satiny, the blankets a fine cotton weave. He pulled everything back, exposing a cloudy-colored interior. He stripped down and got under the sheets. The bed was cold, the mattress comfortable, and though he knew there was no one coming back, he still felt like an intruder.

He reached for the nearby lamp, switched that off and lay there, staring at the ceiling. No wind blew that night, and the in-floor heating didn't kick in right away, so Gus was left with his thoughts in between those crisp sheets.

Tomorrow was the day. He exhaled heavily.

Tomorrow.

He wondered if tomorrow night he would be sleeping in the same bed.

35

The next morning, Gus dressed, used the crapper, and went down to the kitchen. There he ate dry cereal—*Honeycombs*—from the box, while waiting for his instant oatmeal to warm up and thicken. Once the oatmeal was ready, he ate that as well, glowering at the outer gate as if he were standing on guard. It was overcast again, as if the winter hadn't been dreary enough already.

"Today," he whispered, not convinced in the least. A part of him wanted nothing to do with searching houses. Not one damn bit. He finished his breakfast, and gripped the edge of the sink as if about to puke into it.

"You gotta do it," he said, studying the outer gate. "You gotta. Today is it. If you don't, you're gonna be *wishin'* for a can of green peas. I shit you not. You… you don't know what it's like to starve. Oh, you've been hungry. Maybe even real hungry. But not starving. You've been pretty damn lucky that way. And if you don't get over this mental thing stoppin' you, you will. You will fuckin' starve. And I bet whatever's left in the pantry, that starving to death is… is a helluva lot *worse* than being eaten alive. Okay? All right? We doing this then?"

The universe didn't answer him, but he wasn't thinking about staying back and not going.

"All right then…"

His legs only got part of that message, however, as getting to the garage was a challenge. His feet were concrete. He dragged himself through the mudroom, where he scanned for something, *anything*, to distract him from continuing. Anything to keep him occupied for a couple of hours, to help speed the morning away.

Somehow, he reached the garage. The van waited. Gus went to the locker and opened it. Three bottles. Captain Morgan dark rum. Bacardi white rum. Jack Daniels whiskey.

231

It was only 8:40 in the morning, but Gus's recharging nerves demanded action. His hands quivered as he took the Captain Morgan, undid the lid, and poured himself three-fingers. He toasted the other bottles and drank with barely a twitch or shiver.

The rest of the drink went on the nearby bench, next to the bottle. He readied the shotgun and bat, placing them in the passenger side of the van, angled to the floor. Five extra cases of shells came along as well. Having done that, he dropped the Bacardi and whisky in the passenger seat. The rest of his equipment was already in the rear, prepped earlier, but he inspected everything one last time.

Gus returned to the locker and, piece by piece, pulled on the makeshift body armor.

Extra sweater. Inner leather vest that got zipped. Nutsack protector. Leather pants over the jeans. Knee pads and connected shin guards. Boots. The leather coat was tight, even tighter when he zipped it up, but he got into it. He strapped on the elbow pads and tested them with a slap. Then came the neck guard. He appreciated the stiff protection. A mild sweat broke over his brow. His drink waited, and he reached for the glass with shaking hands, which wasn't because of his steady drinking. Holding his drink two-handed, he downed the rest and poured himself a second three finger bullet.

"Fuck it," Gus whispered.

And added two more fingers for overdrive.

Leather gloves, one size only. He bit into them for a test. Nothing tore, although if a zombie did bite his hand, he imagined he would feel it. Could be worse. Could be mittens.

On the verge of overheating and thirty pounds heavier, Gus turned back to the work bench, and the helmet there. The visor was down, reflecting the distorted leather golem he'd become. The door to the house was also there, closed. He couldn't remember if he'd done that or not.

"Losing it," Gus said. He chuckled nervously and swallowed. Despite being two drinks in, his throat clicked.

He stared at his reflection in that black visor, leaned in close enough to see the light in his eyes.

"But I'm doing it," he whispered. "I'm fuckin' *doing* it."

And snatched up the helmet.

Gus fitted that last piece over his head and flipped the visor up. He had the barest chin whisker sticking out from underneath, but whatever.

He hauled himself aboard and settled in behind the wheel.

Closed the door and got his seat belt on.

His breathing increased, close to panting, but that was from moving around. Sure it was. Shit was tight. Jacket and pants. And his crotch felt like it was cupped by a steel ladle. His gloves creaked when he gripped the steering wheel, and he glanced, longingly, at the closed door leading to the house.

Jesus above, he did *not* want to go down there this morning. It was morning, for fuck's sake. *Who* in their right mind would do what he was contemplating doing in the *morning?*

Too cold to go there today, his brain said. *Fuck it.* Fuck it. *Wait it out. You can get into the second season of* Ash versus the Evil Dead. *That's the stuff right there. Go tomorrow. Check out New Cross tomorrow. Tomorrow's better.*

Gus liked that plan a helluva lot more than the current one.

He started up the van instead. Opened the garage door. And backed the beast out into the melting snow.

Even as he lowered the garage door and drove for the gate, that little voice kept right on nagging. *Stop*, it said. *Go back. Wait 'til the snow is completely gone. The roads will be clogged, just you wait. You won't be able to get anywhere, anyway. You're wasting time. Go back inside and throw on some soup for lunch. Get to work on that dark rum. Seriously. You're wasting time…*

The brake pads squealed as the van stopped before the gate.

Gus climbed out, stiff from all the gear he wore, and opened that final barrier to the great outside. Once that was done, he went through the paces of getting the van through the gate and shutting it behind him. By the time he was back behind the wheel, those eight ounces of black rum were landing in great big calming flashes. He recognized and welcomed the spreading, numbing warmth.

And as it warmed him, the voice inside his head frizzled and shrank away into nothing, blasted into oblivion.

Gus pulled the helmet from his head, gasped, and reached for the whiskey. Two swallows and a stinging hiss later, he put the bottle away.

"Needed that," he remarked through clenched teeth.

But not too much. That was the trick. It was a slippery wire he walked, and him without a balancing pole or a net.

Gus drove down the mountain.

He didn't look back once.

The road was knottier than usual, bouncing him in his seat, and forcing him to slow down. Snow still covered the single lane, but the van cut through the middle of that mountain road, momentum and all-seasonals carrying Gus through.

The highway appeared, flooded by a moat of white. He stopped and peered right and left. Both ways were snow-covered but, like the road behind him, it was visibly diminished in the morning light. Except the way into the city looked a little more melted in the center.

The engine rumbling, he looked right, considering the path into Annapolis.

Then he considered left, which led to New Cross.

Pursing his lips, Gus turned left, tires cutting into those treacherous melting lumps. New Cross it was. The little town was the safer play.

Except, not five minutes later, higher up on the mountain, the snow became denser. Taller. Thicker. The larger drifts shaded and protected by forest. The snow lay across the whole of the road and beyond, daring him to take his best shot. Gus felt the greater depths through his steering column and all the way down to the tires, where that white cement clutched at the wheels and kept him straight. He applied the brakes, pumped them, felt them clench and lock, and had a brief sensation of uncontrolled sailing.

Towards a snowy dune that spanned the width of the road.

Gus worked the brakes, staring at that white wall, and bracing for the worse.

The beast stopped two feet away.

"God almighty." Gus leaned forward, inspecting what lay before him. Snow. Far too much snow. A settled avalanche, really. Snaking through the forest and spilling onto the highway. High, unspoiled drifts that buried the road until it curved out of sight.

New Cross was out of reach. *Way* out of reach. And too far to hike.

"Well…fuck," he said, and took two swallows of whiskey. He placed the bottle back before he grabbed the stick. Worked it until he got Reverse, then lowered his window. He alternated between watching his side mirror and sticking his head outside.

"If I get stuck out here…" he warned and then burped.

But it was just talk.

The house was only a short hike away up the mountain. The more he thought about it, the more it appealed to him. A hike all the way back wasn't a bad thought at all. Not at all. He'd lock up the van—out of habit, really—get out with his bottles and go on a wilderness pub crawl. Suck in some of that clean mountain air along the way. That idea appealed to him mightily.

Except…

Except then he would be that much closer to the little can of green peas.

Perhaps even *wishing* for green peas.

As much as he was secretly hoping for it, he didn't get stuck. Didn't even so much as waver. He drove in reverse all the way back to his turn off. It took twice the amount of time, maybe even longer, but he sighted his mountain road, and angled the rear end onto it without trouble.

Where he stopped, the van idling, and thought of grocery stores. They just popped right in there. The big ones. Big risk for big reward. One stop shopping.

He considered the highway into the city.

The city had almost killed him the last time, but there wasn't so much snow on the ground then. There had been plenty of snow since. And all that snow wasn't being cleared from Annapolis's streets. It just piled up and up, and the recent rain might not have made anywhere near the dent he needed to get down there.

That led him to another, more recent thought.

How did *all those dead people do during the winter months?*

He thought again. Hard. Weighing the risk and reward. Hard enough to start shaking his head in disgust.

"Yeah, I know," Gus eventually said to his bottles in the passenger seat. "I'm not drunk enough."

On that note, he grabbed the whiskey, got it opened, and drank down two scalding mouthfuls.

"But I'm sure as fuck stupid."

He pulled back onto the pavement and headed for the city.

Snow covered everything. The highway going down into the valley was bad, but not unpassable, and he could maneuver around the more intimidating snowdrifts. The snow had a sagging ice cream appearance. Most of the roads lay beneath deep drifts, but the wider strips were better. Black puddles formed near the center, and Gus splashed through them. In minutes, the first few homes passed by. Then the forest slowly thinned, replaced by more houses. The roadside obstacles he'd warily come to know came into sight. The traffic thickened, becoming a vehicular slalom run. Beyond all that, the suburbs slowly came into view. Then the city. Houses and buildings lay beneath mounds of powder, and, in some cases, a person could ski off the slopes tethered to bungalows.

Monstrous drifts blocked off driveways. Cars and trucks wore sloppy, receding white caps, and their bases were hidden.

Then he saw them, scattered about.

Zombies.

They noticed the van, just like before. Yet they were unable to do anything. The snow and freezing temperatures had rendered them motionless. Ice caked their hair and faces. Melting snow lathered their shoulders and, in some cases, their entire fronts. They stood like department store mannequins, and yet, as he drove by, those frozen heads detected him. They struggled to turn, reanimating with every drip of water. Snowy sleeves fell as half frozen arms flexed. One gimp slowly twisted its upper body while its legs remained trapped in a thigh high drift. Another zombie sporting a slushy beard, actually fell over and went splat in a dense snowbank, disappearing from sight.

Gus drove by them all.

Winter had indeed done a job on them, and he suddenly liked his chances all the more.

All he had to do was stick and move. Stick and move.

Downtown. The main drag wasn't so blocked with snow, but the smaller two-lane roads and one-way streets were clogged and dangerous looking. More snowbound houses floated by, then a school, half-submerged.

"Where am I going?" Gus asked himself, the whiskey alive and working, shielding yet hindering him.

Then he remembered.

"Right…groceries."

The school was the senior high school. And not a klick down from that, if he could reach it, was a shopping plaza.

In that city block was a local EGA.

That stood for Ernest's Groceries Association, or something like that. The big thing was, after Mollymart East, EGA was the preferred shopping place for groceries. It didn't have the same floor space as Mollymart, but that didn't bother him. They'd stocked the same frozen pizzas and chicken fingers as the bigger chains, and sometimes had better deals.

"Chicken fingers," Gus whispered, and liked very much. "Fuck *me.*"

The plaza came into sight, not quite as buried as suspected, and Gus wondered how the hell that had happened. The parking lot, however, was something else. It was an Arctic icefield.

More importantly, not a deadhead in sight.

"All right." Gus turned onto the parking lot. The drifts became higher, as high as his tires in places, forcing him to slow down and plan his approach. Snow gripped the wheels, but the all-seasonals, god bless their rubber treads, pulled him through. A few hidden potholes made the ride a little more interesting, but he aimed the beast for the EGA entrance.

Which was open and filled with snow, as if the automatic doors had been forced apart. Daylight revealed the EGA's foyer and a mess of trashed materials. The deeper interior, however, was a sunless cavern. There were other shops along the plaza. A Korean food takeout. A pizza place. A walk-in hair salon. A smart phone place. A Royal bank. A Fish King. All had their doors closed and the windows intact.

Creeping over that snow-choked parking lot, Gus pulled ever closer to the open doors. A great slope of white flowed inside the foyer, where racks of packaged bread had been toppled. On the other side, however, stacks of water were untouched. A good sign that the groceries might very well be still inside.

Gus did a ninety-degree turn and backed up to the blocked doors.

He braked and swallowed thickly, realizing he was melting.

"Can't stop now," he said, barely hearing himself.

Within seconds, he was up and lumbering for the back doors. The urge for one last drink got him, however, so he returned to the passenger seat and got his swallow of whiskey. Then two more.

He slipped the bat into a bag, the same one Ray had provided him with, then donned the unit over his head and shoulder like the scabbard of a big old broadsword. He pulled on the helmet and snapped the visor down. Then he picked up the shotgun and worked the pump exactly once.

The rear doors beckoned.

Gus blanked out for a moment, eyeing the exit. He stood there, paralyzed for seconds. His knee joints protested. Sweat streaked for his eyes. His testicles felt jammed into a thimble while the edges of the cup irritated his skin.

Gus pushed all that away and focused.

EGA was a big place, nearly the size of Mollymart East in square footage. He'd never done a place this big before—which was a step up from the sporting store—and that notion froze him in place.

Only for a few heartbeats, and then he reached for the doors.

Which opened with a mouse fart of ungreased hinges.

That single high-pitched note rooted him to the spot. He stood there, blinking as if he just received a thousand raw sparkling volts up his pee-hole. Gus waited for a reaction, and heard none. He shoved the doors open—a little too hard as one rebounded on its hinges, shaking the van.

The entrance lay before him, partially snowed in like some newly discovered ice tunnel. Darkened aisles were barely visible inside. Gus hopped down and splashed slush. Checking his flanks, he snuck inside, every step a soft splatter and pissing him off to no end. He eyed the cases of water. No one in their right minds would leave that untouched. The rest of the foyer had been trashed, however. The shopping carts lay piled up in their corral. Shelves of potted plants had been ripped through, flinging containers and withered vegetation all over the place. The bread lay strewn across the floor. Surprisingly, whoever had roughed up the flowers had not done the same to the bread. The packaged loaves were untouched but had become a science experiment in frozen fungi.

Gus proceeded further inside, shotgun ready, the snow becoming wet floor. He'd make sure the place was clear first.

It got darker.

Fuck, Gus mentally swore and slid up his visor. He couldn't see *shit* with the thing down. Shotgun braced against his shoulder, he snuck forward. A smell hit him, growing stronger with every step. Pungent. And cold. The smell of rotting meat and decay somewhat reduced by winter air.

Daylight didn't reach far into the store, leaving it a shadow-filled hangar. The deeper in, the place became a lightless vault where his every step was a maddening click upon floor tiles, accentuated by his own rabid breathing. The deli section lay to his right, with a selection of packaged sandwiches, or what he thought were sandwiches. The fruit and produce section stretched ahead, empty and quiet. Decomposing fruit resembled charcoaled lumps, barely distinguishable from each other. Bananas had gone to blackened blobs of mush. Plastic containers held pulp that had long since up and expired. Pineapples still resembled pineapples, as did the melons, but only because of their shapes.

With each step, the air became a little denser, the decaying sweetness more offensive to breathe.

The booze in his system kept him on an even keel, but he knew he should've drank more. He scanned for any lurking targets. Gus remembered fish tanks being in the rear, but had no desire to look to see if they were still alive. The bakery was back there as well, but judging by what he'd seen around the main doors, he wasn't interested in funky perishables.

He kicked aside black clumps of matter covering the floor and turned left, where the checkout counters and aisles waited. A sign hung above the first aisle, listing health foods, toothpaste, and medicines therein. Gus stopped and peered down that lightless channel, seeing to the halfway mark where everything became dark. Daylight from the main entrance did not reach the rear, but it didn't matter.

The aisle was empty.

Gus moved to the next one over. He could just make out "Soda Pop and Snacks" and "Chips and Popcorn" on the overhead sign. Since he was close to munching down on green peas just for fun, all that junk food goodness nearly got him misty. He halted beside a stack of energy drinks covered in plastic, and peeked down the aisle.

Also empty.

Well, shit. Two for two. He moved on.

Everyday displays of items on sale or reduced to clear cluttered up the check-out area. A couple of empty shopping carts had been left behind as well. Gus eased by it all, careful not to rattle anything, his senses wired and practically buzzing.

He *knew* he should've drank more.

Next aisle… Dairy section. Also empty. Outstanding. Another long way to the back, and every bit as haunting as the first. Gus could barely make out the contents, but the shelves appeared relatively full. He left everything, however, deeming it all hazardous waste at this point.

There weren't many aisles left. No more than four, and the last one was frozen food, where the upright freezers shone like obsidian. Gus spotted the sign for the next aisle, the lettering impossible to read in the deepening dark, but a stack of the in-store special dropped a hint. Paper towels—piled high. A toilet paper goldmine was no doubt just around the corner, and both commodities were highly prized in the Berry household. He stopped at the corner, peeked around the paper towel stack, and nearly shit his shorts upon seeing a mob of undead shoppers facing—*ogling*—the bare and barren shelves of the toilet paper section.

The sight shocked Gus right down to his boot heels. He jerked backwards, clipping the stack of paper towels with his shoulder.

The household items bounced to the floor in great building blocks of four and two rolls each.

That soft tumble barely made a sound, but the motion of all that falling goodness got the zombies' attention.

Bodies lurched.

Heads swiveled, seeing that weeks-old, in-store special topple.

That was all they needed.

Undead vocal cords alerted the whole pack. Hanging arms rose and pointed. Legs churned into motion as the gang staggered forward to investigate.

Gus almost screamed.

Almost, but he didn't. Instead he kicked at the traitorous packages and broke into a strategic retreat. The first of the morbid shoppers emerged from toiletries, their voices a horrible, windy wailing as if their dead diaphragms powered a section of rotten pan flutes. Their lifeless eyes resembled cigarette burns, and they kicked away rolls of paper towels as they advanced.

Gus didn't even think about shooting.

He ran, instead, fleeing for the distant daylight.

The zombies smacked into shopping carts, knocking over displays in their pursuit, or what sounded like pursuit. Gus moved at a pretty good clip, considering his size and the amount of gear strapped on. He rushed by the produce section and hung a sharp turn for the entrance. The zombies followed but he didn't look back. Didn't even glance.

The EGA was a nest, and he was having none of it.

Ahead, open doors spread wide with its wintry welcome mat, marred by his own boot prints. Beyond that, framed in a gun smoke shimmer of daylight, lay the finish line. The escape pod. The wide open crack of the beast.

Gus lunged aboard arms first, shotgun held high so he wouldn't blow his own head off. Momentum did nothing for him as his leather coat hitched upon the metal floor. He pulled his legs in, knees clacking off the lower lip of the van while the undead's chagrin about missing a quick bite grew louder in his ears.

Only then did he look back.

They came shambling through the foyer, a festering collage of wrecked faces, gaping mouths and gangrenous teeth. Blackened fingernails, horrible bite wounds and missing eyes. All preceded by a noxious cloud of stink that was positively breath robbing. They charged him in a frantic lurch, a drunken hyper-gait, working legs and hips as if hobbled by steel pegs.

Gus rolled onto his side, clutching the shotgun. The nearest deadhead was closing fast. Gus fired from the hip, the kick almost jerking the weapon free of his hands. The lead zombie took the blast dead centre, a juicy crater bursting in the center of its lumberjack shirt. Its unliving carcass flew backwards into the mass behind it and, like a cluster of wobbly pins struck by a bowling ball, they all went down.

Gus pulled himself to his knees, losing the shotgun. He pitched forward, arms out, and latched onto the doors.

More zombies emerged from the entrance, struggling to walk over that livid doormat. Those caught in the blast weren't down for the count. The result—an angry pile-up in the foyer, where arms clawed for a grip of anything.

Gus pulled the van doors shut and locked them. A hand slapped the window and he flinched. The glass didn't break, but he didn't want to find out if it would. He hurried to the driver's seat. He flopped down, started up the rig, shifted and hit the gas.

The van shot backwards.

"*Jesus!*" Gus blurted as the beast crunched into whatever was clawing at her haunches. The ass end rose, as if riding a low ramp. There was a distinctive give, followed by a muffled rattling of bodies, ending with a crash of glass and debris clattering off the van.

Gus rebounded from his seat, then the steering wheel. He grabbed the stick, located the right gear, and hauled his machine out of that mess. The van surged ahead, thumping over whatever was underneath.

Then he was shooting through the parking lot, following his first cut through the melting snow and abandoned vehicles.

Arms locked and pressing himself into the driver's seat, Gus turned this way and that, keeping to his tire tracks, avoiding drifts too risky to plow through. He circled right into an open patch he hoped was pothole free and swung back towards the EGA.

There, at the entrance, zombies spilled into the daylight—falling over moving bodies, waving and gesturing at him. At least three dozen or so corpses.

A determined Gus braked and turned, flinging up jets of slush in his wake, hearing the softer stuff spray against the van's chassis. He zipped past the lead zombies, who swatted at the beast's side as it charged by. A few of them even connected. He drove to the far side of the lot, where he turned again and lined up the group. He hit the gas, getting the rig up to a steady forty which felt like seventy on the sloppy pavement.

The van blasted through the little mob, bludgeoning them off their feet and splattering them like wrecked snow angels. After clearing the group, Gus pulled around, actually fishtailing before straightening up again. Then, with deliberate aim, he battered the ones still standing and ran over the fallen. He cut it close to the entrance, as if shaving away an unsightly hedge.

He did that three times, before circling once more to inspect the damage. All the while, he barely blinked, certainly didn't panic, and stayed in control of his bladder.

Movement in the corner of his eye drew his attention.

Across the street, in ones and twos, others were coming, drawn to the violence.

He had time. Maybe even a lot of time. If he hurried.

Gus stopped at the entrance. Nothing else came out of the grocery store. He parked the van and went for the rear doors. He opened them right over that dewy mess of a zombie he'd gunned down and subsequently ran over. A broad tire tread crushed its head like an ink blot from an overloaded pen, but he still saw a jawbone in there, among other things he didn't need to see. Gus lowered himself onto the gore-colored snow, knowing his boots would need a cleaning before he got home.

Other things moved through the snow. Matter of fact, now that he'd stopped, it looked like a *lot* of things still moved, but nothing stood on two feet. The follow-up passes had crushed legs and spines, demoting the pack to twitches and crawls. Relentless crawls.

Gus aimed at the nearest deadhead some ten feet away, but didn't fire. The approaching reinforcements at the edge of the parking lot stopped him. There were less than a dozen gimps, but if he fired the shotgun, more would come. He placed the weapon back in the van and pulled the bat. He didn't want to trample through the snow to whack the nearby crawlers, so he would let them come to him.

He reached for a flashlight, switched it on and hurried inside the EGA. The whiskey kept him focused, even though his heartrate could recharge a car battery. The first few aisles contained nothing of interest. He did stop at the head of the aisle with all the toilet paper and did a second sweep, confirming what he'd glimpsed earlier. All reserves of bum wad were gone. Pillaged. There might be more out back, but he was on a clock. Gus went for other necessities.

Pop aisle.

Fully stocked.

He grabbed a cart and loaded it up with three cases of ginger ale. The fourth case, and his lower back protested. The fifth case turned his cheeks a blustery red.

Gus balanced the bat across the cart and pushed it back to the van.

The whole operation felt like a run on some daytime game show, where failing meant a fatal zombie dick-chomp. That alone made him go faster, because he knew once a deadhead started on his dick, the bastard wouldn't stop chewing until he reached asshole.

He plowed through the paper towels littering the floor. That was fine. He'd get them on the next run.

Two zombies were pulling themselves along the snow-covered ground when he reached daylight. One was even inch-worming towards him, unable to use its shattered arms.

Gus brandished the bat, hesitated and hammered the inch-worm's skull like it was a shitty hardboiled egg. All movement ceased as the head squished like an oversized tension ball, unable to spring back into shape. The second zombie wasn't much better. That one reached for Gus's ankles, and something about those long, emaciated digits freaked him out something fierce. He whacked the head twice before turning away, glimpsing what spurted free.

"Oh no you don't," he said, smucking a third wormy corpse and stopping it cold. Gus backed off, his frame heaving, and checked on things. Four more were ten feet out, but after that, it got a little better, although that second wave of dead things continued making baby-steps for the van. Even as he watched, one of those zombies toppled over, perhaps hitting a patch of ice and losing ankle support.

Gus reset himself and charged back into the store.

Canned food section.

In heaping handfuls and broad sweeps of his arm, Gus plunked everything into the cart. Tin salmon, tuna fish and sardines. Cans of corn giblets and canned peas and carrots (which he thought were beans, for some damn reason). Cans rattled off the cart's interior until it was half full.

Rushing for the end and banking hard to the left, he stopped and flashed his light over a row of frozen foods. The power was gone but it was winter. Temps were still frigid. He eyed the stacked pizzas, quesadillas, deep fried chicken thingies, and flung open the glass doors.

He raced into the next aisle, nearly wiping out on the curve.

Beans. Beans and *wieners*. Christ all mighty he needed his beans and wieners. Chili. Ravioli. Spaghetti. Meatballs and *gravy*. Jesus, Jesus, with fries you had a *banquet*. Then there was the selection of Kraft dinner and hamburger fixings. Holy shit. He'd bludgeon a fuckin' busload of zombies to get just a box of each. He grabbed several from the shelves. A few cans spilled from the overfilled cart, signalling it was time to leave.

Gus arranged a few packages, hemming in the overflow, and barreled down the lane. He turned sharply without loosing a single item and hoofed it back towards the light.

At the rear of the van, the remnants of the EGA welcome party had pulled themselves closer.

Gus let the cart roll to a stop, using the momentum to pull his bat free. He crushed the heads of four zombies before backing off—staggering really——and checking the parking lot.

The ranks had doubled. Maybe two dozen dark outlines out there, arms swinging, working, as they waded past the outer edge of the EGA's parking lot.

Gus released a grunt of both anguish and exhaustion, but he unloaded the cart, pushing himself, tossing everything into the van. He finished in under a minute, wheezed as if stricken by pneumonia, and checked on the incoming second wave. Seeing there was still some time, he whipped the shopping cart around and, with a deep breath that might've made him pee just a little, pushed it back into the supermarket.

On the way back in, he chucked any paper towels underfoot into the cart.

Frozen pot pies. Sweet and sour pork. TV dinners. *Ketchup!* Sweet gawd almighty and bless your cotton socks he couldn't forget the ketchup! Nor ketchup's tart sister, mustard! Then a couple bottles of mustard pickles which ignited a craving the moment he spotted them.

Then he was in the snack aisle, once considered death row to him.

Now, however, it was a long, sweet and salted, multi-flavored road to mental wellness. Nay. Mental *nirvana.*

Bags of Ketchup chips, bags of All Dressed chips. *Cheesies,* god save a duck. Bits and Bites (he fuckin' *loved* those), as well as popcorn because he was in a grabbing frenzy then, knowing the timer was into the last few seconds, knowing any moment, he'd hear the zombified security forces storming the breach, searching for his doughy ass. And still he was grabbing items off the shelf as he stormed by—cookies, candy bars, candy and even——holy *shit*—beef *jerky*—colon corn at its *finest*—throwing everything into the cart and wheezing profanities as sometimes they bounced back out. When they did, Gus left them and grabbed for more.

In no time he rounded a corner and chugged for home, on the verge of cardiac immolation, wishing he had a dog team helping him along.

Gus plowed through the unmoving mess around the van, actually slipping on a grey arm, stumbling, and bouncing the cart off the rear bumper. He got up, kicked away the offending limb and struggled for breath.

Then he checked the coast.

Three dozen at least, with the lead elements halfway across that windswept tundra belonging to EGA. Gus wished God would do him a solid and strike the whole lot of them down right then and there, but nothing of the kind happened. So he started throwing his latest load into the van, wheezing, snorting as he aimed for bins—missing often and bouncing shit off the floor.

When he finished unloading, Gus whipped the cart around and shoved it inside the store. His arms and shoulders burned. His legs were damn near jellified. He tried to jump aboard the van, failed (unable to get his knee pads above the bumper), wheezed *"Fuck it"* and rolled himself inside like a sunburned beached whale. An unkind surf of cans pushed back, even rolling over him in places. Gus shoved it away in great rattling waves. He got to his knees, turned for the rear doors and faced a zombie police officer with wide, deep-fried eyes and a quivering bottom lip attached by a sliver of meat.

Gus screamed and fell backwards, splashing down amongst his EGA booty.

The zombie clutched his ankles.

Energized by fright, Gus bicycled pedaled, trying to free his legs, yet that undead constable on patrol not only held on but dragged the kicking, gasping house painter a whole foot along the floor of the van…

Until Gus's flailing hands fell upon the hidden barrel of his shotgun.

In a glossy, heavy wave of chips and beef jerky, Gus brought the weapon to bear, aimed over his knees, and fired.

The undead cop blew backwards, as if finger-flicked by the good Lord himself.

Problem solved, Gus stumbled to his feet and closed the doors, noting a few food items had fallen onto the pavement. Dismissing the spillage, he locked the doors and pushed through the considerable haul to the driver's seat.

Sitting down never felt better, but through deep deep gasps of breath, between those life-giving gulps, he saw the stirring might of the city.

It wasn't just the three dozen gimps past the midway point of the parking lot that caught his attention. No sir. It was the *hundreds* of zombie citizens behind them, bleeding out into the streets like an oily seepage.

Winter hadn't buried the entire population.

Gus froze at the sight. Then he started up the van, and with one last look at the army coming for him, he whipped the beast around and started searching for the nearest escape route.

36

As expected, the roads within the city were either partially blocked by melting snow dunes or clogged entirely. Zombies stood in those streets, cold-stricken silhouettes cut off from Gus by the same barriers. He drove on, painfully aware of the trembling in his limbs, from both exhaustion and fright. He'd bashed in the heads of several undead back there, remembering the unpleasant sensations, remembering each decomposing face just before the bat hammered down.

After a minute of driving, Gus spotted an empty alley where the snow was, surprisingly, mostly gone. There he parked the van. Removed his helmet. And immediately reached over and grabbed the bottle of Bacardi. A third of that went down, and only because he had to stop for breath.

At which point he sized up the bottle and saw how much he'd just downed without pause.

"Christ," he growled, wiping at his face.

Then he fumbled for the lock, feeling the oncoming eruption. He popped open the door in time to puke into the street. It was mostly white mush, the breakfast his stomach had been working on before being hosed down with rum. Red eyed and dripping, Gus took another dose and swished it around before spitting everything out. Memories of the zombie cop struck him, and his breath hitched in his throat. He wiped his face before checking on his surroundings.

Still empty. But it wouldn't be that way for long.

The rum helped, tipping the scales back in his favour, bringing him back from nearly losing it in those last few minutes at the store. The cop's staring face and that fat caterpillar of a hanging lip.

Gus drank some more then put the bottle away.

A moment of silence, where he gripped the steering wheel and gazed off into space. No question. He was getting his alcoholic's badge of honor if he lived through this.

The loose goods behind him got his attention then. Half of everything he'd taken from the EGA was on the floor, rattling around with every brake, bump and turn. He'd eventually have to store it away in the bins. Get it all out from underfoot. But then the police officer was in his head again, how he'd shot the thing through the chest, that burst of black sludge flying from the dead man's back. It was dead. Months dead. But the thing was probably already on the prowl again, searching for a person-shaped pizza pocket.

"Not drunk enough for this shit," Gus croaked, his despair leaking through. "Never be drunk enough for this."

But then he clamped down on that shit, and clamped down hard. He wiped his eyes, his nose and mouth. The day wasn't done yet, and he was in the big city. He didn't have near a full rig of goods, but he'd made a start. The EGA would be swarming with dead people now, however, but he felt good. Hell, he felt *charged*. Charged enough to look for another one. Fuck the zombies. Fuck the snow. And fuck the maze that was Annapolis.

Then he realized where he was. Recognized the alley.

"Holy shit," Gus whispered.

Whether it was chance or luck or just blindly following his nose, he had wound up in a part of town not five minutes from his apartment building. A ten-minute drive in traffic, but probably longer in a winter's worth of unchecked snowfall, melting or not. Still, he'd gotten this far, and the rum was kicking into overdrive…

You only came for the groceries, his brain said. *Just the groceries.*

"Yeah, but I'm right *here*," Gus said, and that was that. He'd been wanting to get home, his real home, for so long, to be so close and simply *leave* it? With all his *clothes* there? Just waiting?

No way.

Powered by rum and whiskey, he shoved the horrors of the EGA behind him.

And just a little after twelve noon, he rolled up to his apartment building and circled it twice.

37

Four Brownfield Heights (which Toby referred to as "bunghole delights") was the second building on the left. It stood on a nine square grid apartment complex compound, where each building was separated by small parking lots. There were taller buildings the next row over, but Gus's home was on the third floor of a twelve-unit building. His place was the smaller, two-bedroom affair, but for three hundred bucks more, he could upgrade to the larger, more family-oriented nest.

Nest.

Gus leaned over his steering wheel and sized up the front of the building. Nest indeed.

Opaque windows disclosed nothing of what lurked inside. The main entrance doors were smashed and partially opened by snow and junk covered by snow. There were no zombies around, nor any sign of them. Cars remained in their designated parking spots, underneath thick mantles of soggy powder. When he circled the place, he could go around his building and two others beside it. Snow prevented him from reaching the others, and he had no desire to hoof it through the higher drifts. No footprints marred the snow around his building, but the van's tires spun at times, causing Gus to proceed at a crawl. The lack of zombies convinced him that, if anything, the tenants—his *neighbors*—were either dead, undead and frozen somewhere, or undead and still inside their apartments.

He remembered when Toby was alive, when they were in the suburbs looking for the police. All the houses and the broken windows. Didn't matter if a zombie couldn't open a door, some of them were strong enough to go through the front window. And they did. Maybe even headfirst.

Gus checked his blind spot before turning around. His tires spun on hidden patches of ice, but he got over them, and positioned the van in front of the entrance.

He reached for the Bacardi. A quarter of the bottle gone. Did he really drink all that? Christ almighty. The lid came off in a swirl and he drank more, cringing in between. Then he put the rum away and got up, a little unsteady. He stopped at the rear doors, ready yet far from raring to go. It would be dark in there, but he lowered the visor anyway. His hands didn't shake as he reloaded the shotgun or slung the bat across his shoulders.

One final breath and he opened the doors.

The hinges creaked again in a sick bullfrog *yarp*. Gus pursed his lips in annoyance and slowly lowered himself, for fear of hitting a patch of hidden ice and wiping out. His footing seemed firm, so he checked his flanks and entered the apartment building. Past the snow, the lobby was a mess. Gus flicked his visor up, then down, confirming the dried blood on the walls and floor, where it mixed with the snow melt. Rugs had soaked up their fill, making every step as wet and spongy as an oversaturated moss. Many of the posters and notices tacked to the bulletin boards had been ripped down. The single sofa in the lobby, just past the two elevators, remained intact. There was no security desk, so the elevators, one regular, one freight, were on the right, side by side.

Gus stopped, considered one elevator, considered the noise factor, and opted for the stairs. Sensors activated the lighting when he stepped inside the stairwell. Not a gimp in sight. The enclosed space smelled, however. A nasty, ruptured abscess of a stink that the helmet could not keep at bay. Gus kept the door open, not wanting it to close, and that little bit of motion almost landed him on his face. The rum reinforcements had caught up with him. He was plastered. Pickled. Humming along on Caribbean sunshine and not worried in the least.

He forced himself to focus as the door closed behind him. The lighting system lit up the walls as he hiked to each landing. Three floors up and Gus felt the strain in his legs, having only used the stairs maybe twice in the whole time living here. A power nap was in his future when he got home. One great big snooze that would take him over into the next afternoon. That would be his reward.

Third floor door and he held his breath, to better hear. Nothing, so he let his breath out and pulled the door open.

Into the breach he went.

It smelled better than the stairwell, at least. Beige hallway. Funky red carpet with little blue lightning bolts patterned on it. Grey light came through a window at the end of the corridor, creating a dusty-yet-frosty feel of disuse over the whole empty area. He didn't really see many of the other tenants to begin with, but he knew his neighbors. Now, however, he didn't *want* to see his neighbors. Their doors were closed, so that was fine.

His however…

He passed the elevator doors and went to his… which was locked.

Fuckin' *'course* it was locked. He had the keys back at the house. Wasn't like he was making this shit up on the fly. Things were going just *swell* up to now. Gus rattled the knob again, confirming what he knew the first time.

"Great," he whispered, mindful of the silence. That got him smiling. The other two doors were shut, but he was still worried about disturbing the neighbors.

Still, if anyone was alive, they were behind closed doors.

Gus eyed his doorknob. There was a sliding lock and a chain on the inside as well, but they were only used when he was inside.

"Fuck it," he said, and stepped back.

He brought up the shotgun and blew off the knob in a peppery burst of fragments. The knob bounced off the floor while Gus put a boot to the door, flinging it open. A muscle behind his thigh tightened in pain, warning him not to do that again.

He entered the apartment and stopped, trying to pinch his nose and realizing his visor was down. The apartment reeked. Worse than the stairwell. That was one thing he was starting to realize—dead people stunk. They stunk bad. And the lack of ventilation caused that dead ass stink to simply hang and wait for someone to walk into it, to suck it down. It was so bad, in fact, his eyes became a touch weepy, bringing up the idea of disinfecting his sinuses with some whiskey. Taking the brunt of those daisy killer fumes polluting the apartment, Gus checked out the place through watering eyes.

Umbrella holder. Open closet filled with coats and an orderly assortment of footwear. A picture of a Mediterranean harbor, which was quite nice and momentarily distracted him from the main living room which had a sound bar hooked up to the television, as well as plush furniture. There was also a fine-looking coffee table with a pile of magazines and a remote control. Several withered flowers were arranged near windows, suggesting more than a passing interest in the hobby.

All the while, Gus's mind went blank… until finally asking, in a revving of neurons, when did he get all this stuff?

Which caused him to check the door again.

"The fuck..." he muttered, searching for a number. There was no number, but he was in *his* end of the hall.

"Don't tell me..." Gus looked back into the apartment. He was on the wrong *floor*. He inspected the carpet once more, which remained red with little blue lightning bolts going through it. That wasn't right. Wasn't the carpet on his floor *blue* with little *red* lightning bolts?

"God—"

The zombie shuffled out from the dark bedroom, its decomposing carcass pushing that sickening wall of stink at Gus. Its blackened feet dragged across the carpet, quick enough to keep the thing reanimated on static electricity alone. The zombie was an older man, wearing a grey cardigan and foul red pajama bottoms. The cords in his neck were so pronounced one could probably pluck out a harpsicord tune. He wore dentures, evidently, because there wasn't a single tooth in his mouth as he repeatedly chewed on that loathsome air.

The thing charged in that whispery barefoot shuffle, startling Gus.

But only for a second.

The shotgun blast shook the walls. The zombie flew back and over the coffee table, its lower legs striking the wooden edge. It landed heavily between the sofa furniture, its spine awkwardly bent, its midsection resembling a wet hole of inky tubing. Congealed goop splattered the upholstery.

Gus took two steps and aimed for the head. The deadhead gripped the nearby couch just before he fired, the shotgun kicking hard against his shoulder. The head exploded and the face disappeared, dousing the carpet in a thick rancid pulp.

Everything slowed then, and Gus staggered back until he hit a wall. His breathing raced, the rum's effect diminished. The dead thing didn't move, so Gus eventually lowered the weapon. The banging in his temples, however, was something else.

Nightmares, he thought. *Gonna have nightmares tonight. Booze or no booze.*

Then he realized the banging in his temples *wasn't* his temples.

The noise drew him to the corridor, where the pounding was loudest, coming from the two other doors. The gunshots had roused whoever lived inside those apartments, and they were attempting to come through. That hammering was stunning, furious and frightening.

Gus waited, aiming down the hall, but after a few seconds it became clear they couldn't get out.

And he wasn't going to bother going in. He wasn't even on his floor.

The apartment he'd just invaded, however, got his attention. Ignoring the commotion from the other apartments, he went back inside, trying hard not to look at that appalling mess in the middle of the living room. The place still stunk and was getting worse. He remembered the face just before he destroyed it, and thought maybe, *maybe* he knew the guy.

Randall. Or Rundale. Something like that. Randall (or Rundale) lived by himself, which meant the apartment was empty. Not dropping his guard, Gus went for the kitchen. The refrigerator was one of those big stainless-steel models, with two doors one could open up top and a pull-out freezer below. Gus opened the fridge and immediately slammed it shut, getting both a whiff and peek of the alien mold infesting the plastic interior.

The cupboards were better. An assortment of dried food lay within, canned and boxed. Flour and sugar, cookies. Sauces. There wasn't a lot. Apparently Old whasisface didn't stock up like regular folks did, but there was enough to fill a box.

"I'll be back," Gus informed the contents of the cupboard and left the apartment.

The pounding on the doors continued as he left the floor and rose another level. There were no numbers for some stupid reason, so he figured he was either on the third or the fourth, with the roof right over him. He opened the door and listened, immediately hearing footsteps on the carpet. Footsteps that hastened.

Gus hesitated—just as a tall zombie lurched into sight and reached for him. Gus blasted the thing, slamming it off the wall in a smear and spatter of sludge and wrecked gyprock. The zombie fell and Gus advanced. Only to see a frightening *female* zombie, wearing pink bunny pajamas, speed walk towards him. She had no eyes, and her yawning mouth gleamed with stained dentures. Gus shot her through the middle, the force bouncing her off a wall. The taller zombie croaked nonsense and rolled himself onto his ruined stomach, his arms reaching as if not quite understanding what had happened to him. Gus finished him off with a blast to the head, whereupon he worked the shotgun and sent the spent cartilage flying onto blue carpet with red lightning bolts.

His floor. Or at least he thought it was his floor.

The woman sat up, her bunny PJs tore asunder, the material soaked in tar and her black ribs visible and drooping.

Gus shot her through the face, flattening her in a blink.

All was silent then, but his stomach fluttered with sickness.

"Oh shit." He sized up the two kills. "Oh Jesus. Oh…"

He stepped over to the male gimp, leaning as if staring off a high cliff. His stomach lurched a little more in recognizing the big zombie.

Allen Wolack. His third-floor neighbor. Which made the woman… Gus didn't need to check her out. The bunny PJs gave her away. That was Terri Russell. Terri was a dental assistant while Allen was an unemployed plumber who would do work under the table.

"The shit I pulled outta this guy's shower drain, Gus," Allen would delight in telling him. "Enough to make a fur coat puke. I swear. Must've been about twenty years' worth of pubic hair clogging that thing."

Terri was a sweet lady, too. Always good to have a short conversation in the hallway that never felt forced. Always genuine. Loved to bake cookies. Loved to share, and Gus was right there when he did.

And he'd shot them both.

Or what used to be them.

Nothing else greeted him. In fact, both Allen's and Terri's doors were open, allowing their diseased persons free roam over the whole floor. Gus's place was the only one closed.

"Sorry Terri," he whispered. "Sorry Allen… sorry."

He backed away from the pair. His door was locked, and his shotgun was empty, so Gus took a minute to thumb red shells into the weapon.

"Just shot my neighbors," he said, his voice breaking. "Shot my fucking neighbors. And they were good people."

With a moan, he brought the gun barrel up, to rest against his forehead. He'd hadn't known them for a long time, but in the few years that he did know them, he liked them very much. And he'd shot them. *Not them*, he told himself. They weren't the people he'd known, but their reanimated shells.

They were already dead, his mind told him, taking his side for once.

Or were they? said another part of him, twisting him with guilt.

"They were," Gus said softly, and aimed at his door. "I saw their faces."

He fired, the door shuddering, the inner lock slumping to hang from the hole. Gus pushed it open with his shoulder. Cold, stale air reached him, just enough to let him know he hadn't been living there for a long time. With a last look at the corridor, he entered his home.

The place remained the same. Worn couch and different color recliner, both picked up at a used furniture shop and both great deals. The coffee table had candles spread around its outer ring, and a three-piece stack of cheap coasters. Right across the way was a midsized television perched on a wooden entertainment center, another bargain from the second-hand shop. An old fashion DVD and Blu Ray player sat on one of the shelves there, as well as his toonie collection in a large Blue Rush coffee can.

It wasn't quality stuff, but it was comfortable, paid for with good money earned by doing honest work, and it was Gus's home. Everything was untouched since that fateful night when he was planning on heading over to Tammy's place, to take care of her while she dealt with her flu. He would have been there right when she changed, too, if it hadn't been for Benny calling him up with the Mollymart job. A powerful surge of sadness gripped him then. He missed Tammy. And, as much as a pain in the peehole Benny could be, he missed his old friend and boss, too. He missed them all. Everything. The way it all was…

Be miserable later. Not here.

He hauled his coffee table across and placed it before the closed doorway. The zombies were heedless of such obstacles, so he'd hear one if it tried to come through. In theory, anyway.

His bedroom. Used furniture again. He had the cash to buy new, if it was on sale, but didn't see the need. The stuff he had was fine. A twin-sized bed covered in light sheets and blankets and a mattress in need of its yearly flip. Bedside tables, with a lamp on his side.

Everything the way he'd left it.

Gus went to the open closet, hauled out a stiff suitcase and opened it.

Clothing that fit! Thank you, Jesus, he thought as he packed.

He rolled the suitcase back into the living room. He had things in the bathroom: toothbrush, towels, and what not, but he'd taken replacements back at the house. There was food, and he would take a peek at what was in the place before leaving.

First and foremost, he needed to get his suitcase back to the van. He might even go for a change of clothing right there.

Gus reached the entrance and peeked out into the corridor. Terri and Allen lay on the floor, the smell fouling the air even more. Gus pulled aside the coffee table and door and rolled the suitcase out to the stairwell. After a quick sound check for possible pursuit, he continued down the steps. The heavy suitcase banged off the first step, and a pissed-off Gus hoisted it clear of the rest.

Lobby area, and not a soul in sight. The van was right there, ready and waiting. Little wheels spinning hard enough to fly loose, Gus hauled his suitcase across the floor. His spine creaked and popped but held as he hefted the thing up and shoved it deep into the rear. Then, catching his breath while checking on the coast, Gus went back inside the building.

He returned to his apartment and went straight for the kitchen. He didn't keep a lot of things on hand—didn't have the space for it, really—but his new place had all the space he needed and more. He located the stash of recyclable cloth bags and shook out the first one. The fridge stunk when he opened it, so he slammed it shut and focused on everything else. Hamburger helper. Meatballs and gravy. Chunky soup. Pasta. Cereal. Sugary drink mix. Pens and paper. Scissors. Bandages even.

When he filled six bags, he paused and realized he had the shotgun to carry.

It was awkward, at times painful, with his grip failing enough that he frequently stopped, but he got those bags back to the van. He dumped everything into a bin and, when he was done, stuffed the smaller bags into the duffel bag.

Two swallows of whiskey and a half a bottle of water later, and he went back into the apartment building.

Terri and Allen were dead and gone, but Gus took whatever preserved food they had in their apartments. They didn't have a lot, but he got it all into the duffel bag and carried it, two-fisted, back down to the van. Gus was a little disappointed in the lack of alcohol, as neither one of his neighbors had any in their kitchens. They were both readers, and Terri actually had a collection of paperbacks—military action, crime thrillers, and horror, with the odd auto-biography thrown in there. Allen was more into health, self-help and personal development, which Gus figured would have been more of Terri's thing. Allen did have a nice mountain bike, but Gus left that. Allen also had a wooden baseball bat with an unreadable scrawl across the barrel. Gus left that as well. There was money—Allen had about sixty dollars in green bills on his bedroom dresser, but Gus ignored it.

Back in the van and nearing one thirty, he finished off his water, left the booze, and hiked back into the apartment building.

There were other units to explore.

Gus once again ascended, taking the stairwell, and stopped at what he counted as the second floor. How he fucked that up the first time was beyond him. He eased onto the floor, barely making a noise on the red carpet with the blue lightning bolts. The pounding on the doors had stopped for the time being.

They would start again.

Gus returned to Randall's (or Rundale's) apartment, ignored the sprawled-out corpse, and went into the kitchen. Everything he could scavenge went into the bag, including an assortment of multi-vitamins for people over fifty and a huge bottle of powdered fibre and stool softener.

He got everything downstairs and into the van.

Time, as sure as God was his witness, he felt the time ticking away. One great big countdown to impending doom. Nothing moved on the parking lots, however. Nothing lurked in between the cars and the snow. Nothing could be heard.

Gus packed everything away as quickly as possible and headed back inside.

The next apartment on the same floor was occupied, belonging to a married couple called the Swiss-Morgans-Alfred-Buttons and their teenage son. After blasting the doorknob away and entering, however, he discovered only the Swiss Buttons (as Gus liked to shorten) were home but not the son. Which was just as well. He emptied the shotgun into the two apartment dwellers, knocking them off their feet. Using the bat didn't enter his mind, and he was such a lousy shot, he felt he needed the practice. Once it was over and done with, his chest felt tight, and his shoulder ached from the kick of the wooden stock.

A quick search turned up more non-perishable food, but no booze. Not a full haul, but enough to fill a couple of bags. A flat of water in plastic bottles, with only a handful gone. A case and a half of orange soda. Everything he could scrounge he took, then returned to the van.

The third apartment belonged to the Mattbrooks and as before, Gus shot the door knob off. The Mattbrooks, Cybil and Ernie, were pressed up against the door, preventing him from getting inside while struggling to reach their very much-wanted visitor.

Gus aimed through the initial hole he'd made and fired, blowing both zombies away. He made a mess upon entering, missing both heads as the Mattbrooks, the goddamn Mattbrooks, were a little more well-preserved than the others, and a little more agile. They were *next level* fast, compared to Randall (or Rundale). Gus blew away shoulders and chests, missing the heads entirely and spraying the inner hall in a filthy tar of zombified tissue. In the end, he put aside the shotgun, girded his loins and returned those two reanimated corpses to the earth, cringing at each bone-crunching connection of the bat.

When he was done, a fully sloshed Gus eyed the gruesome scene inside the apartment. If it wasn't for the happy juice in his system, he might've dropped into a corner somewhere and blubbered snot until he lost his mind. Numb as he was, however, he did no such thing, but the sight of all that carnage, and the smell, from two people no less, threatened to turn his stomach.

"I don't need anymore," Gus finally said, shaking his head. "No need to go in there."

But he did. After a quick reloading, he stepped over the bodies as if threading his way through a minefield. Mrs. Mattbrooks— Cybil—glared at him, her head concaved and snarling, her pallid skin and hair spattered with gore. Mr. Mattbrook—Ernie—was even worse, but he had the murderous look of a husband whose wife's dignity had been insulted.

He retrieved more food, including three packages of chocolate and vanilla wafers. The sight of those cookies lifted his spirits. Only for a minute, however, as there were no real spirits of any kind. Not even a single beer.

"The fuck's going on?" Gus muttered after going through the kitchen cupboards. "Doesn't anyone get *shitfaced* anymore?"

Another two bags of goods, which he crammed into the duffel bag. Feeling it lopsided, he struggled back into the hallway, knowing he'd have to clean his boots off in some snow when he got back outside. He hadn't reached his full capacity yet, and the day was getting on, so with a long contemplative (and inebriated) look upstairs, he started climbing steps.

"Hate you," he panted, with each step. "Hate. You. Every fuckin' one."

It was a good thing he'd got some time in shoveling snow. If he'd tackled all of this without that bit of endurance training, he was certain he would've dropped dead long ago.

Breathing hard all the way, he reached the fourth floor.

The duffel bag dropped to the concrete landing, his hand stinging from the load. And if he felt the sting, damn well sure it would've hurt more if he were sober. He pulled opened the door to the fourth floor and a long grey arm shot out for his face, fingers smacking him upside the head and driving it back. Gus slammed against the wall as the gimp—a decomposing Martin Steady, pushed into the stairwell wearing only his pajama bottoms. Putrid substance dripped from the deadhead's face, his eyes a waxy black. The dead thing tackled Gus and sunk stained teeth into his padded neck. Martin bit— and continued biting—until Gus shoved him to the floor.

A pissed off Martin-thing rose to a crouch, all element of surprise gone. He faced Gus and got his filth-soaked head ripped from his shoulders in a single shotgun blast.

Boom.

If Gus thought firing the weapon in an apartment was loud, he'd just been corrected. Shooting the shotgun in the stairwell, in the structure's superior acoustics, buckled him at the knees. In the aftermath of that short-but-extreme struggle, the stairwell door closed with barely a click.

Grunting, groaning, shivering and maybe even having peed himself just a little, Gus straightened. He worked the pump and stood back from the Martin-thing. Young Martin had been a linesman working for the local power company, and beyond that, Gus barely knew him.

"Fuck it," he announced at the closed door. "I'm done. I am *done*. I'll fuckin' come back tomorrow. Or Saturday. Hear me? You undead fuckers. I'm getting the unsweetened fudge butter outta Dodge."

Then he realized the dead Martin Steady had landed on the duffel bag.

"Goddamnit, Martin."

Gus bent over and grabbed an arm. He pried Martin's carcass off the duffel bag, into which he quickly shone a light.

"If you crushed my fuckin' wafers…"

He reached in and felt around for the cookies, found them and frowned. "God *damnit*, Martin."

Not pleased in the least, Gus straightened and waved a hand. "Adios mutton-chops. I'm fuckin' done here."

Smelling zombie shit from somewhere, Gus descended, hoping that whatever it was could be cleaned off in the snow.

Perhaps it was the smell that had distracted him.

Perhaps it was the unexpected tussle to the death with sneaky zombie fuck Martin Steady.

Or maybe it was the booze tipping his senses a little too much in the wrong direction.

Whatever the reason, when Gus walked out into the main floor lobby, the last thing he saw, that he *expected*, really, was the swing of a bat.

Just before it crashed into his head.

38

"Jesus, you trying to take his head off or something?" said a voice.

"Fuck you care if I do?" another voice answered.

"Yeah, fuck you care?" a woman pitched in.

"Well," the first voice reasoned, "for one, *that* ain't a zombie. That's a person."

Me, Gus thought, head rolling on the floor, still in stunned, galaxy spiraling wonderment as to what had happened. Shadows gathered overhead, but damn if he could see details—could *process* details. The faces he saw were as surreal as those in a fleeting, waking dream.

"I can see that," stated by the second voice—the home-run swinger.

"Back the fuck off, Reggie," warned a new fourth voice.

"You back the fuck off, *Jamie*," Reggie, the home run swinger, challenged. "Don't think I don't see what you're doing. I *know* what you're doing."

"Yeah, what's that?" Jamie dared back.

"Shut the fuck up," said the first voice. "All of you. Christ, it's bad enough you're at each other's throats when I'm gone. Figured bringing you along as a team would do everyone some good, but I can see I was wrong."

"You mean so you could keep an eye on us," the woman said.

"Yeah, Al," Reggie added. "You're gonna have to be better than that."

"Look," Al said. "I said I believed you. Okay? Helen?"

"You believe that rat there more than us?" Helen asked back. "And Jamie, for the record, you were there. I didn't *see* you do that shit, but I know you did. We know you did him. But you fucked up. Always five or six clues left behind at a crime scene."

"I think," spoke the one called Jamie, "Angry *Reg* there showed his hand when he clobbered Mister Motorcycle Helmet there."

"Oh you treacherous piece of shit," Reggie said, the heat rising in his voice.

"Knock it off," Al said in a low tone. "Zombies got Bobby. That was it."

"Zombies didn't get Bobby, man." Helen said. "That guy right there did him in and made it *look* like zombies."

"You want to aim that thing, you aim it at him," Reggie added.

"See," Jamie said. "What did I tell you, Al? They got it in for me."

"Shut up Jamie. And both of you shut up, too. Jesus Christ. I thought this was behind us this morning."

"Yeah, well," Helen said. "It's a long ride into town."

"Plenty of time to get your story straight," Reggie accused.

"Fuck you," Jamie warned.

As loopy as Gus was, sprawled out as he was, even he could recognize the unmistakable pause just before extreme violence.

"All right," Al stated in a serious voice. "Helen, you take that shotgun. Slow. And don't challenge me on this. Now, this is what we're gonna do…"

Oh shit, Gus thought, … then realized he might've said that out loud, because everything got quiet.

"You're trusting me with a shotgun?" Helen asked.

"I do," Al answered. "So take that for something. We're going *back* to the house. We're *all* going back to the house. You ride with Deb, in this guy's van."

Gus realized they were talking about *his* van, and tried to say something.

"You taking their side, Al?" Jamie asked, sounding betrayed.

"There *are* no fucking sides, Jamie," Al spat. "We either are, or we are not. Bobby's dead, all right? The morning's moving too fast for me. I got some thinking in on the way over here but it ain't enough. I'm gonna do some *more* thinking on the way back. But we'll get to the bottom of this at home base. Understand? Out here in the wild ain't the place to hold court. Okay? Three of us will go in our ride, and you'll drive. That way I can keep an eye on you and on you."

That last you was directed at Reggie, Gus suspected, and he tried to say something. Nothing happened, but his hand actually rose.

"He's coming around," Helen said.

"Wants to say something," Jamie added.

"Fuck me," Al said. "I don't have time to worry about this guy."

"So what are you gonna do with him?" Helen asked. "You gonna leave him alone with Jamie over there?"

Jamie didn't comment on that, but Gus felt even more tension on the air.

"Leave him," Al said. "He's got his bat. He'll do fine."

"Do fine?" Reggie asked doubtfully. "We're in the fucking city here, Al. I say we take him along."

"We're not fucking taking him along. Not this time. Not after you clocked him upside the head."

"You think taking his ride and leaving him here will win him over?" Reggie asked.

"He'll do fine. Look at him."

"Yeah, sure."

"Button that shit. I'm running out of patience here. He's inconvenienced for the day but look at him. All that leather. Shit. Why didn't any of you fucking geniuses think of that? You're the experts."

"Never said we were experts," Helen said. "Just watched the shows, is all."

"Yeah, well, the *shows* got it wrong," Al said, barely holding back a yell. "Get moving. And Reggie, you watch him. Jamie? I got the keys right here, so you be on your best behaviour. We'll settle this once and for all back at the house. Now get going."

"Muh," Gus said, weakly, waving a hand.

A bearded face loomed over him. "You're coming around. That's a good helmet you got on there. Listen. Thanks for the van. And all the shit. We're loaded up ourselves, so you saved us a lot of work. Look. You still got your bat there, so you'll do fine. Just hunker down and take your shot when you can." The face glanced towards the main entrance. "I can't take you along. Not now. Don't know you. You could be another fuckin' Jamie for all I know. Trust is a little hard to come by right now, which doesn't help either one of us in the least.

"You see what I'm saying here? Give me the day to sort through some shit, okay? Things are a little tense in our group. Someone got killed and there's some clarifying needing to be done. Some follow up questions that need answering. Seriously, I'm doing you a favor. Well, after you get past us stealing your van. Look. Hunker down here and I'll do a drive by in the morning, rain or shine. See if you're still here. Just… just be waiting in the lobby here. If you wanna talk. I just hope you're not another potential nutjob like the one I got on my hands right now. Swear to fuck. These days? Feels like I'm living in an old John Carpenter movie."

"Muh," Gus tried again, but then everything was spinning, and he dropped his head and felt it thump on the floor tiles.

"Tomorrow, then," Al said with a nod.

Then he was gone—or, rather, Gus blacked out.

The gunshots brought him back.

He rolled over onto his stomach and let his head hang between his shoulders. Seconds later, he sat up and pulled the helmet off his head. The lobby couch was right there, so he crawled over and hoisted himself up onto it. His hand probed the right side of his head. The helmet saved him, but the force had still knocked him for a loop. Without the helmet, he would've been dead. As it was, if he remembered correctly, someone had been standing over him, a lot of people, really, but in the end just the one. Some guy who said he'd be by in the morning.

Rain or shine.

There was no swelling, thank you Jesus, but he had one bastard of a headache. He stood, felt a swoon coming on, and sat back down. His stomach relaxed, his vision cleared, and things smoothed out.

Tried to stand again.

And this time, he didn't get the faints, didn't get dizzy. He groaned and vacillated on whether to pick up his helmet, which was a long way down. He did so anyway, without passing out, so that was a good sign. But the headache remained.

Concussion, he figured. *Got a concussion. Great.*

On top of everything else, a concussion was exactly what he needed. What day didn't get off on the right foot without a concussion? It was right up there with breakfast. But then he realized it wasn't morning. And that a lot of daylight was leaking into the lobby.

"Awww fuck," Gus blurted. He wobbled to the entrance, his helmet slapping off his thigh.

His van was gone.

Head pulsating, Gus stood in the doorway, suffering, grimacing, and staring out at the melting winter cityscape. One set of slushy tire tracks was his, parked right up in front of the building, but there was a second set, stopped in front of his van in a T formation. Those tracks did a wide loop and showed both vehicles driving away, their trails plain to see in the snow.

"But…" Gus wailed, staring at how the tracks bled off into the empty distance of the street. "I mean… my… you can't… awww *fuck*."

That last frustrated expletive caused his head to hurt, so he pressed a hand over the point of impact.

A gunshot echoed through the apartment grid, causing Gus to turn in that direction like an old man. Then another. Then… screams.

That confused him, and his bat-clubbed brain wasn't allowing any degree of deep thought at the moment. He started walking between the slushy tire tracks, following them, hearing those screams petering out. The snow cushioned his footfalls and he left wet prints behind him. Clouds had moved in while he was going through the apartments, and though it seemed brighter outside the lobby, Gus realized that these clouds were dire, and darkened the land.

He wobbled in the tire tracks, leaving his own slushy prints. Both sets of tracks deviated off the route, heading in a direction that didn't mean anything to him, except that they were turning off the road with less snow and more houses.

An intersection lay ahead, where both vehicles had gone through and turned right, past a line of mailboxes, toward what Gus knew was a long street of homes. A row of bare elm trees lined the road's edge. He decided on a shortcut and the slush grew into knee high snowbanks as he cut behind an apartment building and trudged over a snowy parking lot, going nearly to his thighs at times. *Dangerous,* he thought. *This is dangerous,* but was unable to pinpoint why, only that he had to stay out of sight. He moved between cars, where the snow wasn't so deep.

At the building's corner, Gus could see the fenced backyard of the next house over, a monster of a two-story Cape Cod with a steep roof, high dormers, and siding all painted a shitty shade of forest green. He plodded across a snowy open space of no more than thirty feet, laboring through much deeper drifts. He moved at an angle, aiming for the front of the house and the corner there. Through the row of trees lining the street, the tire tracks continued on, straight up the middle.

Gus stopped at the corner of the Cape Cod and rested there for a couple of seconds before taking a peek.

There, not quite a soccer field away, over the roofs of buried traffic and through snow covered porch furniture, were two vans, one of which he thought was his. The other one had plowed into one of the many elms lining the sidewalk and had clearly lost that battle. He couldn't see much more than that, because of all the pedestrians crowded around the vehicles. Even as he watched, *more* people were lurching out from between the houses and down the far street, drawn to the accident. Dozens of them walked out from between homes, some of them actually falling as others pushed by, joining the already-impressive demonstration around the rigs.

But that wasn't the worst of it.

Advancing from the far end of the street, just barely seen (and he had to blink and wipe his eyes to make sure), was another mob. An indistinct wall creeping, *bubbling*, towards the stricken vans.

Zombies. Deadheads. Gimps.

Holy shit.

Gus yanked himself behind the corner and panicked, pressed up against foundation as if he alone were holding up the structure. He remembered his helmet, realized he was carrying the damn thing, and pulled it on—which resulted in a dinner bell ringing around both ears. Once secured, he flipped up the visor and scooted the bat free.

The vans. Maybe the lead one skidded into the tree. Maybe those zombies had been in the road and the drivers had thought to plow through. Maybe something else had happened. In any case, something had gone wrong, resulting in one rig slamming into a tree. The others stopped to help, or maybe, maybe it was deep snow and the vans got stuck, and their attempts to get clear attracted the zombies.

Peripheral movement attracted his eye. There, oozing into the street, was a single zombie, shuffling along in the tire tracks left in the snow. Walking in those tracks would help anyone else, but the undead didn't appear to know they existed. It stared ahead, at the commotion around the vans.

Another deadhead appeared behind that lead zombie, the ripped remains of a green shirt hanging off a chest clawed open to the gore-caked ribs. Another two walking corpses appeared right behind the dead man.

The sight of them unfroze Gus, who remembered he was very much out in the open. He watched them, ready to run if detected, and slowly inched his way along the wall, towards the fenced off backyard. Three other rotten bodies waltzed into sight, glimpsed just as Gus struggled through the melting snow and instinctively checked his flank.

His guts went cold.

Risen and mobile, they materialized all around him, moving between houses and buildings, drawn to the two vans and anything else in between. A terrible force of tattered shadows and permanently slouched over corpses, wading through the mounds of powder. All searching for a slab of warm, blood-saturated muscle to claw apart and feast on.

Sooner or later, they would notice him, if they hadn't already.

Gus increased his pace, keeping just ahead of that angle, where the zombies would step into view and perhaps notice him. His feet punched into the white depths and sucked at his legs with every frantic step. His gloved hand ran over the fence, rubbing his fingers. The planks were chin high and fitted tight together, allowing near perfect privacy. He reached the far corner and turned it, spotting a closed gate in the barrier.

One horrific individual, jeans and shirt painted in dried blood, forged through the drifts with chilling stop-motion animation some thirty feet away. Like them all, it was marching for the wreckage, but this one stiffly swaggered into an open back yard filled with snow.

And in plain view of Gus.

If the thing turned its head.

Pressed against the fence and forcing his way along, ripping up a small white surf with each step, Gus reached the gate. He pawed at the latch. Somewhere beyond the house, a slab of heavy-handed meat slapped a metal shell, demanding entry.

And for whatever reason, the bloodied zombie at two o' clock halted, as if seized by a bear trap.

Gus watched the dead bastard, distantly aware of his own frantic breathing. He continued working on the latch. Up and pulled. Then down. Then side to side.

The zombie turned in his direction, slow and ponderous, as if its entire spine was a sloppy fusion of bone and sinew and on the verge of falling apart. A thick wave of platinum hair covered most of its face, except the mouth, which was in full view and open to impossible size.

Gus let out the tiniest of moans and heaved his weight against the gate— which opened all of two inches. Stopped by gathered snow, bracing the portal from the other side.

The zombie's arms lifted, pointing in the living's direction, and one of those arms was missing its entire hand at the wrist. The other hand didn't have any fingers, and that dried-out mitten of meat wore away just a little more of Gus's booze-infused mental armor. Other shapes appeared in the background, lurking at the edges of his sight. Though that handless monstrosity was still thirty feet away, those two stumps shocked him, and any second he expected a shrill zombie scream.

Gus heaved his shoulder against the wood, shoving the thing open a foot. It was a sturdy fence. He squeezed through the gap, his bat scabbard catching on the latch and nearly taking him off his feet. Gus staggered, wheezed in disbelief, and yanked the strap over his head before heaving it outside. He'd get another one.

He elbowed the gate shut and nearly laughed when he saw a sliding bolt lock near the top. He slapped that home and whirled upon the wintry backyard. Wicker furniture held up mounds of snow. Latices were caked white.

Gus hoofed it for that door, his footfalls sinking into deep drifts, each one sounding like muffle gunshots. At times he stumbled and used the bat to keep upright. He stomped over the three backyard steps and across the narrow porch. The doorknob yielded and turned in his grip, but the hinges, on opening, creaked far too loud. Tired and aching, Gus forced himself through with all the stealth he could muster.

Five frosty apparitions could be seen just over the fence, slogging toward the house.

Gus closed the door and put his back against a wall, avoiding windows.

The cold, dusty air of an abandoned house caressed his face.

White kitchen, with a nice little island in the center with a moody dark finish. A set of fine china was on display within a matching brown cabinet. There were bowls upon the counter, as well as a set of large knives in a wooden block. A streak of either flour or sugar was strewn across the floor. There was an archway with a set of swinging doors to his left and a dark hall stretching deeper into the house, the shadows long and dreary in the late afternoon.

Gus checked on his pursuers. The fence stopped them, but their heads bobbed over the top, as if trying to walk through the thing. One had clutched the pointy parts, perhaps trying to climb over or just pull it down. After a few seconds, however, it became clear none of them were getting through. All Gus needed to do was wait until they lost interest or something else drew them away.

The commotion in the street would do just that.

He glanced at the kitchen, his breathing loud in his ears. With effort, he forced himself to hold it, even though the rest of him wasn't on board with that plan.

Nothing moved in the house. Not yet anyway.

Tippy-toeing, or rather heel-stepping, he threaded his way deeper into the house. A den was on his left, along with a set of stairs going up, positioned near the front porch. He continued to a T junction, where one hall went straight all the way to the same front porch. There, the door was curtained, screened, with a mass of zombies parading past.

Not one of them deviated for the house.

Gus let his breath out in a low, satisfied hiss. Mindful of the silence, he carefully stepped back and continued on, following the inner hall to a bedroom, where the foot of the bed could be seen. He noticed two other open doors, one leading to a basement. Gus moved to the basement steps. Check that, and he could relax in the quietest, most secure place in the house. Wait out the flow of zombies marching by the front door and then… well, he'd see. The excitement of the day was catching up to him, however. He wouldn't mind taking a moment to visit the crapper and meditate on everything while moving his considerable bowels.

Tightening his grip on the bat, Gus hesitated, rethought his plans, and instead decided to check out the bedroom, making each step a quiet one. He passed what was a small bathroom, empty and without a shower. It had a toilet, however, a light green porcelain one. There was even water, though the insides of the bowl were streaked with dirt.

As long as you flush, Gus informed the throne, and stepped back out. The bedroom was next.

The two windows in the place had their curtains drawn, darkening the area, making the red satiny décor appear sinister, the material a little too bloodlike. The floor creaked ominously in one place, freezing Gus. He waited for a response but heard nothing, so he continued inside. Clothing for a couple filled the closet. The bed was queen sized, and he lowered himself to his knees, using the bed for balance, and peered underneath.

Nothing.

Rising, knees crackling, Gus stood and exhaled mightily. Downstairs. In the fucking basement. Everyone was down there. That was his bet. Or maybe he'd just find a dead cat. If he was lucky.

Then it hit him.

Perhaps it was getting down on all four to check underneath the bed. Perhaps it was all the excitement during the morning, culminating in being knocked out and having all his shit stolen. Maybe it was the booze or all the zombies moving around outside. Whatever the reason, Gus suddenly had to go, even though he'd already used the crapper back home.

He fought back, however, clenching like he'd never clenched before, and lumbered into the bathroom. A second cramp took him, more powerful than the first.

Oh you bastard, Gus messaged his ass. *You moody asshole. After all we've been through and* now *you need to go?*

A third push for the rear exit nearly caused him to see stars.

And being clunked across the head probably didn't help matters. So without another thought, Gus placed the bat in one corner, behind a lovely stack of two-ply. The business of undoing everything below the waist was a race, however, because with every thing he loosened, his insistent ass pushed harder.

Gus shoved his leather pants to his knees. Then his jeans and his shorts. His guts cramped again in a high-pitched scream of intestinal mutiny, and he practically slammed his buttcheeks down on the toilet seat, completing the connection.

When everything exploded from him.

Gus exhaled, letting everything flow. When the torrent stopped, he took a deep breath, which got everything going a second time. Then a mind blowing third. Then he sat and relaxed, appreciating the moment.

When it was over, he cleaned himself up, stood with everything pooled around his knees, and without a second thought, flushed.

In the stillness of the bathroom, of the *home*, where, outside, reanimated corpses were waiting for a hint of where the living might be hiding, that natural, instinctive, turn and pump of the flush lever sounded like a 747 firing up its considerable jet engines.

And as everything got forcefully shipped out in a muddy whirlpool, Gus's jaw dropped while his balls rose in a counterweight. He stared at the toilet as it sucked everything down and, thankfully, didn't clog.

Unlike the next few minutes of Gus's life.

Which was when he heard the *thump* from upstairs.

Then more thumping, just getting started, really. A slow but steady rotation of bicycle pedals, almost, winding its way across the floor overhead. It came from one end of the house and stopped right above Gus's head, as if losing the scent.

Fuck oh fuck, he thought, and scrambled to pull up his undershorts, jeans, and leather all at once. He did so, but upon a frantic, booze-powered zipping up of his jeans, he nipped his knob. Gus shrieked, a short grunt of tear duct cleansing power, stifled at the last second. He immediately unzipped his tackle, the resulting pain engulfing his penile partner right to the root.

All the while, the thumping continued above, sounding like a drunk person attempting to riverdance in work boots. The noise barely matched the overworked yammering of his own heart. Or the screaming of his wounded manhood. Worse, he discovered he was *bleeding* down there, badly, and one shuddering look at his hand and his knees almost gave away.

Gus whimpered and grabbed a white face cloth. He wrapped the thing around his lad, then did a quick search for something to bind the bandage with. A handful of hair elastics rested on the toilet's flush box. Gus grabbed two and got them on, snapping them around his John Henry. With that secure, but feeling sick and terrified, he finished pulling and zipping up his clothing, then grabbed his bat.

A rolling, tumbling mass bouncing down and off the nearby staircase straightened him. Only a piano would have made more noise, but in this case, seeing how it was so quiet to begin with, it made an unholy racket, complete with a miniature dust cloud rising at the base of the stairs.

Gus slapped down his helmet's visor and waded out of the bathroom towards the porch, where the stairs to the second level began.

Where he stopped halfway, poised, bat raised and ready to smash a mouse if necessary.

An arm flopped into view, the palm up, as if whoever had fallen over the steps had landed on their back. That blue grey flesh was saggy. Doughy. Hairy. Then that arm got pulled in like the two-jointed snake it was and disappeared. There was a rattling of flesh on wood, as something righted itself. Through the beige spindles, a mass flopped upright against the wall. There it skidded, resisting gravity, until it fell over again with a dead man's thud.

Gus hesitated, noticing himself in the inset mirror just underneath the stairs.

That was the second he would later want back.

The zombie doing all the monster-mashing on the second floor pulled itself into the hallway, hauling its mass along on those pudgy arms. It rushed Gus, who backed up with a heartfelt *"Fuck!"* His retreat was a frantic one, and everything in the hallway that could be knocked down was knocked down. And through it all, the zombie rushed forward, held aloft on its elbows, carrying itself in a surprisingly swift crawl.

And if that wasn't horrifying enough, the thing's head—which appeared to be a little old lady—had been plied back. All the way back, so that her skull rested on her upper spine and the sour milk of her eyes, wide and staring, were aimed not at the ceiling but down her nose, locked onto the man in her lair.

Each time she lurched ahead, her hand shot out for one of Gus's feet— who did everything to keep ahead of the spry monster, dodging those fleshy claws and not turning his back.

He banged off a wall, tipped to his left, enough to teeter, and got an even better look of that stretched out expression of horror rushing him.

One of its hands shot out and latched onto his ankle—always the ankles—
—the grip shockingly strong.

Gus was already falling, so he swung the bat on the way down.

And connected, driving the deadhead into the floor. He landed on his side, the thing still clutching his ankle. Those sallow eyes stared at the ceiling as it pulled itself toward Gus. He punched it, creating distance, but the dead lady didn't let go. Somehow, in the narrow confines of the hallway, Gus twisted himself up. The zombie tried biting into his protective kneepads, baring stringy teeth whose roots pushed and popped free of the black gum line.

The zombie continued to bite, however.

Gus shoved the thing away with bat and foot, up against the opposite wall. Then he got a boot to its face, grounding his heel into its lower jaw. Fragments of yellow enamel sprinkled the floor. The zombie released his ankle and flailed at him, swatting his beltline. Gus dropped the bat and grabbed the hand. He plied it back, snapping several fingers. The dead thing thrashed under his boot, perhaps feeling its bones go, but it didn't stop reaching for him. So Gus did the last move available to him—stretching out the arm and doing a boot-stomp to its face.

The first two kicks connected, and the skull crumpled just a bit.

The third kick squashed the face, its slug of a tongue popping forth.

Gus unleased a savage boot stomping then. A horizontal mambo. A fear-injected temper tantrum. And when he stopped, the zombie wasn't moving.

But there was one God-awful mess in the hall.

Struggling to breathe, he grabbed the bat and crawled free of the dripping sludge. A tinkle of breaking glass jerked his head up, whereupon he realized he'd been crawling in the direction of the front porch.

Where at least three zombies were currently knocking on the door. One of them had punched through the glass, its fingertips mashed and dripping.

Gus reversed, double time, halfway back up the hall until he stopped and struggled to his feet. His lower legs were coated in jellified bits that shook and shivered and stuck to his leather. With a glance at the front door (there were twice as many zombies there now) he hurried into the kitchen. A dish cloth hung from the oven door, so he grabbed that and wiped himself down. He tried the taps, but nothing happened, so he chucked the dirty cloth into the sink.

With the hammering intensifying, Gus looked out the window into the backyard.

The zombies there had moved on, perhaps drawn to the commotion at the front of the house.

More glass crashed, drawing him to the hallway.

There, like a giant garden slug with arms, a zombie leaned over the shattered window of the front door and dropped to the floor. Its companions moaned at the landing, their attention on Gus. He retreated as two more attempted to come through.

The one on the floor crawled forward, carrying its carcass over the welcome mat.

Gus went around, into the living room, looked out the window there—where his heart dropped.

Thickening clouds cast a dire, overcast shadow over everything, and the dozens or so zombies deviating from the street and shambling over the Cape Cod's front lawn. A ragged line of them already stood on the porch steps, waiting for their chance to pound on the door.

Movement drew Gus's eye.

Crawling on knees and elbows, the first invader slunk into the room.

Gus clubbed it, dropping the entire unit to the carpet. He nailed it twice more and it ceased moving. A grim moaning rose then, as if the zombies at the door knew one of its numbers, perhaps even a good friend, had perished.

Everything in Gus demanded that he leave, just take his chances and go out the back, to not stop. Thing was, everything he had was in his van, and if he did reach another house, what would stop the risen population of Annapolis from pounding their way inside again? Plus, he had *toilet paper* in his ride. That shit literally didn't get made anymore, and Gus wasn't keen on using his sweat socks when he ran out.

So he smashed out the living room window.

This excited the mob, and even got looks from the ones lining up on the front step.

Gus raked the bat left and right, sending shards flying.

"*Fuck ya!* Ya pack of fucked-up undead *shitheads!* Fuck ya sideways and twice on *Tuesday!*"

And like an audience rushing the stage at a rock concert, they trampled through the snow towards the picture window.

Gus backed away, turned and fled into the kitchen.

He stopped at the back door and regarded the yard. All clear—all the while the front of the house was getting the living shit kicked out of it. Wishing he had something to drink to further fortify himself, Gus whipped that door open.

And slipped and fell down the steps.

He landed on his back, buckled and grimaced, and pulled himself into a sitting position. He hadn't gone ass over tit, but he still landed hard enough to rattle teeth and spine alike. The day was fading, even quicker with the onset of the serious-looking cloud cover. The temperature had also dropped, but Gus didn't think twice on that. He stood, winced, saw steam and tramped through the snow to the backyard gate.

"Anyone out there?" he called. "No?"

He yanked opened the gate. It was indeed clear. Even better, the snow had been flattened. Trampled by the gruesome fivesome once there. Bat in hand, Gus moved outside and sized up the next house over. He stayed low, ran to the corner of the fence, and stepped beyond it.

Dozens of zombies were in the street, the force divided as some headed for the front of the Cape Cod while others were still around the van.

"Hey!" Gus shouted, and clacked the fence with his bat. "Hey! I'm right here, you shitty-assed bastards!"

Some spotted him and immediately stepped away from their groups, arousing interest in the others.

"*Hey!*" Gus roared and grabbed his crotch. "Bite *my bleedin' dick!*"

More of the undead turned for him.

Gus backed up, glanced over his shoulder and saw a handful of stragglers coming from the houses behind him. The way to the next backyard, however, was open.

So he ran.

As best as he could, through snow drifts that reached his knees. Twice his foot got stuck, where he had to lean forward, using his bat for stability, and work his foot free of the icy grip.

"Oh you sonsabitches," Gus yelled, struggling forward. "If I lose a *boot* I'll be *pissed. Pissed* I tell ya."

He reached the backyard of the next house over, which had a much lower fence, and he kept on running, lower legs burning, becoming heavier with every stride. His chest was on the verge of exploding, but he figured he'd simply stop, drop, and croak long before that happened.

Behind him, those taunted few slowly turned the corner of the fence, while those arriving late to the party attempted to cut across the open space.

Gus chugged to the next house over, another Cape Cod, which got him wondering why everyone on this street had a hard-on for Cape Cods.

By the time he cut across the open backyard and reached the far corner, he almost collapsed. His breath came out in angry wheezes, and though it sounded like inarticulate nonsense, he was actually saying *"fuckmegently. Woooofuckmegently."*

Exhausted. He was exhausted. And when he looked around, a wall of zombies pursued him. They struggled through the snowbanks as he'd done, but unlike him, they stumbled and fell, and those behind attempted to walk *over* the fallen.

"Ohnoyoudon't," Gus huffed. *"Fuck*noyoudon't."

That last ejected *fuck* sprayed spit inside his helmet, some of it spattering Gus's upper lip. The dewy moisture surprised him, frankly. He didn't think he had any left.

He lurched around the corner, saw the street, and drew upon the last remaining fumes circulating his empty gas tank. He didn't run but staggered, relying more on mass and momentum than anything else. His breathing was a series of gasless puffing. He buckled down, knowing he'd either get to his van or his heart would simply explode in his chest.

Either way, things looked good.

The van ahead was his, stuck deep in both a snow drift and a log jam of flailing zombies. The other van was on the far side, crashed into the tree, but Gus only had eyes for his beast. The same van that had saved his ass time and time again. The same rig that would save his ass now. If he could reach it.

The snow was beaten down by the undead masses. A few ass clingers lingered around the vehicle, and they came into sight as Gus neared the rear doors.

"Gah!" His feet nearly slipping out from under him as he skidded into a turn, slapping the beast's rump as he staggered along the passenger side.

Ahead of him, a zombie came around the corner.

When it did, Gus knew he didn't have the strength to swing his bat. Hell, he didn't have the strength to even swear at it, which was saying a lot.

He was spent. Done. Over with.

And no sooner did that arisen horror with a leering expression of *wellwell* circle the front of the van—when it tripped in one of the flailing arms of the zombies stuck underneath.

Gus could've laughed. Except to do so probably would mean using the absolute last drop of gas he had.

He clutched at the passenger side door and yanked it open. The zombies pursuing him were getting closer, louder. Gus hauled himself inside, and as he hoisted his boot off the ground, fingers raked the rubber sole.

He plopped down with a boyish squeal, the neck of a bottle digging deep into his ass crack. Ignoring the unexpected probe, he clawed at the door, got a hold of it, and pulled it shut with a slam.

The zombie that had tripped and fallen rose into view, its smiling, rotten face tracking him.

Wild eyed and horrified, Gus ignored it and locked the door. He then awkwardly stretched over the cup holders and locked the driver's door as well. A glance into the rear told him all the shit he'd taken from the apartments was still there. Supplies covered the floor. Also, he blinked twice. Was that his shotgun dumped barrel first into one of the bins? He thought it was.

Gus climbed into the back, hunched over and crashed through everything to reach the rear doors.

Which he locked.

He peered through the glass and saw that his run for the van had not gone unnoticed. All the zombies that had stormed the house were now returning to the stricken vehicle.

Spilling out into the street.

Gus wheezed and stomped back to the bin with the shotgun. Sure enough, it was his weapon, which was curious. He supposed whoever had stolen his rig had their own weapons and regarded his as a backup. A quick look behind the driver's seat revealed his remaining cases of shells as well, so he was armed.

There were dozens of gimps, however. Maybe even a hundred. Far more than he was willing to shoot. Even if he did go on a shooting spree, he'd have to lower a window or open a door. And shooting them would only attract more, so fuck that noise.

He placed the shotgun back where he'd found it. Emergency only. Gus flopped back down behind the wheel. The key fob was in one of the cup holders, which was a win. He started the thing up. Worked the misleading stick until he got Reverse.

And heard the demoralizing spin of tires stuck not only on zombie ass, but ice and snow. That unmistakable sound took all fight out of him, and for a moment, Gus simply sat and stared, hands locked onto the steering wheel, listening to that God-awful whirl and burn of rubber.

Mister Neighborly zombie bashed a hand off the hood, as if demanding service. The expression one of pure evil delight.

Where were those ball-grabbers, anyway? Gus wondered, thinking of the bastards who had robbed him. He looked around. There were plenty of bodies around the crashed van. Some had their heads blown off, others looked like regular zombies. There were a few dressed in winter clothing that were definitely much more recent, *fresher* kills, than the others, not yet risen again.

Gus paid them no further thought. Shit had gone down, and someone had gotten themselves bit or outright killed. Whatever the case, his attention was again taken by Mister Neighborly, smacking the hood on his way around to the driver's side. Each connection quivered the metal. It wasn't a gong the undead dick was hitting, but it had the same effect.

It attracted the rest of them.

Caught in snow and zombies, Gus figured there would be too many coming up from behind him to escape from the rear.

Which meant he was stuck.

Marooned.

All trussed up in a metal box like a goddamn chicken dinner.

He didn't even have the breath to swear on the situation.

Mister Neighborly drifted closer to the driver's side, that decomposing wreckage of a face pressing up against the glass. Gus leaned away because Mister Neighborly, which was an interesting pet name for the undead turd gobbler, smeared his rotten cheek to the left, then right, as if he couldn't quite get a good look at the driver.

When Mister Neighborly went to the left again, however, that whole cheek came apart in a soft, overripe peach of a smear.

Gus looked away, but he still caught a glimpse of teeth through that disintegrating cheek. He exhaled, glanced around and saw the very bottle that stuck its neck up his ass.

"Hello beautiful," he whispered.

A second later, the bottle was in his hand. Rum. His favorite.

"You're my favorite, too," Gus told the bottle of whiskey. Which had somehow landed on the floor. "Make no mistake."

He popped the lid and drank a mouthful, held it for the burn, and then sent it down. One glance at the grinning ghoul outside his window prompted Gus to take a second shot, without barely a flinch.

"Needed that," he said.

No sooner were the words out when Mister Neighborly slapped the window, causing it to shiver, reminding Gus the undead were still outside.

"Left my license at home." He informed the fright and again lifted the bottle. "So fuck off."

More zombies gathered around the front. Something walloped a hand into the side of the van, and Gus jumped at the sound. He settled back, shook his head and drank again.

"Knock yourself out," he said, keeping his eyes lowered. "This thing's got tempered glass."

Three eights of an inch thick, he remembered one of the Mollymart people saying of the grocery store's front doors. He couldn't remember his name just then. Walt? Maybe. Poor old Walt. In any case, he'd misplaced his confidence in the glass. The zombies had bashed through it in only a couple of hours.

Those zombies, however, were freshly turned, Gus reasoned. The ones encircling him now were *not* freshly turned. And judging by the slab of *cheek* hanging off his window…

Gus checked on that, glad to see that chunk of meat had fallen off.

"Yeah," he let out. "I don't think you're going to pound your way through this one. Unless you want to smash yourself apart, you dumb fuck."

Mister Neighborly slammed the driver's window, splaying wide five frost-bitten fingers.

"Do that again, shitpouch," Gus said and took a sip of rum. "Double dare ya."

But Mister Neighborly did better. He hit the glass three more times.

And a second after the third strike, a new hand hammered into the glass, shivering it.

"Fuck you come from?" Gus asked, but didn't like what he was seeing… when he bothered looking, that was.

They had him surrounded. Those gravelly, frost-crusted vocal cords moaned and quivered outside, letting him know they *knew* he was in there. They *saw* him. And that it was just a matter of time.

Before they got him.

More hits. A rabid drumming that erupted just behind Gus, then the other side, then the back. That initial warm-up was all the rest of the mob needed, because whoever was in reach started wailing away, pounding the machine from all angles. They hit metal and glass, the hood and doors. And they sang. A burial dirge of promises, sung in zombie, detailing how they would get inside, eventually. And get him. And eat him.

Gus shook his head and rose from the seat. He stumbled into the rear. The shotgun was right there, and it tempted him. One way to quiet the neighborhood, but he doubted they would run if he did start shooting.

So, considering the day he'd just had, and with daylight fading, Gus cleared away a section on the floor. He threw down some blankets and towels he'd taken from an apartment, folded them up, and sat down. Pulled out the shotgun, and placed it by his thigh. There, he leaned back, opposite the bins, and felt each impact as the undead continued smashing the beast.

He held the rum bottle with two hands, to better control the shakes, and when he drank, he only barely managed to choke it down.

Then he smiled. Even chuckled.

"God love ya," he said to the bottle. "Don't care what anyone says. I'm glad you're here."

The hammering on the van continued, perhaps even louder, and Gus heard it, even felt it through the walls. Given the current situation, stuck as he was, all he could do… was wait.

For the city to devour him.

And while the rum made him even more comfortably numb, overriding his mounting terror and transforming it into a reluctant acceptance of his doom (which he supposed he could speed up with one blast from his shotgun), he failed to notice what was happening outside.

For around that time, in the upper left section of the windshield, above the slapping hands…

A single white flake hit the glass.

39

Tammy's place, her living room, lying on her couch, his head against a pillow propped against her thigh. Tammy rested her hand across the base of his neck, stroking his chin. The TV was on and they were watching some home improvement show.

Gus looked away from the screen and gazed up at the woman who'd somehow seen in him something she liked, something he didn't see, no matter how often he studied his reflection in the mirror.

Hair tickled his face.

Tammy leaned forward, her locks falling around her features, cloaking it in shadow. She smiled at him, wetly, her dark eyes twinkling.

"Something on your mind?" she asked.

"No."

"What is it?"

"Nothing."

"There is," she prodded gently, her smile lessening but still warm. "Come on. Tell me."

"I'm sensing sexual favors if I do."

She drew back, not pleased but not entirely displeased either.

"What?" Gus asked. "Just saying. I got information you want, and you do things I like…"

"All right, out with it."

"Sexual favors?"

"Say what's bugging you and we'll see."

That was good enough for him. So he said what was on his mind, because she'd know otherwise.

"Why are you still with me?"

A bit of a frown then, then she leaned in close once more. "What?"

"Why are you with me? I mean… I'm no prize. I know it. You, on the other hand, I mean, you could do a helluva—"

"Gus?"

"Yessim?"

"You don't know yet?"

"The soap I use?"

"No. Well, yes. A little. But besides that."

Gus waited, looking into her eyes.

"I want *you*, you dummy. You. And only you."

He studied her earnest face. "Must be the soap."

"Must be," her hair tickled his face again.

"Definitely not the way I dress."

"Nope." Then she rose again, looking much more serious than before. "You got a way about you, Gus Berry. You do all the little things right, what's important to a lady, anyway."

That was good to hear, he admitted.

"Look." She pointed two fingers at her eyes, then at his. "No matter how bad things get, or could get, you always seem to break even. You always pull through. So I'm telling you, and you better listen… stay strong. Stay well. And stay… alive. And above all, remember… I miss you."

That caused Gus to frown.

"I miss you something awful…" she said, her voice fading.

He woke… calmly, peacefully, his face mashed into a blanket. It was dark, but he sensed daylight. A dream. Only a dream. Of Tammy. And he pressed a hand over his eyes, trying to commit her face, her scent and touch, and her words, to memory. After a few moments, he smacked his lips and rubbed his beard.

Gus pushed himself up on an elbow, quietly yawned, and stopped moving.

He was still alive.

Even more interesting, it was quiet.

The windows were snow covered, daylight barely glowing through the thick grainy whiteness covering the windshield. The van wasn't shuddering anymore. No moaning. It was cold, however. Really cold. Gus got both hands under him, touching the rum bottle, which rattled across the floor. He grabbed it, held it against his belly, and wondered why the thing was full. Then he remembered. Trapped as he was, he had no where to take a leak, so he'd used the empty rum bottle. A portable toilet of exactly forty ounces and currently filled to roughly thirty-eight—which proved that you only rented the stuff. He vaguely remembered taking a piss in the thing, which was impressive to say the least. As far as he could tell, not one drop fell to the van's floor.

The plastic bottle was sealed tight, not that he was going to open the thing. He didn't need to. There were two empty water bottles nearby, obviously intended as back-ups. And while he marveled over the piss bottle and his dick's unbelievable aim, nothing stirred outside.

All right, he thought, and stood. That action alone dropped a bomb of a headache between his ears and around his upper jaw. He rattled about the interior, his clothing cold and clammy, and even all that moving around failed to draw attention from outside.

Then he saw the windows again, and realized they were crusted over with snow.

Snow.

He'd passed out, certainly. Blind drunk and, ultimately, rocked to sleep by the undead. The pounding had reached a point where, between the booze and the unrelenting beating, he'd simply crashed on the van floor, lying there until they finally got inside… which obviously didn't happen. Then it was morning.

Did the undead lose interest in him? Did something happen to lure them away from the van? Gus made his way to the front and all that motion woke his bladder. He resisted the urge, however, his puzzlement overruling the need.

Still nothing from outside. Not a sound except for the wind, going from high to low before rising again. The loneliest sound in existence. He could barely see through the glass, and certainly not enough to understand what was going on. The dead dashboard and the nearby key fob were right there, and he thought about switching on the wipers. Then he remembered. The gimps had pulled them off.

The door handle was right there, tempting him.

His hand curled around the handle and held on for seconds.

Before releasing.

Gus headed for the rear, his bladder and headache momentarily forgotten. The rear doors were locked and still intact, despite the abuse they'd suffered all through the night. After a moment's hesitation, he unlocked one door and gripped the handle.

He pushed.

The door cracked open like the air lock of some deep space shuttle, and cold air knifed in. Gus fully expected a multitude of fingers to rip the door open and grab him. There'd be noise then, all of it coming from him.

Nothing of the sort happened, however.

Dumbstruck, Gus peeked through that sliver of a crack, into a blustery morning.

There, not three feet off the back of the van, was a zombie.

A *frozen* zombie.

Black eyed and staring, its horrid features twisted into a snarl, the zombie stood with its arms by its side.

And that wasn't the only one.

There were others out there. Dozens, in fact. Maybe even hundreds. All struck motionless.

It was snowing. In fact, snow covered their shoulders and their faces, both partially or the whole thing. Some frozen heads wore white caps that reached their necklines, while others…

Gus opened the door wider, and it thumped against a weight. He waited a second before pushing, then heaving. The weight fell away, resulting in a snow muted *thud*.

Snow. Everywhere. On everything. The cold sparkling, enough to freeze tears.

"Holy shit," Gus whispered in awe.

Late winter storms weren't unheard of, and seldom enjoyed, because they buried spring and all that budding goodness. In recent years, however, they happened more often. Temperatures would plummet overnight. Then, if the province was unfortunate enough, one last smack to the face, a parting reminder from Old Man Winter that yes, Spring was here, and Summer would be hot on her heels, but he and his cousin Fall would return.

Until then… *shovel this*.

The snow continued falling, coming down thicker, driven by a screaming north-easterly gale. The wind whipped snow into Gus's face. The city was out there as well, behind a shifting grey sheet that erased any semblance of a world beyond. Power poles became faint lines. Houses were frosted over. White dunes engulfed cars and trucks.

He lowered his head against the squall, snarling at its building fury, cringing at the flakes lashing his eyes. Gus hung onto the door as he leaned out of the van, spotting the frozen gimp he'd just knocked over, in maybe two feet of snow at least. Snow drifts as high as his thighs in some places, clinging to upright dead people left motionless by the savage overnight drop in temperature. Annapolis citizens, at least the ones thinking they had an easy meal in Gus, had stood, crouched, or fell over flat, succumbing to last night's killer change in the weather. They were in the street, on the lawns, and in between the houses.

"Holy… *shit*," Gus whispered a second time, eying the depth and scope of the storm's wrath.

A blizzard? Perhaps. Definitely a few levels above a mere snowstorm. And the temperature was in the minus double digits. He could tell by his own shivering.

The overcast nature of the sky, the gloomy, ass-dreary heavens above… never looked better to him.

Then—a sense of urgency.

He was already dressed, so all he did was pull on his helmet and gloves. Bat in hand, along with the shovel that he'd tossed in there, Gus dropped down to the pavement, sinking in just past his knees.

How or why snow piles up the way it did, he didn't know. The winds, he supposed. But on this morning, he looked around and saw that while the snow clung to the van's backside, the rear wheels were practically untouched. Going forward would be a problem, but he saw that he could make a channel through the drifts behind him.

A marshmellow world, Gus heard in his head, and smiled.

He didn't know how much time he had.

But he got digging…

40

Snow.

Roads of white, wind scratched to the asphalt in places and buried to one's waist in others.

Where the snow was deep, too deep for the all-seasonals, he got out and dug.

He dug often. Hungover and sweating, he cleared passages just wide enough to drive through. When he drove, he drove until the snow stopped him again, whereupon he would get out and start digging once more.

He drank bottled water when he needed, as well as whiskey. Anything to help keep him warm. To keep him going.

The undead had been thickest around his van, but some time during the night, for whatever reason and well after he'd passed out, the zombies did indeed lose interest in their attempts to bash through the walls. Perhaps it was because Gus had passed out and did not provide any incentive to the mindless eaters seeking to enter. Maybe something distracted the zombies. He would never know.

All he knew—the storm had come, the temperature dropped, freezing them all in place. Trapping the undead legions… and offering a way of escape from the city. Unexpected, and not without some serious hard work, but it was there. He had plenty of water and food, however. And his own spare winter clothes. Also, as fortune would have it, not only did he have what he'd recovered from the apartment buildings, but he had grabbed most everything out of the wrecked van of the looters. Cases of water and pop, considerable stores of tin food, including two cases of cold Moosehead beer. Transferring everything from the wrecked van to his own took an energetic and somewhat paranoia-induced thirty minutes, but he got it all.

And was thankful for it.

When he dug, he took frequent breaks, suffering from a killer hangover but… also powered by hope. It was hard, punishing work, but he kept hydrated and rested when he climbed aboard, only to drive the van ahead. Sometimes it was a few feet. Sometimes farther. Snowdrifts blocked the roads, but he avoided the ones the size of whales and dug through the smaller ones. Still, clearing a path drained him almost to death. Zombies were in those drifts, frozen stiff. Gus bashed them aside with his bat, ignoring the frozen hatred in their eyes.

When he realized they couldn't hurt him, he put aside the bat and used a long screwdriver instead, going in through their eyes. Or their ears. Whichever was softer. Just scramble whatever was inside, working the tool like the crank of a music box, then pulling it free. When he was sure they were truly dead, he dragged them out of the van's intended path.

It all took time.

Wasn't until evening he got clear of his neighborhood alone, when the temperature dropped again, viciously so, forcing him to retreat to the van to warm up. He stayed away from the whiskey and stuck to water, if only to replace what he lost. Those breaks were no longer than half an hour, however, unless exhaustion forced him to rest longer. Otherwise, he dug. Long and hard.

Gus whizzed in the snow when he had to, but miraculously didn't need to use a crapper until that nightfall. When he did, he left the van in the street, and trudged to the nearest house with an open door. After a quick search to ensure he was alone, he proceeded to use the facilities.

That night, around ten, with the temperature and wind dropping, exhaustion finally caught up with him. He changed into fresh clothes in the van, dumping the sweat soaked ones into a corner. A pile of blankets and towels on the van's floor was his bed for the night. He dozed, however, unable to truly rest. Constantly waking, uncomfortable, paranoid…

Sometime around two in the morning, he got up, started up the van for heat, and got out to clear snow. Just wide enough to get his van through. The city remained a white maze of buried patches, rising and falling in great majestic swells. The street he followed, however, would get him back to the outer ring road, which would take him home.

All he needed was to keep on shoveling.

This continued into the next day, and the next night.

An hour after he rose the following morning, just when he thought he was nearly free of the city, a massive snow drift blocked the road. The very sight of the monster destroyed any lingering hope in him.

Gus got out, once again enduring that great ever-chill that touched his bones, and stood in ankle deep snow. The drift shimmed under a rare sun, the snow spanning four lanes and becoming highest on the right side, perhaps nose level.

"The hell…" he muttered in demoralized amazement. How the snow had piled up that fast shocked him. How the snow had piled up that fast right where he needed to get *through* cut his heart out. The van idling at his back, Gus walked up one side of the drift and studied the lay of the land after it. There were no zombies in sight. Not one frozen corpse, which was good. Only a leviathan of a drift. Thickest in the middle, but lowest and thinnest on the left.

That's where he would dig.

Retrieving his shovel once again, he started in, his back reminding him only after three tosses to go easy. There was no going easy, however, not with the size and scope of the monster before him. There was only the stoop, scoop and heave. One after the other, while the cold sweat trapped in his clothing made him feel waterlogged. But weeks of shoveling snow around the house, up on the mountain, had conditioned him—readied him for exactly this effort.

It was still bad, that rhythmic chuffing and tossing, wearing him down, threatening to break his back. When it got really bad, he'd stop, rest for a minute, then carry on.

There was no warmth under that sun, so Gus ignored it, concentrating on the next scoop. Never had he labored so hard in his life. Never had his life so depended on it. Everything leaked sweat, further saturating his inner layers of clothing, chilling him down to his nuggets. When he had enough, he hauled himself inside the van, where food and water and shelter waited. When his clothing got too soaked to wear, he changed into fresh, and rejoiced at the near perfect fit.

Always, after a short rest, he went back to digging.

And at one point, with the sun descending, he hit something the moment he thrust the shovel into the snow. A quick clearing later and he'd discovered the frozen face of a zombie. Not the first, but the first one uncovered on this section of road. Ice filled the empty eye cavities, as well as the mouth. Fearing the thing would rise with the next thaw, Gus got out the screwdriver, and jammed it into the zombie's ear. Two hard cranks sunk the tool deep, and once he'd dispatched the corpse, he pushed it out of the way. All that effort took a lot out of him, so he returned to the van. There, he took a twenty-minute break before getting back to digging.

Eventually, he hit a sidewalk.

Shortly after, he discovered a storm drain. A lower corner above the grate had crumbled away, revealing a dark rabbit hole into the city's sewer system. Gus poked a boot toe into the cavity, pushing some snow inside, but failed to fill it. Not that it mattered if he did, so he left it, and got back to work.

Dig. Drive a few feet, repeat.

Some time after sundown, he turned around, and realized, that the city lights had failed to come on, leaving the whole of Annapolis in darkness. He stopped shoveling and realized the only sounds he heard was that of his own breathing, and the dying wind. The nearby houses became angular shapes within the valley, while the snow looked even colder, and the night became that much lonelier.

"Well… shit." He felt that much sadder. When he was able to see them, the city lights had provided company for him, in a way. Now that they were gone, it seemed like he'd lost yet another friend. Or at least a neighbor. He thought they would go off sooner or later, without the crews maintaining the grid. Now that it had finally happened, it left him depressed. And the cold sunk the feeling deep.

"See ya, buddy," Gus whispered to the city, finally gone to rest. "You were good to me. To us all. Back in the day, that is."

He looked at his feet. Snow clung to his boots and pavement. The drift he was hacking through was far from done. Annapolis had just died, but he didn't let it keep him down for long. There was still plenty of work to do, so he started again, in that great and mysterious dark, pacing himself, trying hard not to think of old friends no longer around.

He became a slow working, shoveling machine.

Perhaps close to midnight, the clouds overhead cracked and split apart. A great shimmering glow spread across the highway and surrounding land. Moonlight and shadow dappled the countryside, transforming the world into an ice blue wonder. The wind had dropped out completely. Silence ruled.

In disbelief at what he was seeing, Gus took a moment to appreciate all that haunting beauty.

Just for a minute, and his spirits lifted.

Discovering an untapped reservoir of strength, he attacked the last few feet of snow. In short time, and with one final toss, he returned to the van and climbed aboard. Switched on the engine and let both the seat heaters and vents thaw him.

Gus eyed the uneven channel he'd hacked out. The moon was so bright that he didn't even need to keep the headlights on, but he did.

"Close," he said in a low voice. "But I'm not home yet."

Shifting, Gus drove into that trench, grateful to be behind the wheel again. The beast pushed through, its sides grazing the snow in places, but not slipping. Gus kept the machine in low gear and eased it along, hoping he would not have to shovel anytime soon.

The van rumbled ahead, leaving the snow dune he'd worked on for what seemed like a very long time. He drove a considerable distance, before having to get out and do it all again.

Some time later, long after the machine's rumblings lessened and flatlined into silence, long after Gus had forgotten about the storm drain…

Something moved within the crumbling hole of the uncovered storm drain.

It was a scrawny thing, dragging a hairless cord behind it. Underfed and whiskers twitching, it crept forward, testing the quiet, emerging from the dark cavity into which Gus had once kicked snow.

The rat took a few more exploratory steps, sniffing as it went.

Making a cautious line towards the zombie uncovered and left behind in the road.

The next morning, with the sun shining into his face, Gus reached the outer ring road.

But the highway back to his mountain hideaway was even more of a chore.

There were no zombies, and the cold spell finally broke, bringing a rise in temperature a few ticks above zero. The snow became heavy with moisture. Gus cleared what he could, taking many breaks, drinking, replacing fluids.

On the fifth day, he finally reached the smothered driveway for his mountain home. When he realized what he was looking at, what it *meant*…he stopped the van, leaned back, and sniffed back snot like a five-year old finding his long-lost puppy.

He had his cry, finished it, and wiped his face dry—or close to dry, ignoring the stink of body sweat coming from his sleeves. With the fresh snow, however, he knew there was no way he could get his ride up the side of the hill.

Didn't matter.

He was home. Strange to say it, but after all this time referring to it as a house, and especially in the days after being trapped in Annapolis, the house *was* home. His *new* home. And he could not have found anything finer.

Nor could he wait any longer.

So he packed up food and water, whatever he could carry in the duffel bag. He got out, locked up the van just because it was habit, and started hiking. He brought the shovel along, for balance, and the shotgun, also stuffed into the duffel bag but careful not to crush his wafers any further. The twelve gauge was merely a precaution, but the shovel… he'd need that most definitely.

At times the snow rose to his waist, as if the whole mountain had been buried by an avalanche. When he had to, he dropped the bag behind him and took up the shovel, digging just enough of a cut to get through. Gus became a robot of sorts, during those hours, his only function to dig, move ahead, and dig again. As before, the drifts rose and fell, and when they fell, the going became easier, and he made better time.

That climb, up a winding mountain road, knee deep—sometimes waist deep—in wet snow, nearly broke him. Nearly.

Six punishing hours later, with the sun descending, he was inside the gate and closing it, barely having the strength to do so. Foot after sinking foot, he staggered towards his house. At times he fell over, the duffel bag dropping beside him. When he did fall over, he slowly picked himself up, dusted himself off, and took the next step.

Until he finally reached the front step. Snow rose to nearly three feet at the door's base, but he didn't care about that. The thing opened inward, anyway. That tall slab of lumber was the sweetest thing he'd seen in a very long time.

He'd made it. He was home.

Home.

Just mouthing the word saved him.

When he opened the door, the trapped heat embraced him like the warmest of blankets. Or a sunny Caribbean beach. Something clicked inside him then, not unlike the snapping of an icicle. Gus shambled inside, his arms and legs so very heavy, and dropped everything with a clatter. He slid the helmet off and disrobed, slowly at first before ripping and peeling everything off his damp skin.

Standing there naked, shivering like a newborn, Gus sank to the heated floor and planted his bare hairy ass upon it.

Heat.

Glorious, wonderous heat.

He would never take it for granted again. Never take leaving *home* for granted again, for when he left it, when *anyone* left home, who really knew if they were coming back?

Then the tears came, and Gus let them flow.

MOUNTAIN MAN: 2ND PREQUEL: THEM EARLY DAYS

Heat.

Glorious, wonderous heat.

He would never take it for granted again. Never take leaving *home* for granted again, for when he left it, when *anyone* left home, who really knew if they were coming back?

41

"Need a bath," Gus blubbered. He didn't know why he was crying, but it was no doubt because of the last five days. Or was it four? Or six? He wasn't sure. He'd been digging for so long, it was a wonder there was anything left to the shovel. And the trek up the mountain was no birthday party either. That he accomplished something significant didn't occur to him. All that really mattered now, was getting that bath.

Knees shaking, he stood, the warm air caressing every crevice. There would be a puddle where he dropped the duffel bag, and there was some frozen chicken fingers in there that needed to be put in the freezer. So he got those out, along with some frozen pizza he'd scored, as well as a couple of Mighty Big TV dinners.

His feet squeaked across the floor as he plodded back and forth through the house, making the more urgent deliveries. It hit him that he hadn't taken a leak all day, and when he finally did, it gushed out of him. Even his piss felt cold.

The upstairs was next.

Every step took his last few ebbs of strength, but every successful flick of a light switch made him smile that much more.

Somehow, he reached the master bedroom. Then the en suite. White tub, with steel rods for gripping and keeping balance. Wide edges for candles if desired. Thick towels. All very fancy. Whoever owned the place had spared no expense.

Gus turned on the hot water and it gushed forth. A feeble adjustment got the temperature just right, and he sat on the toilet (lid down) and watched the steam curl from the filling tub. The sight of that hypnotized him, and he sat, shivering occasionally, until the water level was right where he wanted.

He was thankful for those rods in the tub then, and used them to lower himself into the water, right up to his chin.

Good Lord Almighty.

He even started to sweat, looked around, and saw there were no face cloths or towels within reach. Didn't matter. His eyelids closed.

The cooling water woke him. After a few seconds, Gus washed himself as best as he could. Getting out of the tub was just as hard as getting up the mountain, because he had nothing left. Not a goddamn thing. He got out all the same, and pressed a towel where it was needed.

Last bit. The very last.

The bed.

Or the couch downstairs.

The steps would kill him.

The bed was right there.

With only the light from the bathroom to guide him, Gus went for the bed. Pulled back the blankets, and actually ran a hand over the wonderfully smooth cotton sheets underneath. His bare ass sighed with relief when he sat down on the memory foam, and when he covered himself, Gus sighed as well.

The bathroom light was on. No matter. He'd leave it on, for the night. For Tammy, for visiting him when she did, at his darkest hour.

And for Annapolis, when its own lights died.

There, with the blankets pulled up to his chin, and his hands folded over his belly, Gus didn't have the energy to smile.

So he slept instead.

And slept like the dead.

42

A week later, Gus parked the van inside the garage and unloaded the last of his supplies.

In the days following his return home, the weather warmed up considerably, reaching double digits. The snow melted quickly during that time, creating streams that cascaded from his eaves, which he watched when he sat on the couch.

In the nights following his return home, the lights of Annapolis never came on again, nor did he expect them to.

Some of the frozen food had thawed, much to his disappointment, and he had a drink to mourn its loss. There was still plenty of dry, instant, and tin food, however. And he spent a day transferring everything from the van into the house, where it all got distributed upstairs and below.

It would last him a while, but eventually, it would be all gone.

Whereupon he'd have to go back. Down there. Or somewhere.

At the day's end, Gus sat on his couch, his usual perch, and held a glass filled with Captain Morgan rum. Ice accompanied the drink. The bottle—a forty ouncer—stood right next to a forty ouncer of Jack Daniels. They faced the city. Gus wore his own t-shirt and pajama bottoms, which were both a little loose on him. A side effect of all the exercise he'd done to get back to his newly realized home. Wouldn't be so bad if he could lose weight as fast as he was losing hair. He'd have to be careful, though. Snow shoveling, while an excellent form of exercise, also resulted in a notable number of heart attack deaths amongst seniors. He'd read that somewhere. Or maybe it was on TV? Didn't matter. He wasn't a senior, but his weight probably made him a risk.

But then that thought was gone from his mind.

"Well," he said quietly, after a time, pleasantly buzzed and thinking other matters over. "What did I learn the last time?"

He sipped his rum.

"Not to go down there during winter," he answered and jingled the ice. "Never fucking again."

Another sigh.

"Gotta go back there sooner or later though. Maybe New Cross, but… I'm thinking the city. It's all down there. In the big shops. And the small shops. Yeah… that might be an idea. Convenience stores. They're like mini-grocery stores. They got it all. Or at least most of it. Bet I can score a nice haul from any one of them. Less floorspace to check on too. Be faster. Everything's on a clock. Get inside, check it, clear it out—if I got to—then load everything aboard before they show up. Because they will."

Gus eyed the remainder of his drink. Half empty. It was half empty.

"Convenience stores. Then the houses," he continued. "Each one has a little stash in them. Each and every one. Like a little surprise package. Hit the ones on the edges first, where they're spaced out more. Get what you can and move on. Lots of grub in those, and the preservatives in them? Should be good for a year or two. At least."

He took another sip, just enough to sting his tongue, but these days, the sting barely bothered him.

"All right. Going forward, that's the plan. The big plan. Hit the smaller places first. Big places only if I got to. Stock up on everything, until…"

He couldn't finish the sentence. Didn't know how. Didn't matter. That would be his plan going forward. Until he could figure out what to do next.

Another little drink, just a little, and an idea popped into his head. Food supplies were one thing… but there were other things he'd need. Important things. Like medicine and such. And he remembered one place, in particular.

It wouldn't happen this day, or tomorrow even, but sooner or later…

Gus nodded to himself.

He'd check out the hospital.

About the Author

Keith C. Blackmore is the author of the Mountain Man, 131 Days, and Breeds series, among other horror, heroic fantasy, and crime novels. He lives on the island of Newfoundland in Canada. Visit his website at www.keithcblackmore.com.